BRODY

THE LANDER SERIES

Westmorland Publishing

BRODY

THE LANDER SERIES

A NOVEL BY

CARRIE CHESNEY

WESTMORLAND PUBLISHING

ISBN:978-0-9822029-2-0

WESTMORLAND PUBLISHING

Paperback First Edition: December 2009

Dedication

This book is dedicated to the love of my life, Lance. You have taught me so much about love, patience, and forgiveness. Thank you for giving me a love that is celestial every single day.

Acknowledgements

Cover Art: Jeanette Pitt

OTHER BOOKS BY MS.CHESNEY

THE LANDER SERIES:

CHRISTOPHER
BRODY
JENNIFER

CO-AUTHORED WITH THOMAS LYNN

THE SECRETS OF BLANEY'S MOUNTAIN

AUTHORS NOTE

I want to take this opportunity to thank all of my LDS readers for their past support. With respect for their standards and beliefs I wish to warn them that unlike other volumes in the Lander series, this book does contain what some may consider sexually explicit content. I have not written graphically for the sake of any gratification, but to serve a social purpose which the storyline will bear out. It is not my intent to offend, but to educate and hopefully assist women who have difficulty dealing with intimacy due to sexual abuse.

CHAPTER ONE

February 8, 2003

She lay naked on the bed, listening. Unable to see, unable to move. Hearing remained her only useful faculty. Oh, she could still smell and taste and feel, but those senses brought no pleasure. Everything smelled stale, and dank, and rancid. The things he forced her to swallow made her gag. As for feeling, she felt the bruises, the burns, and the little critters that climbed around her scalp, driving her mad with the itching.

She cried perpetually the first two days, but it exhausted her and accomplished nothing. With no perception of day or night, time quickly became irrelative in her life.

Duct tape held her eyes firmly shut, like the strip covering her mouth. A self-locking plastic tie wrap like those used by police for handcuffing secured her hands behind her back. Nylon rope bound her ankles, so they could easily be undone to allow her to walk to the toilet when he was around to let her use it. On occasion, he stayed away too long, and she urinated in the closet he kept her locked in. She remembered the first time with clarity.

"What's all this on the floor?" he bellowed as he kicked her in the side.

She cowered into the corner in fear, wanting to say she was sorry, that she couldn't hold it any longer, but with her mouth taped shut she was unable to reply.

"Well, I guess if you want to act like a pig, you can live like one." From that time on he left her to lay in whatever body functions puddled around her.

Her life became one endless, repetitive cycle. After the first week, her fear waned as the monotony increased. Hope of rescue faded, and she became apathetic to his customary routine. Each day he opened the closet door and declared the exact same words. "I wonder if I'll kill you today?" Considering the alternative, she began to wish he would just do it and get it over with. Surely death had to be better than what life was offering.

Things grew worse when he starting bringing friends to take a turn at her. With her only weapons, her arms and legs, immobilized, fighting back remained next to impossible. Realizing early on that he enjoyed her struggle, she ceased to respond and allowed her mind to take her to another place where she wouldn't have to suffer the indignity.

Today, he finally made his first mistake. His cell phone rang, and rushing out in flurry to respond to a call, he failed to lock her back in the closet. She estimated about fifteen minutes passed since his departure. His complete lack of schedule or routine left her uncertain where he went or when he might return. The only thing certain was when he did, she would be beaten and raped. Again, and again, and again.

Realizing her luck and how short her window of opportunity might be, a small glimmer of hope finally sparked in her heart. The will to survive caused a rush of adrenalin to surge through her veins as she stretched her arms back and down, hooking her wrists around her hips and beneath her thighs. Drawing her knees as close to her chest as possible, she struggled to pull her feet up and through the space between her arms. The exertion left her panting – difficult to do with her mouth effectively gagged, but the effort finally paid off.

With her hands now in front of her, she ripped the tape from her eyes and mouth. Her world of black onyx slowly dissolved, and the dim light of the night sky peering through the dirt-smeared window made her wince. Seconds ticked by, but she couldn't afford the time required to allow her vision to adjust. She needed to vacate the premises quickly.

Feeling in the darkness, she manipulated the rope until the last knot fell loose, and she kicked it free from her feet. The absence of heavy breathing nearby let her know she had been left without the watchful eye of the guard dog – another unprecedented circumstance. She knew the power of his teeth; her legs bore the open wounds made by his incisors.

Still naked, she stumbled outside into the night air and shivered almost instantly, not certain if it was due to the cold, the adrenalin, or the fear.

When her captor found her gone, he would track her down and beat her. Maybe even kill her this time. If she had to die, she would rather it be from the elements and not at his hands. Given a choice, she refused to allow him that satisfaction.

With no idea where she was, she had no inclination for direction. Following the laneway to the highway was just asking for him to find her. No, she needed to go cross country and find whatever shelter she could until she was far enough away to risk the main roads, if she found any.

She felt certain she was no longer in Oregon. Her ride in the trunk of his car after her abduction lasted much too long; maybe a full day or more. A full moon lit the countryside, and she saw the outline of mountains in the distance and plenty of wide open space offering no camouflage or protection from the elements. She wondered where she was in relation to the mountains; east or west of the range. Was she in Nevada or Utah, Montana or Colorado?

As the circulation to her unbound limbs increased, so did her speed. Her feet sprinted across the frosted ground, the bitter cold forcing its way into her bones.

Making her way across the prairie, she glimpsed a light in the distance. As it drew closer, she recognized it as the headlamps of a vehicle. Not willing to risk being spotted, she lay down on the frozen earth and waited, shivering, until it disappeared.

Rising slowly, she resumed her journey, racing as fast as her tired and weakened body would allow. Her muscles cramped quickly and felt atrophied from the prolonged bondage. The cold continued slowing her progress, and her teeth chattered so hard she felt sure they would break.

After traveling for what seemed like forever, her body betrayed her, giving out when she needed it most. It did not seem to matter that she was an athletic girl who ran every morning. Cold air penetrated her lungs in large gulps while she ran, chilling her from the inside as well as the outside. Somewhere along the journey the shivering stopped and fatigue won out. Collapsing to the ground, she lay still a moment and tried to breathe. Even that required too much effort.

Inching along the ground at a turtle's pace, she heard another car approaching but could not fight anymore. Not an ounce of stamina lingered to draw on. Utter exhaustion enveloped her. She hoped he would simply kill her this time and be done. Death seemed preferable to the alternative. With those final thoughts her eyes closed, and she fell unconscious at the side of the highway.

•

Deputy Brody Ashton finished his shift shortly past eleven. The evening had been uneventful for the most part, which suited him fine. He pulled his Avalanche out of the parking lot at the Fremont County Sheriff's Office on Railroad Street in Lander, Wyoming, ready to head home. Flipping on the heater, he hoped to soon feel its effects. Even though it was a bitter night, the ground lay bare. Being early February, he knew plenty more snow would fall before spring made an appearance.

Nudging a button with his knuckle, the CD player came on, and Kip Adams serenaded him as he passed through town headed northwest on Highway 287. Kip was not only his favorite singer, but also a close friend, having gone to school with him.

Singing along to the music as his fingers tapped the rhythm on the steering wheel, he noticed something curious at the edge of the highway.

"What the heck is that?" He pulled off to the shoulder and directed his high beams at the questionable heap. Peering through the windshield, he recognized the outline of a human body.

Getting out of his vehicle, he flicked on his flashlight and approaching with caution, found a woman lying unclothed. If not for her arms extended above her head onto the macadam, he would never have seen her in the pitch black night. A layer of frost already covered her bare body.

He knelt and touched her, to his shock detecting a faint pulse from her carotid artery.

"Holy Hannah! She's still alive!" he murmured.
Pulling out his cell phone, he called the Sheriff's Office.

"Jennifer, it's Brody."

"Hey, Brody, you just left here less than a half hour ago. Missing me already?"

"I'm 10-8, and I have a naked woman!"

"Too much information. You don't need to call in to report your sex life. We prefer you keep that to yourself." Jennifer enjoyed teasing Brody, well aware he was blushing even though she couldn't see him.

"Ha ha," he muttered sarcastically. "Listen, Jen, this is serious. I found her about fifteen miles north on 287, unconscious with her wrists bound. Obvious hypothermia, advanced stages. I'm transporting her down to LVMC. I'll leave a flare at the side of the road so the boys can rope off the area."

"Negative. Do not transport. I'll send a cruiser and call for the ambulance to retrieve her."

"It would be faster for me to drive her there."

"Move her as little as possible. Jostling her around can cause cardiac arrest. Do not transport."

"Body heat and A.R.?" he asked as he strode quickly to unlock the back of his truck.

"You got it. You just gotta manage to do both at once."

"Yeah, right. How am I supposed to do that?" He reached inside and pulled out a wool blanket he kept for winter emergencies and a sleeping bag still there from his camping trip two weeks earlier with his brother.

"Come off it, Brody. Use your imagination. Don't you ever kiss while you're having sex?"

Brody brushed aside her flippancy. "Thank you, Jennifer. I don't need you to draw me a picture."

"Well, apparently you do," she smiled, then grew serious again. "Hey, Brod, know who it is?"

"No idea. Hard to tell at this point anyway. She's been pretty badly beaten."

"10-4."

Brody quickly spread the woolen blanket on the ground next to the victim and gently rolled the body onto it. He knew she needed to be handled delicately, and that the body core was the most critical part to warm immediately. Quickly unzipping the sleeping bag, he draped it over his shoulders before opening his shirt and dropping his pants. The bitter night air caused him to shiver immediately, and he dropped to his knees and lay on top of the woman.

He lifted her bound hands, looping them around his neck and wrapped the sleeping bag snugly around them both, huddling them closely together. He tilted her head back with his left hand while his right hand gently pressed her nose closed. Very slowly, he breathed his own warm air into her lungs at her own rate of breathing.

Her frigid temperature shocked his body as he pressed against it, but he remained consistent with his efforts, developing a steady rhythm. He heard a vehicle door slamming shut and soon a pair of feet appeared in front of him.

Tara Shepherd stared down at him. When Brody lifted the blanket from their bodies, unbidden thoughts raced through her mind in spite of the seriousness of the situation. As a rule she behaved in a totally professional manner, but the visual that greeted her swept away all sense of decorum. Her eyebrows rose in surprise, and words spurted out before she could stop them.

"Geez, Ashton, didn't know you were so desperate for a woman that you'd settle for an unconscious victim. Even got her hands tied up I see. Wow, I'm just learning new things about you by the minute, aren't I? Bit cold to be doing it out here tonight though, I'd say."

"Tara, just get the gurney."

"Got it right here, and by the way, dropping your pants is going well beyond the call of duty."

Brody felt embarrassment color his cheeks, and he mentally cursed Jennifer for instilling the picture in his mind in the first place, certain it never would have occurred to him otherwise.

Tara turned as her partner, Justin Cassidy, opened their new hypothermia bag on the ground beside them. Brody helped transfer the cataleptic body to the carrier and then lift it onto the table. Tara extracted a pair of scissors from her pocket and removed the plastic cord binding the wrists. After zipping the woman into the bag and strapping her down, the paramedics hastily wheeled her to the ambulance.

Tara didn't hesitate to look back to see Brody's naked backside in a totally non-professional way before climbing in beside the victim. Justin slammed the doors shut behind her, and she immediately focused on her patient, slipping the oxygen mask over the mouth and nose and turning on the warmed oxygen. Opening a flap on the side of the bag, she inserted an IV cannula into the patients' arm and started a drip from a pre-warmed bag of dextrose/saline that hung in an insulated warming bag. Getting the IV started proved difficult with a body so cold. She knew oral and tympanic temperatures would both be inaccurate, so she settled for taking blood pressure and pulse, both of which were very low.

Back at the roadside, Brody could not get his clothes back on fast enough, certain particular body parts were in serious danger of frostbite. Not bothering with the buttons on his uniform shirt, he zipped his coat over top.

He dug into the back hatch of his vehicle for flares to mark the site. Before he had a chance to light them, the red lights of a cruiser rolled in behind him.

"Hey, Brody, what's up?"

He quickly relayed the few details of his brief encounter.

"I'll show you where I found her. Maybe you can pick up the trail when it gets light. Not much wind tonight, just cold. Hopefully that'll help preserve your evidence until daylight. I'm gonna follow her to the hospital and see how things work out."

"Okay. Where was she?" asked Deputy Rhett Owens.

Brody pointed out the spot, and they easily saw the body imprint in the frost and a trail of her footprints. Deputy Patrick Danvers knelt with his flashlight to take a closer look, but the beam was insufficient to be of much help. Even if they brought out high-powered lighting, there was still too great a chance they would miss important evidence that might be easily found otherwise. There was also the fact that the footprints of the officers would obliterate things, compromising the crime scene. Protocol required they wait until daylight. They would have more manpower then to scour the area for possible clues relating to the crime.

"Let's hope the frost holds up 'til morning when they get out here. You get going, Brod, we'll talk to ya later."

"Thanks, Rhett, Patrick. I'll see ya."

Getting back into his truck, he shoved the heater all the way up, slapped his blue flashing emergency light on the roof of the truck, and drove like a demon to Lander Valley Medical Center.

CHAPTER TWO

A doctor and a team of nurses stood ready and waiting when the ambulance arrived at the Emergency entrance. Tara jumped out of the back of the vehicle, reciting the patient's vitals as she helped steer the gurney down the hallway and into a treatment room. Once inside, Tara and Justin stepped back and allowed the trauma team to do their job. Not wanting to crowd the staff who needed to maneuver quickly, they vacated the sterile room.

Justin stopped at the nursing station to complete the necessary paperwork while Tara ventured farther down the hall and let herself into the supply room. Shelves laden with boxes of vacu-packed syringes and needles, plastic tubing, latex gloves, and various other paraphernalia offered her everything she needed to restock the ambulance.

Trying to balance the unweildy load in her arms, she managed to pull the door open. Her elbow flicked the light switch off and she stepped out into the corridor, nearly bumping into Brody. His hand reached out to steady her, and he caught the box that slipped from the top of the pile.

With a smile, she thanked him before standing on tiptoe to whisper near his ear, "I couldn't help noticing, Deputy, that you have a really nice butt. Really nice. Made my night." She turned and sauntered down the hall.

He watched her go, like she had every confidence he would. Without looking back, she gave a little wave over her shoulder, letting him know that she knew.

Shaking his head in amusement, he smirked before slipping into the treatment room to linger in the background. The sight of the medical team, hasty and efficiently dealing with the patient instantly pulled him back to the gravity of the crime, and he hoped the victim would survive. He retreated to the corner, trying to be inconspicuous. Apparently to no avail.

"Victim have a name, Brody?" Dr. Shepherd called out.

"Jane Doe. What you see is what I found."

The doctor dropped his voice as he addressed his team. "We need to intubate her. Her breathing is too shallow, and sinus rhythm is pretty sluggish. Her arterial PO2 levels are also way down," he told the nurse. To Brody he added, "It's a good thing you found her when you did, or she'd be in the morgue. Hopefully we'll be able to avoid that."

The nurse filled a syringe with 2% Lidocaine to inhibit mucosa production. When she tried passing it to the doctor he shook his head, refusing it. "Can't use it until her temp goes up. Her metabolism's too slow to process it. Why don't you get the ECG hooked up, Lisa. Make it a 12 lead. Wanda, get me a rectal temperature - that's what we have to rely on. Make sure you find one with a low scale, not a standard. Call the lab to send a phlebotomist down to try and draw some blood. I want a

CBC, BUN, creatinine, electrolytes, sugar, platelets, PTT, prothrombin tine, amylase and liver function." He flashed his penlight in his patient's eyes. "Pupils are dilated and unresponsive." His glance slid down the remaining length of the body. "Lisa, still writing those orders down? I think we should add HCG, all STD's and HIV."

Dr. Matt Shepherd began to insert the laryngoscope into her throat. "Meghan, this scope is too big. Get me a smaller one, a Miller please."

She passed him the tool he required, and he deftly inserted it down the patient's throat.

"Okay, give me a 7." He reached his hand out, and she passed him the requested endotracheal tube which his experienced hand deftly guided past the vocal cords and into the lungs. He pulled the scope out, then listened to her stomach and chest with his stethoscope to ascertain the tube went down the trachea and not the esophagus.

"It's in. Hook her up to the warmed oxygen, 42 Celsius with 50% humidity."

"Her temp is 30 degrees, Doctor."

"That's not great. We have to get her back up to 37.5. Wanda, I need you to put in a bladder catheter and take the first few ounces of urine in a specimen bottle for a urinalysis before you hook it to the bag. Meghan, I need a nasogastric tube. We're going to try a gastric/bladder lavage. Lisa, open that IV line to run faster and have more heated dextrose saline ready to go. She's seriously dehydrated, and we've got to get fluids into her." When taping the tube to the side of her face, he noticed he was not the first in line.

"Brody, come on over here, and take a look at this. See the adhesive and threads still attached? She's had her eyes and mouth taped shut."

"To face the weather out there tonight with no covering, she was obviously pretty desperate to get away."

The doctor held out the stiff hand for observation. "Damn. Some of her extremities have frozen. Lisa, call down to maternity and have them set up the whirlpool tub, about 38 degrees. As soon as we can get her temperature up a few degrees we'll need to quickly thaw her hands and feet, hopefully save them. When she gets down there, make sure the jets are turned on low to keep the water circulating. Keep her immersed for about twenty minutes."

Lisa finished making her notes and headed off to do as instructed. Matt turned back to Brody. "She'll be lucky if she doesn't lose them. At least she won't be awake to feel the agony when they thaw." He moved further down the body. "As you can see, there are multiple contusions all over her. See these circular blisters on the breasts? Cigarette burns. Deep rope cuts at her ankles. I'd say she was bound for quite a long time. Maybe days."

Wanda spoke up from her position. "Dr. Shepherd, I think she needs vaginal and perineal stitches."

The more Brody heard and witnessed, the redder his fury became. Sometimes the hardest part of his job was staying removed – not allowing himself to be emotionally sucked in. Cases like this made it close to impossible, but he consciously erected the wall, distancing himself from the horror. "Let's just hope when she wakes up she knows who did it to her."

The phone in his pocket jingled a tune. His cheeks flushed, well aware a reprimand was on its way. "I know, no cell phones in the hospital. I'll take it outside." He left the trauma room, checking the caller ID as he went. Pressing the button to turn the service off, he repocketed it. He should have remembered that magnetic fields in hospitals suck a phone battery dry in no time.

A cold gust of wind swept through the hall and Brody turned to look in the direction of the electronic doors at the emergency entrance. Seeing Tara coming back inside from the bitter night, her cheeks rosy, he approached her.

"Hey, Tara."

"Hey."

"Was that your way of asking me to go out with you?"

"Wow! He's hot AND smart. Winning combination, and something quite rare in the male species."

"When?"

"When are you off?"

"Tuesday is my last night, then I get seven days off."

"I get off Wednesday. Food and bowling at the Silver Spur. 6:30."

"I'll be there."

Without another word she smiled and went back outside. Brody grinned after her, then remembered what he was supposed to be doing. Using the phone at the nursing station, he called headquarters.

"Fremont County Sheriff's Department. How may I help you?"

"Hey, Jen. Brody here."

"How's she doing?"

"Doc Shepherd's working on her now, but she's in bad shape."

"I'm sorry to hear that."

"Yeah. Listen, somebody there just tried to call me."

"It was me. I was just wondering what you're up to Thursday night?"

"Got no plans. What's up?"

"Thought maybe we could drive up to Riverton, take

24

in a show, maybe go for a drink afterwards?"

"Sure. I'll pick you up at 6:00."

"Terrific. See ya later."

"Hang on a minute. Is Rhett back there yet?"

"Sure is. Want me to connect you?"

"Please." Brody heard the phone ring, and it was picked up by his friend.

"Deputy Owens."

Brody relayed the doctor's observations. "Her body is still too cold to collect evidence of rape. Probably be a few hours yet before they can do it. Anyway, they have to submerse her in water so we'll lose the trace." His fingers pushed his hat back, and he rubbed his forehead as he spoke. "Her temperature is something like 84 degrees, and they can only bring it up by two or three degrees an hour. Any faster will cause her heart to stop. So, probably about five hours before she's back to the land of the living."

Rhett took notes as Brody talked. "Give me an age guestimate."

"I'd say probably early to mid-twenties, Caucasian, about 5 ft.6. Light brown hair. Can't give you an eye color; haven't seen them."

"Okay, I'll check with missing persons and have them put it on the wire. Maybe somebody out there is looking for her."

"You know, Rhett, if she escaped on foot, you have to wonder how far she could actually travel in these circumstances. Looks like we have us one sick puppy in our jurisdiction."

"Sounds like it could get pretty nasty. We've got to find this guy. Could be one of our girls next time."

"I don't even want to go there. Just seeing this woman is making me sick. Pull it back, Rhett."

"I hear ya." Rhett paused a moment. "Hey, what are

you doing next Sunday?"

"Ain't got no plans yet. Whatcha got in mind?"

"Snow's good up in the mountains. Wanna go boarding?"

"Sounds great. I haven't gotten up there nearly as much as I wanted to this year. I'll put it on my calendar." Brody was about to hang up but stopped. "Hey, Rhett?"

"Yeah."

"Guess who asked me out tonight?"

"Well, it can't be Jane Doe. I give."

"Jennifer Dexter."

"Lucky devil. Where you going?"

"Movie and drinks. Should be all right."

"Have you taken a good look at her legs? I dream about those legs. How much will it cost me to take your place?"

"Rhett, why don't you ask her out if you like her?"

"She's way outta my league."

"I don't know about leagues. I never think about that kind of thing."

"That's because you don't have to."

"So, guess who else asked me out? This one'll surprise you."

"Nothing surprises me about your dates anymore. Who?"

"Tara Shepherd."

"Shoot! She's one fine looking filly. Curves in all the right places and a real pretty smile." Rhett pictured her in his mind. He always considered Tara a woman worth the trouble. "What's she want with an ugly buck like you?"

"Got me beat. I'd better go now."

"Talk to ya later." Rhett hung up the phone and wondered what it was about Brody that consistently drew women to him. He found it rather irritating now that he thought about it. Brody never asked a woman out, yet he dated more than anyone else Rhett knew.

Brody extracted his PDA from his pocket and entered his dates for next week. Ladies tended to get irritated if you showed up late, or worse, not at all. He bought this little gadget just to keep track of them all. As he tucked the stylus into his pocket, he wandered back to the treatment room. The door opened, and Dr. Shepherd came out.

"She's in pretty bad shape, isn't she, Doc?"

"Yup. She should be all right now, for the most part anyway. I just hope she can make it back."

"How do you mean?"

"Back to being a normal person. One who isn't terrified every time a phone rings or a man passes her on the street. She may never feel safe again, and that's where the real rape takes place. You see, Brody, it's not the physical, it's the emotional that gets destroyed."

"I hope she's willing to press charges. I'd really like to lock this guy up and castrate him while I'm at it."

Matt nodded knowingly as he removed the stethoscope from his neck. "I feel that way every time a rape victim comes in the door."

"But you can't collect the rape kit until she's awake, and you have her permission."

"That's the rules. I can do a pelvic exam to check for damages. That's about it."

"It's really too bad. After all she's been through, it would probably save her a lot of humiliation having it done while she's asleep. Besides, once you get her into the whirlpool, we'll lose our evidence."

Matt thought about it a moment. The young deputy presented a strong argument. "I'll tell you what. I'll bend the rules a bit here. If we can save her any more trauma, then we should. I'll collect the evidence when I

27

go back in. When she wakes up, I'll speak with her. If she gives the okay, I'll hand it over to you. If she doesn't, then I'm sorry, but it will be in the garbage."

"Thanks, Doc. I appreciate that." He touched a finger to the brim of his hat in deference.

"You can go in. Meghan's with her. I have another patient to see, then I'll be back."

Brody strode into the treatment room and saw the patient now had a clean white sheet draped over her body. "Hey, Meghan. How's she doing?"

"I think she's coming along pretty well. Her vitals are stabilized. Her temp is up to 33 degrees now, so that's pretty good. She's starting to look better, not quite so white. We're taking good care of her. Dad really is a great doctor. I'm lucky to be able to work with him."

Matt came back in and pulled a stool to the foot of the table. "Meghan, I want you to get me a rape kit."

"Yes, sir. But, she's not conscious yet," she argued.

"Meg, don't question. Just do as I've asked."

"Yes, sir." Meghan reddened at the reprimand and followed orders.

Matt extended the stirrups from their recessed location under the table. He lifted the patient's legs into them, then dropped the end of the table to provide himself easier access, all the while keeping the sheet draped modestly over her.

She returned with the kit and handed it to him. He opened it and passed her envelopes. "Do it very gently, Meg. Her fingers can be easily damaged," he cautioned.

"Yes, sir." She set the open envelope under the fingertips and one by one gently scraped underneath each nail, dropping any residue into it.

"Brody, I'm gonna have to ask you to step outside while I do this. I still need to respect her privacy as much as possible."

Brody left the room, and Matt took out the fine tooth comb which he drew through her pubic hairs, looking for any that did not belong to her. "Looks like we've hit the jackpot here."

When he completed the job he closed the envelope and placed it in the bag. He took the speculum to the counter and let hot water run over it to warm it before inserting it into her. Reseated, he examined the surface and found tears in the vaginal, anal and perineal areas. He collected vaginal fluid samples on swabs and enclosed them in their tubes. When he finished examining her, he stitched up the tears.

"Meggie, put this away in a cupboard until she gives permission for the police to have it." He saw the relief on his daughter's face, and further explained, "I thought it would be easier for her not to suffer through the indignity of it. Now she can go to the whirlpool."

"I'm sorry I questioned you, Daddy. I should have known you'd never do anything wrong." Meghan labeled the specimens and put them away in the cupboard before going to her father and sliding her arms around his waist.

"That's okay, Meggie. You're a good nurse, and I understand your questioning it. That's the morals we've raised you with, but you have to remember it's not your place to second guess a doctor. He hugged her tightly to him. "I love you, Meg." He kissed the top of her dark head and took pride in his precious little girl. "We make a good team, you and me."

Nurses took the patient to the maternity whirlpool, and Matt suggested he and Brody get some coffee. They walked to the staff lounge where the doctor poured them each a cup, adding milk and sugar to his own. Brody took his straight black.

After a few minutes of musing, Brody said, "You

know, your daughter sure has a sassy mouth on her."

"Which of my little darlings would you be referring to, as if I didn't know?"

"Tara."

"Of course, Tara. She's just like her mother. I'd like to say they mellow with time but it just isn't true." He got a lopsided grin as he talked. "Angie is just as sassy and bossy and fun as she was the day I met her, and you know, I wouldn't want to face a single day without her."

"It really happens does it?"

Matt looked at the young deputy, waiting for further explanation.

"Love, marriage, happiness."

"Sure it does. It's not easy, especially in jobs like mine or yours. It's easy to get involved in the job, and you don't want to take home the horror you see. You want to leave it, no, you need to leave it behind. To them it means you're not sharing."

Matt sipped his brew, then continued. "The important thing is priority. You have to make the marriage the priority, not the job. It's all in how you look at it. I love medicine, and I always have, but would I be happy being a doctor without Angie? No way. I'd be miserable. Next question. Could I do any other job and be happy as long as I have Angie? Absolutely. She's the thing that means the most to me, and I treat her that way. Even during my residency. I had a lot of forty eight hour shifts, but two whole days without her? No way."

He sat back and grinned as memories flooded his mind. "She still giggles about the fact that we knew every closet in this hospital. Of course a few times my pager interrupted us with an emergency, but generally, we got to enjoy a few minutes together. It let her know I was crazy about her, so she was never jealous of the job. It's all in learning the balance."

"You know, Doc, that's some of the wisest stuff I think I've ever heard. You should counsel guys in jobs like ours on a regular basis. Probably save a lot of relationships from heading down the drain."

Matt laughed at Brody's suggestion and took another swig of coffee. "So, did Tara ask you out?"

"Yup. How'd you know?"

"It's known far and wide that Brody Ashton never asks a woman on a date. Makes you pretty revered amongst the males in this county."

"Holy Hannah! Everybody knows that?"

"It is a small town, Brody. What's your secret?"

"Danged if I know. I haven't got nothing figured out. Women just come up to me out of the blue and ask me out." He sat back on the sofa and tipped up his hat with his knuckles to scratch at the head underneath. "Sometimes I know 'em, sometimes I don't."

"Yeah, back when I was young it was Bill Clayton. Even Angie used to have a crush on him. He took her to the movies when she started high school and that sealed her future. After that she was asked out by just about every jock in the school. I guess I can't complain. He got the looks, but I got the girl." Matt drained his coffee cup and rested it on his knee. "Listen, about going out with Tara, good luck. Wish I had some advice for you, but I don't."

Brody smiled and carried his mug to the sink where he washed it out. As they stepped back into the corridor they saw the patient returning to the ER.

"You can go in with her, Brody. I'll be along in a few minutes."

"Thanks, Dr. Shepherd."

Brody pushed the door open and went in. The consistent bleeps of the heart monitor kept a steady rhythm with a staccato beat in the sterile room. The walls were freshly painted in a soothing shade of blue. The patient lay on the trauma table, still as death, her pale skin reminiscent of the snow covered mountains. A shiver crept along his spine, and he prayed the case didn't turn into a homicide.

Meghan Shepherd stood at the end of the table, bandaging the patient's feet.

"Hi, Meg. How's she doing?"

She glanced up briefly and continued carefully putting pads of gauze between each toe so they wouldn't stick together, then bandaged the foot.

"She's holding her own. It'll be awhile before she's safely out of the woods." Fantasies of the deputy played in her mind while she cut a piece of surgical tape to secure the dressing. Tucking her scissors back into her pocket, she asked, "Say, Brody, I was wondering ..." her gaze dropped shyly to her feet as she second-guessed herself before drumming up the courage to go through with it. "Would you consider going out with me? On a date?"

"Sure. Are you free Friday night?"

"No, I'm working," she frowned. "What about Saturday? Maybe we could go out in the day and do something. If there's snow, we have some snowmobiles out at my Grandpa Hathaway's ranch. If there isn't, well maybe we can find something else to do."

"That sounds great. Why don't I pick you up about ten, and we'll really make a day of it."

She blushed with pleasure. "Thanks, Brody."

"Hey, no problem. We'll have a good time together."

Matt came back in, and seeing his daughter's smile and florid cheeks, knew without asking. Another of his daughters had a date with Ashton. He had only one more daughter to go and wondered when she would take her turn. Shaking his head, he smiled. He may well end up with Brody Ashton as a son-in-law one day. The question was, which daughter would it be?

CHAPTER THREE

She lay on the bed, listening. Female voices drifted in and out, but that did not make sense. No one but the scum and his friends came around. Excruciating pain engulfed her when she tried to move; so much more than usual. A consistent beeping in the background irritated her. An alarm of some sort maybe? Whatever it was, somebody turn it off. Everything seemed to be floating. Someone moaned. Who could that be?

Tormented by the itching on her head, she lifted a hand to scratch. Though her mind was still foggy, she comprehended her arms no longer seemed bound together. A hand took hold of her wrist and gently urged it back down.

"Try not to move your hands," a man's voice softly told her, but she continued to float, not yet alert enough to make sense of it.

"You gonna wake up yet? I've been waiting a long time."

Her heart sank as memory permeated the mist in her mind. "Please, no more. Just kill me. I don't care anymore. Please, just kill me," she wished, unaware her thoughts slipped through her lips as raspy gurgling noises.

Sensing her distress, he sought to reassure her. "I'm not gonna hurt you. I'm here to help. You're in the hospital now. Can you open your eyes?" he asked.

Agonized expressions flitted across her bruised face.

"It's safe to open 'em. Give it a try," he encouraged.

Open her eyes? Was it possible? She battled her way through the haze, struggling to lift her heavy lids. She had not been allowed to see for so long.

"Take your time." He patted her shoulder reassuringly. "You're safe now. No one's gonna hurt you. Okay? You're safe. You don't need to be frightened anymore."

Eyelashes began to flutter, and slowly her eyes peaked open. Blurry at first, things gradually settled into focus. She shifted her gaze, searching for the owner of the deep, friendly voice. A large man with blond curls and a thick blond moustache stood beside her. A warm smile spread across his face when she looked at him, and a dimple appeared in his right cheek.

"Aha! Emerald green, same as mine. I've been wondering what color those eyes of yours are." His expression grew more serious and sympathetic. "I guess you're hurting, aren't ya? I'll find the doc and tell him you're awake." He left her side and went to the door. Poking his head out into the hall, he saw Dr. Shepherd at the nurses' station making notes on a patient's chart. "Hey, Doc, she's awake."

Safe? Was she really and truly safe? Her chest heaved as relief flooded through her, filling every corner of her soul, and a tear slid unbidden down her cheek.

A man she presumed was the doctor came into the treatment room, a stethoscope hanging draped around his neck. "Well, young lady, you've kept us pretty busy around here." He put on his stethoscope and leaned closer to listen to her heart. Her instinctive withdrawal from his touch stopped him.

"Just a minute," he said. Understanding immediately that she would be more comfortable with a woman, he went to the door and called Meghan in to take the vitals.

A nurse in purple scrubs came into the room, her long brown hair clamped up on the back of her head. In soothing tones, she approached the bedside and introduced herself. "Hi, my name's Meghan. I've been looking after you since you came in last night. I'm just gonna check a few things and see how you're doing." With a friendly smile, she listened to the heart and lungs and took the pulse, blood pressure and temperature. She slipped the doctor the paper with the results recorded on it.

Matt looked at the numbers, made a decision and nodded. "Okay, Meg, let's extubate."

She gently removed the surgical tape holding down the tubes on the woman's face while Matt leaned on the bed railing and spoke to his patient, explaining the procedure to her.

"I'm gonna take this contraption out of your throat, so you can breathe on your own." He turned the oxygen off and disconnected the vaporizer. "Take as deep a breath as you can, and when I start to pull this out, I want you to exhale with as much gusto as you can muster."

She nodded slightly, and moments later the tube was out. She coughed for a moment, sending pain shooting through her chest like a thousand sparks of fire.

The doctor maintained eye contact with her and pointed a thumb at the blond man stationed at the foot of the bed. "The deputy here found you last night with some pretty advanced hypothermia. Now, we have another tube running into your stomach. If you promise me you'll drink like you've spent a month in the desert,

I'll remove it, too." When she nodded in agreement, he clipped off the lavage fluid and extracted the tube from her nasal passage.

"Meg, we'll go with nasal prongs now."

Meghan connected the tubing to the oxygen and slipped it over the women's face, placing the small air jets into her nostrils. After clearing away the excess paraphernalia that was no longer needed, she stepped toward the door to leave when her father stopped her.

"Meghan, stay please."

She turned back, fully cognizant of his reason for asking. "I'm just gonna get her a warm drink to soothe her throat. I put one in the microwave for her when I heard she was awake." She stood at the doorway, waiting for his permission before proceeding.

Matt nodded his approval. "All right, but leave the door open, please."

With the doctor busily making notes on her chart, the patient turned her attention to Brody who moved to stand at the side of the bed. With effort, she managed to whisper, "Thank you."

"Hey, no problem. I'm just glad I found you in time. My name's Brody. Brody Ashton." He doffed his hat. "Nice to meet ya. Have to say, I'm sorry it's under these circumstances. Now, we know who I am, and your name would be…?"

"Lindy." She struggled to swallow. "Lassiter."

"Lindy Lassiter?" He repeated, wanting to make certain he heard her correctly. She nodded as Meghan breezed back into the room with a steaming mug in her hand.

"I've brought you some warm cider. It should make your throat feel better and help warm you. Let's sit you up, first." Meghan pushed a button on the bed's control panel, raising the head to an upright position. Smiling, she wrapped an arm around Lindy's shoulders to help her sit up further, while lifting the cup to the young woman's mouth.

Lindy took a tentative sip. Finding it not too hot, she drained half the mug before relaxing back on the pillows. "Better, " she croaked and smiled tremulously in gratitude.

Matt allowed her to settle before taking control again. "Good. Now, if Brody will excuse us and wait outside, we'll discuss what's going on with you."

Nodding, Brody gave a shy parting smile and did as requested, stepping into the hall. Curiosity tempted him to stand outside the door and listen, but his integrity would not permit it. Closing it firmly behind him, he went in search of some fresh black coffee. It had been a long night. Normally, he did not wait at the hospital to see how things turned out for a victim, but this one was different. He felt more involved, reasoning it probably had something to do with taking off his clothes. Shrugging, he strolled to the doctor's lounge and poured himself a cup of hot brew. A telephone on the table in the corner by the couch caught his attention. Picking it up, he pushed a button for an outside line.

•

From the vantage point of her bed, Lindy looked expectantly at the pair in scrubs at her side. Meghan stood next to her, smiling, while the doctor pulled up a stool to sit on. She gave them her undivided attention.

Matt looked up from the chart, pen in hand, and tucked his reading glasses into his pocket. "We still need to get your temperature up another few degrees. Your fingers and toes were completely frozen. The tendons, muscles, tissue and blood vessels will probably be damaged to some degree. You'll notice they're bandaged. It's important that you be careful with them. They'll be swollen and blue for about a month. If we can prevent infection, and no gangrene develops, there's a good chance you'll keep them. It's been known to happen."

He spoke compassionately, yet gave it to her straight. "Now, as for the rest of you, you arrived badly dehydrated, so the IV stays in. Along with that, you have to drink as much as possible. We have a catheter in the other end, so if you need to pee just go right ahead. No worries there. It may feel strange at first, but you'll get used to it. You won't be able to get up for the bathroom anyway. You're confined to bed."

A shudder of revulsion ran through her as the doctor's words paralleled memories still too fresh of not being permitted to use the bathroom when the need arose. "If you need to pee just go right ahead. It may feel strange at first, but you'll get used to it." No, she never got used to it. Pulling her mind back to the present, she tried to concentrate on what was being said and make sense of it. The only thing that truly mattered was that she was safe.

"Now, I need to discuss things more personal." His voice took on a gentler tone. "Lindy, I'm sorry, but it's evident you've been badly brutalized and raped. You have two broken ribs and a hairline fracture in your collarbone. If you'd rather not discuss it with me, I can leave, and you can talk to Meghan, or I can have someone from the Women's Crisis Center come in to see you."

She swallowed. What did it really matter? Any shred of dignity she ever held had been stripped from her. "It's all right, but I would be more comfortable if Meghan stayed." She looked at Meghan pleadingly, and the nurse reached down to brush some hair from her forehead.

"Lindy, I don't know how you feel about pressing charges against whoever did this to you. When I examined you for injuries earlier, I stitched up all the places they tore you open, and collected evidence with a rape kit. I haven't handed it over to Deputy Ashton yet, and if you don't want to press charges, I'm not permitted to give it to him."

"They?"

"I found evidence of more than one rapist. I'm sorry if you didn't know that."

She closed her eyes and took a deep breath. "I did know. I don't know how many. Maybe four or five."

"I'm so sorry," Meghan said. Unable to hold her patient's bandaged hand as a gesture of comfort, she made do with gently rubbing the girl's upper arm.

"Is there anything else I need to know?" Lindy asked.

"I've ordered blood tests for HIV, STD's and pregnancy. I expect they'll all come back negative right now, but you'll need to be retested again down the road. I can give you a drug so you don't conceive from this, but it's only effective if taken in the first five days after the rape. Also, if you're not allergic to penicillin, I'll give you a dose to take care of possible STD's."

"I've been raped daily for at least three weeks now I think." Her voice was passionless, as though she harbored no feeling whatsoever regarding the crimes against her.

Meghan glanced at her father, barely managing to stop herself from gasping aloud. Turning to her patient, she sought to offer reassurance, knowing full well it was too little, too late. "You're safe now, Lindy. It's all over. No one can hurt you here, and we'll be keeping you for at least a month."

40

Relief transformed Lindy's features. "Thank you." Her head settled back into the pillow, and tears swam in her eyes, slowly starting their cascade. Silent tears. She allowed the words to roll around in her mind. Safe at last. She held in her hands the power to see the scum put away for what he had done. It would put her through more hell, but she refused to allow someone else to go through the same thing because she had been too cowardly to stop him. Power – it was something she had been denied for too long, and reclaiming it felt good.

She stared into space, her words soft, as though talking to herself. "I got away. I ran until I couldn't go any farther." She paused a moment, then turned and looked squarely at the doctor. "Tell the deputy to come in. I want to talk to him."

"If you're sure." Matt stood and paused, giving her a chance to reconsider.

"Yes, I'm sure." Her voice was firm; her decision quickly made.

"All right. After you've talked with him, somebody will be along to take you to your room." He left in search of the deputy.

As Meghan held the mug for Lindy to take another drink, respect for her patient swelled within her. "Not that my opinion counts, but I think you're doing the right thing. I know it's got to be hard, but I really admire your courage. You're sure lucky Brody's the one who found you. He's stayed with you from the time they brought you in last night. The police usually come back later when we notify them the patient can talk. He's been pretty worried, though."

The deputy rapped on the door and poked his head in.

"Come on in, Brody."

He strolled into the room and sat on the stool Matt

left vacant near the foot of the bed. Taking his hat off, he said, "You know, Lindy is a much nicer name than Jane Doe. Besides, we meet too many girls with that name in my line of work." He smiled, trying to relax the tension in the room. "Mind if we talk?"

Lindy nodded, feeling numb enough to deal with the circumstances. She looked at the nurse from the corner of her eye, and as much as she would feel safer with her in the room, she wasn't sure how the girl would take hearing the details. "Sure, that would be fine. Meghan, I think I could use some more hot cider if you don't mind. I'll be fine with the deputy."

Meghan took her cue and crossed the room to the cupboard. She pulled out a white paper bag with the rape kit in it and handed it to Brody. He nodded his gratitude and tucked it in his bulky coat pocket. As she left them alone, she made a point of propping the door open for Lindy's sense of security.

Reaching into his pocket, he pulled out his pad and pen. "We'll be seeing a lot more of each other, so for now you can just tell me the things you're comfortable with."

She gave a quick nod of assent.

"Okay. Why don't you just start talking, and I'll take notes. How about starting with where you live?"

"I'm from Portland. My dad left when I was small—I don't remember him, and my mother died of cancer last year. I don't have any other family. When I finished school I put the house on the market and decided I wanted to start fresh in a smaller town. You know, a Mayberry kind of place. So, I was going to drive until I found something that suited me. Then I'd look for a job and settle there.

"On January 14th, I stopped for gas near Baker City, Oregon. It was one of those rest stops that has a few

42

small fast food restaurants, so I went inside to buy some lunch. When I came out, I never made it back to my car. I was grabbed, drugged, and thrown in a trunk which is where I woke up. My eyes remained taped shut from that time until I escaped last night, so I can't give you visual descriptions of them. There was a dog left guarding me most of the time, too."

Brody hurriedly took notes as she spoke, pleased that she seemed able to tell him the things he needed to know without a lot of prodding.

"Can I ask something?"

He looked up from his notepad. "Sure. Anything you want."

"Where am I? I've been wondering that forever."

"Well, as a matter of fact, you've landed yourself in Mayberry, Wyoming," he smiled.

She blinked at him, startled, and he laughed. "It's actually called Lander. But you don't come any closer to Mayberry than this. It's a great town. Lived here all my life and don't ever wanna leave."

"Wyoming? I'm in Wyoming? I guess that makes sense. I saw the mountains in the distance when I escaped. My other question is, what's the date today?"

"Today is February 8th."

"I see." She bit her bottom lip as she quickly tried to calculate in her mind. Suddenly weary, she sighed heavily and asked, "Is that enough for today? I'm getting tired."

"Just two or three easy ones if you can. I need your date of birth."

"June ninth, 1980."

"Is there anyone out there looking for you? Someone we should notify?"

"No. I said goodbye to everyone. No one expects to hear from me."

"All right. So your car is still back at that highway gas station?"

"Unless they've had it towed away. It has a trailer hitched to it carrying everything I own in it. And my purse…I don't know what happened to it. It had some money, my identification including my medical insurance information, and I don't know. I guess nothing else that was important."

"I'll see if I can locate the vehicle for you. Hopefully, it hasn't been vandalized."

"Thanks. I'm sorry, but I'm just so tired. Can we talk again tomorrow? I may be a little stronger by then and able to tell you more."

"Hey, you've done great. You're a brave lady."

She smiled weakly. "I don't know about that." She closed her eyes a moment, then opened them again and watched as he put his notepad away. "Deputy?"

"How about calling me Brody? We'll be seeing a lot of each other over the next few weeks. I'll be your first friend in Mayberry," he grinned. She was one heck of a brave woman, and he admired her spirit after all she'd been through.

"Okay, Brody." She turned away and paused, then looked back at him. "Thank you. For last night. Just before passing out, I thought about dying. Almost wishing for it. Thank you for stopping and saving me."

"Well, I sure hope you never think of it again, but if you do, just make sure you pass out on that same highway when I'm heading home from work. I'll stop and save ya again."

He smiled, and she gave a weak laugh. "Destined to be my hero, are you?"

"Sure. Hey, don't give it another thought. Just work at getting better." He stood and took a step back from the bed.

44

"Wait a minute. You were on your way home from work?"

"Yeah, why?"

"Meghan said you stayed here all night."

"Meghan shouldn't be giving all my secrets away," he blushed.

"Thanks, Brody. My first friend."

"You're welcome. Get some rest now." He smiled at her, and watched as she closed her eyes, almost instantly asleep.

Meghan arrived with the fresh cup of cider as Brody was leaving the room.

"Catch you later, Meg. I'm gonna head on home to catch a few hours of sleep before I have to be back on duty."

"Okay, see ya, Brody. Thanks for staying with her. That was right caring of you." She flashed him a smile of admiration.

Pushing his hat back on his head, he headed down the hall and outside into the frigid February morning air.

CHAPTER FOUR

Lindy awoke in a private room with a spectacular view of the Wind River Mountain Range. For a woman who lived in a world of abysmal darkness with her vision denied her for so long, she couldn't imagine waking up to a more glorious site. Relaxing into her pillow, she drank it in.

The door opened interrupting her brief reverie, and a woman with a cheerful smile breezed into the room. Lindy noted jeans and sweater under the suede coat. Must not be a nurse, yet she seemed confident that she was in the right room.

Setting her purse on the window ledge, the stranger introduced herself as she removed her coat and hung it on the back of a chair. "Hi, Lindy. I'm Gina. It's a pleasure to meet you. I'm so glad I've found you awake. Can I get you anything?"

Wondering how the woman knew her name, she asked in a leary voice, "Are you a nurse?"

"Yes, and no. I am a nurse, but I'm not a hospital employee anymore. A few years ago my mother became quite ill, so I left my job here to care for her until she passed on. Since then I work for people who require home care."

The young woman eyed her suspiciously, uncertain about the stranger and her motivation for being here. "I'll be here at least a month, so I don't think I'm in the market for home nursing."

"Well, that's not the only thing I do. I got two phone calls early this morning to come and see you."

"Two?" Lindy's brows knit together in disbelief. "I don't even know anyone in this town."

"Well, one was from Dr. Shepherd. We worked together quite a few years."

The door opened, and Matt Shepherd entered as if on cue. "Good morning, Lindy. I see you've met Gina."

Lindy lay silent, her eyes shifting back and forth between the doctor and the woman, uncertain of their agenda.

"Hi, Matt. I just got here, myself," the woman smiled with familiarity.

He smiled back and turned his attention to his patient. "I thought I'd better come up and vouch for her. After everything you've been through, I'm sure you'll be wary of strangers for awhile."

Absolutely right.

"I called her to stop by, figuring she might be able to help you. She's from the Women's Crisis Center."

Her reserve slowly dissipated with his corroboration. "Thanks, Dr. Shepherd. I appreciate you taking the time."

"Not a problem. I have to run now, though. My wife is home waiting for me." With a smile and a quick wave over his shoulder, he was out the door, and the women were once again left on their own.

So, her name was Gina, and since she was offering and Lindy's throat felt dry, the girl asked, "Actually, if you don't mind, I'm supposed to be drinking a lot of fluids. Would you mind getting me something warm?"

"Sure thing. You just sit tight. I'll be right back."

Lindy glanced at all the tubes and monitors and knew she didn't have any other choice. It wasn't like she could get up and go anywhere.

Gina walked down the hall with purpose. Inside the patient's kitchen, she went straight to the cupboard where she knew the hot chocolate powder was kept. It only took a few minutes to microwave some milk and stir in the drink mix. She could have made it with water, but that poor girl needed the nutrients. Adding a few cookies to a small paper plate, she carried the snack back to the sunny room and placed it on the tray table.

"I made you hot chocolate, which sounds good on a day like this. It's pretty cold outside. Would you like to sit up more?"

"Yes, please." She held up her bandaged hands. "Even with electric controls, I'm afraid I've been rendered incapable."

Gina elevated the head of the bed, then perched gently on the edge. She lifted the mug and held it for Lindy to drink, then settled on the chair next to the bed.

"You said you got two phone calls this morning about me."

Gina smiled, "The other was my son insisting I get over here and become your second friend in town."

Lindy's eyes lit with surprise. "Deputy Ashton?"

"Yes, Brody called before I even had the coffee pot on. Told me I'd better hustle right on over here and meet you. Something about being Aint Bea from Mayberry."

Lindy giggled. "Thank you for coming then, Aint Bea. I told him I was looking for a place that reminded me of Mayberry to settle down in, and he said I'd found Mayberry, Wyoming."

"Well, he oughta know. He works for Sheriff Taylor."

"Are you serious?"

"Matter of fact I am. Sheriff Laramie Taylor."

"Maybe I really did land in Mayberry." Growing more serious, she speculated, "Or maybe I'll wake up and find out this whole thing has been nothing more than a nightmare."

Gina sat back, silently waiting. In her experience, victims often did better if left to talk on their own.

Lindy swallowed hard and tears began to well before holding her hands up to view. "Look at this. If my hands don't heal, how will I ever play the piano again? How will I turn the pages of books? What will I do with myself?" She stared at her hands, for the first time considering the impact it would have on her life. Even though her life had been saved, she felt her whole world falling apart. "I'm sorry. I shouldn't be sitting here feeling sorry for myself. I should just be grateful to be alive, shouldn't I? Anything beyond that is a gift, isn't it?" She looked at Gina, wanting answers.

"I suppose. It depends on how you look at things. Nobody can have everything they want, and nobody can be happy all the time. That's reality, and I suppose there's a good reason for it. If we were always happy, we wouldn't appreciate it because we'd have nothing to compare it with. If we had everything we wanted, we wouldn't ever learn the difference between want and need.

"On the other side of the coin, I think we're all entitled to happiness in our lives. We need things that will enrich us and offer us some kind of pleasure. If we've been blessed with talents, it's important to be able to explore and cultivate them. Have you played the piano a long time?"

"I started taking lessons when I was four. My mother

taught me. I took more advanced studies in university and gave lessons to help pay my way through school. I don't think there have been many days of my life that I haven't played."

Gina waited to see if she would say anything more, but she stayed silent. Leaning forward, Gina rested her hand on the young woman's arm and spoke with conviction. "Lindy, you've been through so much these last few weeks. You've had a lot of things stolen from you, and you know what? You can be mad about it. You can be sad about it. You don't have to apologize to anyone for anything. You haven't done anything wrong. Nothing that's happened to you has been your fault. None of it. You have the right to feel whatever you feel. You have a right to let it out. You had everything taken from you, but now it's safe for you to take your rights back again."

Lindy dropped her head and started to weep. Gina wrapped her arms around the girl and held her. Weeping turned to sobbing, and Gina held her without a word, just letting her cry. She knew this was just the first of many bouts of tears Lindy would suffer through. When the crying began to wean off, she dried the tears and wiped Lindy's nose.

Sniffling, Lindy leaned back into the pillows. "Thanks. That felt pretty good."

Gina gave her a bite of cookie and another drink of her hot chocolate before settling back into her chair. "Purging is good. Holding it all in never helps. It all comes to a head and has to be let out eventually. Lindy, anything you say with me, stays right here between us. No one else will ever hear it. If you want to talk, you can. If you don't, that's okay too. Sometimes you need a best friend to talk to, and other times, well, it can seem easier to talk to a stranger."

"I think I do need to talk. Maybe it will help straighten things out for me." Keeping her eyes cast down, she let her story unfold, telling Gina about being kept in the closet, about the filth, about the repeated rapes and sodomy and how she learned to deal with it. She told the things she could remember about the man who kidnapped her, and the friends he brought around, about the dog attacking her.

Keeping her eyes down for fear of seeing the revulsion on Gina's face, she talked about the never-ending darkness, about not knowing anything about her surroundings. She went from numbness to choking on the words and crying and back to numbness again. She talked about that last day, when he forgot to lock her back in the closet. She talked about her cross country journey through the freezing dark night.

Gina sat quietly and listened. She had heard a lot of rape stories over the years, but never one like this. She found it difficult not to cry herself while listening. When the story finished, she sat stunned for several minutes before she could find her own voice.

Sitting forward in her chair, she put her hand securely on Lindy's arm and squeezed it comfortingly. "Lindy, do you understand that you didn't deserve this? That none of this was your fault? He's a very sick individual. He's not normal, and what he did to you was not normal. This was all about power and violence. It has nothing to do with the way a relationship between a man and a woman is."

Lindy sort of nodded and sort of shrugged.

Gina kept her anger in check, but spoke with conviction. "I want to hear you say it, Lindy. Say 'it's not my fault, and I didn't deserve it.'"

Lindy finally lifted her eyes and looked into Gina's. "It's not my fault, and I didn't deserve it."

"You remember those words, and you learn to believe them. Now, I want you to stop feeling you have to bear this on your own. You've shared it with me, and now I'll help you through it. We'll work at it together."

Lindy gave a weak smile, grateful for Gina's kindness. "I actually do feel better after talking about it."

"Good. Sometimes we need to say things out loud, so we can hear it. It makes it a more real thing to deal with and easier to get through and put away. Now, I'll bet what you'd really like more than anything else is a bath."

Lindy's eyes opened wide. "Yes! Can I?"

"You bet you can. I'll get a wheelchair and take you down to the hall to the tub. I know they soaked you in the whirlpool last night, but it hardly counts if you weren't awake to know about it. Besides there's nothing like a good bath to relax and feel clean again."

After retrieving a chair from down the hall, Gina lowered the level of the bed, making it easier to transfer her patient. When they arrived at the tub room, Lindy looked at her feet and suddenly wondered what to do about them.

"Don't worry about that, honey. They can get wet. I'll put on dry bandages when we're done, okay?" Gina turned on the water and rigged the harness that would lift Lindy. "This is gonna feel so good being in nice hot water." After transferring her to the tub, she stripped off her own sweatshirt, revealing a Tee-shirt underneath that made it easier to get her arms wet. She dipped a fresh white facecloth and a bar of soap into the water, rubbing the soap over the cloth until it frothed. "You've got a lot of bruises, so I'll try to be gentle."

"No, just scrub. I don't care about the bruises."

Gina understood the need to feel clean. She had seen women who removed layers of their skin with scrub brushes, in an attempt to wash the emotional filth away. Trying to be mindful of the broken bones, she started on the back and shoulders, glad Lindy could not see her cringe upon discovering the black and blue outline of a boot print splayed across the kidney. She blinked back her own tears and nudged at them with her shoulder trying to wipe them away as she scrubbed.

Lindy sat silent under her ministrations, craving the small sense of absolution that came with the cleanliness.

Gina noticed the infestation in her hair without surprise. "We have some chemicals in the ER to take care of your little visitors. After I'm done washing you, I'll leave you to soak for a bit while I go get them. How's that?"

"Sounds wonderful. I really needed this. It feels so much cleaner than a bed bath." As gratitude welled in her chest, she whispered, "Thank you."

Gina scrubbed her arms and face, trying to be gentle on the burnt breasts. She managed to scrub Lindy's inner thighs and genitals without embarrassing her, simply by keeping casual conversation running throughout the task.

When she was finished Lindy lay back in the tub, and Gina turned on the whirlpool jets to help her relax before heading to the ER for the delousing chemicals.

Basking in the deliciously hot water, Lindy thought of all the times she would have given anything for a steamy bath or shower, just to feel clean. Tears came unbidden and ran of their own accord.

When Gina returned she noticed the tears but said nothing, focussing on getting Lindy out of the tub. Her hair would have to be washed over a sink.

When the job was finished and they returned to the room, Gina sat the wheelchair by the window, allowing

Lindy to look outside while she changed the bedding in an effort to prevent a re-infestation. She brushed out Lindy's shoulder-length brown hair and used a fine tooth comb to pick out as many nits as she could find.

"So Lindy, tell me what you studied at school besides piano."

"I finished my master's in library science. I have such a passion for books. Since I spent so much time in the library growing up, my mother suggested I make a career of it."

"We have a lovely library here in town. In fact, they recently built on an addition. When you're released from here, I'll take you to see it." She tucked her into the clean bed and planted a kiss on the girl's head. "Right now, I think you're very tired and should probably get some more sleep. You can dream about happy things, because you're safe, and he can't ever hurt you again."

"Thanks, Aint Bea." She gave a genuine smile this time, then laid back and closed her eyes. Sleep came easily and for the first time in a long time, undisturbed.

•

Brody arrived at his parents' house in Lander at two thirty. With half an hour to spare before work, he wanted to check in with his mother. Knowing how efficient she was, he knew she would have already been to the hospital to see the victim. He wanted her professional take on it.

"Hey, Ma. It's me. Where are ya?" he hollered as he came in the front door.

"Kitchen. Come on in."

He ambled into the kitchen and stopped at the fridge. Helping himself to the leftovers from last night's dinner, he made a thick roast beef sandwich and sat down at the table to enjoy it. His mother poured him a glass of milk and set it in front of him.

"So, did you get in to see her?"

"Sure did." Gina bristled at the mention of it.

"And?"

"And what, Brody? I saw her." Tension and indignation flared without warning as she spoke. She could not help it. Her mind was incapable of putting away the things Lindy had confided to her, and it ate at her heart. Her words came lashing out, laced with the anger that consumed her. "I saw her bandaged hands and feet. I saw the physical and emotional scars that she'll bear the rest of her life. I saw the agony she's suffering. I saw a pianist who wonders if she'll ever play again. A librarian who wonders if she'll ever be able to pick up a book. A runner who wonders if she'll ever walk again. A woman who's had more indignity thrust upon her than any human should ever have to bear. So what exactly is it you want to know, Brody?"

"Ma, why are you shouting at me? I didn't do it to her." Brody sat back, stunned. He studied his mother's pained expression. "You're really upset. I've never seen you like this before, and you've done this kind of counseling for years. You always manage to keep a detachment."

"Well, I'm sorry. I've never seen a case like this one. Maybe heard of them in a distant sort of way, but never actually seen one. And so help me, don't you dare ask her to tell you about it. Not one single detail. Do you understand me?"

It was not often that Gina spoke to him like he was still a little boy, bossing him as though he had no choice but to do as he was told. But whether she liked it or not, he was a grown man with a responsibility. In a voice that came out quiet amidst the surrounding tempest, he told her simply, "Ma, you know I gotta job to do."

"Not one detail, Brody Ashton. Do not make her live through that horror again. If you want to know something, well, never mind, I can't tell you. But so help me, Brody, when you catch the son of a... "

"MA!" Brody exclaimed, shocked by his mother's display of pure rage.

Gina clutched the back of a chair and took a few deep breaths to calm down, then, in an even tone of voice said, "Brody, hear me well. When you catch him, I don't want you to bring him in. Just kill him. No questions asked. Just put a bullet straight through his filthy head."

"Ma, I'm sure I'd like to but...."

"Brody, don't mess with me today. I said kill him, and I meant it. I promise you, even God will shake your hand."

Brody left his parents home full of questions he dared not ask. He had suffered his mother's wrath before, and it was not pretty. It did not happen often, but when it did, he wanted to be on the other side of the globe. He drove to the station and checked to see if the lab reports were back on the evidence he dropped off on the way home that morning. As Dr. Shepherd suspected, they had solid proof of three different attackers. He could not help flinching when he heard the news.

With the reports in hand, he strode through the deputies office to his desk and dropped heavily into his chair. Clearing away some of the clutter, he pulled blank forms up on his computer screen and started filling in the paper work with the details acquired thus far.

A girl pushed through the door and headed straight for his desk, a large manila envelope in her hand. He smiled at her, although he had never known her to smile back in the seven years he worked for the Sheriff's office.

"Thanks, Marnie."

"No problem, Deputy."

Brody opened the envelope, and pulled out a stack of 8 x 10 glossies Meghan had taken of the abuse. He scrutinized them and saw a great deal more injury than he noticed when he had been there, leaving him feeling sick by the time he dropped them on the desk top. Leaning back in his chair, he ran a hand over his face.

His mother was right. This superseded any rape case he had ever dealt with before. The fact that the violations perpetuated on this scale over a period of weeks worsened it. He stroked his blond moustache as he meditated on it. Picking up the photos, he stuffed them back in the envelope and dropped it in the bottom drawer of his desk.

Hating to admit it, Brody acknowledged this case was bigger than him. He pulled out his directory and looked up the number for the FBI office in Denver. Even though Lindy was safe at the moment, the incident had crossed state borders, and kidnapping was a federal offence. The phone was answered on the third ring.

"FBI. How can I direct your call?"

"This is Deputy Ashton in Lander. I have a kidnapping to report."

"One moment, please."

Brody heard another ring, immediately answered by a crisp, male voice. "Agent Northrup."

"This is Deputy Brody Ashton in Lander, Wyoming. I'd like to report a kidnapping."

"Go ahead, Deputy. What's the situation?"

"I have a twenty-three year old woman from Portland, abducted just outside of Baker City, Oregon on January 14th. She's been held somewhere in this vicinity. She was able to escape last night. I found her lying at the side of the road, naked and unconscious with severe hypothermia. She was totally disoriented during the escape and has no idea where she was held."

"Deputy, I'll be there tomorrow morning, about ten o'clock. See you then."

Brody knew local law officers and federal agents were often predisposed to feel an animosity toward one another but he felt relieved to have Special Agent Northrup on the way. He hoped to be allowed to assist on the case, but placing it in the hands of experience helped him breathe easier.

Plunking his hat on his head, he stalked out to his cruiser. Like his mother, he knew better than to become personally involved in his cases, but without question, he agreed with her. This one was different.

Parking the car in front of Chocolates for Breakfast, Too, he went inside and laid out the cash for a three pound box of hand dipped chocolates and three boxes of herbal teas. With the gift-wrapped candy in hand, he headed south to Lander Valley Medical Center.

CHAPTER FIVE

Brody knocked at her hospital door just as Lindy wakened from a nap. With an apologetic smile, he poked his head in the room. "Hi. I know I wasn't supposed to come back until tomorrow, but this is my tomorrow. Can I come in?"

Blinking her eyes against the afternoon sun that streamed in her window, she squinted at her guest. The hat on his head made it easy to recognize the officer who saved her life.

"Deputy. Sure, come on in." As he entered the room the door sailed shut behind him, and she felt a moment's panic. Being alone with a man, any man, in a closed room sent shivers racing through her. "Could you please leave the door open?"

Brody witnessed the moment of fear that streaked across her features. Instantly aware of his mistake, he caught hold of the door before it could close all the way and propped it open before approaching the bedside.

"How you feeling? You're sure looking better than last night."

"I'm not sure I can answer that. I just seem to drift in and out of sleep. I guess it's all the drugs they're pumping into me."

"I brought you something." With a shy, lopsided grin, he held the box out in front of him in offering. Her face lit with surprise, and he was immediately taken by the transformation. She had a beautiful smile, and he felt gratified to see it.

"Thank you. That's very nice of you." Her eyelashes fluttered as she fought back a wave of emotion. Kindness had become foreign to her. Holding up her heavily bandaged hands to demonstrate her point, she told him, "I guess you get the honor of opening it, since I don't have any hands." She dropped them back to her lap and admitted, "Honestly, I don't know if you're a day early or not. I'm afraid I don't know one day from the next anymore. I have no sense of day and night. Time has become completely elastic. Five hours can pass in ten minutes and ten minutes can feel like ten hours."

Brody nodded, knowing he couldn't begin to comprehend the many ways her world changed over the past month. Hoping to distract her from her misery, even if only for a few moments, he set the box on her tray table and opened it for her.

As the contents were revealed, her eyes grew large with pleasure, and she smiled unabashedly at him.

"This is the best gift in the world. I have a major chocolate fetish. I'd live on chocolate if I could get away with it. However, I insist on sharing with my hero."

"No, they're for you."

"I'm afraid eating it would totally embarrass me if you weren't having some too. I sort of," she paused, uncertain how to reveal her uncontrollable habit, "make noise."

He watched her wince at the revelation and was instantly intrigued. "You make noises while eating chocolate?"

She looked at him sheepishly. "Well, I don't actually

60

eat it. I savor it."

Determined to keep her spirits buoyed, Brody figured he may as well find out first hand. He tossed a chocolate in his mouth, then chose another and held it to her lips. He smiled at her, and she smiled back as she opened her mouth to accept it. The moment it touched her tongue, her eyes drifted closed. Brody pulled up the chair and sat, resting his elbow on the bed and propping his chin on his hand while he stared with anticipation.

"Mmmmm!" she purred. He watched as her bottom jaw worked slowly back and forth, but he could see she was not chewing. She took a deep breath and let out another sensuous "Mmmmm." Her breathing picked up its pace a little, and a small whimper of pleasure escaped. The tip of her tongue slipped out and delicately licked at her lips, which she then pressed together and rubbed back and forth. When she finally swallowed what little remained of the confection, she let out a sigh of completion. She opened her eyes and found him gazing at her in rapt fascination. Color quickly crept up her cheeks, and she dropped her eyes. When she dared look up again, he had still not moved a muscle.

"Hello. Earth to Brody."

His eyes remained glued to her mouth while he searched for his voice and finally murmured, "That was the most fascinating thing I've ever seen in my life. And you do that every time?"

"Unfortunately," she confessed.

"Heck, nothing unfortunate about that. Nothing at all." Refusing to take his eyes from her, his fingers reached blindly for the box and fumbled for another chocolate, tossing it into his mouth before quickly retrieving a second one to feed her. He sat mesmerized while she repeated the ritual. When she finished he still sat motionless. "Wow. I could sit here all day and watch this. Holy Hannah, I know guys who'd pay to watch this."

"So you think I should take up eating chocolate as an occupation and charge admission? It does sound like a great way to break the bank. Of course, if I did nothing but eat chocolate all the time, I'd end up being one of those people that gets so fat they can't get out of their bed. Bet it wouldn't hold the same mystique then, would it?" She grinned at him, and he snapped out of it, laughing at himself. "It's a natural reaction I'm afraid."

"I have to admit, I'm definitely in favor of natural reactions." He leaned back in the chair and folded his hands over his stomach, relaxing.

"You're back in uniform. I presume that means you must be on the job."

"I am, but this is an unofficial visit. I just wanted to check on you, see how you're doing. No questions."

She dropped her eyes to stare at her hands. "Thank you for that." Struggling to maintain her composure, she fought through her self pity for something conversational. "What's it like outside?"

"Just about the same as the last time you were out there, 'cepting a bit of sunshine. Not much going on out in the world today."

"Your mother came to see me earlier."

"How'd that go?" He balanced his Stetson on his knee and ran his fingers around the sharp rim.

She turned her attention to the window, fixing her gaze on the mountains in the distance. "Well, I don't know how she felt about it, but it was really quite wonderful for me. She's very kind and…smart. Yes, she's really smart. She somehow seemed to know and understand what I needed before I did. I felt much better by the time she left. I hope I didn't scare her away."

He thought of his mother and smiled. "Takes an awful lot to scare my mother, Lindy. She's a gutsy lady."

Needing to change the subject, she said, "She told me she was the nurse that helped when that country singer, Kip Adams, was born."

"Yes, she did."

"Did you ever know him?" Uncertain how to make small talk with someone she did not really know, she tried to remember things from previous conversations to draw on.

"We were good friends all through school, so yeah, I knew him then and still do. Chris hasn't really changed since he became famous. He's pretty much the same guy. Just has a bigger bank account than all the rest of the town combined."

"Chris?"

"His real name is Chris, and that's what he goes by when he comes home. He only uses Kip professionally. Sort of keeps a line there for him; helps him sort out his life."

"I guess that makes sense."

"Yeah, if somebody says 'Hey, Kip,' he knows it's someone who only knows him through his work. If somebody says, 'Hey, Chris,' he knows it's a friend. He's had a rough few years. Just got divorced. I think he's out on the road touring right now."

Lindy nodded as she listened. Okay, with that subject exhausted, what could she talk about now? "I hear you work for Sheriff Taylor." A smile tickled her lips.

"My ma told you that?" He chuckled. "Yeah, I told you this was Mayberry, didn't I? We had a barber named Floyd too, but he's retired now."

Lindy giggled. "I thought she was joking when she

told me, but when she insisted it was true, I had to laugh. I've got to say, I hope you're a better deputy than Barney Fife."

"If I wasn't, I wouldn't have a job. Sheriff doesn't go around doing our job for us here." He studied her a moment, and said, "You have a wonderful smile. It's nice to see it."

"I suppose it beats looking dead, doesn't it?" she quipped soberly. They sat in silence a few minutes, and she felt herself quickly standing on the precipice of depression and self-loathing. Don't fall, Lindy, don't do it, she told herself. She blew out a deep breath of resolve and asked, "So, what kind of things do you do when you're off duty?"

"I run every day. I like just about anything athletic, pretty much whatever's going on. I'm going snowboarding next Sunday with one of my friends from work. I bought an old Victorian out in the countryside that needed lots of renovating, and I'm having a great time with it. I like working with my hands. Designing and choosing things for it, you know, cupboard doors and knobs and door handles. Send me to the lumber store, and I'm in paradise."

He talked so easily about himself, and she warmed to him. "You're a very busy man."

"For the most part I like to be."

"I think you're too busy to be hanging around here. You should probably be out there giving someone a ticket."

"I am right where I want to be. Never too busy for a friend, so enough of that. Now, tell me all about Lindy. What does she do with herself?"

Lindy frowned at her bandaged hands. "I'm afraid I don't have an answer for that any more."

"Okay, then tell me about Lindy Lassiter in Portland.

Who were you before you came to Mayberry? Hey! Lindy Lassiter of Lander! Sounds kinda cool, doesn't it? Like it's meant to be."

"I guess if my goal in life was to become a tongue twister it'd be pretty good," she smiled. "Hmm. Lindy Lassiter of Portland just finished a Masters in library science. I love reading. I taught piano classes. I ran every day. I like a good game of tennis, spinning, cross country biking, swimming, and as you've seen, chocolate. I love movies, and I see a lot of them. I like going to concerts--everything from rock to Bach. I love ballet and live theatre, and I've always wanted to go white water rafting. How's that for a mixed-up girl?"

"It doesn't sound at all like a mixed-up girl. It sounds like an interesting, diversified girl. I think it's great having a lot of interests. I guess because I'm that way too. Hey, that one thing you said, spinning, is that like with yarn?"

"No, it's like an aerobics class on a stationary bike. It's a real tough work out, but it feels great." To her amazement, Lindy felt comfortable with the young deputy. His natural manner and easy smile set her at ease. Surprised, she found herself starting to open up to him, wanting to prolong the visit. "So, I guess you like cop movies, huh?"

"I like adventure, comedy, mystery. I can handle a movie just fine with nobody in a car chase or shooting people up. I'm not saying I don't enjoy those on occasion, too, but it's not the only thing I enjoy. Even a chick flick can be good if it makes her get all soft and snuggly."

"Is there a special her?" she wondered, eyebrows raised.

"Nah, just going with the flavor of the week. Haven't met the right gal yet. But when I do, that's it. I'm getting married and settling down. I know it would make my mother happy. What about you? I figure since you picked up and left town, there wasn't anybody special there."

"No, I spent most of my time with school, and when Mom got sick, well, I looked after her, too. I had to cut back my schedule. Never had the time to get serious with anyone, but I'm not worried. I've got lots of years to find someone, or maybe I'll just be happy on my own. I'm sure it won't be easy finding a guy interested in a girl with no fingers or toes."

He swallowed hard, uncertain how to reply to her dose of reality. "Hey, I'm sorry about that." He leaned forward and set his hand on her arm. "I don't know how it feels, and I won't pretend I do, but I can imagine how awful it is for you. I know you've got a few weeks of uncertainty ahead. If you want to talk, I'm a good listener."

"Like your mother, huh? Thanks for the offer. If I need you, I'll let you know."

He looked around the room, wondering what would keep her mind off her troubles for the time she would be confined here. "Don't you have a TV in this place?"

"No. They cost money, and since I'm broker than a piece of smashed pottery until I get my things back, I won't be having one. I'm amazed they're even letting me stay here without my insurance information."

"Don't worry about that. I told them it's pending. It just means I'll have to get out there and find your things for you. I guess I should probably get going and do what I'm paid for."

"Thanks for coming by, Brody. I appreciate it. And thanks for not asking about…you know."

"Are you kidding me? I wouldn't admit it to most people, but the truth is, you're looking at a man who is still afraid of his mama. If I was to upset you the teapot would boil over, and there would be big trouble. She frequently tells me I'm not too big to go over her knee, and I tend to believe she means it. Besides, I really just wanted to see how you're faring."

He twirled his hat in his hand for a minute before giving her the update on her case. "There's a special agent coming from the FBI tomorrow. I'm afraid you'll probably have to talk to him. He's from the kidnapping unit, so hopefully he'll help us put away the guys who did this to you." About to rise to his feet, he changed his mind. "Hey, can I watch you eat one more chocolate before I go?"

She rolled her eyes and smiled, shaking her head in amusement. "I never turn down chocolate."

He selected a runny maraschino cherry and set it on her tongue. Captivated, he watched as her eyes closed and her jaw started to slowly move just the slightest bit. "Mmmmm," she started. Then she sighed and moaned and "Mmmmm"'d again. At the end, the tip of her tongue appeared and licked her lips. They pressed together and rubbed back and forth. Opening her eyes again, she saw the fascination on his face, and started to giggle. "Go to work, Deputy. Enough lollygagging."

Pleased to see her laugh, even for a brief moment, he stood. "You're right. I'm off. That's really an incredible thing to watch, you know. You've got it down to an art."

"Bye, Brody," she prompted with an eyebrow raised. As he turned to leave, she stopped him. "Hey, Brody? Thanks."

He heard the sincerity in her voice, and knew a lot of emotion was tied up in that single word. He tipped his head in acknowledgment. "No problem. See ya later." He pushed his hat on his head and left her. His determination to do whatever it took to close the case, hardened.

Lindy lay in her bed, looking at the empty doorway. His visit had brought a pleasant respite. Something to draw her attention from the horror that was her life. Now he was gone, and there was just her and the memories. Tears started to pool in her eyes as she studied her hands, distraught by the thought of never having their use again. Would she ever spend a day of her life not haunted by the events of the past month? It didn't seem likely. A quiet sob escaped on her breath.

•

By the time Brody's shift finished he managed to locate her car, which amazingly, still sat where she left it. Her purse had been found in the parking lot the day of the abduction and turned in by an honest citizen. Her identification and cash were still safely tucked inside. With part one of the problem solved, he needed to figure out how to get them to Lander.

The meager night shift officers started to drift into the station. Brody heaved a sigh and began clearing things off his desk.

"Hey, Brody. How's it going?"

He glanced up at his sandy-haired friend. "Pretty good, Rhett. How 'bout you?"

Rhett dropped into his chair at his desk across the aisle from Brody's and twitched his top drawer open to find a stick of Juicy Fruit gum. Unwrapping the foil, he answered, "Can't complain. How's Jane Doe?"

"Jane Doe is Lindy Lassiter from Portland. She survived the hypothermia okay. Her hands and feet are bandaged up. Doc Shepherd says they'll have to wait a good month to see if she gets to keep 'em or not. As for the other, well, Ma went to see her today."

"And?"

Brody hesitated, still disturbed by his mother's reaction. "Ma says it's the most horrendous story she's ever heard and threatened my life if I ask Lindy to relive any of it." He hunched forward and spoke in a quiet, confidential tone, his brows creased in memory. "I saw the photos. It's a lot worse than I glimpsed last night. She's got a coupla broken ribs from being beaten. Raped every which way from Sunday. I'm determined on this one, Rhett. We've got to find and stop them before they can do it to someone else. He's in our back yard now, and I don't want him going after the women of Fremont County. Got a fella from the FBI coming in tomorrow morning to take over."

"Any new leads?"

"Detectives went out this morning but could only follow the footprints for a distance before they disappeared. They said sometimes she seemed to be going in circles. Probably confusion from the hypothermia. So, we have no idea where she was held, and I don't think she'll be any help on that score. Poor woman, didn't even know what state she was in."

Brody propped a foot up on his open drawer and sat back in his chair, tapping a pen on his knee. Staring at the calendar on his desktop, an idea formulated. "Hey, you've got next Monday and Tuesday off, right?"

Rhett studied him through narrowed eyes. "Whatcha got in mind?" Wary of his friend's unpredictability, he made it a practice to always ask before committing himself to anything with Brody.

"How about a trip to Baker City?"

"Where the heck is Baker City, and since I don't even know where it is, the next question is how far is it, and why do I want to go there?"

"Baker City, Oregon, is where she was kidnapped. Her car and ID are still there. Thought maybe we could ask some questions, and bring her things back with us." Tossing the idea casually on the table, he picked up a handful of paper clips and started linking them together.

"Again, how far, and when did the sheriff's department become a vehicle delivery service?"

"Just under seven hundred miles, and because I want to help. Geez, after all she's been through, somebody ought to help her out. Besides, I'm conducting an investigation here, remember? Only makes sense to make some inquiries at the abduction point."

"Okay, that's why you want to go. Why do I want to go?"

Brody decided it was time to bring out the big guns. "I'll tell you what. You meet me in front of LVMC tomorrow afternoon at about five o'clock, and I'll take you to meet her. Once you've seen this girl eat chocolate, you'll do anything for her. Most erotic thing I've ever seen."

"Eating chocolate? You're losing your mind, Ashton."

Convinced Rhett would capitulate after witnessing it for himself, Brody prodded him, "Meet me there, and see it for yourself. She's not even trying to be sexy. It's all natural. Totally amazing to watch."

Rhett chuckled at Brody's apparent enchantment. "I'll be there, but I think you have a few screws loose, buddy. Anything else new?"

Brody thought for a minute, then his face lit. "Guess who asked me out last night?"

"You already told me. Jen and Tara. I admit, I'm jealous. No need to gloat."

"No, somebody else. You won't believe this one."

"Yes, I will. Listen, you left here at eleven o'clock last

70

night, and on the way home got asked out by three different women? I wish to heck you'd marry one, and let somebody else have a chance in this town. So tell, who is it this time?" Rhett put his feet up on the desk, resigned to hear of the latest conquest.

"Meghan Shepherd."

"The shy one? She's pretty cute."

"Yeah. Nice girl. Gonna see her Saturday. If we get some snow we're going snowmobiling out at the Hathaway ranch. Should be fun." Brody dropped the remaining files into his drawer and locked it with a small silver key on his key ring.

"Wait a minute. You're gonna date sisters? I don't think that's the smartest thing you've ever done."

Brody shrugged it off. "I'm heading out. Think I'll actually try to grab a few hours of sleep tonight. Hopefully, nobody'll jump in front of my truck needing to be rescued on the way home. I spent all night at the hospital."

"Drive safe."

Brody shrugged into his large navy parka and ventured out into the cold night. While the engine warmed, he got out to brush the new fallen snow off the windows. Climbing back inside, he turned on his Kip Adams CD and listened while the engine hummed. When the heat finally warmed the interior, he drove across town and out into the countryside to his old farmhouse.

Bone tired, he trudged up the back steps and entered his kitchen. Before even taking his coat off, he put a cup of water into the microwave and heated it for some chamomile tea. Doffing the winter outerwear while the seconds ticked by, he padded in his socks to drop some soft classical music in the stereo. The microwave beeped and he pulled out the hot water, dropped the tea bag in, and went to lounge on the sofa with his feet up on the coffee table. The tea and music relaxed him to the point of feeling drowsy.

Placing the now empty mug on a table top, he closed his eyes and listened to the music as a vision of Lindy eating chocolate danced in his head. He saw the bruises on her face, her hands looking mummified. As he drifted into slumber, he witnessed Lindy walking across a half-full parking lot. She had something in her hands--a bag. Closer scrutiny revealed the logo of a submarine shop. In her other hand she carried a paper soft-drink cup.

Her soft brown hair shone in the sunlight, falling around the collar of her Melton bench coat. She appeared happy, self assured… but wait… two men followed behind her, rapidly closing the distance between them. Brody tried to see their faces, but they remained blurred. He tried shouting to warn her, but no sound would come out. He tried running to save her, but his leaden legs felt glued to the pavement.

Helpless, he witnessed one of the men grab her from behind, covering her mouth and nose with a cloth in his hand. In mere moments, she passed out cold. His companion helped lift her into the trunk of a car, and they rummaged around before closing the lid.

When they climbed into the front seat and started the engine, Brody tried to at least determine the make and model. They pulled out of the parking lot in a dark green Caprice Classic. He squinted to decipher the license plate number, but the car grew distant quickly, and he was unable to make out even the state. Frustration enveloped him as he struggled in vain to pursue them. They were getting away. They had kidnapped her, and they were getting away. He watched the whole thing transpire, helpless. Alone, he stood in the parking lot shouting for help at the top of his lungs. No one heard him. No one came to help.

The sound of shouting jolted him awake. Realizing he was in his living room, he gave his head a shake to clear it, then took his mug to the kitchen sink. After locking the back door, he headed upstairs for the night.

Seated on the edge of the bed, he unlaced his work boots, then stripped off his uniform. As he dumped it in the laundry basket on the floor of his closet, he acknowledged gratitude for a mother that still did his laundry.

With the light out, he climbed into his queen size bed, pulling the blankets up around his neck. Cold winds howled against his window, making him glad a new furnace kept the house warm. Unable to shake the disturbing dream, it weighed heavily on his mind thwarting any attempt to sleep. Lying with his eyes closed, he recalled occasional dreams in the past that related to work. The difference this time was he had never stood by, impotent to stop the crime before. He debated how much was his imagination, and how much was real.

Although beyond exhaustion, every time his eyes closed his mind replayed the scene.

"Is it like this for her? Does she relive it every time she closes her eyes? Does it haunt all of her dreams?" he wondered, feeling a new empathy for Lindy. If what he envisioned bothered him to this degree and kept him from sleep, then how much worse must it be for her? Was she reliving all the brutality and the raping? His stomach rolled over and clenched, leaving him sick at the thought.

When sleep finally embraced him at four in the morning, he knew he would not find peace until he closed the case.

CHAPTER SIX

Gina walked to Main Street and headed for The Whippy Bird. The silver bell tinkled as she pushed the door open, and Joanna Hathaway glanced up and smiled from behind the counter where she penciled entries into a notebook.

"Hi, Gina, how are you this morning?"

"I'm doing just fine, Joanna. I don't mind the cold so much when I've got some nice fresh snow to go with it." She wandered among the racks, fingering clothing as she went. "I'm in the market for some pretty nightgowns for a girl in her early twenties, and I could use some help. I guess you probably heard about Brody rescuing her the other night out on the highway."

"Matter of fact, I did hear something about it. He found her laying by the road unconscious? How is she?"

"Yes, poor dear. Her name is Lindy Lassiter. By the time Brody found her she was almost dead from hypothermia." Gina shook her head in sorrow. "She's a lovely girl. Her mother died last year and left her on her own. She'll be in the hospital for at least a few weeks, and I thought she'd probably be more comfortable in something nicer than those hospital gowns."

"Perfect timing. I just put some pretty new ones on the rack this morning." She directed Gina to the back corner where the night apparel was displayed.

Gina started sliding hangers along the bar, browsing through the various styles. "Well, this one's pretty. The flannelette will feel nice on her skin, too. Anything in a green? Lindy's got lovely green eyes."

"How about this one?" Joanna held out a navy and green plaid nightie with pin tuck pleats across the bodice and a large dust ruffle around the bottom.

"Oh, I like that. I'll take that one, and this one, and maybe one more. How about that lilac colored one? I think it would look lovely with her complexion."

"All right. I'll take these things to the counter for you. Anything else?"

"Well, let me think. Slippers are out of the question. Her feet are bandaged up. Maybe a nice bathrobe." She wandered to the robe rack and found a rich emerald green velour with a zipper down the front. "I think this one's perfect." Gina lifted it from the rack and carried it to the cash register. "I guess that's all she'll really need in the hospital."

"How's she doing, Gina?"

"Her fingers and toes were frozen solid. Matt says he'll have to wait a least a month for the swelling to go down before he knows if she'll be able to keep them or if they'll need to be amputated. It's the saddest thing I've ever seen, Joanna. She's an accomplished pianist and a librarian. If she can't ever use her fingers again, her greatest loves will be lost to her. My heart just breaks for that child. She's so sweet."

"If there's anything I can do, let me know." Joanna offered. She took Gina's MasterCard and ran it through the machine, then handed it back. The cash register spewed out the receipt and Gina signed it, handing Joanna back her copy. "If she doesn't like any of these, you can bring 'em back."

"Thanks, Joanna."

Gina left the shop and dropped into Corner Drug next door. Picking up a basket inside the door, she browsed up and down the aisles, picking up hair care items, baby powder, oil, toothbrush and paste, deodorant, some cologne and a few cosmetics. She knew that when a woman looked good, she felt better.

Tossing her purchases on the front seat of the car, she headed to the hospital.

•

Brody came in from his morning run, sweaty and breathing hard. Taking the stairs two at a time, he went into his bathroom and turned on the shower, letting the water heat up as he doffed his sweat-soaked clothing. As the room filled with steam, he stepped into the tub and let the hot water runnel down his chest. He felt driven to run an extra mile while thinking about the case of the frozen lady. The exercise helped work out some of the tension, and now the water relieved the stress further. He shampooed his blond hair and lathered his body with a bar of Zest. After rinsing clean, he toweled dry and decided to put his uniform on, even though he was not scheduled to start until three.

By eleven o'clock he sat at his desk at the Sheriff's Office, going over his notes on Lindy's case. Glancing up, he spotted an unfamiliar face heading his way. He rose to his feet and extended his hand. "Special Agent Northrup? I'm Brody Ashton."

"Deputy. Just call me Northrup, or Bracken. Either one's fine," replied the tall, dark haired agent.

"Okay, Bracken. Call me Brody. Everybody else here does."

"Fine. Let's see what you've got."

Brody pulled an extra chair to his desk, and with the formalities out of the way the two men went straight to work. He handed the agent a legal size yellow folder. "I made a complete duplicate of the file so you could have your own working copy for reference."

Bracken sat back and eyed the officer, sizing him up before asking, "Brody, are you wanting to work this case with me?"

"I'd like to if it's all right with you. Since I'm the one who found her, I'd like to see it through."

"Great. Let's get started." They opened their folders and reviewed the contents in their entirety. It did not take an incredibly long time.

"Well, let's go see where you found her." Bracken stood and shrugged his shoulder in a circular motion, working out the stiffness. The men chatted amiably as they drove through the town and headed out northwest of town in the cruiser. Seeing the police markers still at the side of the road at the site, Brody pulled onto the shoulder and parked. Bracken wandered around, crouching down to look where footprints no longer remained. A blanket of fresh fallen snow covered Fremont County stealing any traces of Lindy's passage.

He looked at the surrounding landscape to see if he could scope any possible locations for her imprisonment, but was met with a wide open prairie at the base of the foothills. "Well, I guess there's not much to be learned here. We might as well grab some lunch and discuss how to proceed. It's your town. Where do we eat?"

"How hungry are you?" Brody grinned.

Bracken laid a hand on his stomach, and felt the

rumblings. He missed breakfast to catch the early plane. "I guess I'm hungry enough."

Getting back in the cruiser, Brody started the engine and turned the car back toward town. "Good. Then today we eat at Judd's Grubb. People come from all over for their burgers. Massive things."

"Sounds good to me. Drive on."

•

Lindy lay in bed staring vacantly at the television when Gina walked in. "Hey, you got a television. That's great."

"Gina! I'm glad you came." She tried to sit up, but winced in pain and relaxed back against the pillows again. "I think Brody had something to do with the television. He asked yesterday why I didn't have one."

"I've brought you something." Gina set the bags on the chair by the window and one at a time, pulled the nighties out to show Lindy. The girl's eyes lit up at each new item displayed.

"Oh, Gina. They're beautiful. Thank you so much. I'll pay you back as soon as Brody finds my stuff. I do have some money in the bank.

"You'll do no such thing, Missy. This is a gift, and I was happy to do it. I also stopped in at the drugstore and picked up a few things." She dumped the contents of the bag into Lindy's lap on the bed.

Lindy's eyes glistened with tears.

"Well, I've never seen anyone cry over getting a hairbrush before," Gina teased.

"It's just, you're being so nice to me. It's been so long since anyone's been this kind." Lindy swiped at her eyes with her swaddled hand.

"Oh, darling." Gina sat on the edge of the bed and

embraced the young woman, mindful of the injured ribs and collarbone. "Life is gonna get better from here on. I promise you it will. It's gonna take a bit of time, but you'll somehow manage to put all this behind you and find some happiness in the world."

Lindy sniffled and relaxed, being careful not to bump her hands. It seemed so long since anyone cared enough to give her a hug. Gina provided the emotional medicine she needed to heal her soul as well as her body.

"Now, I didn't know about shades for makeup, so if you don't like this, I'll take it back and exchange it. That's not a problem." She held up the blush and the lipstick showing Lindy the shades.

"Try a bit on my arm," Lindy suggested.

Gina brushed a bit of blush on her arm, and it blended perfectly.

"I think you did a better job than I do. I've never managed this good a match. I like the lipstick, too."

"Good." She sat back and smiled, happy her small gifts brought so much pleasure. "Would you like a trip to the bathtub today?"

"Yes, I would, but maybe not just yet. Can we talk for a bit first?"

"Sure we can, honey." Gina pulled a chair next to the bed and sat, leaning forward with her arms resting on the mattress ready to listen. "Something particular on your mind, or do you just want to chat?"

Lindy stared hard at her lap, and her brow furrowed as she dredged up the courage to talk about it. "Last night, I kept waking from nightmares. I relived it all over again. I'm so frightened to go to sleep. I'm afraid those things will be there waiting for me, every time."

Gina nodded. She expected it. "It's because it's still so fresh, honey girl. I wish I could just push a button and say it will never happen, but you know it doesn't work that way. As happier things start to happen in your daytime, those night-time hours will begin to grow easier. The nightmares will probably still come from time to time, but with less frequency as time goes on." She spoke with conviction, willing the young woman to believe her words. "What we need to do is infuse your mind with good things that will push the horror away. Was there a specific event you were remembering?"

"Yes." Lindy felt a knot in her throat, choking her. She swallowed hard as she fought to say the words. "It was one time when he brought a friend. It was so painful; I could feel myself being ripped open. I could scream all I wanted, because my mouth was always taped shut unless they wanted fellatio. They were so amused when it made me vomit. I would imagine I was somewhere, anywhere else. I tried not to struggle, to just leave my body, but that time it was so painful. Maybe that's why that particular incident is so vivid. Because I couldn't disappear."

"That sounds reasonable."

"When he pulled me from the closet that day there was something different in his voice, in the atmosphere. Sometimes others were there, but I never knew it unless they spoke. But that time, he brought someone new. The man didn't say much, but he was so vicious, so cruel. I sensed he wanted more than the rape. He wanted to hurt me, to cause pain. I was scared for my life that day. I honestly believed he would kill me. The things he did, the way he did them – at one point he strangled me until the scum made him let go."

Gina tried not to be affected by what she was hearing, to stay in a capacity where she could comfort and counsel without falling apart. "You survived it, Lindy. You didn't die. You came out of it, and you're safe. I know it's so difficult after what you've been through, but you need to remember — you won. You got away because you were smarter. They tried, but they failed. You're stronger. You're the winner, Lindy." Gina leaned forward and firmly clasped Lindy's forearm. "You're the winner."

Bravely, she lifted her eyes and blinked at her tears. "I never thought of it like that."

"I know it's hard to pull a positive thought from all the filth. But that's it, Lindy. You beat them at their game. You have to keep that in mind and find satisfaction in it." Gina moved onto the bed and collected Lindy in her arms, hugging her close and whispering assurances to her. When she felt the trembling settle, she pulled back and looked into the girl's eyes, needing to talk business. "Lindy, there's a man coming from the FBI."

"Brody mentioned that."

"Would you like me to talk to him? I can tell him the things he needs to know so you don't have to go through it again. He'll probably still have some questions for you, but I can tell him the worst of it. I won't go into the details of the rapes. He doesn't need to know all that."

Relief visibly flooded through Lindy. "Oh, would you?"

"Of course I will. And when he does come to see you, I'll be right here with you if you want. Whatever you need, you just say the word, honey."

Lindy lay back on her pillows and ruminated quietly. Finally, she turned to Gina and said, "I think I'm ready for that bath now."

After the bath Gina dropped a fresh new nightgown over Lindy's head, careful to pass the IV bag through the sleeve and rehang it. Toweling her hair almost dry, Gina took the brush and pulled it gently through the light brown tresses. The ends curled under softly, and she selected two hair clips to pull it back on the sides.

With the hair complete, Gina brushed on some mascara and blush, and ran the lipstick over Lindy's lips. A little spray of cologne, and Lindy felt pretty and feminine -- something she had not felt in a long time. Gina held up a mirror, and she smiled faintly when she saw herself. "I almost look like me."

"Most of the bruises will be gone by next week, and then you'll be Lindy again. In the meantime, what I'm seeing is still pretty."

"Thank you, Gina. You always know just what to say and do. You've helped me so much."

"Honey, you deserve some looking after and pampering. You're such a sweet girl." Gina sat on the edge of the bed and rested a hand on her arm. "I'll always be here for you, whenever you need me. I'm just a phone call away. Day or night. You hear me? We're gonna become fast friends, you and me."

Lindy felt overwhelmed by the kindness. No one had paid attention to her since her mother's death. Her entire life it had been just the two of them, and her mother's passing left a gaping hole in her life.

Frowning, Gina said, "Hey, hey, now. Tears are gonna ruin that make up job. What is it?"

"I miss my Mom. You're so much like her, and I've been so lost since she died last year. It's a terrible feeling when there's not a single person in the whole world who loves you."

"Oh, honey." Gina wrapped her arms around Lindy and held her for a long time, realizing just how sad and lonely the girl was, aside from trying to deal with the rape. She was right. It would be horrid having no one care. She thought of her own two daughters, and wondered who would love them through something like

82

this if she was not around. Her maternal soul opened, and accepted Lindy into her fold, already loving her.

CHAPTER SEVEN

"Hi, Lindy. I thought you could use some color to bighten things up in here." Meghan Shepherd arrived in jeans and a sweatshirt carrying a floral arrangement.

Lindy turned from her view of the mountains and smiled shyly. "Oh, hi. Meghan, right?"

"That's right. How are you feeling today?"

"Just fine, thanks."

Meghan stood at the foot of the bed wearing a skeptical expression. "Now tell the truth. How are you feeling today?"

Lindy sank back into the pillows and admitted, "I hurt just about everywhere. My feet, well I'd hate it, but in reality I think I could handle not being able to use them again. It's the idea of losing the use of my hands that's so distressing. Thank God for anti-depressants. That and the fact that people here have just been so kind to me."

Meghan checked the IV drip against her watch and made an adjustment to it before settling in the chair Gina left beside the bed that morning. "It's nice to see you looking fresh and pert. It sure beats the way you arrived. That's a pretty nightie."

"Gina Ashton bought it for me. She came yesterday and today. She's quite wonderful," Lindy smiled. "She made me feel comfortable right away."

"I'm glad. Gina's a great lady," Meghan smiled and hesitated. "Have you been able to talk to her?"

"Mm hmm. You know, somehow she made it easier," Lindy said with wonder in her voice. "She says when I think about it, I should talk about it instead of trying to keep it bottled up. After we talked yesterday, I felt as though a huge burden fell from my shoulders. It doesn't take away all the anxiety by any means, but I don't feel so alone with it anymore."

Meghan sat forward and lightly rubbed Lindy's arm in comfort. "I'm glad. We see a lot of patients who won't talk, and it just makes it that much harder for them to deal with it." She spotted a box with a familiar label sitting on the side table. "Hmm. I see treats from Chocolates for Breakfast, Too, no less. Hand dipped at the store; very expensive and worth every penny."

Lindy turned to glance at the box as Meghan spoke. "Brody brought me those. I wish you hadn't told me they're expensive. Now I'll feel guilty every time I eat one, but since you brought it up, we ought to break them out right now. Want one?"

Meghan blushed and stammered, "I'm sorry. I wasn't trying to imply…"

"I know that. But let's have some anyway. You know, I can't have any unless somebody is here to feed them to me, and I am such a chocoholic."

"Okay." Meghan lifted the box, and opened it to display them to Lindy. "Pick one. Just like playing battleship. Letters down the side rows and numbers across the top."

Lindy started counting in her head. "Okay, I'll have

C5."

Meg picked up the designated chocolate and fed it to Lindy, who began the routine of savoring it. She watched with amusement. "Hey, I like chocolate, but you're making me think I'm missing out on something important here."

"Okay. I'll give instructions. First, you must never bite it. Take the chocolate and place it on your tongue." She watched as Meghan placed the confection on her tongue. "Right. Now, let it sit there for a moment, and then slowly rub it between your tongue and the roof of your mouth. It will gradually dissolve so you can swallow it."

"Mmmmm." Meghan swirled it around. "Ohhhh." After swallowing, she looked at Lindy with large round eyes and said, "I see exactly what you mean. That's wonderful."

"Glad you like it. Now I'll have E3."

The girls sat and ate chocolates until Meghan felt certain she had added five pounds to her hips.

Lindy licked her chocolate and sought something to talk about. Small talk had never been one of her fortes. "So, Meg, since I don't see a wedding ring, I presume you're single."

"I sure am. Not in a rush."

"Dating anybody special?"

"Nobody steady. But I do have a date on Saturday."

"Good. What's his name?" She soon felt comfortable chatting with Meghan, who she presumed to be close in age.

"I can do you one better. You've met him. Brody Ashton."

Lindy's eyebrows lifted ever so slightly. "Very nice. Think it'll turn into something?"

"Not likely. Brody has a reputation known far and

wide. The funny thing is, he doesn't even realize the whole town knows."

Lindy's interest peaked. "What does everybody know?"

"Brody has never, and I mean NEVER, asked a girl for a date in his entire life."

"He's shy?"

Meghan scoffed at the idea. "Hardly. The thing is, he's never had to. He's always been asked by the girls."

Lindy's eyes enlarged as she sucked on a chocolate, amazed by the information. "You're kidding me!"

"And now, I have finally joined the throng of many. We have an all day date on Saturday. Then I found out he has a date with my sister, Tara, this week too. You know, it's not even like he's drop dead gorgeous. He's just such a great guy and so personable. He attracts females like flies to a dung pile." She giggled. "Well, I guess that wasn't the most flattering comparison, was it? No, when you ask Brody for a date, you know not to put your heart on the line, or it'll be broken for sure. I guess, though, there are many that hope they'll be the one with the magic whatever it is he's looking for."

"I love small town gossip. I grew up in Portland, so I've never had the opportunity. I'm tired of the big city, though. I was looking for someplace small to settle now that I'm alone."

"Did you just get out of a relationship?"

"No. My mother passed away last year. She was the only family I had."

Meghan's forehead creased with sympathy, "Oh, Lindy, I'm really sorry. How awful for you. I can't imagine being without a family. Well, you've already met half of my family."

Lindy looked at her, puzzled. After being in town only a day, she had not met many people. "I don't think so,

Meg. You must be mistaken".

"No, my sister, Tara, brought you in the ambulance and looked after you until you got here. I guess you didn't actually get to meet since you were unconscious. Then, Daddy looked after you when you got here. My other sister, Paige, works here too, but I don't imagine you've met her yet."

"Dr. Shepherd?" Lindy asked, surprised.

"Yup. That's my dad. I'm so lucky to work with him all the time. He's a great doctor."

Lindy smiled. Life in a small town where everyone was related to someone.

•

Three o'clock found Brody seated at his desk with Bracken Northrup, calling for aerial photos of the county to be brought to him. They poured over each one with a magnifying glass, making note of every building within a five mile radius of where he found Lindy. He knew five miles was beyond generous, but he chose to err on the side of caution. Going by the things Lindy and Gina told him, he ignored homes and their immediate outer buildings, hunting for places more remote. They made a list of properties and the approximate building locations.

The phone on his desk rang as Brody rolled up the maps. He reached absently for it. "Deputy Ashton."

"Brody, I was talking to Lindy today."

"Ma, is this important? I'm kinda busy here."

"I wanted to tell you she gave me permission to tell the FBI fella the details of her captivity. I thought it might be easier for her if he doesn't make her relive the worst of it."

"Thanks, Ma. I'll send him over for dinner. Six o'clock

okay?"

"That's fine. Are you coming too?"

"Sorry, can't. I've got other things that need doing."

"All right, then. Talk at ya later."

"Bye, Ma." Brody hung up the phone and drew a map for Bracken. "You're invited to dinner at my parents place. My Ma's gonna love you. Bracken is an Ashton sort of name."

"What's that mean?"

"All the kids in our family have names that start with B-R. Be careful, she might try to adopt you."

Bracken laughed and put the map in his jacket pocket. "Say, what's the 411 on the girl out at the switchboard. I noticed her when we came in."

"That is Jennifer Dexter. Yes, she's single. No, she's not attached. I have a date with her this week, but it's just a movie and drinks. She's a terrific gal. Lot's of fun, good sense of humor, and she's got some pretty terrific legs."

"I definitely noticed those. So she's open for hunting season?"

"Yep. You gonna be in town long enough for hunting?"

"With game like that? I'm sure I could arrange it."

Brody raised an eyebrow. "Good luck then." He checked his watch and found it close to five o'clock. He needed to hustle or he would be late meeting Rhett. "I have to head out now. I have a few things to take care of on some other cases. I'll be back later. Enjoy dinner. Ma's a great cook." Pushing his hat on his head, he gave a farewell nod as he headed across the squad room and out the door.

Rhett stood waiting inside the front lobby of Lander Valley Medical Center when Brody arrived. "This has got to be one of the dumbest things you've ever gotten me to do, Ashton. I can't believe I even showed up."

"I know you think I'm exaggerating, but just you wait and see. I have every confidence you'll be impressed."

"By a woman eating chocolate."

"Correct."

Rhett gave Brody a dubious look. He could not believe watching anybody eat anything was that interesting. They walked to the medical wing and up the stairs to the second floor. Brody stopped and knocked at the third door from the staircase. A voice invited them inside, and when Brody pushed open the door Rhett got his first look at Lindy Lassiter. She lay watching television in a semi-upright position.

When Lindy saw Brody arrive with a friend in tow, she silently thanked Meghan for taking the time to brush her hair and put fresh lipstick on her so she at least looked presentable.

Brody's eyes reflected his surprise before he quickly hid it. "Hey, Lindy. This is my friend, Rhett Owens. Rhett, this is the Legendary Lindy Lassiter of Lander, in lavender."

Rhett gave Brody a quirky look, and Lindy giggled, "Try saying that one five times real fast." Her eyes met those of the man who stood just under six feet with a leaner frame than Brody. "Hello, Rhett, it's nice to meet you."

"Pleasure's mine, I'm sure," Rhett brushed a finger against his hat brim.

"How you doing today?" Brody asked.

"Bad night, pretty good day, all things considered. Thanks for asking, Mr. Studmuffin." She tried to hide her grin as she watched his eyes become saucers and his cheeks turn bright red.

Rhett could not help himself. He tried to look away, but still he laughed. "Hey, Brod, you didn't tell me she knew ya so well."

"Shut up, Rhett." He turned his attention back to Lindy. "And where did that come from?"

"Hey, I've been in town for over twenty four hours now. I've heard the town gossip," she teased.

Brody opened his mouth to reply, but nothing came out.

"Ooooh, burn!" Rhett chuckled, thrilled to witness the moment. "Hey, Brody, it's a deal." Turning back to Lindy, he told her, "Brody and I are going to get your car and your other stuff for you."

Her attention riveted to Brody with excitement. "You found my things?"

"Yes, ma'am. It took all my training and skill as an investigator, but I found it all right."

"Where?"

"Right where you left them," he chuckled, glad to be the bearer of some good tidings for her. "Say, you're looking awful nice today. Vast improvement over those hospital gowns, don't ya think?"

"You're mother's doing. She brought me some really nice things. I just love her. You're very lucky. Enjoy her while you have her. She reminds me a lot of my mother."

"She's got pretty good taste. My sisters have never returned anything she's ever bought them."

"I didn't know you had sisters. I guess we talk about me too much."

"I have an older sister, Brooke, who's married with two rugrats. Then I have a younger sister, Bronwyn, and a younger brother, Braden. None of us live at home any more, though."

"It must be wonderful to have siblings." Lindy's melancholy made her sensitive to the things she missed in her own life.

"Only if ya like 'em. Brooke was a real bossy brat growing up. Still is a lot of the time," he grinned and pulled a second chair to the bedside. "I guess we all get on pretty well. Ma wouldn't let it be any other way."

Lindy turned to Rhett who wore a pair of jeans and a denim shirt under his heavy suede coat with sheep's wool lining. His cowboy hat sat balanced on his head at a angle that portrayed confidence. "So, Rhett, how is it you and Brody know each other?"

"We work together, ma'am."

"So, you're a deputy, too?" she asked, her voice losing its color.

"Yes, ma'am." He watched her face swiftly change from pleasant, to crestfallen, to agony.

"I see. So, I guess you fellas are here on business. You want to know about the rapes and the beatings. You want all the dirty little details." Tears sprang to her eyes and coursed down her cheeks. She could not bear to look at them. Once they knew, she would be too ashamed to ever face them again. She felt the world rolling over, and an overwhelming darkness fell over her spirit. As the sobs broke free, she wrapped her arms around the pain of the broken ribs. The pain in her spirit was far worse and she grit her teeth as uncontrolled screams came ripping out of her.

Rhett and Brody looked at each other in shock. Brody tried to comfort her. "NO! No, Lindy, that's not why we're here. It's all right, Lind. We're not gonna ask you anything."

She could not hear him, deep in her own world of horror. Brody moved on the edge of the bed and tried to put his arms around her to comfort her. She struggled to get away, trying to break free. "Don't touch me! Don't touch me! I hate you! I hate you! I hate you!"

"Lindy, it's me, Brody. Please, Lindy,…"

She attacked him with her elbows until he pulled his arms away and held them up in the air as though he was under arrest to show her he had backed off. Turning to Rhett, he said "Get a nurse in here." Scared, he leaped to the far corner of the room and snatched out the cell phone he knew he was not allowed to use. Lindy cried and screamed, flailing her arms while he dialed his mother's number.

He kept it short. "Ma, Lindy needs you. Stat!" Flipping it shut, he repocketed it.

She had felt him pawing at her, trying to restrain her, but she was not tied up any more. She fought back. She would never let him do it again without a fight. "No! No! I'll kill you first. Get away from me."

Brody stood bewildered as he watched her. Rhett returned with a nurse who raced to Lindy's side, speaking in a calm, soothing voice, but she was inconsolable. The nurse withdrew a hypodermic needle from her pocket and was about to inject it into Lindy's IV when Brody stopped her. "Please, her rape counselor is on the way. Just wait a few minutes for her."

"It's just enough to relax her, not put her to sleep."

Within moments the screaming stopped, but he could see she still was unaware of the reality around her. She lay curled up in the fetal position, closed in on herself.

Gina barreled into the room, tossing her purse into the corner and sat on the bed with Lindy. Over her shoulder she commanded, "Brody, get out and take Rhett with you. NOW!"

Brody and Rhett stood in the hall outside her room, both badly shaken. Rhett slumped against the wall with his arms folded. "Holy Hannah!"

Distressed, Brody ran his hand through his hair over and over. "Yeah. The happiness thing is a facade. She's trying, struggling to cope with what went down. I'm amazed she's been doing as well as she has. She's a strong lady. And she's got Ma in her corner. She's a survivor, but it's gonna be a long road."

•

The sedative took effect, gradually relaxing Lindy emotionally, mentally, and physically. Through the fear and confusion, a voice soothed her, assuring her she was fine.

Gina held her and rubbed her back. "There, there, honey. It's all right now. Nobody's gonna hurt you. Gina's here with you now, baby. It's just you and me. We're safe now, Lindy." Feeling the security of Gina's arms around her, Lindy grew calmer, and her focus on the room around her sharpened.

"Gina? Oh, Gina! Thank you for coming. Thank you," Lindy cried. "He wanted to hurt me again. He tried, but I wouldn't let him."

Gina continued holding her and rocking her back and forth. The crying gradually wore down to sniffles. "It's okay, honey. I'm with you. Are you feeling a little better now?" She pulled back so they could look at one another.

Lindy nodded.

"Do you want to talk?"

"I saw him. He was here, and he tried to touch me. He wanted to hurt me again, Gina. He wanted to hurt me." She started to gasp for breath again as the fright seized her.

"All right. Calm down. What was the last thing that happened before you saw him? Was Brody here?"

Lindy thought about it. "Brody?" She paused, "Yes, Brody was here with his friend. They wanted to ask me questions about the rape. That's what it was. They wanted me to remember it all."

"It's okay now, Lindy. Do you know that Brody wouldn't hurt you?"

"I think so. He's been very good to me. I don't think he'd hurt me."

"No, honey. He never would." She felt the girl relax in her arms and she gently laid her back against her pillow to rest. "Will you be okay for a few minutes if I go out of the room? I won't be long. I promise you. Brody's out in the hall, and he's very scared for you. I just want to tell him you're all right."

"Yeah, I'll be fine. I'm okay. Please come back." Shivers still ran across her skin.

Gina kissed her cheek and went out into the hall where her son and Rhett Owens waited.

"Brody what in the name of heaven did you think you were doing? I told you…."

"Ma, we didn't come to question her. We just wanted to visit. As soon as she found out Rhett works with me, she assumed we wanted to question her, and she freaked. It wasn't our fault. We didn't say nothing to instigate all that. Honest."

"You have to understand, it was a natural assumption on her part. No offence, Rhett, but why are you here?"

"We came to watch her eat chocolate, Ma."

Gina glowered at her son with disgust, and he felt ten years old again. "Brody Ashton, that is the most asinine thing that has ever come out of your mouth!"

"That's what I told him, Mrs. Ashton," Rhett chirped in.

"Shut up, Rhett. You sound just like Eddie Haskell!"

"Sorry, Mrs. Ashton." Rhett hung his head at the reprimand, and realized he did sound like a suck up

95

teenager.

"Ma, I want to tell her I'm sorry. Can I just do that?"

Gina glared at him while she considered his request. "That's her decision to make, not mine. I'll ask if she'll see you, but I wouldn't count on it. She's too shaken up. You have to realize the memories are still so fresh and overwhelming in her mind, they tricked her into thinking you were the rapist trying to attack her again. In the future, don't presume to touch her in any way without asking her first."

"I'm sorry, Ma. Tell her I'm sorry. I'd never hurt her."

"She knows that, dear. You need to understand she has no control over things like this. Her mind plays tricks, and her body plays tricks. She's ruled by fear, no matter how good a show she puts on."

CHAPTER EIGHT

Lindy lay on her side with her back to the door, wanting to shut out the world. Gina sat next to her, gently caressing her back. "Feeling better now, sweetie?"

Mortified by her outburst, Lindy gave a small nod.

"Honey, Brody and Rhett didn't come to question you. They just came to visit – purely social. He feels real bad they upset you." A gentle smile lifted the corners of her mouth. "Ya know, I think you scared them almost as much as they scared you."

She closed her eyes in dismay. "Oh, Gina. I'm so embarrassed. How can I ever face him again? He's going to think I'm a total nut case. He'll never come back."

"You have no reason to be embarrassed. Brody's a big boy. He doesn't know exactly what you've been through, but he knows it was horrendous, and from there he can use his imagination. He knows a trauma like this can play all sorts of games with your mind." Gina placed a finger under the girl's chin and lifted her face until their eyes met. "Don't underestimate the man. He cares a great deal about what happens to you. If you're up to it he'd like to come back in. What do you think?"

"I don't know." She sat in silence a moment while considering it. "I suppose. I'll have to face him sooner or later anyway."

Brody timidly pushed the door open and stuck his head in, the question in his eyes. Gina gave him a nod. With a few quick strides he stood next to the bed with Lindy's back to him. Twirling his hat brim nervously in his fingers, he spoke with contrition. "Lindy, I'm sorry we upset you. I promise ya, I won't ever ask for the details of what happened. I know it's difficult for ya." She turned to look at him, and he saw tears glistening in her eyes.

Feeling the flush that colored her cheeks she answered in a small voice, "I'm sorry, too. You've been so good to me."

"You don't have to apologize for nothing. I honestly like you, Lindy, and I'd never hurt you. I want you to know that."

Sensing that emotions had found their equilibrium, Gina slipped out of the way, and Brody moved in to sit on the chair so he and Lindy could face one another. "I'm sorry I touched you. I was just trying to comfort you. I didn't mean to scare you. I didn't know it was the wrong thing to do."

She heard the regret in his voice, and it touched her heart. "I guess there are still some things too fresh that need to heal. I didn't mean to scare you, either."

"Heck, don't worry about me. I'm fine. Still friends?"

"I hope so. I'd hate to lose my first friend in Mayberry." She attempted a half smile. "What must poor Rhett think of me?"

"Poor Rhett got a little more than he bargained for. You sure know how to make first meetings memorable."

"Oh, no." She lifted her bandaged hands up in front of her face. "Please, tell him I'm sorry. Now he'll never come again, either. I certainly can send them running, can't I?" she cringed.

"Oh, I think I can promise he'll be back. He came to watch you eat chocolate."

Gina glared at him in disgust. "Brody!"

Spreading his arms as though in explanation, he tried to justify himself. "Well, Ma, I can't help it. It's true." He turned back to Lindy. "I told him it was something spectacular that he just had to see."

Gina threw her hands up in resignation. "Oh, good grief! Well, I think things here are better now. You gonna be all right, Lindy?"

"Yes, I'll be fine. Thank you for coming so quickly."

"I told you I would, honey. You get some rest, and don't let this guy stay too long." Gina kissed her cheek and frowned over her shoulder at her son before leaving. "Brody, behave yourself."

Lindy stopped her at the door. "Gina, maybe you can tell Rhett the coast is clear. I won't throw anything at him."

Gina left the door propped wide open so Lindy wouldn't feel confined with the men. She spoke briefly to Rhett with a wagging finger on her way out. He peeked in and cautiously approached the bed. "Everything okay?" he asked quietly.

Tension hung thick in the air. Needing to dispel it before she caved in to humiliation, she determined to brighten her spirit whether she felt like it or not. She would force herself to pretend, at least for the duration of their visit, that all was right in her world. "Yes, much better thank you. I apologize for what happened. Didn't mean to scare you."

"Don't worry about it."

"Please, come in and sit."

Rhett dragged a chair from the corner to sit by Brody.

In an attempt to break the ice she told him, "I understand you came to see me eat chocolate." She tried to smile but it faltered as her eyes fell to her lap. "I hope you don't mind if I'm not really up to a display at the moment."

Rhett felt the crimson creeping from his neck to his hairline, and he glared at Brody. "Lindy, I don't know what my good friend here has been saying..."

"It's all right, Rhett," she assured him. "I'm aware of Brody's little fascination. He thinks I should sell tickets." Her spirits lightened in spite of her grief as she remembered Brody's face when he watched her. The tension in her muscles relaxed, and her body slowly unfolded. "Oh, and speaking of entertainment, thank you for the TV, Brody. It's provided a wonderful diversion. Sometimes I just stare at it without seeing it, but occasionally it pulls my concentration, and that's good. I can't spend all my time inside of myself, or I'll never get out."

"I was happy to do it," he smiled. In an effort to continue distracting her, he informed her, "Hey, Goober over here is the one I'm going boarding with on Sunday."

"Goober!" Rhett looked at him puzzled.

"I see. Well, Goober, was it Barney's idea to go snowboarding, or did you have to ask him?"

"It was my idea." Rhett said, still uncertain how he got to be Goober.

"That's very interesting." A smile tickled the corners of her mouth. "So, it isn't only the women who have to do the asking for a date with Brody, it's the men too!"

Rhett laughed while Brody looked embarrassed all

over again. "Whoa! Burn again! I like this gal, Brody."

"Yeah, that's the great thing about my friends. I can always count on them to make me the punch line." He shook his head and chuckled.

"You're lucky he could fit you in," she told Rhett. "The way I hear it, he's a busy guy. Even planning to date sisters this week. I'm not certain, but I don't think that sounds like a good idea," Lindy advised. The lighthearted banter gradually wiped the darkness from the edges, and she smiled without pretense.

"That's what I said. Just looking for trouble, isn't he?" Rhett confirmed.

"Hey, it's not my fault they both asked me. And it's not like I have a problem asking women to go out with me."

"Is that right? Do tell," she prodded.

"I guess it started in high school with Mandy Howser. She asked me to a school dance. Then the next week, Shelley Jensen asked me to go ice skating. Ever since then, I've just always been lucky enough to have a date whenever I wanted to go out. It's not something I control, ya know."

"Well, I've never asked a guy out before. So, I guess we're equal on that one. Of course, I don't have a date five nights a weeks, either," Lindy told them.

Rhett sat back with his arms folded, smirking. He liked the direction the conversation was weaving. It was always fun for him when women picked on Brody and caused him to blush.

"That's an exaggeration. It's hardly five nights a week."

"But certainly often enough that you're kept quite busy," she retorted. "So what about you, Rhett? Do women throw themselves at your feet as well?" She eyed him with interest, not wanting to leave him out of

101

the conversation.

"No, that's strictly a Brody thing in this town. I'm afraid I'm from the old school where I'm supposed to ask a woman, but I s'pose I don't do a whole lot of that."

"Oh. Sorry, I didn't know." Her mouth quirked slightly in embarrassment.

Brody loved the turn of the tables. "Hah! Burn, Owens! She thinks you're gay!"

Now it was Rhett's turn to blush. "No, that's not what I..." he flustered. "I'm straight. I just, well, ..."

"What he's saying," Brody interpreted, "is that he's shy. He gets tongue-tied around women."

"Ahh." Lindy scrutinized his discomfort and smiled warmly, all teasing evanescing from her voice. "Then I feel sorry for all the women missing out, cause I think you're a nice guy."

Rhett gave a half-grin and sought to turn the attention away from himself. "So, now that you're in town, are you gonna ask Brody here out on a date?"

"Absolutely not. For a lot of reasons."

Brody raised his eyebrows in surprise, wondering what she so adamantly disliked about him. "Such as?"

"Well, first, I was raised that if a man wanted to see me, he would ask me. I was never allowed to even phone a boy. My mother didn't want me making a fool of myself chasing after someone who wasn't interested. Secondly, I never do anything just to be part of the gang. I'm an individual. The fact that he's dated every other woman in this town is no reason for me to jump on the bandwagon. And third," she held up her hands matter-of-factly, "I have nothing to offer him or any other man any more. I don't expect I'll ever date again. It's going to be hard, but I'll just have to find other things to fill my life."

Brody leaned forward, his laughter evaporated.

"That's just nuts, Lindy. You're a real pretty girl. There's probably a hundred guys in this county who'd love to go out with you. I've never met a guy who said, 'I'm marrying her cause I'm in love with her fingers. Or her toes, either, for that matter."

"That's nice of you to say, Brody, but the fact is, I'm damaged goods—physically and emotionally. I'm too much trouble. Don't try to put rose colored glasses on me. Unrealistic hopes won't help me. I have to accept reality and deal with it. A smart person can't fool themselves forever. And besides, the fourth reason I would never ask you out is that you'd accept it as a sympathy date, and I would hate that."

"That's just not…"

"Stop it, Brody. Not another word."

Rhett sat back, disgruntled. "Shoot. Here I was hoping we were getting her into a chocolate mood, and now she's all upset again. I'm never gonna get to see it."

Surprised by his response, she laughed spontaneously. "Rhett, if you will be so kind as to raise the head of my bed up, I'll eat one just for you. I'm warning you in advance, however, it's not a big deal. He's just being silly."

Rhett pushed the control button on the siderail of the bed until she was in a more upright position. Brody picked up the box of candy and settled on the foot of the bed to watch, careful not to bump against her feet. Lifting the lid off the box, he gave her a bewildered look. "Hey, there's a whole lot gone."

"I told you I love chocolate. Don't be so surprised."

"It's not that. It's just that," he frowned, "shucks, I didn't get to see it."

Lindy rolled her eyes and shook her head. "Give Rhett a chocolate," she instructed.

Brody held out the box and Rhett took a piece, then he took one for himself. After careful selection, he chose one for Lindy who savored it while both men stared attentively. Upon swallowing, she opened her eyes to find them both sitting in a trance-like state. With a sigh, she said, "Give me another one, Brody. You are the silliest men I've ever met." Opening her mouth, she waited while he set a cherry cream on her tongue and ate it as an encore performance.

Brody sensed that although she was smiling and playing along with them, she was tired. "Thanks, Lindy. I promise ya I won't bring anyone else to see it. We should get out of here and let you get some rest." As he stood to leave, a nurse came in with Lindy's dinner.

She eyed the tray and lifted her eyes hopefully, unable to remember the last time she ate palatable food. "Actually, if you have the time and don't mind, I could use some help with dinner."

"Sure. I can handle that." Brody salted and peppered the vegetables and fed her with anticipation, somewhat disappointed to discover she did not respond to regular food the same way she did to the candy. As he held the fork to her mouth, a memory thrust itself to the forefront of his mind with alarming speed, and his hand trembled. "Hey, Lindy. You know when you stopped around Baker City to get gas?"

She swallowed before acknowledging. "Yes, and to get something to eat. Why?"

"I was just wondering; what was it you got for lunch?"

"That's a strange question. I got a submarine sandwich and..."

Brody's hand dropped, spilling kernels of corn all over the bedspread as he interrupted, "...and a drink in a red, plastic cup. You were carrying them to the car, and you had on a dark blue wool bench coat."

"That's right. How did you know that?" she asked, stunned by his revelation. "Did you find a witness?" Her eyes lit with hope.

"I gotta go." Brody grabbed his coat and practically ran out the door, not slowing until he reached the parking lot and climbed into the cruiser. Dizzy, he dropped his head against the steering wheel. Everything felt off balance. What was going on here? Nothing like this had ever happened to him before, and it scared him.

He headed back to the station as the snow continued to fall. Seated at his desk, he ran his hand through his hair over and over as he wrote down every detail he could remember from the dream. The two most important things remained unclear — the license plate and the men's faces. At least he knew what kind of car they needed to look for. It was not much, but it was more than he had before. He noted as much as he could remember about the perps: height, weight, body structure and hair colors. Finished, he sat back with satisfaction. The only thing that troubled him now was how to explain the new information to Special Agent Bracken Northrup. If he told the truth, the agent would write him off as incompetent, and he would be off the case so fast he would feel his butt hit the pavement. His only option was to keep it under his hat for now and try to follow up on it himself until he could come up with a rational explanation.

Stuffing his arms into his coat, he pulled the zipper closed to his neck as he stalked back out into the cold night to patrol the highways he was responsible for.

•

Snow continued falling, but the temperature did not

105

drop as low as it had the last few days. At eight o'clock Brody pulled onto a side road which gave him an open view of the highway in both directions. An hour later a truck turned onto the road and did a u-turn, pulling in to park behind him. The driver hopped out from behind the wheel and approached the passenger side of the cruiser. The door opened and the man climbed in next to Brody, pulling the door firmly shut behind him.

Brody glanced at him briefly before averting his eyes back to the highway. "Rhett."

"Brody."

"What's up?" He screwed the lid back on his coffee thermos.

"That's my question. The way you lit out o' that hospital room, somethings going on."

"Is that what you thought?"

"No, that's what I know. You can't kid a kidder. What's going on?"

Brody sat silent, reluctant to tell his friend the truth. Silently he weighed his options. With a sigh, he knew if he could not tell Rhett, he could not tell anyone. Considering the truth, secrecy offered a safer alternative. However, he also knew Rhett would not leave until he had answers. "It sounds crazy. I wouldn't believe it myself if it hadn't happened to me." He drank the coffee and stared straight ahead out the windshield, shaking his head in disbelief.

"Talk to me, Brod. What is it? Your face went whiter than this snow. You almost looked scared. For that matter, you're still not looking too good."

He breathed heavily, debating what he should say. "You tell no one. I mean it, Rhett. Nobody."

"Right."

His voice dropped almost to a whisper as he admitted, "I saw it happen."

106

Rhett leaned closer to hear him. "Saw what happen?"

"Lindy's abduction."

Rhett's brows lifted as he sat back in surprise. "You want to explain that one? I thought she was abducted back in Oregon, and I know you ain't been to Oregon lately."

Brody leaned his head back against the headrest and closed his eyes a moment before launching into the story of his dream.

"Geez, no wonder you freaked. It's amazing you can recall the details so vividly."

"Are you kidding me? It scared the heck out of me. Kept me awake most of the night. The question is, why? Why did I see what I did? And why were the important things blurred? What was the point?"

Rhett did not understand it, but neither did he doubt his friend.

With his story laid open for speculation, Brody sat up and got back to the business of daylight that he could justify. "Northrup and I made a list of all the outbuildings within a five mile radius of where I found her. Tomorrow we're gonna start checking 'em out, see if we can find where they held her."

"You start your days off tomorrow."

"Don't matter. I have to close this case, Rhett, and fast. You saw her today. He almost killed her. I can't let it happen to anyone else. It has to end."

"I'll meet you tomorrow morning, and we'll split the list," Rhett said.

"You don't have to do this."

"I know, but after all, I've seen her eat chocolate, too."

CHAPTER NINE

A blinking red light on Brody's answering machine greeted him when he arrived home. He hit the button and listened while grabbing a beer from the fridge.

"Hey, Brody. This is your cousin, David, from Arizona. Listen, I've got a job in Lander. Just wondering if you can put me up a few days until I can get my own place. Give me a call, and we can get together for a couple o' beers. I'm staying at the Maverick Motel. Talk to ya later."

David? Brody had not seen David since he was about seven years old. He would call him tomorrow afternoon. The farmhouse boasted five bedrooms— plenty of room for his cousin to bunk down for awhile.

He guzzled down the beer and left the empty bottle on the counter next to the sink, deciding a hot shower would help him relax before sleep. The case left him tightly wound, and after two nights of very little sleep he needed a good full night.

Steam filled the bathroom quickly while hot water sprayed across his broad shoulders and ran down his muscular body. As he bent to rinse the lather from his blond curls, he mentally designed a new bathroom with a showerhead mounted to the ceiling instead of the wall. Since he planned to renovate the room anyway, it might as well be suited to his height.

After toweling off, he tossed the dampened bath sheet over a hook and plodded to his bed with bleary eyes. Exhausted, he dropped onto the soft mattress and tugged the flannel sheet and feather duvet over his naked body and settled, ready for sleep.

Visions of Lindy once again filled his mind. He admired how pretty she was as he sat next to her, her hair shiny and pulled back in clips with just a bit of makeup to mask the pallor of her skin. Her full lips smiled. He respected her monumental efforts to survive her ordeal. She still had a long road ahead of her, but she faced it valiantly, and it impressed the heck out of him.

Without warning, her spirit crashed. She crumpled before his very eyes. He knew she no longer recognized him when he touched her. He needed to be careful about physical contact in the future. He never wanted to see her frightened like that again. The terror in her eyes had been real, and it alarmed him.

Suddenly, he saw her lying on a filthy bare mattress with her eyes taped shut. He stood and watched as she was raped, unable to help her, as though he himself was bound. Struggling against the restraints, the sight made him vomit in the corner where he stood. Her screams, muffled by the duct tape over her mouth, tore at his soul.

The rage, the anger the rapist exhibited, filled the room. His attack was brutal, bruising her with every thrust. Brody felt his own body fill with her agony. "No" he shouted. "Stop! Get off of her! Get off!" He continued to fight against the ties that bound him, but to no avail.

He could not break free any more than she could, no matter how hard he wrestled. "I'll kill you! When I get my hands on you, I swear I'll kill you!" he vowed. He watched with misery as the violator burned a cigarette hole on her breast before dragging her to a closet. When the door opened, a fowl stench filled the room, and he saw her limp, abused body bounce off the wall when she was tossed in.

Abruptly, he found himself seated at the table in his mother's bright, cheerful kitchen

"Brody, when you find him, I don't want you to bring him in. I want you to kill him."

"Yes, Ma. I'll kill him. He'll never hurt Lindy again."

•

Tuesday morning Brody called Agent Northrup to arrange a breakfast meeting for nine-thirty. When he arrived at the Showboat Diner, Rhett and his partner, Patrick, were already seated. The waitress distributed menus as Brody joined them. Without bothering to open it, he ordered steak, eggs and home fries.

"Patrick, good to see you here."

"Rhett told me what you're doing. You know the old adage: More hands make lighter work, or something like that."

"Thanks for coming."

The FBI agent arrived minutes later. Brody quickly took care of the introductions. "Bracken Northrup, this is Rhett Owens and Patrick Danvers."

Heads nodded a curt greeting. Bracken reached into his jacket pocket and took out the list of buildings to be investigated, while Brody turned to a fresh page in his notebook and pulled out his favorite gold Cross pen.

Bracken included all three officers in his gaze. "We'll

divide the list up four ways. We've noted every building not in the immediate vicinity of the occupied residences. We need to physically get inside each of these buildings to check them out. We're looking for any evidence that she was held there captive, or even that it's had recent inhabitants."

Brody added, "There was also a guard dog there, so possibly any dog feces, although with the snow of the last two days, that might not be glaringly apparent."

"Hey. This is Wyoming. If you don't like the weather, stick around five minutes, it'll change," Rhett quipped. He was right. The close proximity to the mountains could significantly alter the weather in the blink of an eye.

Brody broke down the list, keeping the assignments grouped geographically. "Okay, here's the sheets."

"I'll take the Monaghans' ranch. I have to stop out there today anyway." Patrick reached out, and Brody handed him the appropriate list. He quickly scanned it and nodded, "I should be able to get all these done today, don't you think?"

Brody agreed. "Some places'll be obvious it's not what we're looking for, but don't be too quick to discount a place. If you have any question in your mind, look deeper. I do know that the place had a small bedroom with a closet. I can't tell you much more than that."

"Don't worry, Brod. We'll find it."

"I hope you're right, Rhett. I really hope you're right." He silently prayed that some progress on the case would stop the nightmares. The waitress arrived balancing plates heaped with hot food. The men pocketed their individual assignments and dug in with hearty appetites.

Patrick finished his coffee and stood to leave. "I'll let you know if I find anything, otherwise, I'll see you back at the grind next week."

"Thanks for coming out, Patrick. You're a good man." Brody gave him a two-fingered farewell salute.

Northrup took a final bite of sausage and pushed his plate away. "I should head out and get started, too. Listen, I'll give you each my card. If you find anything relevant, call my cell. Better give me your numbers, too." Bracken quickly keyed their cell numbers into his Blackberry organizer before leaving the remaining two deputies on their own.

"You get some sleep last night? You're not looking great," Rhett remarked.

Brody motioned for the waitress to refill their coffee mugs. She smiled, ready to happily chat for a few minutes, but the stern look on his face told her they were still talking business, so she quickly moved on to the next customer.

It was obvious to Rhett his friend was troubled. He leaned forward, quietly waiting as he stirred sugar into his cup.

Brody heaved a sigh and dropped his voice to a murmur. "I had another dream." His eyes skittered around the room, making sure no one could hear him. "I know this sounds crazy, but I'm thinking I might need to go for counseling. This is really eating at me. I've gotta talk to Ma first, see if she'll confirm some things for me."

Rhett's brow furrowed. "I don't understand."

"Remember how the first dream was so detailed, so vivid, like I was actually there watching it happen?"

"Considering how shaken up you were, I'd say it was pretty real for you. What happened last night? Same dream again?"

"I saw it."

"The kidnapping?"

"No. I saw her being abused, raped, other things.

112

Things I never even dreamed of – well, consciously at least. No wonder Ma insisted I couldn't ask Lindy to relive it. Even in my dream, I puked right there in the room. I struggled, wanting to save her, to kill him. I couldn't move, like I was tied up or something, but I felt every emotion she felt. This whole thing is just too bizarre for me. It's tearing me up, Rhett."

His friend sat silent, staring into his cup as steam curled up from it. He had never heard of anything like this happening in real life. He could buy it in a Bruce Willis movie, but here in his world, in Lander, it was a much tougher sell. If anyone but Brody said it, he would have scoffed at the whole thing. But Brody never lied, and his distress was visible. Rhett watched the man's hand tremble as he lifted his cup to drink.

"Maybe counseling is a good idea. Not 'cause you're nuts or nothing, but what you've seen is so real to you that you're seriously affected by it. You know, they do rape counseling for the victim's family and partners as well as the victim herself. Maybe that's what you should look into."

Brody's forehead creased with worry, and his fingers traced over his moustache again and again as he ruminated. Finally, he nodded with an expression of resignation. "You know, that's a good idea. Hadn't thought of that. Ma will know who to talk to." Sliding from the booth, he reached for his parka.

"Hey, Brod, before we head out I wanted to ask ya, do you mind if I go down to the hospital to visit Lindy?"

Brody shrugged, finding the question odd. "You don't need my permission. I just found her, I don't own her. Go ahead. That kid can use all the friends she can get."

Rhett pulled the list from his pocket and stood to tug on his own coat. His shift ended three hours earlier, but he would search every building on his page before he found his way home to bed. And when he awoke later on, maybe a trip to the hospital would be in the cards.

•

Brody left his snow-covered boots at the door before strutting into the kitchen to check out the refrigerator. He found his mother at the sink, peeling potatoes. "Hey, Ma. You'll never guess who left a message on my machine yesterday."

"Well, if I'm not gonna guess, you're gonna have to tell me."

"Cousin David from Arizona. I haven't seen him in what, twenty years or so? Says he's got a job here and asked if he could bunk out at my place. When was the last time you talked to his mother?"

Gina stopped peeling and looked out the back window as she tried to remember. Two goldfinches fluttered in the heated bird bath, and she smiled to see them cavorting about. "I don't know. I guess it's been quite a few years since I've heard from Zita. I suppose if Uncle Ed hadn't moved down south when we were kids we would have gone to school together and been a lot closer, but that's not how it happened. Anyway, I'm glad he called you. It'll be real nice for you two to get to know one another."

"Yeah, I'll give him a call later on." He foraged a piece of leftover cherry pie from the fridge and carried it to the table. Pouring a glass of milk to wash it down he heartily feasted, oblivious to the fact that he finished a huge breakfast only half an hour earlier. Hunger, however, was not his true motivation. He concentrated on the cherry sitting on his fork tine, trying to summon the courage to tell his mother the real reason for his visit. "Hey, Ma, can I talk to you about something?"

She immediately detected the apprehensive tone in her son's voice. Snatching the tea towel from the counter, she dried her hands and joined him at the table. "Something troubling you, Brody? What is it?"

"It's about Lindy. I don't really know how to explain this and sound sane. I had a dream the other night. I saw her abduction. When I asked her a few questions yesterday, her answers confirmed the things I saw. It was so real, Ma. Like I was standing right there."

Her head tilted as she studied him. He refused to look up, embarrassed by his dilemma. Gina reached across the table and placed her hand on his wrist in comfort. "Well, it's unusual all right, but to be honest with you, I've heard of things like this before."

"You have?"

"Yup." She hoped the reassurance would help him relax.

"There's more." He fidgeted uncomfortably in his chair. "Last night, I saw the rape. I was there in the room, watching it all happen. I fought like crazy to help her, but I couldn't move. I shouted, but they didn't hear me. I saw the tape over her eyes and mouth. The things they did were so atrocious it made me sick. He finished by putting another cigarette burn on her breast and threw her into a closet. I wish I could say, 'It was just a dream, and I'll get over it.' But it's not that way. The impressions were so strong. For some reason, I'm witnessing the crimes. It's got me all tied up in knots."

"I can see that, and your reaction is perfectly understandable."

"Seeing as much as I have, I can't pretend it didn't happen. Ma, I can't get the images out of my mind. It's eating at me."

She closed her eyes and cringed. "I'm so sorry you had to witness it. The imprints are on your mind now, and it's a lot different than just knowing it happened."

Looking lost and forlorned, he finally raised his eyes to meet hers. "What should I do?"

"I suggest you see Richard Collins. He's very good. That's who Matt Shepherd referred Lindy to. Sexual crime is his specialty."

"Thanks, Ma. I'll give him a call." He paused and closed his eyes. One deep breath followed another. "I understand why you didn't want me to ask her about it. It was worse than anything I imagined. No wonder she risked that bitter night air to escape."

"She's gonna need a lot of support for a long time. I'm thinking of bringing her here when she's released from the hospital. She has nowhere else to go, and we've got the room."

"I think that's a great idea." Brody smiled at his mother. "You're a special lady, Ma."

"Get on out of here. You've got things to do."

"Love you, Ma." He stood from the table and bent to kiss her cheek, leaving her to her day.

With his assignment sheet clipped to the dashboard, he turned onto the highway heading northwest of town to begin his quest.

•

They would search here sooner or later, and he wanted all trace evidence gone. With steaming water, detergent and bleach in the bucket and a scrub brush in his gloved hand, he scoured the bedroom, including the mattress, determined to eliminate all fingerprints and semen samples. Of course, if they brought Luminal there was nothing he could do about that, but there would be no blood samples and no way to identify the attackers. The odor of the vacant room nauseated him.

The closet was the worst, and even though he wore a mask over his mouth and nose, it made him gag repeatedly.

When he finished, no visible evidence of her captivity remained, and he hoped no microscopic evidence either. He managed to escape without suspicion after the other abductions and rapes in Pennsylvania and Oklahoma. He was determined not go to prison this time either.

CHAPTER TEN

Tara was already seated at a table at the Silver Spur Lanes when Brody arrived. Her eyes sparkled, and her radiant smile made him smile in spite of himself. He admired the way her effervescent energy and love of life tended to spill over and enveloped those around her.

"Hey, handsome. Glad you made it."

"I wouldn't stand up a girl as pretty as you," he winked. Sitting across from her, he smiled at the waitress who arrived with beer and ribs for both of them.

"Thanks for ordering, Tara. You must have been here awhile now waiting on me." He checked his watch to see how late he was.

"Not to worry. I got here early, so I figured I might as well get the order in. I knew you'd be hungry when you finally dragged yourself in here."

"Smart girl. Thanks."

"So, have you been back to the hospital to see your victim?"

"Yup. Stopped in on my way here tonight."

"How's she doing?"

Brody leaned back in his chair and swigged down

some cold beer before answering. "She works hard to keep her spirits up with visitors, but who knows how dark it is for her when she's alone. She survived one of the worst crimes I've ever seen. It's gonna take a lot of time before she'll have any semblance of a normal life again. Ma's working with her, too. She absolutely adores the girl."

"So, I guess outside of the crime, you haven't really had a chance to talk to her and find out what she's like."

"Don't you talk to your sister? Meghan visits with her. They're becoming quite friendly, those two. You should meet her. I think you'd like each other. Quite frankly, that girl can't have too many friends. Her mother died last year, and she has no family. I think that got Ma's maternal fires burning."

Tara cleaned the meat off a bone with her teeth and wiped barbecue sauce from her mouth with her napkin. "It must be difficult to go through something like this alone. Maybe I will go see her. But you know, if she and Meg get on well, I don't know how I'll fare. Meggie and I are like day and night."

"You're both beautiful, happy, spontaneous girls. You just show it in different ways. Meg is shy, and you're more spirited. No reason she can't like you both. I do."

Tara looked over Brody's shoulder and an eyebrow raised. "Hey, who's that over there with Jennifer Dexter? I've never seen him before."

Brody turned and saw Jennifer putting on her coat to leave. When he saw who was with her, he cocked an eyebrow of his own and smiled. "Name's Bracken Northrup. Federal man. He's here to run Lindy's investigation."

Tara shrugged and glanced at her large-faced masculine watch. "Our lane is ready in five minutes. Are you gonna be finished with those ribs by then, or do you need some help?" She reached across the table, teasing.

He slapped her hand away and grinned. "You bet I am, little lady, and I'm gonna beat the pants off you."

"Promises, promises."

Brody gaped at her in mock surprise, and she gave him an openly sensuous look. "You are something to be reckoned with, Tara Shepherd."

"You bet your britches I am. And maybe later, I'll let you demonstrate that mouth-to-mouth on me that you were doing the other night."

He chuckled at her flirtations as he chewed the meat off the final rib. Wiping his fingers, he tipped back the last of the beer and stood, pulling her to her feet. They wandered through the crowd to their appointed lane with his hand riding on her lower back. They bowled two games and true to his word, he won both times. He had to admit, however, that she gave him a real run for it and did not let him win easily.

"Okay, you won. I guess that means I have to pay for the first round," she conceded. They put their coats on and walked out to the parking lot.

"I'll take you up on that, but there's only gonna be one round. You live in town, but I have a drive to get home, and I'd like to be sober enough to handle it."

"Do you like to be sober all the time?"

"Why do I have a feeling you're not talking about alcohol?" He looked down at her out of the corner of his eye. He knew Tara Shepherd's reputation as a wild girl. "No, I don't always like to be sober, and I think you know that. What's on your mind, girl?"

"Oh, nothing. Yet."

"What's that mean?"

"Are you gonna go out with me again?"

Without answering, he opened the passenger door of

his truck for her. She stepped up onto the first step so she was almost face to face with him. He turned to walk away, but she grabbed his jacket and pulled him back. She wore a teasing smile as she gazed up at him through her thick lashes.

"Whut?" he drawled.

Instead of speaking, she took hold of his coat with both hands and pulled him closer, setting her lips on his and instantly seeking admission, which he freely gave. Sliding her hands inside his coat, she wrapped her arms around his broad chest and let her hands roam up and down his back.

He participated eagerly. Tara could ignite any man's fire, and he was not immune to her charms. When the cold finally became stronger than his libido, he pulled away and looked into her eyes.

"So, are we going out together again?" she repeated.

He smiled and said, "I think you can count on it."

"Good. How about Friday night?"

"Works for me." He kissed her one more time and gently pushed her inside the truck. They drove to the Hitching Rack for some music and a drink. At a table in the back corner, Brody ordered a rye and ginger while Tara opted for cherry whiskey and coke. They talked and laughed and danced a two-step. She tried to coax him into a second drink, but he remained steadfast.

Upon returning her to the Silver Spur parking lot to retrieve her car, she treated him to a make-out session that left him in an uncomfortable state for most of the drive home, despite of the cold.

The house was dark and empty as he inserted his key in the lock at the kitchen door. Stepping inside, he flicked on the light switch, shrugged off his coat and dumped his keys on the table near the back door. The flashing of the little red light on his answering machine caught his eye, and he hit the button to listen while he took off his boots.

His ears perked up as soon as he heard Patrick Danvers voice. "Hey, Ashton. Sorry I didn't catch you. I found a place that could be the one you're looking for out at the Clayton ranch. Give me a call tomorrow, and I'll take you there. Up to you if you want to bring along the FBI guy or not. It was the only place on my list that fit the profile. Talk to you later."

Brody had not found any place suitable on his own list. If there was no news from Rhett or Northrup, then Patrick probably located the right place. He hoped so.

The machine gave a little chirp before the next message. "Hey, Brod, just reporting in. Nothing on my list panned out. Sorry, buddy. Let me know if you found anything. I went to see Lindy tonight. Easy to talk to, isn't she? Talk to you later."

Chirp.

"Howdy, Brody. This is David. I guess we're playing phone tag here. Listen, I got your message about staying out at your place. Thanks. Maybe you can leave me a map at the motel desk tomorrow. I'm working as a ranch hand for a fella by the name of Hathaway. Hope to see you tomorrow night."

The Hathaway ranch was only about eight miles from the Clayton ranch. He would stop by there tomorrow to meet David and give him a map and a key. That way David could let himself in while Brody was out on his date with Jennifer.

The answering machine continued. "Hey there, sexy man. I just put on some silk baby dolls and on a cold night like this, well, I guess I'll need an extra blanket for warmth, won't I? I just wanted to thank you for tonight. I had a really good time with you, and I'm looking forward to Friday night. Good night, Brody. You really do have a great butt! Can't wait to get my hands on it!"

Brody chuckled. "Tara, baby, I don't think you'll be needing no extra blankets. You're hot enough to warm up the entire town." He smiled as he hit the rewind button before turning out the lights and heading upstairs to bed.

After two nights of disturbed sleep, Brody finally succumbed to a long, deep sleep, undisturbed by dreams or nightmares or "real life" experiences. His body and his mind recharged, and he slept until the morning sun sat high in the sky.

Stretching his shoulders, he wandered into the bathroom to shower off the last remnants of sleep and get ready for the day ahead. Feeling clean and fresh, he pulled a pair of Wranglers from his drawer and added a western shirt, rolling his sleeves to his mid forearm. Downstairs in the kitchen, he microwaved his frozen pancakes while making a cup of instant coffee. The microwave dinged and he took out the overly hot plate, scurrying to drop it on the kitchen table. Grabbing a fork from the drawer, he sat down to look through yesterday's mail: another credit card application, a hydro bill and a six-month free trial to a new health club in Riverton. Two were filed in the garbage can and the other in his accounting drawer.

He checked his palm pilot to see his agenda for the next two days. He needed to get in touch with Bracken, Rhett and Patrick, and fit in a visit to Lindy. Maybe pick up some more chocolate for her. He remembered the key for David and put a stop at the Hathaway Ranch on his list. Tonight he was taking Jennifer to Riverton. Tomorrow he might finally have some time to work on the house before going out with the Hot Tara Shepherd again. Wondering what she had up her sleeve, his mind replayed her message on the machine last night, and he smiled.

Back to the schedule. Saturday was the soft, quiet Meghan Shepherd and Sunday with Rhett, whom he knew without a doubt would not be nearly as much fun as Tara.

•

Rhett sat in the passenger seat of Brody's truck as they followed Northrup and Patrick out to the Clayton ranch. Brody placed a call to Bill Clayton to inform him they would be on the property. It was the smart thing to do considering trespassers were reckoned fair game in Wyoming.

Pulling off the highway, they headed cross-country toward the Wind Rivers. A speck on the horizon gradually grew into the building they sought. The snow had melted a bit under the morning sun, and barren patches of land presented themselves as dirty smudges on the white panoramic canvas. A laneway approaching from the north became evident as they neared the cabin. Brody pulled up beside Bracken's rented Lexus and parked. The officers all climbed out of their vehicles and began to examine the exterior surroundings.

"Hey, Brod, look at all the dog feces over there. And it don't look like it's from no toy poodle, either."

"Point one." He began to mentally count the substantiating clues as he circled around to the front of the building. Frozen tire tracks etched deeply into the earth. A vehicle had obviously been here during a recent thaw to make the deep ruts in the mud. "Point two."

Bracken stepped onto the small front stoop and opened the door. The others followed him inside. As soon as Brody crossed the threshold a bolt of adrenalin shot through him, and he reached out to brace himself against the wall. Rhett noticed his reaction and laid a hand on his shoulder, quietly asking, "You okay?"

"Yeah, fine." He collected himself quickly, not wanting the others to know the effect being here had on him. His eyes perused the cabin layout in one quick sweep. There were three closed doors. The first opened to a bedroom, and he knew right away it was not the one. The next door revealed a bathroom. He stood at the third and swallowed before opening it. Gripping the handle, he twisted it and pushed the barrier wide. "Point three." His heart jumped into his throat, choking him. There stood the bed, and he recognized it immediately, but something was not right. He entered the room and positioned himself in the corner, viewing it as he saw it in the dream. The closet was where it was supposed to be, and the bed and mattress were the right ones, but in the wrong location.

"It's been moved," he muttered

"What's been moved? What are you talking about, Brody?" Patrick stood inside the doorway.

"The bed. It should be on that wall. Somebody's moved it and cleaned the place."

"How do you know it's been moved? You been here before?" Bracken was puzzled by Brody's seeming adamance.

"Trust me. I just know." He pulled open the closet door. "Look in here. It's clean. You can still smell the bleach." He suddenly felt the walls closing in on him, as though all the oxygen was vacuumed from the room, and his chest felt ready to explode. "I've gotta get outta here," he gasped as he pushed past the others and on out the front door. Once outside, he sucked in the fresh mountain air letting the frigidness of it burn his lungs. The sky was grey, and he could smell the snow that would be falling later on. The bitter bite of the wind felt good on his face.

Bracken followed him outside and pulled out his cell phone, placing a call to the local FBI office. He requested a forensic team to do a sweep on the cabin and make prints of the tire tracks. "Where the heck are we, Ashton?"

The tall, blond officer took the phone and gave directions. The team arrived within the hour and went straight to work.

"How far do you figure she ran to get to where you found her?" Bracken asked.

"Round about a coupla three miles. It's amazing she made it that far in those conditions. Her body was covered with a layer of frost."

Bracken allowed his gaze roam over the countryside as he shook his head in wonder. He couldn't begin to fathom what it must have been like for the victim to make that midnight escape into the frozen hell that awaited her.

Eager to leave, Brody and Rhett got into the truck, not waiting for the evidence to be collected. They remained silent until the truck was back on the main highway and heading into Lander.

"You okay?"

Brody stayed mute for several minutes before finally answering his friend. "I don't think so, Rhett. I can't begin to tell you what it did to me being in that room, recognizing everything: every picture on the walls, every scratch on the floor, and knowing what that closet looked like before somebody cleaned it."

"I'm sorry, Brod. Where we going now?"

"Ah, shoot. I almost forgot." He slowed the truck and made a U-turn, heading back out into the countryside. "I have to stop out at the Hathaway's. My cousin just moved here from Arizona, and he has a job out at their ranch. He's gonna sack out at my place, so I have to drop off a key to the house."

"Never heard you mention him before. You guys close?"

"Nah. Haven't seen him since I was just a little kid. Don't really remember much about him, but he's family, and I have the space, so why not?"

At the silver mailbox with HATHAWAY emblazoned on it sitting at the side of the road, Brody turned into the laneway and drove to the main yard behind the house. As they climbed out of the Avalanche, Tara's grandfather emerged from the stables. Age had not yet bent the back of this hard working rancher. He still stood tall and covered the stable yard in long strides, a friendly smile greeting his visitors.

Brody clasped the extended hand warmly. "Mr. Hathaway, how you doing?"

"Can't complain, Brody, Rhett."

"I understand you have a new ranch hand here. Fella from Arizona?"

"Yes, I do. David Whitson. He in any kind of trouble I should know about?"

"No, sir. Dave's my cousin. He's gonna be staying at my place, so I dropped by to give him a key."

"Right then. He's over in cattle barn three. Go on ahead."

"Thanks, Mr. Hathaway. I'll be seeing ya Saturday. Meg invited me to come out for the day with her."

"Well, that's just fine. But listen, Brody. You be careful with that girl. She's her grandpa's little sweetheart, and I don't want her to be one of the grieving women left in your dust."

"We're just friends. Meghan knows that. But if I need to make it clear, I will. I'm not ready to settle down with anyone yet."

"All right then. You know, Tara's different. She's stronger, can take care of herself, but Meggie is my little softie, and she hurts easy. Paige, well, she's her own story. I've never met a more accident prone girl in all my life." He shook his head in wonder as he recalled the long line of broken things left in Paige's wake.

"Thanks for the advice. See ya later." Brody wiped at his brow, making his escape with Rhett quick on his heels.

"Who's tonight, Brod?"

"Jennifer."

"Ah, yes. Lady of the legs. I can just imagine those legs wrapped around me."

"So, ask her out."

"Not in the mood to be laughed at."

Brody stopped at the barn door, his hand clasping the handle and turned to look at his friend. "Ask her. You may be surprised. If you don't grab hold of her, I think Agent Northrup just might. Then you could be out of luck for good. Grab your chance while the grabbings still good."

They strolled inside and found David unbaling hay for feed. He glanced up at their approach and grinned widely when he saw who it was. He lifted his hat and wiped the sweat from his brow with the back of his arm, leaving dark hair askew. He pulled the off his leather work glove and happily pumped his cousings hand.

"Great to see you, Brody. Thanks for helping me out."

"Glad to have you. And to make it easy, I live right down the highway there. Second house past the third side road on the right. It's an old white clapboard. Name's on the mailbox. Go ahead and let yourself in. I'll warn ya, I'm doing a lot of work on the house, so it's in a perpetual state of repair. But there are three available bedrooms on the second floor and one on the main floor off the kitchen. Take your pick. They're all empty."

"I surely do appreciate it. Any house rules?"

"Clean up your own mess, and personally, I never bring women home."

"Never?"

"Nope. I make it a point to go to their place. Then if I want to go home, I can. I can't ask a lady to leave on her own at two in the morning if I don't want her to stay. Besides, any who did stay would see the renovations and start coming up with all their own ideas to make it a dominion they can rule and reign. No, thanks. My place is my refuge when I want to get away from it all."

"Good thinking. I can live with that. So, you're a deputy, huh?" David asked.

"Yup. This here's my friend, Rhett. He's a deputy, too. I usually work the afternoon shift, so you'll have most evenings to yourself. I get home about eleven thirty."

"Well, this is great. Thanks a lot. I think it'll work out well for both of us. You can leave me a note telling me what my expenses will be. Include my share of utilities and things. I'm not looking for a free ride."

"Okay, I'll do that. Listen, we should head out and let you get back to work. I guess I'll see ya when I see ya."

"Right. Thanks again."

Brody and Rhett retraced their route into Lander, the miles clicking by unnoticed as they talked, the dismal sky threatening to ply them with freezing rain.

"Seems a nice guy," Rhett remarked. "Ya never know how these things are gonna work out, do ya? Sometimes best friends can't even share a place without being at each other's throat. Ya just gotta go into it and hope for the best."

"Yup. That's why it's good we work different shifts. Both still get privacy. I hope it works out okay."

"I'm getting hungry. How about the Breadboard? Hot soup and a sub sounds good to me."

"I'm up for that." Brody parked the truck and they hurried inside for comfort food as the cold drizzel began to fall.

CHAPTER ELEVEN

Brody tucked the last bite of his bread bowl soaked with gravy into his mouth and chewed thoughtfully. "Think I'll stop in and pick up some more chocolates. Lindy's just about out, and heck, that's the best entertainment I get all day. Besides, she deserves some special treatment. She's working so hard to get through this. That girl is determined to pick her life up and do something with it."

"She's a great lady. I hope she gets the feeling back in her fingers, even if she can't walk. It's a damn shame this had to happen to such a good person."

"I know what you mean. Not that you want it to happen to anyone, but it always feels worse when it's someone special. And Lindy is a great person. She worries about taking too much of Ma's time. She actually feels bad for needing. I guess after taking care of a sick mother for so long, she's used to being on the giving end and has trouble sitting on the other end of the stick."

Arriving at Chocolates for Breakfast, Too, Brody chose a five-pound box of soft centers; maraschino cherries, chocolate truffle, lemon, strawberry and hazelnut cream. He hoped to witness more of this box's consumption than he did the first one.

They returned to the truck, and Brody drove the few short blocks toward the center of town before parking again. Not sure where they were going or why, Rhett dutifully followed. Brody opened the door of Main Street Books and waltzed inside.

"Whatcha looking for here?"

"Lindy likes to read, but she can't turn the pages, so I thought I'd bring her something I could read to her. I don't know who she likes, so I'm gonna jump off the haystack on this one, and hope I land in a good place." He ambled to the new releases shelf figuring he stood a better chance of striking something she had not yet read. Settling on the latest by Harlan Coben, he took it to the cashier.

The men separated after leaving the book store. Rhett reclaimed his own car from the Sheriff's Office around the corner, and Brody headed south on Buena Vista Drive to the medical center.

Arriving at the hospital, he stopped at the front desk to inquire about Dr. Collins. He learned the doctor practiced in Riverton but came to Lander two afternoons a week. Brody booked an appointment for the following Friday. There was no question in his mind he needed it after the morning spent at the cabin. He could not even explain to Rhett the anxiety and terror that clung to him after the ordeal.

Taking the staircase at the end of the corridor up to the second floor, he consciously willed the stress of the day's findings to drop from his shoulders. Lindy needed to be lifted up, not pulled down. When he opened the door to her room he found her laying with her back to him, crying. Immediately concerned, he quietly asked,

"Lindy, can I come in?"

She looked at him over her shoulder, "Oh, Brody!"

He crossed the room in three steps and set his gift on the chair. "Can I help?"

She nodded and reached her arms out to him.

Hanging back timidly, he remembered the rules and asked first. "Is it okay for me to hold you?"

"Please."

He shucked off his coat and dropped it in one fluid movement as he sat on the side of the bed. Pulling her close, he folded her in his arms and held her snugly against him. Her arms wound around his neck, her face buried in his large chest.

"Hey, now. I've got you, Lindy. I'll hold you as long as you want me too. I won't leave ya, honey."

She continued to weep, and he kept one arm securely around her while he tenderly stroked her hair, laying his cheek against it and surrounding her with his comfort. More than once he felt moved to kiss her head, as though she were a small child. But she was not. She was a full grown woman, and she needed him right now. It was not often he felt needed like this.

The crying became sobbing, and he reached over to her bedside table to bring the Kleenex box to her. He could not remember ever hearing either of his sisters cry so hard before. He pulled a tissue from the box and held it to her nose for her, wiping it dry. Then his arm wrapped around her again, cocooning her in his safety.

"Oh, Brody. It was so awful. So...awful."

"I know it was, honey, but it won't happen again. It's all over, and you're safe now. I'll hold you until you can believe it. I'm here for you, Lindy. You don't have to be scared anymore."

The experience was new for Lindy. Never had a man held her so close and offered her comfort before. She always suffered through her heartaches on her own. She lifted her face to look up at him, her cheeks wet, and told him, "Your arms feel so good."

Brody looked into her eyes, and he ached to give her whatever she needed. She lay her head on his chest, gazing up at him. He witnessed all the pain swimming deep in her eyes.

"Lindy, what he did to you, it wasn't sex. It wasn't love making. It was violent and angry and something you didn't deserve. But it wasn't sex. Do you understand that?"

"Mentally. Try telling that to my emotional self. He hurt me, Brody. He did so much."

"Ssh. It's okay. I know, hon. You don't need to tell me."

She pulled back and looked at him, her brows frowning in fear. "Your mother told you?"

"Ma didn't tell me a thing. She's kept your confidence."

"Then how can you know? I haven't told anyone else."

He pulled another Kleenex from the box and blew her nose again. "Now you've hit on something I'm not ready to talk about yet. Just believe that I understand more than anyone else can. I'm hurting over this whole thing, too. Lind, I need to be here for you. Not out of some sense of duty or pity. There's a connection between us that I can't explain, even to myself. I have to be here to share this with you."

She shook her head in bewilderment. "I don't understand, but I'm glad you came when you did. I feel a strange kind of connection, too. Do you know that the only person who ever held me while I cried was my mother, and then your mother?"

"I'm glad I was here. I know it's hard for ya, and of

course when you're alone it just rises to the surface wanting you to deal with it. My mom is great, but I'll be here for ya for the rest of your life. You can call on me for anything. I'll try to give you whatever you need."

"Thank you. I don't know when I've ever had such a good friend in such a short time. I'm growing comfortable so quickly with you, Brody. Someday I just may want to talk to you. I'm too afraid to right now."

"What frightens ya?"

"That you'll be so repulsed that you won't be able to look me in the eye anymore. That you… I don't know. I'm afraid to lose you as my friend. I have so few, and what you think of me matters."

"Oh, I'm repulsed all right, but not by you. Lindy, there's nothing you can tell me that will make me turn away from ya. Those things were done to you. You didn't have a choice in the matter. I hate the things he did, but that doesn't make me hate you. And honestly, there's not much ya can tell me that I don't already know. I hurt for you, but nothing lowers you in my esteem. Nothing you need to be ashamed for me to know."

"Thank you." She tightened her arms around his neck and hugged him close. He kissed her forehead, and when she finally let go he moved off the bed to sit on the chair.

"Look what I brought for the princess today." He held out the heavy box of chocolates.

"Brody, if you keep feeding me chocolates I'll be two hundred pounds by the time I get out of here. Then I'll really have to run to get back into shape."

"You can run with me. How many miles do you do a day?"

"Five."

"Then I guess I'll have to start working if I'm gonna

keep up. I only do three."

"But you do other things, too."

"Yeah, I have a weight machine I use."

"Well, it works. You deceptively look like a big cuddly teddy bear, but you're rock solid."

Brody scrunched his face in distaste. "Geez, Lindy. Don't go telling a lawman he looks like a teddy bear. It's not an ego booster."

She shrugged, seeing his point. "How tall are you anyway?"

"Six foot three."

"You see, I knew you were up there somewhere with your own climate. Not like we little people, down here. Is your brother tall like you?"

"Braden? Not quite, I guess he's about six one."

"But your mother isn't a big woman. How did she manage to get you out of there?"

"I wasn't born this size, ya know," he grinned. "I was a lot smaller as a matter of fact. Only about four foot ten."

"Okay, I deserved that."

She smiled, and he was happy she could. She had a beautiful smile, and it looked a lot prettier than the tears he walked in on.

"Hey, I brought something else, too. If you've read it, say so, and I'll take it back. I didn't really know who you like, so I took a shot in the dark."

"Harlan Coben. Ooh, good choice. Have you read him before? His book Tell No One had me biting my nails."

"Good. I thought maybe I'd read you a chapter a day until we finish it. Sound okay to you?"

"You're really too good to me you know."

He gave her his mischievous grin. "Why do you think the women ask me out?"

"Is that what you're shooting for here? 'Cause it won't work, you know. I told you, I don't ask men out."

"Ah, shucks. I'll just keep being wonderful, and maybe you'll change your mind."

"You're gonna have a long wait, Officer. Who's tonight's lucky lady?"

"Jennifer Dexter. She takes care of the dispatch and switchboard over at the department. I think Rhett has a thing for her, but he's too chicken to ask her out. Last night she went out with Agent Northrup, the FBI dude who's here to run your case."

"So, you'd go out with a girl you know your best friend has a thing for?"

"He never mentioned it until after I told him about the date. How was I supposed to know? I'm not a mind reader. I'm more of a stupid cupid."

She laughed at him. "So, where are you going with her?"

"Riverton. They have two theatres there. We'll go see a movie, then maybe have a drink and head home."

"Wow! Two theatres! Aren't there any in Lander?"

"Sure. We got the Grand. But if you've seen what they're showing, that's it. In Riverton, you get a choice, you see. You can go to the Acme or the Gem. So really, it's a choice of three movies. I don't even know what's playing. I'll let her pick."

Lindy giggled.

"What's so funny?"

"I'm sorry. I know I'm spoiled. I'm used to being in the land of the Cineplex or the new mega theatres going up. You have a choice of about ten films in one location. If you don't see what you want there, you just go half a mile down the street and choose from another dozen. That's how I've managed to see so many movies."

"Okay, city girl." He stared at her for a moment,

trying to think of a equalizing rejoinder. "Well, we have a video store. So there."

"Okay. I guess you win," she smirked. "I sure can't beat that. One whole video store. I guess I'll learn to not even try competing with you. So, tell me about last night. What did you do?"

"I ate some ribs and bowled with Tara Shepherd. Beat her both games, and then we went over to the Hitching Rack and had a drink. Then I dropped her off at her car and went home."

"Did you have a good time?"

"Course I did. I told ya, I won both games."

"I'm seeing a new side of Brody Ashton here. I didn't realize you were so competitive. Merciless. I guess if you're gonna catch up to my five miles, I'll have to push myself to seven. I have to stay ahead of you at something."

"I like a woman who's not afraid to push the line. But, my dear girl, I'm afraid you're so far ahead of me at so many things that I'll be eating your dust for many years to come."

Curious to know more about his date, she asked. "So, no juicy details?"

"I said I dropped her off at her car and went home."

"That doesn't mean anything. I've dated men in a car before. I know what can happen."

"We kissed, and that was the full extent of it. But it was enjoyable," he grinned.

"Are you going to see her again?"

"I think so. Tomorrow night."

"Ooh. Twice in one week. Is that unusual?"

"Never thought about it. Not if it's the only person I'm seeing, but since we're not exclusive, I guess it might be unusual. Can we talk about something besides my love life?"

"But it's so fascinating."

Feeling himself starting to writhe on the hot seat, he picked up the book and opened it to chapter one. "I think it's time to start this book now."

"Wait a minute. That's not the beginning."

"Yes it is. Says right here, Chapter One." He held it up to show her.

"Brody, that is not the beginning of the book. First comes the acknowledgements and the dedication. I always read those. The author puts them there for a reason, you know."

With a sigh, he leafed back the few pages to the very beginning. After reading the pages he felt superfluous, he asked, "Now can we read the story?"

"Absolutely."

Turning onto her side, she snuggled down under the covers and watched him as he read to her.

CHAPTER TWELVE

"Well, let's have the story. What movie did you see?"

"We're gonna go through this again?"

"Come on, Brody. I have no life here. I have to live vicariously through you. Now spit it out. Start to finish."

Brody sighed as he dropped into the chair. Balancing his hat on his knee, he ran his hand through his hair in a feeble attempt to bring some semblence to his curls. She looked at him expectantly, and he knew there was no way to escape the conversation. Surrendering to the inevitable, he gave her what she wanted. "I picked her up at her place at six thirty. We had a nice drive to Riverton. Good conversation. Jen's got a good sense of humor, and like you, she's always trying to make me blush, which by the way is pretty easy, so you don't have to try so hard."

"And then..."

"And then we went to the Gem and saw the new Hugh Grant movie. It wasn't bad."

"I love Hugh Grant. He plays such wonderfully vulnerable characters that you just have to fall in love with him every time."

"Yeah, whatever. I think he's too English."

"Did you have popcorn and stuff, or go for the starvation thing."

"I paid to get in. She bought the eats. Then we came back to town. I don't like driving if I've been drinking, and I always limit myself to one. I've pulled over enough drunk drivers in my day. I have no desire to be one of 'em."

Another example proving he was very much in control of his life and not easily swerved from his course. She admired that about him. "Okay, so what did you order?"

"I had a Bacardi and coke, and she had a sling."

"She was hurt?"

"No, a Singapore Sling."

"Hmm. Fruity."

"Yup."

"Do you always drink rum?"

"No. When I was with Tara I had a rye and ginger. I like variety. Don't want life to get too predictable and dull."

She nodded, tucking away a new fact about her friend. "Ahh. I like an occasional Golden Cadillac but usually just a nice white wine."

"I keep some wine at home. It's nice for winding down when I get home from work on occasion." He propped his feet on the bars on the side of the bed and relaxed. "A glass of wine, some nice soft jazz, I can handle it."

"Sounds nice, but we aren't done with the date yet. What happened after your drink?" she prompted, steering the conversation back to last night. Lindy enjoyed hearing about his life. Her own was so empty; the days seemingly endless and alone. The time she spent with Brody provided her with her only break from the memories and pain that enveloped her the rest of the time. She craved the company and the respite it offered her.

"I drove her home and said goodnight."

"Did you walk her to the door?"

"Of course I did. It was a good night. Jen's a nice girl. Fun to be with."

"Get on with it. Did you kiss her?"

"A friendly kiss. Nothing hot and heavy. It was nice."

"Just nice? That's it?"

"Nothing wrong with nice."

Her eyes dropped, and she paused before confiding the thoughts of her heart. "I suppose. Personally, I wouldn't be satisfied with nice. I'm waiting for the kiss that's gonna knock my socks off. The kind where you hear music when there is none, and your knees get all weak, and you know that you're sunk forever, because you've just found true love."

"You believe all that?"

She met his gaze. Was she a fool? Probably. And yet, a part of her refused to relinquish all her aspirations to the rapist. "Yeah, I do. I have to believe in good things, or I won't make it. It may sound unrealistic, especially considering everything I've been through lately. I guess all my hopes and dreams need to be re-evaluated now. But in a perfect world, I hoped that one day I'd be kissed by the right man, and all that would happen for me."

Brody felt a bolt of admiration shoot through him, amazed at her strength.

"But enough about me, let's get back to you. What's Jennifer's best feature?"

"Rhett says it's her legs. I guess I'd agree with him. She does have pretty spectacular legs."

"What about Tara Shepherd?"

"What about her?"

"What's her best feature?"

"Ooh. That's harder. It depends on whether she's walking toward me or away from me. She's pretty much a package deal. But if I had to pick just one thing, I'd probably go with her breasts, and before you ask, that's a clothes on observation."

Lindy frowned at him, disappointed. "You're such a male."

"Don't ask if you don't want the answer. I think it's story time." Attempting to wiggle out of the heat, he picked up the novel and began to read.

Before leaving later that afternoon, he decided to talk to her seriously. He sat forward and clasped her wrist gently. "I wanna tell you something about the case before I go. Are you up to hearing it?" He watched closely to see if her face and her words said two different things.

She contemplated it before agreeing to listen.

"We found where you were held. It was all scrubbed down by the time we got to it, but the forensics guys are pretty thorough. They nabbed a few things that will be of help. They've identified a few strands of your hair which proves you were there. It's a good step forward, Lindy."

She held a brave face in spite of the tears that glistened in her eyes just waiting to fall, and a trembling lip that told him more than anything else. He saw the change in her expression as a thought occurred and she looked at him, puzzled.

"Wait a minute. You've been off the last few days. When did this happen?"

"I've been working with Northrup during my time off. I want to put an end to it, so you can get on with your life. I want you to be able to feel safe and happy again. I hate what they did to you, Lindy. I hate that they're still

143

out there." A sour taste filled his mouth, and he felt a knot twisting in his stomach.

"You're doing all this for me?"

"Course. You deserve the best."

That was all it took for the rain to fall. She produced a torrential downpour, and he sat on the bed. Feeling a safety with him she couldn't explain, she leaned readily into his arms, and he rocked her while she cried.

"We're moving along. I don't want you to hurt anymore. It's gonna be okay, honey. I promise you, I'll put an end to it." He allowed her the time she needed to grieve.

Lindy felt something with Brody she did not experience with anyone else. So small in his massive arms, she felt secure, like he was blocking out the rest of the world. A sense of trust steadily flourished; surprising her. Trust was something she felt certain she would never feel towards a man again. Brody was different. She knew he would never hurt her as he kissed her head and stroked her hair. His touch was gentle and comforting, not at all aggressive or threatening.

He bent his head to kiss her forehead and held her tighter. "Lindy, I won't be here again until next week. Probably Tuesday. I don't want ya to worry, and I don't want ya to think I've deserted you. I'm going to Oregon to get your stuff."

"All right. Thank you for telling me. I hate to be a burden to you, you know. I realize you already have a very full life without me, but…" she dropped her eyes, embarrassed by the admission, "…you make me feel so safe, Brody. The only time I feel it is when you're with me. I need that."

He held her close as he thought. "I feel something special with you, too. There's some kind of connection I can't explain, but I think it would be wrong to be anything more than friends. Don't you agree?"

"Yes. I know you're right." She was clinging because he rescued her, because he treated her so well. Her head knew it. "I'll be all right. Don't worry. You should get going. You have a date to get ready for tonight. Remember, I'll expect a full report next week."

"You've got it, Lovely Lindy Lassiter of Lander. When I get back you'll be able to have your own things around you, and that's got to feel better." He stood to go, and she gave him her best imitation of a smile. "Talk to you later, Princess." He bent to place a final kiss on her forehead. "Look after yourself."

•

Brody picked up the ringing phone in his kitchen.
"Hey, Brody. Bracken here."
"Hi. What's up?"
"I did some work on the computer last night and came up with some pretty interesting things. I found two other cases similar in every way to Lindy's, both unsolved. One in Oklahoma and the other in Pennsylvania. The only difference between those cases and this one is that Lindy escaped. The others weren't so lucky."

"I don't like the sound of that. Let's nail this guy before he moves on and starts again."

"I'm all for that," the agent confirmed.

•

Passing through Baker City, Rhett stayed on the highway until they were six miles out of town. A highway rest station loomed on the left and he pulled into the parking lot.

He noticed Brody's white-knuckled grip on the armrest as he parked. "You okay?"

"Sure."

"Okay. So I'll ask you again. You okay? This is like the cabin, isn't it. It's just the way you saw it." Rhett knew his friend well enough to sense the tension escalating through him.

"It's the same. I stood right over there and watched it happen. It's so frustrating to see everything so clearly except the things I need to identify the men. I almost wish I could dream it again so things would come clearer. You can't believe how maddening this is."

"Let's go ask some questions. Probably won't learn much, but it never hurts to ask."

Brody had already contacted the local sheriff's department and learned no calls reported the incident, and they had no knowledge of it. That meant there were probably no witnesses. Except him, and he was not much help at all.

Approaching the service station, Brody went into the office while Rhett spoke to the young fellow working the pumps. Brody got nowhere. Rhett learned the man remembered Lindy because he filled her tank and was surprised to notice the vehicle still in the parking lot that evening when he finished work. The only thing that made her stand out from others he attended that day was her U-Haul trailer. Otherwise he would not have noticed her at all.

The deputies drove back into town, discouraged by the lack of leads they gleaned but not surprised. Tired and hungry, they pulled into the parking lot of the El Erradero restaurant to devour a hot Mexican meal. If they could not move forward in their investigation they could at least satisfy their stomachs.

146

"What do you want to do, Rhett? Stay the night here in town or what?"

"I could go for another hour or two. Want to start back and find a place to stop along the way? Make tomorrow's journey that much shorter."

"Good idea. Then I might get back in time to see Lindy."

"You gonna see that doctor your mother mentioned?"

"Friday. Hope it helps. It's haunting me all the time. Can't shake it."

When the waitress arrived to clear the table they both ordered fried ice cream to finish off the meal.

Changing the subject, Rhett said, "I like Lindy. She's easy to talk to. Doesn't make me feel all fumbled up inside. Not like Jen or Tara. Maybe I'll drop by tomorrow night to visit her, too." He turned the idea over and nodded to himself in approval, deciding he liked the way it looked.

Brody agreed. "In the rare moments she feels comfortable enough to be herself, she's fun. I took another box of chocolates last week. Hope she still has some left by the time we get back."

"I have to give it to you there, Brody. You were right about the chocolate."

The ice cream arrived, and they dug in like they had not yet eaten. "I knew the chances of learning anything new today were slim, but I was really hoping there'd be something. Sure wish I could go back and give her some good news." He spooned another mouthful of the cold confection.

"We'll nail 'em, Brody. I can feel it. It may not be this week, but we'll close it."

"They didn't close the ones in Pennsylvania or Oklahoma, did they?"

"That's because we weren't on the case. We're just

the ones to nab these guys."

"I sure hope you're right about that, Rhett, cause things won't be right until we do. I can't rest until they've been put away. I want these dreams, or whatever they are, to end, and I have a feeling that closing the case is the only thing that's gonna stop 'em."

When they finished their ice cream, the men paid the bill and walked outside to the parking lot. Rhett got in his car.

"When you're ready to stop, give me a flash with your lights, and I'll pull off at the next place we come to."

"Sounds good. If you want to stop and I haven't flashed, just go ahead and pull off. I'll follow. We'll stop at Boise if not before." Brody unlocked Lindy's car and climbed inside, grateful the keys were in her purse and not her coat pocket when she was abducted. It saved a lot of time not needing a locksmith to make a new set.

Rhett pulled onto the highway and drove into the darkness. Brody stayed close behind. His watch showed ten o'clock before they finally stopped for the night. The exit they turned off at provided a Best Western, and they got a room with two beds. February was not a big month for tourism which left the parking lot fairly sparse.

They took their overnight bags upstairs to the fourth floor. "I'm gonna grab a quick shower and then hit the rack." Rhett carried his bag into the bathroom and closed the door.

Brody grabbed his cell phone from his coat pocket and stretched out on the bed. Quickly clicking in his mother's number, he kicked his shoes off and they fell to the floor at the foot of the bed.

"Hi, Ma. We made it to Baker City and picked up Lindy's stuff. Didn't learn nothing new though."

"I'm glad you got it. I'm sure it will help to give her

some peace of mind."

"You sound worn out, Ma. Busy day?"

"Bad day. Matt Shepherd called this morning when he was doing rounds. I spent the day at the hospital."

"What happened? It's not Lindy is it?" He felt a tremor of fear run through him.

"I'm afraid so. She spiked a fever of 103.8."

Brody sat up quickly as he listened, the creases in his forehead deep with concern.

Gina continued, "When Matt checked her over, he found gangrene had started on her left foot. He had to amputate a toe. Only one so far. Now she's back on IV with an infusion of antibiotics to fight the infection. She's not doing well. The fever's causing her to be delirious, and unfortunately that means living through parts of the rape again. Of course we need to break the fever, but the main concern is keeping an eye on the foot and hoping it doesn't spread."

"I can't believe this, Ma. Hasn't she been through enough already? When will it stop?"

"I don't know, son. I'd sure rather it was sooner than later. How are things with you? Where are you staying tonight?"

"We've just stopped for the night. I guess we're as far as Boise. We've gotta get some sleep. We were on the road fourteen hours today. We'll start out at sunup, and I'll be back there as soon as I can."

"You don't need to rush, Brody. There's nothing you can do."

"I should be there for her."

"Honey, she's not your responsibility. You don't have to be there to make everything better, you know."

"I know that, but there's something there, Ma. I think it's the dreams. It's caused some kind of connection I can't explain. Aside from that, she's a friend." He

149

flopped back across the bed, keeping his feet firmly grounded on the floor. "Until this case is closed and I've taken care of this with Dr. Collins, I need to be there for her."

"Just be careful, Brody. I think you know what I mean."

"I do. We aren't gonna go getting romantical just because I'm the one who saved her."

"All right. As long as you keep your head on. I'll probably spend most of tomorrow at the hospital with her. No need for you to rush. Just drive safely."

"Okay, Ma. We've still got almost ten hours on the road ahead of us, so we'll take it easy. All right?"

"Good. I'll see you when you get here."

CHAPTER THIRTEEN

Brody pulled into his driveway at four-thirty Tuesday afternoon. After driving Lindy's car and trailer into his barn, he closed it up and went into the house, taking Lindy's purse with him. He would have to remember to take it to the hospital the next time he went.

In the kitchen he put a cup of water in the microwave and made himself a hot cup of chocolate. The drive had been long and cold, and he wanted to warm up a bit before heading back out into it.

He leafed through the mail he picked up from his box out at the road on his way in. Nothing required immediate attention. Looking around, he detected small signs of his cousin. David had chosen the main floor bedroom. That was good. They would be less likely to disturb each other with this arrangement.

Warmed and ready to go back out into the world, he drove the Avalanche into Lander, stopping on the way to pick up some barbecued ribs from the Silver Spur before heading south on Buena Vista Drive. He reached for the shopping bag on the floor of the passenger side which held Lindy's purse and took that, along with the rib dinner inside with him. He harbored every intention of sharing if she was up to it.

He found Meghan in Lindy's room reading a book while Lindy slept. Stepping closer, he asked about Lindy in a whisper. Meghan pointed to the door, and they went out into the hall to talk.

"She's doing much better today. Her fever's down. Not as much as we'd like, but when she's awake she's lucid. Not having the hallucinations any more, and that's good. She knows about the surgery and seems okay about it. Are you gonna be staying awhile?"

"Yeah. I thought I'd stick around a coupla hours. I haven't been in since last week. Been to Oregon with Rhett to pick up her stuff from the road stop where she was abducted. Luckily, it was still there, and no one tried to break in to steal anything. Listen, while I'm thinking of it, I've got her purse here. Do you wanna get out her hospital insurance information?"

"Not really. Some women are pretty sensitive about other people going into their purse." She hesitated, looking over her shoulder at the patient. "I guess she can't do it herself with her hands the way they are anyway, so…okay, I'll do it. Then, if you don't mind, I think I'll go on home. I have to be back here on duty tonight at eleven, and I could use a few hours sleep."

"Go for it. I'm not back to work until tomorrow night." He turned his attention to Lindy. "Anything I need to do for her?"

"I don't think so. If she needs something she'll let you know. Just play it by ear. She's been asleep for about two hours now. She'll probably wake up soon."

"Thanks, Meg. I really appreciate you being a friend to her."

"Well, I'm not doing it as a favor to you, ya know. I like Lindy. We get on well together."

"Yeah, she's remarkable isn't she?"

"She is. I'm gonna grab my things and get going."

They went back into the room and Meghan collected her coat and purse. Brody stood waiting, and they gave each other a friendly kiss on the cheek before she left.

He seated himself beside the bed ready to keep his vigil. Moments later, she opened her eyes and blinked at him.

"Brody?"

"Hey, Lindy. I'm back. How's it goin?"

"Not so good. I'm a girl with nine toes."

"Ma told me when I called last night. I'm sorry, hon. Let's hope the antibiotics stop the infection from spreading. Hey, want some good news?"

"Yes, please."

"I've got your car and trailer out at my place, and I brought your purse to you. Hope you don't mind, but I asked Meghan to get your insurance information out."

She gave a brief nod of acquiescense. "I don't know how to thank you, Brody. You've been so good to me."

"Shucks. It ain't nothing. Hey, look at this. Your dinner tray is still here. Let's see what it is." He lifted the cover from the plate and found congealed creamed chicken on a biscuit. "Well, you can have this. I'll bet it was probably good while it was still hot. I'd be happy to feed it to you, or you can have some barbecued ribs that I brought."

"Really? I love ribs." Her eyes sparkled for just a moment before clouding over again. "I guess it's kind of messy for a girl who can't eat with her fingers, isn't it?"

"Nah, ribs are supposed to be messy. That's the fun of it. Hang on." He stepped to her sink and washed his hands before retrieving the still warm bag of food. Taking out the covered dish, he opened it, and Lindy's senses were instantly assaulted by the enticing aroma of barbecue. He took out a rib and teased her with it before holding it to her mouth.

"Oh, Brody, this is so delicious. Hands down, it's the best thing I've tasted in months, with the exception of the chocolate, of course. These ribs are enough to make a person settle down in Lander."

Brody chuckled as he chewed. "Thought you'd like 'em." He held more out to her with his right hand while feeding himself with his left. When they had both cleaned the meat from the bones, he pulled another container filled with a tossed salad from the bag. He poured a ranch dressing on it, and they ate it along with their ribs. By the time they were through they both had sauce on their mouths and chins, and Brody had some on his moustache. They giggled at each others' mess, and Brody started to lick his fingers.

"No fair. I don't have any fingers," she complained.

He held out the hand he was not working on, and Lindy happily licked and sucked the sauce off of those fingers. What started as fun suddenly shot arousing sensations through Brody. He looked at her in surprise, and he wasn't laughing any more. She noted the sudden change in his demeanor.

"Dang it, Lindy!" he whispered as he moved toward her. With his clean fingers tucked under her chin, he leaned her back into her pillows and gave her a gentle kiss. She responded to the tenderness with a small sigh, and the sound of it undid him.

He pulled away and buried his forehead in the pillow next to her. "I'm sorry," he whispered in her ear. "I shouldn't have done that. Can you forgive me?"

"Last time you were here I thought you said you didn't want this for us."

"I did, and I meant it. I still believe it's wrong, but we have something I don't understand. Lindy, you have to

154

know that I would never hurt you." He stood abruptly and turned to the window, his hand rubbing the back of his neck. "I'm no good at this stuff. I don't know how to talk about feelings."

"Brody, I know you wouldn't hurt me. I never feel better, never safer, than I do when you're around. I feel different with you than I ever have before. At a time in my life where I shouldn't even want to be in the same town with a man, I want you to be here. It feels good when you hold me. That's the only thing in my world I'm not confused about."

He sat on the chair resting his hand on her arm. She rolled onto her side to face him.

He leaned forward and kissed her again, softly. "You're beautiful, Lindy," he said quietly. "I wish things could be different." His fingertips softly stroked her cheek, and she wanted to stay just like this forever. Finally, he pulled away, and gave her a half smile.

"Tell me about your trip. How did it go? Let's face it. It had to be better than my trip from Baker City."

"Nothing nearly as exciting as yours was. Twenty-four hours of driving in two days, most of it through mountains. We stopped long enough for dinner last night—Mexican. Then we started straight back. Tonight I have to get to bed early and catch some sleep. I go back on duty tomorrow."

"You went to a lot of trouble to do that for me, and on your time off no less. I really appreciate it, Brody."

He sat back and crossed his legs. "Don't even think about it. I think Rhett might come in to see you tonight."

"Good. Rhett's come by a few times. He sent me that bouquet of pink roses over there. He's a really nice man."

Brody turned and eyed the flowers with surprise. Rhett never mentioned that he had been in to see Lindy more than one time, and he sure never mentioned the flowers. Not like there was no time to discuss it. They just spent twelve hours together in a car.

Turning back to her, he faked a smile. "That's nice. He's a good friend to have on your side."

"He's easy to like, makes me laugh a lot. He said the next time he comes he'll be bringing a surprise. I wonder what he's got up his sleeve?"

"His arm."

"That was bad. Anyway, I'm glad you're both back. I've had a few other visitors while you were away. Meghan was here earlier, and she came in on the weekend. Says she had a really fun time on your date and that you're very attentive."

"Good. Who else came?"

Lindy grinned mischievously. "Another friend of yours— Tara."

"That girl is a whirlwind. Did she tire you out?"

"Not at all. She cheered me up considerably. She's very outgoing, isn't she? She told me so many funny stories that my poor broken ribs hurt. I really like her a lot, and I think she liked me too. I can see why you like dating her." Dropping her voice, she whispered conspiratorially, "I checked it out, and I have to agree with you. Even from a woman's point of view, she does have great breasts."

"Lindy!" Brody turned bright pink again.

"Well, you said it first. I'm just agreeing. Now Meg, I would say it's her face. She has beautiful, soft features. Who are you seeing next?"

"Me and Tara are seeing each other Thursday afternoon."

"Aha! Tara again. That makes three times in about a week, doesn't it?" Her eyes dropped a moment and then she looked up at him through her dark lashes. "Do you kiss Tara the same way you kissed me?"

"None of your business. Have you met with Dr. Collins?"

"Yes, twice now. He wants to work on helping me feel secure as a woman again. We're working on the guilt thing right now."

"Good. Ma said he's the best at this kind of thing. I suppose she's been in today."

"She spent all day yesterday with me. She's actually been here every day since I arrived. I really love your mother."

"Yeah, well, she's pretty crazy about you, too. I've never seen her connect with another patient like she has with you."

"Thank you for sending her. I owe you so much. I'll never be able to repay all the kind things you've done for me."

"Don't expect you to. Listen, I gotta head out now. I have a few things I need to get done tonight before I can go to bed."

"All right. Thanks for coming and brightening my day, and thank you for dinner. That was outstanding."

"One day I'll take you there to eat, and you'll have it hot from the grill."

"It's a deal. Night, Brody."

He left the warmth of the hospital and burrowed his neck deeper into his parka as he walked out into the cold night air. He needed to figure out how to remove himself from temptation without hurting her feelings. It would be one of the most difficult undertakings he had ever attempted.

CHAPTER FOURTEEN

Rhett pushed the door open and popped his head in to see if Lindy was awake. To his pleasure, he found her sitting up in bed watching television. "Hey, Lindy."

Pleased at the prospect of company, she gave him her brightest smile. "Hi, Rhett. Come on in."

He pushed the door open wider and entered toting a box and a shopping bag.

"What have you brought with you today?" she asked with interest.

"I brought my DVD player and some movies along with popcorn and soda. Thought maybe we could have a movie night if you're up to it."

"Sounds terrific. I love it."

Rhett felt an inside thrill at her evident pleasure. He hoped it would make her happy. "Listen, I'll hook up the machine while you pick a movie. Then I'll go down to the patients' kitchen to pop the corn while the trailers run. Okay?"

"Wonderful."

He quickly made the attachments to the television and plugged in the machine, then brought the bag of movies to the bed and spread out the selection for her to peruse at length.

"I can't believe you brought this many, Rhett. Let's go for a comedy. I could use a laugh."

"Then I recommend this one." He picked up Planes, Trains and Automobiles. "Just happens to be my favorite."

"I saw that once when I was about fourteen, and I remember doubling over with laughter. Good choice."

Rhett put the disk into the player and pushed the start button. "I'll be right back."

Five minutes into the trailers he returned with two bags of fragrant popcorn which he poured into a large bowl he brought along and opened two bottles of pop, putting straws in one of them for Lindy. He gently placed the bottle between her mittened paws so she could lift it and drink when she wanted. He understood her need to be able to do something for herself. Seated on the chair next to the bed, he stretched his arm out to put some popcorn in her mouth.

Weighing her own anxieties against the awkwardness of being fed, she made a resolve. "I think it might be easier if you sit on the bed with me. If that's okay with you," she hesitated.

"You sure, Lindy? I don't want you to feel uncomfortable."

"It would be easier for you to feed me, wouldn't it?"

"Yes, you have a point there."

"Just take your boots off so you don't make a mess on my bed, please." She wiggled sideways to make room for him. Rhett was safe. She trusted him not to make any moves on her.

He kicked his boots off in record time and sat beside her, his long legs stretched out on the bed.

"If you start to feel uncomfortable, you say so and

we'll rearrange things here." He put more popcorn into her mouth and some into his own, and they settled in for an evening of light- hearted laughter. As the evening wore on, he was pleased to find that she allowed herself to relax next to him and a few times leaned her head against his arm.

When the movie ended, he finally found the gumption to ask the question that plagued him. "Lindy, about you and Brody…"

"What about me and Brody?"

"Are you two, you know what I mean?"

"Brody and I are friends. No more, no less."

Relief coursed through him. "I guess I should get things cleared up and let you get some rest."

"Do you have to go?"

"No, I don't have to. I just didn't want to tire you."

"Would you mind staying a bit longer? I like you being here."

"Sure, I'll stay." He looked down at her snuggled up next to him, her emerald eyes sparkling with a gentle smile tugging on the corners of her mouth. Plucking up his courage, he bent his head and kissed her, tenderly and respectfully. Nothing aggressive about it.

Lindy appreciated his gentleness. He was a kind man, and she was lucky to have his attention, all things considered. A wave of dizziness washed over her and left her breathless.

"Want another movie?" he asked.

"No. I'd rather just stay like this and talk if that's all right with you."

"Yeah. It's very all right with me. You're feeling pretty warm. Are you feverish?" He frowned as he felt the heat emanating from her skin.

"Yeah, I guess I am a bit."

He started to pull away from her.

160

"Rhett, please don't go."

"I'm not going anywhere. Don't worry." He pushed the call button for the nurse, then went to the bathroom sink. He filled a basin with cold water, grabbed a clean face cloth and came back to her. Tossing the empty soda bottles in the garbage, he made room for the basin on the night table. He soaked the cloth and squeezed out the excess water to sponge her face when the nurse came in.

"Do you need something in here?"

"I think her fever's going up again."

"I'll get the thermometer." Seconds later she was back and sticking the scanner in Lindy's ear. "She's back up to 102. I'll check on Dr. Shepherd's orders."

Rhett kept dipping, squeezing and mopping. "We'll look after ya, Lindy. Don't worry."

"I'm not worried." She gave him the best smile she could muster as her eyelids fluttered.

He knew the fever could be a sign the infection still rampaged through her, and it scared him. "Work with me here, will ya? I'm doing my part, trying to cool ya down. You have to start some positive thinking so this thing doesn't stand a chance of surviving. We've gotta fight this, Lindy." He bathed her wrists and the inside of her arms at the elbows, then pulled the sheets down to let her body heat escape and wiped behind her knees.

"That feels good, Rhett." Her eyes drifted closed, and she slept by the time the nurse returned to add an infusion to the IV.

•

Brody pulled into his driveway and parked. Finding David's blue Neon there pleased him. Maybe they could get to know each other a bit. Tromping up the steps to the back door, he found his cousin sitting at the kitchen table reading the paper.

"Hey, Brody. You just getting back from Oregon?"

"Nah. Got home a coupla hours ago. Been to see a friend. Long trip, though. I'm pretty bushed tonight. Wanna grab a coupla brews and move to the living room?"

"Sure." David opened the fridge and pulled out two cans of Coors, and they flopped on opposite ends of the sofa. "That Meghan gal you were with the other day at the ranch? She's quite a looker, isn't she?"

"Yeah, Meggie's pretty. A really nice girl too."

"You guys steady?"

"Nah. I'm actually seeing more of her sister, Tara, lately. Going out with her again this week. Totally different girl than Meg. Have you met Meredith Hathaway out at the ranch yet? She lives there—cousin of Meg and Tara."

"Haven't been introduced, but I've seen her in passing. Looks pretty young still. I like girls a little older. Late twenties, maybe thirty. A little experience under their belts. I'm not into virgins."

"This is a small town, so it's not like you can sleep with a different girl every week without everyone knowing about it. It's usually considered more acceptable if you're seeing someone steady."

"The curse of a small town. I lived in Dallas and Vegas for awhile. Plenty of anonymity. I guess I'll just have to adjust to small town rules. It's not like I haven't lived them before."

"Lander's a nice town. Full of good people. I'm sure you'll find some little filly here that strikes your fancy. Try going to the Hitching Rack or the Shady Eagle. Lots of the single girls go there weekends. You get to see who's hooked up and who isn't. Good music, too."

"Sounds like a plan. When do you go back to work?"

"Tomorrow afternoon. Then I'm on for ten days straight. It all works out. When I get a few days in a row off, I usually get something accomplished here on the house. I didn't get nothing done last week. Spent my off time working a case which I really can't talk about, so I shouldn't have brought it up. How are you doing out at the Hathaway's?"

"They seem like good people. The work's okay, and the other hands are pretty easy going. Not like trying to break into a closed circle. Met a coupla guys I went out with on the weekend. I think it's gonna be fine."

"Good. You getting settled in here?"

"Yeah. Man, you sure have a lot of frozen dinners."

"I don't cook. If I don't eat at Ma's or a restaurant, my friendly microwave is my only alternative. When the smoke rises to the ceiling, I know it's done."

"Maybe you should consider finding a girl to keep around permanently."

"I've been thinking about it."

"And? Got one in mind?"

"Yeah, I guess I do. She's not ready right now, though. Too much baggage to deal with first. Who's knows what'll happen down the road. She messes up my head, that's all I know."

"Ouch! Gotta watch out for that kind. Next thing ya know, ya can't think of nothing else but them all the time. Pretty soon they've got ya standing in a church before you even know what day it is."

"Yeah, I think she's definitely that kind."

David took a long pull on his beer and said, "Probably a good idea to pull back for awhile then. If she's the right one now, she'll still be the right one then."

"That's pretty much what I figgered. We'll just play it out and see what happens." Brody stood up and

163

stretched. "Well, I know it's still early, but I'm in desperate need of sleep, so I'm gonna hit the hay. Go ahead and play music or watch television. Whatever you want. It won't bother me none."

"Sure. Have a good night."

Brody dragged his feet up the stairs and sat on the edge of the bed. His boots dropped to the floor, followed by his Wranglers. He wanted a shower, but was too tuckered. Falling into bed, he found sleep in minutes.

•

Matt Shepherd arrived to check on his patient at eleven o'clock. He unbandaged her feet and studied them while she continued to sleep. "I don't know, Rhett. I'm not seeing any further damage. Let's hope we can beat this infection before it beats us. I don't want her to lose anything else. Why don't you head on home now?"

"I'd rather stay and help try to bring the fever down if it's all right."

"Okay, go to it. She sure is lucky with the friends she's picked up here." He gave Rhett's shoulder a squeeze before leaving.

After hours of mopping her hot forehead, Rhett checked the clock. Three a.m.. He took the basin to the sink and dumped out the now warm water, refilling it again with cold. As soon as the cloth came into contact with her skin, it heated again. Carrying it back to her bedside, he continued as he had been for hours.

At six in the morning the fever broke, and Rhett, who had been up for twenty four hours and on the highway driving for ten of them, laid his head down alongside her and drifted off to slumber.

•

Gina walked into Lindy's room Wednesday morning, surprised by the picture that greeted her. Lindy lay fast asleep with all the covers thrown off, and there was Rhett, a damp facecloth in his hand fast asleep with his head nestled next to her hand.

Gina quietly crept closer and touched his shoulder. "Rhett." She gave him a gentle shake, and he groggily lifted his head.

"I'll get her fresh water," he muttered. He tried to stand and take the basin, but she stopped him.

"Rhett, what are you doing here?" she asked him quietly.

"She had a fever spike last night when I was visiting. I stayed to sponge her down. It finally broke about six this morning."

"You stayed with her all night?"

"Yes, ma'am. I guess I should head home and get some sleep now that she's out of danger." He rubbed his eyes.

"I think that's a good idea. I'll stay for the day. She'll be fine now. Thank you, Rhett." Gina stepped to Lindy's side and laid the back of her hand against a cool cheek.

"Good night, Mrs. Ashton."

"Good night, Rhett. Can you get home safely?"

"Yes, ma'am." His feet shuffled as he made his way to the door.

Gina bustled about, tidying the room. When she settled in her chair, Lindy awoke, letting out a deep sigh before finally opening her eyes.

"Gina? What time is it?"

"Just past nine. How are you feeling?"

"Fine. A bit hungry, but other than that I'm fine. I had some weird dreams last night, but I can't really remember any of them. Rhett came last night and brought his DVD player so we could watch a movie. Funny, I don't remember him leaving. I must have fallen asleep. I guess I make pretty lousy company."

"Rhett just left about ten minutes ago," Gina told her.

"What?"

"You ran a fever last night. He stayed all night to look after you, wiping you down with a cool cloth until the fever finally broke a few hours ago."

Lindy's eyes mimicked an owl's as she stared at Gina in amazement. "He stayed all night? I can't believe it. Boy, when Brody said this town was full of good people, he meant it."

"There are plenty of people here who care about you, Lindy. You've got yourself quite a fan club," she smiled. "What can I get you this morning?"

"Looks like they've left my breakfast tray. I'm sure it's all cold by now, but we can see if anything's salvageable."

Gina lifted the cover off the tray. "Lucky this morning, Honey-girl. Muffins and juice." She lifted the glass for Lindy to drink and peeled the paper from a morning glory muffin. Finding it still warm, she split it and spread some margarine on it. Lindy loved the rich warm flavor and ate eagerly.

"Well, I'm glad to see you eating after that fever last night. Won't hurt you to take some extra liquids in, either."

"Yes, ma'am."

"Let's see how things look today." Gina unwrapped Lindy's feet first. "Hmm. Pretty good. No sign of gangrene in any of the other toes. That's good news." She left them unbandaged to allow them exposure to the air while she unwrapped the hands. She gently held the fingers as she studied them.

"Gina!" Lindy's eyes lit with wonder. "I can feel that!

166

My fingers are starting to get feeling in them."

"Honey, that's wonderful. You may just get them back after all." Gina hugged her tightly, and for the first time Lindy was able to hug back without feeling like her hands were encased in boxing gloves.

"Can we call Brody and Rhett and tell them?"

"We can call Brody. Poor Rhett is just crawling into bed." She picked up the phone from the bedside table and dialed.

Brody answered on the third ring. Gina put the phone next Lindy's ear so she could talk.

"Brody?"

"Lindy? Is that you?"

"Yes, it is. I've got such great news. I wanted to call you right away."

"Good. What is it?"

"I'm starting to get the feeling back in my fingers."

He could hear her smile over the phone. "Lindy, that's marvelous. I'm so glad you called. This is the best news. My whole day is gonna be better now."

"Brody, there've been plenty of times in the last week that I wished you hadn't found me. But right now, in this minute, I'm very glad you did. Thank you."

He heard the choke in her voice, and his mother took the phone from her.

"Morning, sweetie. I think she's a little overwhelmed, and she has every right to be. She can't move them yet, but the fact that feeling is returning is a sign that the nerve connection hasn't been completely severed. We couldn't have asked for anything better than this. Hey, you won't believe who I found here this morning." She told him about Rhett's night vigil.

Brody did not know how to react to the news. He was surprised, and yet somehow, he was not at all surprised. Rhett was the kind of guy to do something like that. Brody was just not too sure he liked it. Maybe he was over-exaggerating the situation in his mind. Surely Rhett did not see her as anything more than a friend. But those flowers on the window sill...

"Tell Lindy I'm real happy for her, Ma. Maybe someday we'll get to hear her play the piano."

"Will do. Talk to you later." Gina hung up and gave Lindy another hug, rejoicing that today's tears stemmed from happiness for a change.

CHAPTER FIFTEEN

Brody walked into Lindy's hospital room at nine o'clock that evening and stopped short. He tried to take it casually, but there was Rhett, stretched out beside her on the bed, watching a movie with her. They had popcorn and drinks, and she looked sort of cuddled up against him. Brody felt the green monster rising up inside, and he struggled to stuff it back down.

"Hello, Rhett. I didn't expect to find you here. Is it okay to come in, or should I come back another time?"

"Hey, Brody. We're just watching a movie." He lifted the remote and stopped the DVD player, then spoke to Lindy in a quiet voice Brody could not hear.

"Come on in and sit down," she invited with a smile.

Brody moved to the chair beside the bed and sat. Rhett did not move. He stayed right where he was snuggled up against her, looking quite comfortable.

"I was really pleased that you called this morning, Lindy. It's such great news, and I know it's just the beginning of good things for you."

"Your mother left things unbandaged for a while today. It felt so good. They're still purple and swollen,

169

but I was so surprised when I could feel her touching me."

"Hey, you'll be tinkling the keys in no time. I can't wait for the first concert."

Lindy shifted a bit so she faced him more easily, but Rhett didn't move a muscle which irked Brody no end.

"I still have a long way to go before a concert. I'll probably require some physio to get these babies back into use. Then I suppose I'll have to learn to play again, you know, getting the fingers in sync with the brain and being able to get a good octave stretch again. But thanks for the vote of confidence. It is appreciated. Did you work on the house today?"

"I was gonna, but I realized you might have stuff in that trailer that doesn't like the cold for any length of time. The rental company is just tabulating the days, so I unloaded it and put all your things in one of my empty rooms and returned the trailer to the local dealer. I explained what happened and how it was held in police custody for awhile, so he's only charging ya until January eighth."

"You're kidding! Brody, that's great. Thank you so much. You know I appreciate all the things you do for me."

"Yeah, I know. Hey, I thought if I came in before work tomorrow we could kill another chapter of the book. Sound all right to you?"

"Sounds very good."

"Well, I guess I should get back to work." He stood, reluctant to go.

"Okay. I'm glad you stopped in, and I'll see you tomorrow afternoon."

Brody turned to walk away when she reached an arm out to stop him. He leaned over, and they kissed each other's cheek. He gazed down at her with a smile and cupped his hand on her cheek.

"You take care of yourself, princess." He started toward the door. "See ya later, Rhett."

He waited until he got outside before he let the steam roll out of his ears.

"Damnation!" He punched the roof of the car before climbing in. "Well, it's your own fault, Brody. You knew ya had a hankering for her, and you did nothing about it." Then he answered himself. "I know, but I didn't expect her to take up with somebody else so fast, and I sure didn't expect it to be my best friend."

Late in the evening, his radio paged him to settle a domestic dispute. When he arrived on the scene, the wife was on the floor being pummeled, and a small child cowered in the corner. Already on edge, Brody dealt harshly with the abusive husband, laying a good right hook and an upper cut on him. He cuffed him quickly and tossed him in the back of the cruiser where he could do no further harm, then called social services to take care of the woman and child. He stayed until they arrived before he took his prisoner in and booked him.

•

"Thank you for staying with me last week, Rhett. It means a lot to me."

Rhett leaned down and kissed her head. "Good. I like you a lot, Lindy. What I mean is," he paused and grabbed hold of his courage. "Lindy, would you consider, you know, going out with me when you get out of here?"

"I think this is already our second date. I'm happy being with you. You make me comfortable. I'd like to see more of you."

"You would?" His face registered genuine surprise.

"Why do you sound so shocked? You're a good man, and you're very gentle. Those kind of things go a long way with me. Not to mention you're good looking."

"I am not."

She tipped his head to look at her. "Yes, you are, Rhett. You have a lot to offer a woman."

He felt his heart burst at her words. "Ah, shucks. Lindy, you're so precious." He lowered his mouth to hers and kissed her tentatively while he stroked her cheek gently, almost shyly.

She knew he was nervous with women, but she also knew he was worried about frightening her. She applied a bit more pressure to the kiss, and his heart rolled over.

"Lindy, I could be happy kissing you for the rest of my life and never stop. But as much as I want to, I'm afraid it's working overtime on me. I know you're not ready, so I'll be satisfied just having you near me."

"You're the best of men, Rhett Owens."

He accepted the compliment and sat back, smiling. He was dating Lindy Lassiter, and she was a terrific girl.

"Hey, Lindy. Brody seem all right to you when he was here?"

"You noticed it, too? I thought he seemed like something was bugging him, but he didn't want me to know about it."

"Ya don't think he was mad about me being here with you like this, do ya?"

She saw the worried expression on his face. "No, Rhett. I don't think that bothered him at all. He's just a friend. We don't have any claim on each other. He saved my life, and I'm grateful, but that's it. Besides, he's still seeing Tara Shepherd. I think they're becoming a thing."

"That's good. I think Brody and Tara make a good

couple. Not often he settles down to one woman. I think I might just follow his lead."

She smiled at him and thought more about Brody. She saw the unhappy shock when he walked in even though he masked it quickly. If he was interested in her he had plenty of opportunity to say so, yet he never had. Maybe Rhett was the one for her. It was worth finding out. Certainly better than spending her life alone if he was willing to accept her under these conditions.

"Lindy, would you like to do something different next time I come?"

"Well, it's not like I can play crokinole or anything. Did you have anything particular in mind?"

"Not really. I just didn't want to bore you." He watched his finger trailing up and down her arm. "You look real pretty tonight." He lifted his hand and ran strands of her hair through his fingers. "Your hair's so soft and shiny."

"Ah, but the real question is, are my legs as great as Jennifer's?"

He turned bright red and looked ready to die when she laughed outright.

"It's okay, Rhett. You haven't had a chance to see my legs at their best and in action. I'll wait until then before I expect an answer."

"Damn that Brody. I'm feeling pretty foolish right now."

"Don't. I'm the one you're dating, not her. And you're not dating Tara either in spite of the fact that she's a total package, although Brody thinks her breasts are her best feature."

"Why would I want either of them when I could be with you? You're a total package, Lindy. You don't make me feel insecure, although a little embarrassed right now, but I'll get over it."

She sat up and looked into his eyes. "I wish I could touch your hair, Rhett. I wish I could offer you more than a simple, chaste kiss, but I'm not ready."

"I know. Don't worry about it. We need time to get to know one another better anyway."

She kissed him softly, and all was right in his world.

•

Brody sat finishing his paperwork when Rhett came in to punch the clock. Brody tried to ignore him, but he came to the desk and sat on the corner.

"Hey, Brody, how'd it go tonight?"

"I've not had a good night, Rhett. I beat the crap outta some guy who was beating on his wife. I'm going home and put on my runners and do a coupla miles."

"At this time of night? It's pretty dark out there."

"I know what it's like at eleven o'clock at night. I'm out there in it almost every night."

"Brod, something bugging you? You seemed a bit off tonight at the hospital. It's not about me and Lindy is it, cause I asked her if you guys had something going on, and she said no."

Brody slammed the filing drawer shut and lied. "No, Rhett. It's not about you and Lindy. I don't want to talk about what's bugging me, okay?"

"Sure. I'm glad it's not about us, cause we've decided to see a lot more of each other. I'm so crazy about her already. I think she might even be the one I'll settle down with. Man, can that woman kiss!"

"I'm happy for ya. I'm sure you'll be as cute as the couple on the cake. And as for kissing, I'm dating Tara Shepherd. I'm pretty sure I'm not missing out on too much. No offence intended." With that he pulled his coat on and stalked out the door, leaving Rhett to daydream of Lindy on his own.

•

Tara finished work half an hour earlier and had just crawled into bed, when she heard pounding on her front door. It was probably one of her sisters this late at night. When she opened the door of her converted garage apartment, Brody wrapped his massive arms around her waist and lifted her off the floor. He kissed her hard and passionately. She pushed the door shut over his shoulder, and he carried her straight to the bedroom. She helped him quickly undress, and he was on top of her and inside of her, exerting his energy.

"Oh, Tara, I need you. I need you, Tara. I want you so bad baby."

"You've got me."

When the initial stress worked it's way out, he took the time to fulfill her needs.

When they both lay spent and satisfied, he pulled her up against his side and held her snugly. "Can I stay the night with ya?"

"Yes."

He kissed the top of her head and fell asleep with her in his arms. He felt her get up in the morning to use the bathroom before she slipped back in beside him. He got up half an hour later to use it. She went into the kitchen and poured two cups of coffee, bringing them back to the bed.

With the pillows plumped up she leaned back into them, the blanket pulled up to her waist while she blew on her mug. Brody came back into the room and relished the view of her best feature. He climbed onto the bed on all fours and kissed each one before scrambling back under the covers. He picked up his coffee cup and drank before leaning to kiss her good morning.

"Brody, am I missing something?"

"What's that, darling?"

"Well, I know we had a date for this afternoon, so were you just arriving early or what? It's not every night a man comes to my door and climbs on top of me without even saying hello."

"Sorry about that. Howdy, Tara."

She smiled and giggled. "So are we gonna be lovers on a regular basis, or was this a one time thing, or what?"

"Well, I'm not in love with you if that's what you're asking." He took another sip of coffee.

"I don't recall asking if you were gonna marry me. I asked if we're gonna be lovers."

"We've seen a good bit of each other the last few weeks. We're attracted to one another, right?"

"Right."

"I've been thinking about ya a lot, and yes, I want us to be lovers." He set the mug on the side table and slid down onto his side, his head propped on a hand. "What do you want?"

"I want the same thing. I like you being here in my bed with that cute butt of yours." She gave a teasing smile, and he took the cup from her hand and set it down.

"Get over here, woman." He took hold of her waist and pulled her on top of him, then stopped abruptly. "Hey, Tara, I hope you're on the pill cause I didn't use anything last night, and you didn't stop me."

"Yes I am, or I would have."

"Good." He pulled her mouth down and kissed her while she had her way with him.

176

CHAPTER SIXTEEN

David Whitson had been in Lander a full month when he saw Meghan Shepherd's car pull into the yard at the Hathaway ranch. He pulled off his heavy leather gloves and waved. Two women emerged from the little blue Toyota and wandered toward him.

"Howdy, Meghan."

"Howdy, David. This is my younger sister, Paige. I don't know if the two of you have ever met before."

David stuck his hand out to Paige. "Wow. Are all the pretty girls in Fremont County members of the Shepherd family?"

The girls smiled at the compliment.

Meghan asked, "Are you gonna be finished here soon?"

"Yeah. I have about half an hour left on the clock, and then I'm a free man. You have something in mind?"

"Paige and I are gonna go riding. Holden Nichols is coming with us. Want to come along and make it a foursome?"

"Well, let me get this straight first. You're talking about horses, not sex, right?"

Paige burst out laughing, and Meghan tried to keep a straight face. "Yes, we're definitely talking about horses, you fool."

"Well a guy can always hope. Sure. Sounds like fun. Plans for after?"

"Not really."

"Then maybe I can convince you both to join me for dinner in town. How's that sound?"

Meghan nodded, and Paige stood biting her lip. He reached over and tugged her blond pigtail.

"What about you, Smiley? You gonna let me take you to dinner?"

"I tend to get hungry so it sounds good to me. You know how to two-step?"

"Sure do, little lady. You pick the place, and that's where we'll go. I'd better get my work done so I don't keep y'all waiting. Pretty fillies tend to get skittish when they're left waiting too long." He gave Paige another playful tug on her braid and headed back to the barn.

A sudden scream rent the air, and he turned to see Paige laying flat out on the ground. He ran back to the sisters to offer assistance. "What happened?"

"Paige stepped on a bit of black ice and fell."

"You okay down there?" he asked as he stood over her looking down.

"Sure. I have built in bounce-ability. Actually, I came with a pillow stuffed down the back of my jeans to save my coccyx in anticipation of an event such as this."

He laughed and offered both hands to help her back to her feet. To his surprise, when she stood she turned and lifted the back of her coat and sure enough, there was a cushion tucked into the elastic waistband on the back of her pants.

"See? Told ya I was okay."

Startled laughter filled the air, and David wiped the

tears from his eyes before they froze on his face. He could not remember ever seeing anything so funny before. Paige Shepherd was an absolute hoot. He just might need to hook his trailer to that girl for awhile. She promised to be totally unpredictable, and he certainly liked that in a woman.

By the time he finished his chores, he headed for the barn where the domestic horses, as opposed to those raised for sale, were kept. The girls came out with four horses already saddled. Holden arrived a few minutes later, and they all climbed into their saddles and headed at a canter west toward the mountains.

David loved it. It was a part of the ranch he had not seen yet, and it presented an open vista for miles. He could get a real lay of the land from here. They rode through a small copse of trees, and things seemed to be fine until, for some reason, Paige's horse started to bolt. It brushed so close along the side of a tree that poor Paige was scraped off it's back and left behind on the ground. If he had not seen it with his own eyes, he would not have believed it. Dismounting, he bent down to look at her. She did not look hurt, nor did she look angry.

"You okay, Paige?" he dared to ask.

"Darn horse. She does it to me every time. I'm the only one. One of these days I'm gonna stop bringing her apples. I hope you don't mind riding double, David, cause I'm afraid I won't be seeing Bellybutton again until we get back to the stable."

"Bellybutton? Who the heck named the horse that?"

"I did. When she was a new foal she kept poking me in my bellybutton, so I stuck her with the name. Think that's why she always scrapes me off?"

David took his hat off and ran his other hand through his hair. "Miz Paige, I'd be delighted to have you ride back with me. You know, we've just met and already I know that I've never met a woman in my entire life quite like you."

"Yup, they broke the mold when they made me. And I've broken everything else since." She took the hand he offered and climbed up into the saddle in front of him. They talked all the way back to the stable, and David thoroughly enjoyed her ongoing chatter. He looked forward to an interesting evening with the Shepherd sisters.

•

Submerged in an abysmal blackness, Lindy struggled to drag herself across the floor, solely reliant on her sense of direction to guide her. She guesstimated another six feet to reach the door. He was gone now, but she still needed help. Rage and fear mingled together in her throat, choking her. Her smothered screams and cries went unheard. Any sense of security developed over the past month in Lander lay shattered. There was no such thing as safety any more.

It should be easy to crawl the short distance, even without the use of hands and feet for propulsion, but every muscle in her body screeched with pain, marking each inch achieved with agony. Muffled voices from the hallway meant the door was getting closer. So close and yet miles away. Just keep moving, just keep moving.

When she finally touched the finish line, she wriggled around and used the heels of her feet to bang on the door. To bang and bang, seeking a Savior who would arrive too late.

•

He tilted his head to the side, first one way, then the other to stretch the tight muscles in his neck as he wandered down the hall. A floral painting by Canadian artist Mary-Dawn Roberts drew his attention, and he stopped to admire the soft pastel shades swirling together to create a soothing garden for the beholder. He appreciated it when hospitals made the effort to create a relaxing atmosphere for patients and their families who spent so much time within its walls dealing with serious personal traumas.

Glancing at his watch, he marked the time and smiled. Over the past half hour the halls vacated of visitors, with only the skeleton night staff remaining. However, he anticipated things would liven up again very shortly. Oh, how he hoped he would be there to witness the tumult that would ensue.

Ducking inconspicuously into an empty examination room in the emergency department, he slipped the latex gloves from his back pocket, and dropped them into a garbage can to intermingle with the dozens of others already disposed of there.

A few steps down the hall, he shoved open the rest room door with his shoulder and stepped into a cubicle. He took the condom from the sandwich bag in his shirt pocket and dropped it into the toilet, watching to make sure it disappeared when he flushed. Confident that he once again managed to foil the police's chances at collecting identifying evidence, he smirked as he opened the door and blended in with the evening milieu.

•

Brody looked at his watch when the call came from Jennifer Dexter over the cruiser radio. "Brody, you'd better get over to LVMC. Something about Lindy. They wouldn't be specific but said it was an emergency."

"Thanks, Jen. I'm on my way." The siren blared and the lights flashed as the speedometer climbed rapidly higher.

·

When dinner finished, David drove the Shepherd sisters to the medical center where he learned they were both employed. Meghan was scheduled to work that night, and Paige wanted to see her father who was a doctor there. David waited around more than an hour so he could drive Paige home. Sifting through the emergency waiting room magazines, he saw Brody burst through the front doors and run off at full speed down the hall with a security guard trying valiantly to keep up. No opportunity to say howdy. He would have to ask what the big emergency was later on at home.

·

The security guard stood waiting for him. "I had them call for you, Brody, cause she's been asking for ya. I know you're close friends with her."

"What's going on? I was only told there's an emergency." Brody jogged down the corridor to the staircase, forcing the man to run alongside him to maintain the conversation.

"She was attacked tonight. We figure whoever it was came and went using this staircase. The nurse said no visitors went past the station that she didn't recognize, and they'd have to if they used the elevators."

Brody stopped in his tracks, and the guard bumped into him. "Attacked?"

"Yeah. She …"

"What the hell's going on around here? How could someone just walk into a hospital and attack her? Where was everyone? I want answers, and I want them fast."

The guard stuttered in embarrased confusion, not having the answers required.

Enraged, Brody pounded open the stairwell door and took the staircase in leaps. Exiting on the second floor, he ran the short distance to her room. Sounds of crying and screaming carried through the door, the only word discernable being his name. He burst into her room and planted himself on the edge of her bed. With a clear recollection of the last time he tried to touch her when she was panicked, he held back cautiously.

Timidly, he placed a hand on her. "Lindy? Lindy, honey?"

As she turned toward him, he saw her nightgown ripped open down the front. "Brody? Brody, help me, save me!"

He closed his eyes in pain and put his arms around her, and she clung to him. "All right, Lindy. I've got you now, baby. You'll be all right now," he cooed.

"Please save me. Please save me." Her whole body trembled convulsively.

"I'm right here with you, sweetheart. Nobody can touch you now that I'm here. I'll protect you. You're safe with me now."

Dr. Matt Shepherd came into the room and injected a bolus into the IV.

Brody turned to the doctor and stated emphatically, "I'm not leaving her here, Doc. I'm taking her where I know she'll be watched over twenty-four/seven."

"I understand. She'll settle down in a moment. But before you take her anywhere, I need to collect another rape kit." Matt spoke softly, grieved for what this young woman had just suffered, again.

It hit Brody like a cataclysm to realize she had been sexually violated again. He lay his head against hers and cried with her. "Ah, geez, no. Oh, Lindy. My poor darling girl. I'm sorry, honey. I'm so sorry." He held her as tightly as he could, irrationally hoping if he held her close enough, it would all go away like it never happened.

Matt arranged the bedsheet to protect her privacy during his examination. "Okay, Lindy, I need you to scoot down on the bed. I'll finish as quickly as I can."

"Lindy, do you want me to call Rhett?" Brody asked as he helped her lay back on the bed.

"No. I don't want him here, please don't call him."

"Are you sure, honey?"

"I don't want him, Brody. Please. Only you."

"Okay. Whatever you want. Do you want me to leave the room while Doc Shepherd takes care of you?"

She clutched at his arm in desperation. "No, don't leave me. Please don't leave me, please don't." Her voice grew agitated, and her eyes filled with panic. "Don't let go of me."

"All right. I'll stay right here with you. I won't leave your side, honey. I promise." He folded the front of her torn gown closed to protect her modesty while his other hand rhythmically caressed her cheek.

He braced his arm across her on the other side of the bed to act as a visual barricade between her and Matt, and asked the nurse to pack Lindy's things. "Just leave a fresh nightgown for her, please."

The sedative started to take effect, quelling some of her anxiety, though she continued shaking. "Just relax, Lind. He'll be finished soon. Then we can leave."

"You'll stay with me?"

"Of course I will. You know you can trust me. I won't leave you."

"I'm scared, Brody. I'm so scared."

"I don't blame you. You have every right, but you know you're safe with me, don't you?"

"I trust you. Only you. I want you to stay with me."

"I'm not gonna leave you, sweetheart. I promise you."

His fingers stroked across her brow and down her cheeks to gentle her. "Lindy, I need to ask you one thing. Do you know who it was? Did you see him? Was it the same guy?"

Closing her eyes to shut out the memory, she shook her head. "I was asleep when he came in. The lights were out, and the nurse closed the door so the traffic in the hall wouldn't disturb me. I was wakened by the tape being pressed against my mouth and eyes. I didn't have to see him to know it was the same man. He said it again – 'Will I kill you today?'"

Brody pressed his lips together, trying to subdue his fury.

"I'm finished here, Brody," Matt said as he pulled the sheet down over her legs to cover her.

"Lindy, I'm not leaving. I just need to step into the hall with Doc Shepherd for instructions. While I'm doing that, you let the nurse help you into a clean nightgown, and then we'll go. Okay? We'll leave in just a few minutes. I promise you." He maintained eye contact, so he knew she was listening. She nodded and reluctantly released her grip on him.

Brody stepped into the hall and walked to the nurses' station. "Be with you in just a minute, Doc." He picked up the phone and called the Sheriff's Office. "Danvers, please."

Jennifer detected the distress in his curt speech.

185

"Brody? Is Lindy all right?"

"No, she's not, Jen." He tried to maintain control, but she heard the tremor, and it worried her. "I don't have time to talk. Put me through to Patrick, now." The phone rang as he was patched through.

"Danvers."

"Patrick, Brody here. Listen, we have a situation here at LVMC. I want you to get over here as quickly as you can."

"That's not our area. You know that. It's police turf."

"Do not, I repeat, DO NOT say anything to Rhett. It's Lindy. She's been attacked again, right here in the hospital. She doesn't want him to know, and I'd like to honor that request."

"Was she...?"

"Yeah. Doc Shepherd will have the kit ready when you get here. I haven't had time to ask any questions, and I'm not gonna. That's why I want you here. I'm taking her out of here, but come tomorrow morning I'm gonna want some answers and a lot of 'em. When I find out who did this, I'll personally castrate him. Better tell Jennifer to send Northrup. It's his case."

"I'm on my way. See you in five." Patrick hung up the phone and grabbed his coat off the hook as he ran past it.

"Hey, Patrick, where we going? Wait 'til I get my coat."

"It's all right, Rhett. I'll take this one on my own."

CHAPTER SEVENTEEN

Jennifer turned in her chair by the switchboard as Deputy Danvers burst through the doors from the squad room.

"What's going on, Patrick?"

He quickly glanced over his shoulder to be sure no one else could hear. "Lindy Lassiter was just raped at the medical center. She doesn't want Rhett to know. Call Northrup, and tell him to get down there." He took off at a run into the dark, cold night.

Jennifer registered the shock, then set it aside to deal with after she did what she needed to do. She quickly keyed in the number to Bracken Northrup's cell phone from memory.

"Northrup."

"Bracken, Lindy Lassiter has been raped down at the hospital tonight. Brody's there, and he wants you."

Bracken flipped his phone off without another word. The switchboard in front of her rang instantly.

"Hey, Jen. This is Rhett. Any idea who just called Patrick?"

"Sorry, Rhett. They asked specifically for him so I

patched it straight through. Don't know who it was."

He should have known it was a lie. The switchboard had call display. She crossed her fingers that he wouldn't remember that fact until after she was off duty.

•

Brody placed one more call. "Hi, Tara. I won't be able to make it over…I know. Me too…I couldn't really say. I'm on a case…I don't really have time right now...See ya later."

Brody hovered outside Lindy's door talking to the doctor when Patrick and Bracken appeared. "She okay, Brody?"

"Hell no! Would you be?" He stared at the floor with his hands on his hips. "Sorry, Patrick. Thanks for coming." He silently fumed before sputtering, "this should never have happened. After everything she's already been through we should have had round-the-clock protection posted at her door."

Patrick clapped a hand onto Brody's shoulder. "Be reasonable. You know our department doesn't have that kind of manpower."

Bracken added, "Besides, it's been a full month since her rescue. Even if there had been security posted here, it would have been withdrawn by now. We had no reason to believe the unsub was still in the area. According to his M.O. he should have moved on long ago."

Brody ran his hand through his hair in frustration as he introduced the doctor to the men joining them.

"Bracken, you know Doc Shepherd? He's been looking after Lindy. I'm taking her out of here, Doc. Not that you don't have a real nice place here, but she'll sleep a whole lot easier at my folks' house, and so will I.

188

Ma was gonna take her home when she got released anyway." He turned his attention to the agent. "I'll take her statement tomorrow. Right now, you fellas pick up this guy's trail before he gets away again. Pull the security video, and see who's on it."

"She must have gotten a look at the guy this time. Can she give us any leads?"

Brody shook his head in dismay. "No such luck. He taped her eyes and mouth again while she was sleeping."

Patrick jerked his head in frustrated anger. "Damn, this guy is good at covering his tracks. I'll talk to ya later, Brody." He went to the nurses' station and began his questioning.

Bracken stared at the floor. "There's no way this should have happened. It goes completely against the grain. Here, in a public place? How could he get away with it? Rapists generally seek private locations where there's no chance of being caught. This is way too bold a move." He chewed at his bottom lip as he considered the situation. Coming back to the present, he turned to the deputy. "Hopefully, we'll put this to an end soon. You go ahead and take care of her, Brody. I'll be in touch tomorrow." Bracken noticed the security guard standing nearby, his head hanging sheepishly. They exchanged a few words before striding to the elevator together.

With the law enforcement people dispersed, Matt Shepherd gave his instructions. "All right, Brody. I'll sign her out. I'm giving you some prescriptions for her, and I'll notify Dr. Collins. Here's a sleeping pill and some pain meds to get her through the night. Before she leaves I'll give her a pill that should hopefully prevent her getting pregnant, although I didn't find any traces of semen. He's ripped the catheter out, and I'm not gonna replace it. She'll either have to be carried to the bathroom, or be given a bedpan. Gina can manage. I want to see her one week from today."

Brody looked through the open door to see Lindy sitting in a fresh nightgown, staring vacant and listless.

"How do I ever make her feel safe again? I promised her she was safe here. How will she ever trust me now? I'm frightened for her."

"Be there when she needs you, and give her time. Maybe you should consult with Dr. Collins."

"Is it okay for her to have a bath or shower? She's gonna want that."

"She can bath. Getting wet isn't the problem, standing is. She's not ready to be on her feet yet."

They went back into the room together. Matt handed Lindy a pill and a glass of water before Brody wrapped her tightly in a blanket, making sure her feet were securely tucked in. He scooped her into his arms, and the nurse looped the bag with her belongings over his fingers.

The cruiser was parked immediately outside the front of the medical center. He set her inside and closed the door, then walked around and climbed in on the driver's side.

"Where are we going?" she asked nervously.

"I figured you'd probably want to be with Ma. She planned on taking ya home to live with her when you got out of the hospital anyway."

"Will you stay?"

"I will if you want me to," he assured her.

The very sound of his voice calmed her—strong and confident, yet soft spoken. She snuggled up closer against his side, wanting to be absorbed into his large safe haven so the rest of the world would be shut out forever. "Yes, please. I need to know you're close by."

Brody drove to the Ashton house and carried her into the dark interior. The light from the street lamp glowed through the front window, guiding him to the sofa. "I'll get Ma. You sit tight."

He saw the light in his parents' room suddenly flood through their doorway into the hall.

Gina came out pulling on her robe. "Brody, what are you doing here this time of night? Everything all right?"

Brody spoke quietly, "Ma, I've brought Lindy. She was raped at LVMC tonight."

Gina put her hand on the wall for support as the shock of his words hit her. "I don't believe it." She raised her teary eyes to his and saw the grimness written there. "That poor child. Go fill the bathtub. The first thing she'll want is a bath." She pushed past her son and fled to the living room where she cuddled the quivering bundle on her sofa in her arms. "There, there now, darling. Let's go give you a bath."

"Thank you, Gina," Lindy cried.

Gina called Brody to carry Lindy to the bathroom.

He knelt in front of her, laying a hand on her arm as he spoke. "Lindy, I'm going to the station for a few minutes while you talk with Ma." He watched as fear resurfaced on her features. "Don't worry, I'll be back. I have to talk to Rhett. He needs to know, Lind. I won't let him come over, but I have to tell him what you've been through and where you are. You don't have to see him until you're ready."

As much as she hated it, she knew he was right and nodded in agreement as tears rolled down her cheeks. "Be kind, Brody. He's gonna be hurt by this."

"I will be. Don't give it another thought. You just stay with Ma. I won't be too long," he told her. With a nod to his mother, he left to give them privacy.

At the Sheriff's Office Jennifer was already gone

from the switchboard, so he went straight back to the squad room where their desks were. The officers on the night shift started to pour in.

"Rhett, can I talk to you a minute?"

Rhett sat back in his chair and saw right away something was wrong. Brody's face was tight with worry. "Sure, Brod. What's up?"

"Let's go into Laramie's office." He walked past Rhett and led the way, closing the door when Rhett followed him in. He grabbed a chair and signaled for Rhett to sit also.

"Rhett, I need to tell you what happened tonight, and it's not easy."

"This have something to do with the call Patrick took earlier?"

"Yeah. I'm the one who called him." He swallowed the lump in his throat to get the words out. "Rhett, it's Lindy."

Rhett felt the blood drain from his face as alarm shouted to every nerve in his body. "What's happened?"

"She was attacked tonight. Right there in her room."

He started to stand. "How did this happen? I have to go to her."

Brody reached out and grabbed Rhett's arm. "No. She's not doing too well. I took her to Ma's place now. Lindy specifically asked me not to call you. She doesn't want to see you right now."

"But," Rhett stammered, feeling useless and bewildered.

Brody placed a hand on his friend's knee. "Rhett, I know you care a lot for her. She knows that, too, but she's having enough trouble dealing with herself without worrying about anyone else. She'd be too concerned about your hurt, and she can't cope with that right now. She knows you want to be with her, but you have to back off and give her time. She'll let you know when she's ready. In the meantime, you can call Ma for updates."

"I want to be there for her, help her, Brod."

"She knows that, buddy, but she can't deal with any one else's hurt but her own right now. She has to be able to work her way through this and decide what she wants to do. Who knows? She might not even be able to be in a relationship for a long time after this. There's no predicting where she's gonna land emotionally."

"So I don't get to see her, but you do. Tell me how that's fair."

"There's no pressure from me. I'm not the one she's supposed to be falling in love with."

"We aren't at that stage, yet. We only just started to date. Maybe five or six times."

"Right. And you're not already crazy about the woman. Come off it, Rhett. You know what I'm telling ya. She needs the space to work things out."

"Yeah, I s'pose I do. Tell her I'm here if she needs me. I won't push it. Geez, Brody, how did this happen? This is Lander. We're a safe, happy town. Things like this don't happen here."

"Wish I had the answers. I'm as ripped up by this case as anyone. I'll tell ya, it's hell seeing her like this. Oddly enough, I almost think it's gonna be harder to recover from this than from her abduction. She's only just gained back a sense of security, and to have it snatched away again like this has her lost and scared. Praise God, she has Ma."

Brody stepped around Laramie's desk and opened the bottom drawer. He pulled out the bottle of twenty-five-year-old whiskey and poured two fingers into glasses. He sat back down, handed one to Rhett and tossed the other one down his own throat, savoring the way it burned on the way.

"We've got to find the sleaze ball that did this, Rhett. It's the only way she'll ever feel secure again."

Brody left the cruiser at the office and drove his Avalanche back to his parents' house. He found his mother and Lindy sitting on the sofa. Exhausted from all she had been through, she relaxed the moment she saw his face.

"Everything all right?" she asked.

"Rhett's real worried, but I asked him to give you some space. He understands."

"Thank you, Brody. Gina, would you mind if I spend some time with Brody now? You can go get some sleep. I'm sorry I've disrupted your night."

Gina put her arms around the young woman and kissed her. "Don't you be sorry for a thing, darling girl. You're home now, and we'll take care of you. Don't stay up too late. I'm willing to bet Matt gave you some sort of tranquillizer, and you'll be nodding off soon." She kissed her son as she passed by and left them alone.

Brody sat on the sofa. "Can I get you something?"

"No. Will you just hold me for awhile? I feel safest that way."

Brody lifted her in his arms and carried her to the brown suede Lazy-boy chair. Sitting down, he leaned back and cranked the handle on the side so they were cuddled together in it. "This better?"

"Perfect. Thank you, Brody. You've been so good to me tonight."

He did not answer, sitting in silence while running his hand up and down her back. She snuggled in tighter with her head on his shoulder.

"Why do I feel so safe with you?"

"I'll never hurt you, Lindy."

"Yes, I know that, but I know Rhett would never hurt

194

me either, and I don't feel this same safeness with him. You're the only one. Why is that?"

"I don't know. Maybe it has something to do with the strange connection," he mused. "Lots of things I can't explain. Like how I feel we've been friends for years instead of just a few weeks. Like how sometimes you know what I'm thinking before I do. Like how we have the same taste in just about everything. It's like we were meant to meet and become close friends."

She tilted her head and placed a tender kiss on his neck. "My hero."

He kissed her forehead, and in the silence that ensued he heard her breathing change and knew she was finally asleep. He closed his eyes, knowing he held something precious in his arms.

At three in the morning Gina found them there. She took the blue plaid mohair throw blanket from the sofa and covered them before turning the light out and going back to bed.

CHAPTER EIGHTEEN

Gina sat at the table in the kitchen feeding Lindy a plate of pancakes when they heard the front door open and felt the quick cold breeze that came with it. A young woman appeared pulling off her coat and hat.

"Lindy, this is Brody's younger sister, Bronwyn."

"Hi. It's nice to finally meet you. Brody and your mother have both spoken of you often. I almost feel like I already know you." She smiled as Bronwyn sat at the table next to her.

"Likewise. Mom said she was bringing you here to stay, but I thought that wasn't supposed to be for another week or so."

Gina quickly intervened. "There were problems at the hospital, Bron, so she came a little early. That's all. Why aren't you at work?"

"Parent-teacher interviews today. I don't have any until after lunch." She turned her attention to Lindy. "I guess they told you I teach first grade."

Lindy nodded. "Is it a lot of fun, or an ongoing headache?"

"For the most part I have a blast, but there always

has to be one little pinhead that just annoys the heck out of you. Ask me in ten years. We'll see if I'm still having fun then."

Gina took the empty plate to the sink and washed it, leaving it on the drain board to dry. "Listen, Bron, since you're here I'm gonna take advantage of you and run out to pick up some things at the drug store. You'll take care of her?"

"Sure. Go ahead, Mom. We'll be fine together." She turned to Lindy, "Can you come into the living room?"

"I'll take her in before I go," Gina said and relocated Lindy to the sofa before pulling on her coat and boots.

Bronwyn took a clean mug from the cupboard and poured herself a cup of coffee.

"Want some coffee, Lindy?"

"No, thanks. I just finished."

Bronwyn brought her mug and settled in the Lazy-boy chair so she could get to know her family's newest friend. She knew something of the girl's background and admired the courage her mother spoke of.

"So, whatta ya think of my big brother?" she asked with a coy smile.

"That sounds like a loaded question."

"Just wondering."

"Don't really know how to answer it."

"Listen, I know my mother adores you and so does he, so we're bound to become good friends. I just wondered if you only see him as a friend, or if you're interested romantically."

"You don't mince words, do you? Brody is dating Tara Shepherd, and I'm dating Rhett. Does that answer your question?"

"Not one bit. Brody and Tara don't mean a thing. They aren't in love, they're just passing time until something better comes along. Tara could never be more than that to him. She's not the kind of girl Brody wants to settle down with."

Lindy's ears perked up, and her face betrayed her interest. "Oh, really? What makes you say that?"

"Tara's a very social person. She likes to go out every night of the week. Well, she can't because she works evenings, same as Brod, but she would if she could. She always needs to be entertained. My brother isn't like that. He goes out on dates and stuff, but he's just as happy sitting home with a book or the TV. He'll settle with a girl who's a homebody like he is."

"You seem to have put great thought into it."

"Doesn't take a whole lot of thought. Brody and I are like twins. We enjoy the same things. We have the same sort of needs. Tara's fun to pass time with, but she's not a keeper. Not in Brody's book." She picked up the warm mug and drank.

"Have you told him that?"

Bronwyn laughed. "Don't need to. I know my brother. Tara's good sex. End of attraction."

Lindy looked at the hands in her lap uncomfortably. "Well, nobody can ever say that about me."

Suddenly recalling who she was chatting with, Bronwyn wanted to smack herself across the face for her lack of sensitivity. "I'm sorry, Lindy."

"It's okay. I don't want people to tiptoe around me."

Bronwyn hesitated for a moment in uncertainty, then plunged ahead, deciding that continuing the conversation as a sign of accepting Lindy's will was better than uncomfortable silence. "So what about you and Rhett?"

Lindy breathed a sigh of relief, glad Bronwyn had not succumbed to awkwardness. "Rhett Owens is just about the nicest man I've ever met. I'm lucky to have someone like him interested in me."

"Ouch." Bronwyn winced and looked at Lindy through squinted eyes.

"What?"

"Well, that sure said a lot."

"That was two simple sentences, Bronwyn."

"Yup. 'He's very nice. I'm lucky he likes me.' Sorry, but that doesn't sound like a love match to me."

Lindy contemplated just how much she could reveal. "I'm still trying to sort things out. I'm thinking that I don't think I want to see either Rhett or Brody for a few weeks."

"Why is that?"

"I have to figure out what I want and what's real. Here I've stumbled on two wonderful men. One is currently seeing someone else, and we're the best of friends. The other wants to date me, and I think he's getting serious."

"So what's your problem? No conflicts there to resolve."

"I want to love Rhett. He's so good to me, and I truly couldn't ask for a better man. Again, I'm lucky to have a decent man willing to take me and all my problems on. I'd love to fall in love with him and live happily ever after. If there was no Brody, it would probably happen that way."

"What about Brody?"

"With Brody I don't want to chance losing a special friendship by pushing for something he doesn't want. He thinks it would be for all the wrong reasons. But, Bron, every time he walks in the door I feel like somebody's just turned on the Christmas tree. It's something I've never felt before for anyone. I want him to be with me all the time. I feel that spark that I can't seem to find with Rhett, and it makes me feel so guilty. Maybe in time I can develop that kind of feeling with Rhett, but right now it just isn't there no matter how much I wish it was."

"Can't pick and choose who it is the heart goes hankering for I guess. So, let me get this straight. You like them both a lot, but you could fall in love with Brody. However, if he doesn't want you, then why ruin a good thing with Rhett that might turn into love down the road."

"Thank you. That's my inner turmoil succinctly put."

"You know Brody won't look at you as long as you're seeing Rhett. Against his code of ethics. He'd never do anything that might hurt his best friend."

"I realize that, too. Nor would I pursue him as long as he's seeing Tara."

"Forget about Tara. I told you, it's the sex. She's not an obstacle."

"She's giving him something I can't, Bronwyn. What man with a single hormone in his body leaves good sex for no sex?"

They both sat and ruminated on it, rolling it over and over in their heads.

"It's a gamble. You can stay with Rhett and hope you fall in love someday, or you give him up and chance losing both. Rhett won't take you back if you want him after Brody turns you down. He won't settle for being second prize."

"He shouldn't settle for it. He's a good man and deserves better. I don't know, Bronwyn. I feel something with Brody that I can't explain, but the reality is that the whole idea of it being a choice is nothing more than a fantasy anyway. In the real world, Brody will never want me in that way. He doesn't want something used and dirty. So like I said, I'm lucky to have someone as good as Rhett care for me in spite of it all, and I need to work at falling in love with him."

Bronwyn stared at her in shock, too stunned to come up with an answer. She was saved by the front door opening and Gina coming in, her cheeks bright red from the cold.

"How are things going here?"

"Just fine, Mom. Come and sit down. I'll get you some hot coffee." She stood and headed to the kitchen. "Lindy, want some now?"

"Maybe I will, thanks."

Gina sat down on the sofa at Lindy's feet. Bronwyn handed her the coffee, and she warmed her hands around the mug. Bronwyn set Lindy's mug on a tray table beside her with straws in it, then went back to retrieve a fresh cup for herself before reclaiming her chair.

"Lindy and I were just discussing the men in her life."

"Ahh. Rhett and Brody. I've been waiting for this discussion. I knew it had to come sooner or later."

"What do you think, Ma? Does she have a chance with Brod?"

Lindy looked at Gina and waited nervously for the answer. When one didn't come right away she jumped to conclusions. "It's all right, Gina. I don't blame you. I'd want better for my son, too, if I had one. It doesn't matter anyway."

Gina's head jerked to stare at her, anger blazing in her eyes. "Don't you dare talk that way Lindy Louise, because it sounds to me like you're saying I don't think you're good enough for my son. Brody's love life is his business. and I steer clear, like I do with all my children. But if I had something to say, I'd say he couldn't possibly find a better woman to build his life with than you. You listen to me. What happened to you is not your fault. It doesn't make you less worthy of anyone's love, and it doesn't make you any less wonderful. I love you like a daughter, and I'll not allow anyone, least of all you, to put you down like that. Do you hear me?"

201

Lindy sat with tears burning her eyes. "Yes, ma'am."

Gina moved next to her and held her. "You're so good, Lindy. You're a beautiful young lady with a very special spirit."

Lindy's dam burst and she cried, purging more of the hurt that built within.

"My sweet girl, you didn't deserve it. The dirt is his, not yours. You have to believe me, honey."

Lindy cried harder while Gina held her. Bronwyn quietly got her things and left.

●

"I'm sorry, Brody. You can't see her. Lindy doesn't want to see you or Rhett for a least two, maybe three weeks. She has a lot of therapy with Dr. Collins lined up, and she starts her physio next week with her feet and hands. It's a lot for her to deal with."

"I don't see what that has to do with me. Me and Lind are just friends. We hang out together."

Gina stood firm with her arms planted across the doorway blocking his entry. "I'm sorry, son. I'm just the messenger."

Brody slapped his leg with his hat. "I don't understand this. The last time we were together…"

"I know. You held her and fell asleep together. Who do you think put the blanket over you? Brody, you gave her what she needed that night. Now she needs something different. You asked Rhett to give her space to heal. She's asking you for the same thing."

"All right, Ma. Listen, I've brought some boxes of her clothes from out at my place. I unloaded all her stuff there to take the trailer back. Tell her if there's anything she wants, just give me a call. And, Ma, tell her I miss her." He pushed his hat back on his head and scuffled back to the car feeling dejected. He was not used to Lindy turning him away. He spent time with her every single day since the night he found her with the exception of the weekend he went to Oregon. She was always happy to see him before, and he could not fathom what changed since he left her that morning.

With misery as his companion, he drove to Rhett's place. "Hey, Rhett."

"Hey, Brod. Seen Lindy today?"

"She won't see me neither, so I guess we're in the same boat." He flopped down in the chair. "Sucks don't it?"

"Yup. One thing to tell somebody else to back away. 'Nother thing to be told it yourself, ain't it?" Rhett offered him a cold beer.

"Kind of early in the day to start with this, isn't it?"

"Not on a day like this."

Brody took the bottle and twisted off the lid. He let the cold liquid drain down his throat, but it did not make him feel any better. Life without seeing Lindy every day would be empty. Heck, wasn't she gonna miss him?

•

Brody sat hunched over on the foot of the bed as he talked on the phone.

"What have you learned, Bracken?"

"It happened somewhere between nine-thirty and ten o'clock. The nurse heard her pounding on the door with her feet at about five past. She crawled across the room and tried to get the door open, but with her hands bandaged she couldn't manage. The nurses didn't notice anyone who shouldn't have been there at that time of night, but admittedly, they were at the other end of the hall distributing meds and before that the floor was flooded with visitors.

"I've watched the surveillance videos from the elevator areas and the parking lot for an hour each side of the incident and saw nothing suspicious. The night nurses were able to identify every person on the videos as visitors or staff they were familiar with. He had to have used the staircase at the end of the hall near her room. There's no camera in that area, so he could easily make it in and out undetected.

"The rape kit confirmed the rapist is one of the same men who held her in captivity. He left another hair behind that matched. There was only one attacker this time, but I'm sorry, Brody. We don't have any new leads."

"Right. Thanks for your help, Bracken."

"One thing about all this bothers me."

"Just one? A hell of a lot about all this bothers me."

"Granted. I don't understand why no attempt was made to kill her. That would be the usual M.O. in this kind of siuation. If he was worried she could identify him, he would have done away with her without giving it a second thought. He killed the others in the past. So why not Lindy? Why chance leaving her alive to possibly identify him or remember something that would help us target him? It doesn't make any sense. There was no one there to interfere or stop him, so what was his motive in this attack? That's what we have to figure out."

"The bugger is cocky. This was no random attack. He's been watching. He knew where to find her and when she would be most vulnerable. He just wants to show us he can do it right under our noses and still get away with it. Damnation!"

"We WILL nail this guy. Gotta get back to work. Talk to you later."

Brody clicked the button to disconnect and dialed Deputy Danvers at home. "Hi, Patrick. Brody here."

"Hey. How's she doing?"

"It's gonna be hard for a long time. Just when she was starting to feel comfortable and work things through, this happens. Northrup brought me up to speed on the investigation. One thing we do know now is that the perp is still in the area, and he's keeping an eye on Lindy. I'm damned if he'll touch her again, though. God help him if he tries, cause I'll kill him."

"Don't blame you a bit. Where did you stash her?"

Brody lay back on the bed and curled his free arm up over his forehead. "Over at the folks'. She and my mother are pretty tight, so it was a given. She's taking it pretty rough. Refuses to let me or Rhett see her."

"Sorry to hear it. So, you talked to Rhett?"

"Yeah, I went to the office last night and had a word with him. He's torn up about it, too, but he took it pretty good. Didn't try to punch me or nothing."

"It's a bad business all around. We need to catch the guy soon, and get him off the streets. Let's hope he doesn't start looking around for a replacement in her absence."

"He's gotta make a mistake before long, and we'll get him. Talk to ya later, Patrick."

•

Days turned into weeks. The investigation went cold again, and Bracken finally returned to Denver without successfully closing the case, a thorn that dug deeply into his conscience.

Brody grew more miserable as each day passed until he gave up spending time with anyone but himself. He set his hands to working on his house. After finishing the grouting on his new ceramic-tiled floor in the kitchen, he sat out on the steps of the back porch. When his sister's car pulled into the driveway he did not bother getting up. Instead, he remained rooted to the step and waited for her to come to him.

"Howdy, Brod."

"Howdy. What are ya doing out here?"

"Saw Lindy today. See Lindy every day in fact. We've become quite good friends. Thought I'd come and talk to ya."

"Glad somebody gets to see her." He leaned forward, supporting his elbows on his knees and started to scrape the grout from under his nails. "How's she doing?" He managed to sound almost disinterested.

"I think she's doing a lot better. You're pretty miserable. Is that 'cause you don't get to see her?"

"Shut up, Bron."

"Just asking. I know she's been missing you an awful lot' That's all."

Brody eyed her and then turned away again. "Her choice. She knows all she has to do is call, and I'll be there."

"You like her a lot, don't you?"

"We're friends."

"Don't see ya pouting if you don't get to see Rhett. I think you care for her. Much more than friendship."

"Butt out, Bron."

"She's walking. Her feet are doing real good. A few more months, and she'll be able to run again. She said you told her she could go running with you."

"Yeah, so?"

"So how do ya feel about dancing?"

"What?" He looked at her like she was still his annoying little sister.

"I suggested we all go out together as a group, you

206

and Tara, Lindy and Rhett, and maybe I'll ask Justin Cassidy to come with me. We can go to the Shady Eagle Friday night. Lindy was excited about the idea. She can't dance up a storm or anything, but she can go if she takes it easy. What do you say?"

"Lindy's gonna go?" He watched his sister's head bob up and down. "Okay. I guess we can do that. I'll call Tara."

"Brod, you and Tara, you're not serious are ya?" She said it more as a statement than a question. "It's really just the sex, right?"

"Like I'm gonna talk to you about it."

"Want to know what Lindy said to me? I asked her how she felt about you, and she said she wants to be more than friends, but that you'd never want something used and dirty like her, so she'll try to fall in love with Rhett cause he's willing to take her anyway."

His temper flared so suddenly he felt ready to hit something. She held her hands up defensively, knowing exactly what he was feeling. "Hey, I didn't say it, she did. She believes you see her that way."

"Damnation."

"That's what I thought. So you'll come on Friday night then?"

"I'll be there. Maybe I'll ask David if he wants to come and bring Poor Paige."

"Well, good. Now, show me what you've been doing with the house." She stood and held a hand out to him. He took it and walked around to the side porch to go inside so he could show her the fruits of his labor for the past three weeks.

CHAPTER NINETEEN

Rhett was elated when Lindy finally called to invite him to dinner at the Ashton's. He looked in the mirror for the fifth time before deciding the reflection was not going to get any better. Stopping at the florist on the way, he picked up a small spring bouquet. She answered the door when he got there, and it thrilled him to see her on her feet for the first time.

Dinner was served shortly after his arrival, so they sat with Mike and Gina and enjoyed the meal Lindy helped prepare. She could not control small motor skills yet, but she could do larger things. She could break the lettuce for the salad and roll and cut the biscuit dough.

Mike offered to help Gina with the clean-up afterwards, freeing Lindy to go to the back yard with Rhett. She showed him the seedlings she planted in the garden, then they sat together on the garden swing.

"You're looking real good, Lindy."

"Thank you, Rhett. It's good to see you. I've missed you."

Rhett put his arm around her, and she knew he wanted to kiss her. She let him—just a small kiss. "I've missed you a lot, Lindy. It was hard not seeing you."

"For me, too, but it's what I needed. I had so much pain inside, still do. But I had to learn to deal with it, and I couldn't do that if I had other people needing my attention. I hope you understand."

"I do. I'm just happy to see you feeling so much better."

"Rhett, I want to talk about us." She reached for his hand, and for the first time he felt her slender fingers in his. "Rhett, you mean so much to me."

"I feel the same way, Lindy."

Her face grew sad. "But all I'm feeling right now is friendship. You don't know how much I wish it was something more, but right now that's what it is. That's one of the things I had to sort out. I couldn't cling to you just because I needed your strength. I'd rather keep you as my good friend with honesty than to misuse you and lose you forever."

"Wow. That's not exactly what I was hoping for."

"I know. Please be my friend, Rhett. I know that what I'm saying hurts, and I'd give anything not to hurt you. I care so much for you. Who knows what the future holds? Maybe when I'm more secure with who I am, when I'm more sorted out, I'll be ready. But right now I'm not."

"Lindy, can I ask you something honestly?"

"Of course you can. I won't lie to you."

"Are you in love with Brody?"

"I don't know, Rhett. I haven't figured that out myself yet. I can tell you he's never asked me to be anything more than a friend. And even if I find that I do feel something for him, he's with Tara, and I won't interfere with that." She leaned her head on his shoulder, and he put his arm around her. "I do know that you're both very important in my life, and I hope you'll still want to do things with me."

"I'd rather have your friendship than not have you at all."

"Good. How about being my date Friday night? Bronwyn suggested we go as a group to the Shady Eagle. I can dance now, as long as nobody steps on my feet."

"I'd love to go with you."

"You're the best, Rhett."

He brushed her forehead with his lips, and she pulled her feet up on the swing. He used his foot to swing them slowly back and forth. The motion was soothing, and the warmth of the April evening allowed them to stay out and enjoy it longer.

•

Brody pulled the Avalanche into the parking lot of the Shady Eagle. When Tara reached for the handle to get out, he stopped her. She saw he had something on his mind. "What is it, Brody?"

"Tara, about tonight. I won't be going home with you after."

"Oh. I was sort of counting on it." She leaned over and started to kiss his neck, trying to change his mind.

"Tara, cut it out. I'm trying to say something here."

She sat back on her seat and looked at him. "This is it, isn't it, Brody? We've had our run."

"I think so. You've been great, and I've loved being with you. I hope you enjoyed it, too, but we said at the start…"

"I know. It's okay, Brody. I'm not totally surprised. I've felt you pulling away for the last few weeks."

"I'm sorry, Tara."

"It's okay. Let's go inside and enjoy the evening." She kissed him, and he kissed her back, tasting her for the last time.

"I think I'll miss you, Tara."

"Not nearly as much as you've missed her."

His eyebrows raised in surprise. She got out of the truck and he sat, staring at the empty seat. Maybe she knew him better than he knew himself. With a shake of his head, he got out of the truck and went inside with her. Rhett and Lindy were already there with Bronwyn and Justin.

Brody could not believe the surge of excitement that escalated inside of him when he first set his eyes on her. She and Rhett were walking to the dance floor. He led Tara to the table where Tara sat next to Justin. They always had plenty to talk about since they worked together every day. Brody strolled to the bar and ordered drinks. While waiting for them he saw David arrive with Poor Paige. Having her along could make for an interesting evening.

Balancing the drinks in his hand he made his way back to the table and sat down next to Tara, placing her drink in front of her. David sat next to him. "House is looking good, Brody. Haven't seen ya to talk to ya lately. You must be coming up for a few days off soon."

"Yeah, starting today. Five days. I should get a lot done. I'm finished with the kitchen now, all but a slap of paint. Think I might go outside now that the weather's good and do some work out there." From the moment he sat down his eyes remained glued to the dance floor.

Lindy tried to pretend Brody was not there. She came with Rhett, and she was going to pay attention to him, but she could not help her eyes sliding to the table every few minutes trying to catch a glimpse of the broad shoulders and blond head. His laugh boomed out over the music, and it made her smile. She missed Brody.

When Rhett took her back to the table she found she

was seated exactly opposite him. Close enough to look, but too far for one-on-one conversation.

He smiled at her, unable to believe how great she looked, all flushed from the dancing and the excitement of being out for a fun evening with friends for the first time in months.

She smiled back before turning to listen to something Bronwyn was saying. When she glanced again, she caught him still staring at her, biting his top lip as his finger ran around the rim of his glass. Around and around and around.

Rhett saw the way Brody looked at Lindy and the way she looked back. He stood and took Poor Paige to the dance floor, and Brody asked Tara to dance. A slower song started to play and they began to do a Texas two-step around the floor. Tara was a smooth dancer, and it was always good to have her in his arms for a song like this.

"It's okay, Brody."

"What is?"

"You don't have to pretend you're not looking at her. Why don't you ask her to dance?"

"I brought you tonight, Tara. If I wanted to be with her, I would have asked her instead."

"You're a lousy liar, Deputy."

"Okay. So maybe I'll dance with her later."

"What's with your cousin taking my baby sister out?"

"I hear David and Paige have gone out a few times. He gets a kick out of her."

"I'll bet he gets more than a kick. Probably an elbow, a knee, and a few black eyes."

"Poor Paige."

"That's what they say."

When the song was over, Brody and Tara returned to the table. David asked Bronwyn to dance so Brody moved over next to Justin, and Paige scooted around to sit next to her sister. They chatted happily when Meghan, the third and final Shepherd sister, showed up with her date. There was no room for more chairs, but as long as two people stayed on the dance floor and the rest played musical chairs, they all sat together at the same table. Brody decided it was a good thing Tara was okay with things or it could be trouble for him having three of them ganging up on him.

Shortly past ten o'clock Bronwyn wound her way around the table to her brother. "Dance with me, Brody." He vacated his chair which was quickly filled again. As soon as they hit the dance floor she informed him, "Want to talk to you."

"Bout what?"

"You haven't asked Lindy to dance. You haven't even spoken to her."

"Night's not over yet."

"We've been here for two hours. All you've done is sit and stare at her. Never figured you for a slow starter, big brother."

"You've got a wise mouth."

"Had a good teacher." She twirled under his arm. "So, when we're finished, you ask Lindy to join you on the dance floor. I'm gonna put on a song special for the two of you. If you don't, she'll believe you don't care. She'll give her heart to Rhett, and you'll be out in the cold for good."

"You're not gonna look good walking around with your nose all swollen and bent crooked."

"What are you talking about?"

"People who stick their nose where it don't belong are likely to get it busted."

"Hah! As if. This song is just about finished. I have to get to the juke box. You go get Lindy. Say you love me."

"You love me."

"Yes I do. Now go." Bronwyn deserted him and made her way to the jukebox, pushing people aside to get to the front.

Brody ambled through the crowd toward the table and stood next to Lindy. She looked up at him, and he held his hand out to her. She smiled and took hold of it. Leading her to the dance floor, they arrived just before the next song began to play.

The first notes sounded, and Brody could not help smiling. You Shouldn't Kiss Me Like This by Toby Keith. He put both arms around her waist, and she slid her arms around his neck. He looked into her eyes and sang to her. She smiled and felt as though the song had been chosen especially for them. Something did feel different tonight, like electricity the minute he took her in his arms and looked into her eyes. It only took a moment, but she was lost on the dance floor, spinning around in his arms.

"They'll never believe we're just friends, Lindy."

Her fingers began to stroke his neck caressingly. "Are we? Just friends?" She was not sure if anyone else was even in the room with them anymore. He lowered his head to hers, and she swallowed hard. Lifting her mouth to meet his, she let him kiss her while they danced in circles, around and around and around.

With her arms circling his neck, he lifted her off her feet, and she lifted his hat off as she looked into his eyes. He kept kissing her, still spinning slowly in the circle, her feet dangling in the air, never wanting to stop. The rest of the dancers stopped dancing and backed away, watching. The only sound in the room was the jukebox, which started the same song all over again. Brody and Lindy only knew they were there, together at last, and it seemed as though they waited their entire lives for this moment.

When he finally pulled his mouth from hers, he looked into her eyes, her beautiful tear-filled emerald eyes, and the words spilled from him effortlessly. "I love you, Lindy."

She laughed and cried all at once. "I love you too, Brody." He closed his eyes and kissed her again, spinning her around the floor.

The bar roused with applause for the happy couple. Bronwyn stood at the edge of the dance floor and cried, happy her plan worked out. Rhett, seeing them together like this, knew they could not help the way they felt for one another, and his heart forgave them. He turned to Tara and offered to drive her home later.

Lindy reluctantly pulled away from Brody's lips and looked into his eyes.

"How was the kiss, Lindy? Was it just nice, or did it knock your socks off?"

"You've definitely knocked my socks off. I feel like I'm floating six feet off the ground."

"That's six foot three, honey."

She tossed her head back and laughed, and he kissed her again. In the midst of the kiss, a thought suddenly struck Lindy and she pulled away again. "Brody, what about Tara?"

"I already told her it's over. What about Rhett?"

"I told him two days ago."

"And you've kept me waiting since then? Never mind. I love you, Lind."

"Love you back." She tightened her arms and let him start kissing her all over again.

When they finally left the dance floor and made their way back to their table, their friends all stood and applauded them. Lindy was pleased to see that included Rhett and Tara.

Rhett extended his hand to Brody and they shook. "No hard feelings, Brod."

"Thanks, Rhett. I never planned this. I never wanted to interfere with you two."

"It's okay, you didn't. I'm glad to see two of my best friends find happiness. Sit down. Let me buy you a drink."

Brody did as directed and sat down, pulling Lindy down on his lap. She looped an arm around his neck and kissed his ear. He turned, catching her lips with his. The music was loud, but he still heard her sigh. He moved his mouth to her ear. "One more drink, and we're out of here, honey."

"Good. I think we have some catching up to do."

Rhett came back with the drinks, and Brody talked with him while Lindy visited with a happy Bronwyn. Fifteen minutes later, he asked if she was ready to leave. They stood and said their good-nights.

When they got to the Avalanche, he opened the door and kissed her before she climbed in. Getting in behind the wheel, he leaned over and kissed her again before asking, "Where do you want to go, honey? My place, your place, or somewhere else?" His hand reached for hers and he marveled at being able to hold it without it being swaddled in bandages. He lifted it to his lips and kissed each fingertip.

""I love you, Brody, but I'm not Tara."

"I'm not sure what that means, but I'm glad you're not Tara. I broke up with her because I wanted you. I've missed you so much."

"I'm glad, because I missed you something fierce. What I'm trying to say is that I want to be with you, but I'm not ready to sleep with you. I don't know when I will be, so I'll understand…"

"Darling, you're not telling me anything I don't

already know. I wasn't asking you for sex. I was saying I want to be with you, hold you close, and tell you the things I'm feeling inside. You know that doesn't come easy for me. We have so much to say, Lind."

Moonlight shone through the windshield and cast a glow on her that caused her eyes to sparkle gloriously. "Let's go back home then. If your mom and dad are still up we can go down to the rec room."

"That's fine. We can put some music on down there and dance some more. I loved holding you in my arms." He turned on the ignition, and within minutes they pulled into the driveway of the Ashton home. He opened her door and held her hand as they walked to the house.

Gina was just turning off the TV when they strolled in. "Hi, kids. Didn't expect to see you home so early."

"Hi, Ma. Me and Lindy are going downstairs. You don't need to come down to chaperone. We're definitely gonna be making out, but don't worry. Lindy'll line me out if I try to go too far. Won't you, sweetheart?" He leaned down and kissed her tenderly.

Lindy tightened her arms around his waist. "Count on it, big guy."

Gina smiled, happy to see they finally found their way to each other. Lindy beamed, and Brody grinned like a fool. She kissed them both and headed off to bed, leaving them on their own.

CHAPTER TWENTY

Brody dropped the Toby Keith CD in the machine, and it started to play. He turned to her and smiled. "I think they're playing our song, Lind."

She went willingly into his arms and lifted her mouth to his. He loved everything about her. Her softness, her smell, her taste, her giving. "Lindy, honey, you shouldn't kiss me like this unless you mean it like that."

She looked into his eyes and took his hand, pulling him to the sofa. She knelt on it and waited while he sat, then settled herself on his lap. Her arms wound around his neck, and her fingers found their way into his hair.

"I do mean it like that." She brushed her lips lightly across his, and he reached for more but she pulled away slightly, teasing.

"Oh, Lindy," he whispered.

She responded instantly to her name on his breath, tightening her grasp on him and pressing her mouth more firmly to his. His tongue slowly traced along the length of her lips, and she parted them for him. His hand gently massaged the nape of her neck, and she became more receptive. She was amazed such a large man could be so gentle and unintrusive with his loving. He took it bit by bit, never pushing for more than she wanted to give. When she released the kiss, he moved his mouth to her neck, intoxicated by her scent.

"Brody, wait."

He immediately pulled his mouth from her neck and held her. "Too fast, honey?"

She leaned her forehead against his. "No. I've just dreamed of this so often, I can hardly believe it's happening. Brody, do you know that I'm in love with you? I mean really, deeply in love for the first time in my life."

"Yeah, I think you told me that," he smiled, "but you can tell me again. I love you, Lindy Lassiter. I don't want anyone else but you. I've been missing you so bad."

"You believe I love you for the right reasons now, don't you? I know I still have a lot to work through, but I know I can do it if you'll wait for me."

"What I know is that I hurt not being with you. Don't think I can live through another day without you in it. I promise, you have my love and support through this. Honey, I want you to know something I firmly believe in my heart." He looked intently into her eyes making sure she was listening, really listening, to what he wanted to say. "You're my princess, Lindy. There is no other woman on this earth as beautiful or as virtuous as you are. Finding you was a gift from God."

Sighing with pleasure at the relief his words brought to her heart, she kissed him long and slow. "You know, I've never kissed a man with a moustache before." She ran a finger across it and let her finger trail down to his bottom lip.

"And?"

"It's my Brody. Your lips are so soft. I want to kiss them forever."

"Mmm. Good 'cause that's how long your Brody

wants to kiss you." He grazed his mouth slowly across her cheek. "You're so beautiful, Lind. Best thing you ever did was send me away these past few weeks. Taught me that I don't want to go on without you."

"Then it was worth it. And you know what? It taught me the same thing." Her fingers sifted through his curls. "Your hair's even softer than I imagined it would be. You can't believe what it means to finally be able to touch it, to touch your face, to hold your hand."

He wanted to touch her in return, but worried about moving too fast for her. "So, you seem okay with kissing. That's a good thing."

"I'm very okay with kissing you. Probably because kissing was never a part of the attacks."

"Good, 'cause I don't know what I'd do if I couldn't kiss you." His fingers tangled in her hair and pulled her to him again. His lips softly cushioned hers, and she felt herself melting, knowing she found her way home at last.

•

Brody climbed the stairs from the basement Saturday morning, and his mother looked at him in surprise. "Did you stay over?"

"Yeah, it was pretty late when we said good night, and I wanted to be with her today, so I figured I might as well stay." He dropped some bread into the toaster and poured a cup of coffee while he waited.

"So are you two dating each other now?"

"She's the one, Ma. You okay with that?"

"You mean 'The One'?"

"Yup. Probably marry her before the end of the year."

"Brody, I'm thrilled. She's an angel, and she

deserves someone who'll treat her that way. I believe you will."

"Thanks, Ma." He buttered his toast and brought it to the table to sit with her. Unscrewing the lid from the honey jar, he drizzled the liquid across his toast. "She up yet?"

"I haven't seen her. You must have stayed up late. She doesn't usually sleep in."

"We had a lot to talk about. Been three weeks, ya know."

"I think I hear her," Gina told him as she got up to carry her mug to the sink.

When Brody finished breakfast, he wandered down the hall in search of Lindy. He found her seated on her bed with Gina massaging her feet.

"You're gonna have to take it easy today. No long walks," Gina told her.

"I know. They really hurt last night, but it was worth it."

Brody's large body loomed in the doorway. "Morning, Lindy. You never said nothing about them hurting ya last night."

"Well, they didn't hurt when I was dancing with you, cause that was like floating."

"Yeah, I seem to have that effect on women."

Gina rolled her eyes. "The big lug has all the prowess of a bull."

Lindy laughed and looked up at him. The moment their eyes engaged they were lost in each other.

Gina spoke, and when she did not get an answer she looked at them, first one, then the other, and quickly determined that any attempt at conversation was pointless. Standing, she reached for his arm and tugged him into the room. "You rub her feet," she told him as she left.

He sat at the foot of the bed and took his mother's place. He picked up Lindy's feet, kissing the right and then the left, and then he crawled on past them until he was stretched out on the bed. She scooted down to lay next to him, and he took her in his arms.

"Good morning, darling." He softly kissed her smile. She set her hand on his cheek, and her thumb stroked a portion of his moustache.

"So it wasn't a dream, huh?"

"Nope. It's all real. You still love me?"

"Totally." She closed her eyes again and enjoyed his kiss. "You taste like honey."

"Aw, shucks. You say the sweetest things. I suppose we should get up so you can eat. I have someplace I wanna take you today."

"I could just have you for breakfast," she teased.

"Cut it out, Lind, or I'm gonna start pulling your clothes off." He gave her one last lingering kiss before climbing off the bed, tugging her along behind him.

After breakfast they said goodbye to Gina, who shouted a reminder that Lindy should not be on her feet too long. He tucked her into the Avalanche and drove through town, heading out on the highway.

"Oh, Brody, look at that Victorian. What a pretty house."

"Want to take a look?" To her amazement he pulled into the driveway. His eyes scanned the property. "Doesn't look like anybody's home. I guess we can just walk around the yard and look at it."

"Isn't that kind of rude?"

"Heck, no. People like to know their house is appreciated." They got out of the truck, and he toted her across the lawn.

"I love the wrap-around porch. And the turret corner in the front is classic. They just don't design grand

222

houses like this anymore."

"What would you do with it if it was yours?" he asked.

"I'd put gingerbread with spindles all around it, and I think I might paint it white or soft blue."

"Sounds good to me. Come on." He led her up the front steps. "What about the porch?"

"I'd hang some swings. It'd be a wonderful place to bring a book on a summer afternoon. And I'd probably put some planters along the ledge filled with something that would cascade out of them and maybe some wisteria to climb the pillars. And then I'd put a row of lilacs out there," she pointed along the side of the property. "This place is loaded with potential."

"That's what I thought, too, Lind." His hand grabbed hold of the front doorknob, and he opened it. "Come see the kitchen."

"Brody, do you know these people? We can't just go walking in when they aren't home."

Her protests fell on deaf ears as he pulled her through the house to the kitchen. "Do you like it?"

She could see that it had been newly remodeled. "Wow!"

He beamed with happiness. "It's yours, Lindy. This is my house. I hoped you'd like it."

"Brody, I love it. I can't believe it. This wonderful house is yours?"

"It's mine for now, but soon it'll be ours. We'll do all those things you said, Lind. The swings and the planters and the gingerbread. I'm so glad you see it like I do." He lifted her to the countertop and set her on it. "I love you, Lindy Lassiter of Lander." He held her tightly against his chest, then bent his head to kiss her. "I'll make this place into a castle for you, Princess."

"It already is. Wherever you are is home to me."

His eyes lit with sudden excitement. "Wait until you

see this, honey. You're gonna love it." He kissed her again before taking her down from the counter and leading her through the house. He stopped abruptly. "Close your eyes. No peeking."

He guided her around a corner and a few steps later came to a stop. "Okay, open them."

Lindy opened her eyes and could not believe it. She stood in the center of a large room lined with bookshelves. "A library? We have a library?" She flung herself at him in joy.

He caught hold of her and swung her around. "Can't have a librarian without a library, now can I?" He basked in her assault of kisses. "Honey, keep this up and I'm thinking we should go upstairs and see our bedroom right about now."

"Okay, I'll behave myself. Show me the rest of the house, and I'll try to stay calm and respectable," she grinned.

"You don't have to do that. I like your wild side just fine. Hey, know what I liked about last night?"

"I'm almost afraid to ask."

"When we were kissing you started to make those same sounds you make when you eat chocolate. Nearly drove me out of my mind with excitement. You make restraint very difficult."

Lindy became serious as she wandered to the window and leaned against the bookcase, looking out into the yard. "I'm sorry, Brody. You can't begin to know how it hurts me to not be able to give you more. Now that we've committed ourselves to each other," she turned and looked back over her shoulder at him, "we are committed, aren't we?"

"Very committed."

"Good. Now that we've committed ourselves to each other, there's nothing I want more than to be free

224

enough to be your lover. I'm no different than you, Brody. I feel those same desires and needs, I'm just too afraid to let go."

"I want more than a lover, Lindy. There's a lot more to a relationship than sex. You have all the other things I want and need. The rest will fall into place when it's right. I'm not in any rush, long as I get to hold you close to me and know that you feel the same as I do."

"You're the very best man I've ever met. I'm not sure what I did to deserve you, but I'll try so hard to be worthy of your love."

Brody crossed the room and turned her into his arms. "You don't have to try at all, Princess. I give it to you freely. Don't you know how wonderful you are? I've never met a woman who's all the things you are. I'll love you forever, Lind."

She looked into his eyes, and her own became misted. To have a man love her this purely was almost more than she could take. She had suffered through the worst moments of her life, and came out the other end to have Brody. Her arms wound around his waist, and she laid her head on his chest. He curled a hand around her head, holding her securely to him.

"Tell me what you see for the library, honey."

Lindy stepped back and let herself feel the room. "I'd build a window seat in between the shelves there and put in a bowed window."

"Agreed. I want to strip the paint off all this shelving and stain and refinish it. Give the room a warmer feel."

"Yes, and, I know it's a lot, but is it possible to put in a fireplace?"

He was amazed that her vision for the room mimicked his own. He had already begun studying about fireplaces. "Baby, you're right on. And the master bedroom is right above us, so I was thinking of putting a fireplace in there, too."

"That would be spectacular. Show me the rest." She tucked her hand in his, and they toured room by room, looking and talking and dreaming.

"My house in Portland should sell soon. I want to use the money from the sale to help pay off the mortgage here."

"We'll talk about it."

She looked at him with confusion. "What is there to talk about?"

He led her to the couch in the living room and sat. "Lind, it was a real matter of pride for me when I got the mortgage for this house."

"So what does that have to do with me helping to pay it off?"

"I want to pay the mortgage off with my own paycheck. I know that may not be the smartest move financially, but it's the way I want it."

"So you're saying it's our house, but I can't help out. How am I supposed to feel like it's ours then, Brody?"

"I didn't say you couldn't pitch in, I said the mortgage is mine. You can buy all your lilac trees and whatever else you want. You can buy furniture and paint and books for our library. It will be our home, Lind."

"Okay, then make me feel better. Let's go buy our lilacs."

"Now?"

"Right now. I want proof that I can be part of it."

She dragged him to his feet and led him out to the truck. He drove down the road to Sprout's Greenhouse and bought bushes in every shade there was. Lindy would have beautiful lilacs all through her house and still have plenty left on the bushes outside.

With Lindy as foreman and Brody as cheap labor, they spent the afternoon planting the fifteen bushes along the southern edge of the property. When that was done he put in her pink and white peonies across the front of the house.

"I've had a wonderful day. It feels like we're turning your house into our home. Thank you for letting me be a part of it."

"It's gonna be beautiful when we're done."

"It already is. I'll be very happy living here with you. Should I go put some dinner on?"

He felt certain that TV dinners were not on her agenda, and that is the only thing his kitchen offered. "No. Let's drive into town and have steak. I'll just run upstairs and get cleaned up." He kissed her happily and stripped off his work gloves.

Lindy meandered around the porch, smiling as she listened to him singing in the shower through an open window. He was happier than she had ever seen him, and believing she was the impetus for that joy elated her. She stood admiring the bushes they planted together, knowing that in thirty years she would stand on this porch and look out at them, remembering this day; the first day of her new life with Brody. She lost herself in her dreams, and before she knew it a pair of massive arms from behind encircled her, pulling her against him.

A warning bell sounded deep inside her, and instinctively she tensed until her brain reassured her it was only Brody, allowing her to relax.

"What are you thinking about, darling?"

"Us. Our life together in this house. I can see it all -- you and I sitting together in the evenings on our porch swing, watching the kids playing in the yard. A little girl with blond curls like her daddy's runs up with tears to tell you her brother's picking on her. And you know how boys are, but she's your little angel, so you pick her up

227

and go read him the riot act. She can rule the world from her daddy's shoulders."

Brody felt his heart pounding and his throat constricting as he looked out at the scene she shared with him, and he continued the scenario. "And right over there is where you'll be teaching the girls to play hopscotch. I can see you turning the skipping rope while they do that French skipping."

"You mean Double Dutch," she corrected with a grin.

"Yeah, that's it. And I think maybe the older one's gonna have her mother's brown hair, done up in pigtails, cause pigtails never go out of style."

"And over there is where I'll pitch a thousand baseballs to our son while he practices batting. It's a good life, Brody."

"It's the very best life, Lindy. As long as we're together, we'll have everything." He kissed the top of her head, and she smiled when he bent to draw his lips slowly across her neck, wanting to skip dinner and have her instead.

CHAPTER TWENTY-ONE

Brody spent time with Lindy every day for three weeks following their declarations of love for one another. He never expected love to be so consuming. He counted the minutes at work until it was dinner time so he could eat with her, or the end of the shift so he could spend time with her before heading home.

Wednesday was his first day off, and it went without saying he wanted to spend it with her. She remained limited in the tasks her hands could perform and the amount of time she could stay on her feet. He stayed mindful of her restrictions and often ordered her to sit and take off her shoes so he could massage her feet. As he contently rubbed, he summoned his courage to broach a subject that played on his mind frequently. At a moment such as this, maybe he could manage to make it sound nonchalant.

"Hey, Lindy, I was thinking. How'd you like to come out and spend the night at the house?"

Lindy dropped to gaze to her lap, and although she tried to mask it, he saw the fear that sprang unbidden to her eyes.

He scrambled to clarify his request before she grew any more uncomfortable. "Honey, I'm not talking about sex. I just thought it would be nice to hold you and feel you next to me."

She smiled tremulously. "You sure?"

"Very sure. I know you're not ready for the rest, and I won't put you in that situation."

She saw the concern on his face and felt his sincerity. "Okay. I'll pack a bag and tell Mom and Dad so they don't worry." Living with Brody's parents made her feel she had a home. They easily slid into being parents to her. When Mike asked if she wanted to call him Dad, she broke down and cried.

"Really? I've never had a father before."

He hugged her and said, "You do now, honey. Gina and I both love you. You're part of our family."

Brody spoke, bringing her back to the present. "How 'bout you go pack then? I'll tell Ma.

She nodded eagerly and smiled when he pressed his ritual kiss to each foot before giving them back to her. She thought her foot ugly with the toe missing, but Brody never seemed to notice.

After a quiet dinner at the Oxbow, they drove out to the Victorian. Lindy felt a thrill every time she saw the house and still found it hard to believe she would one day live within its walls.

She took her shoes off and carried them when they stepped onto the grass. He took them from her and dropped them on the porch. They walked out to the property line to check on the new shoots sprouting on the lilac trees. As the sun set they sat on the steps by the back door and held hands. She leaned on his shoulder, and they watched the changing colors that washed the sky in a warm silence. When twilight settled around them and crickets started their evening song, they abandoned the step and went inside.

Collecting a chilled bottle of wine and two glasses, he carried them to the living room and was unwrapping the cork when she stopped him.

"Brody, David will probably be coming home soon. Why don't we take this upstairs?"

Pulling her to him, he kissed her. "I love you, Lindy Lou."

"Source of all my joy," she answered. She took the bottle from him, and taking his other hand, led him up the staircase. She set the bottle on the dresser and picked up her overnight case. "I'll just be a minute. I'm going to get ready for bed." She smiled and took the case into the bathroom with her.

A few minutes later she returned wearing a white nightgown with a deep flounce around the bottom and Battenburg trim on the bodice with small white buttons down the front.

Brody felt his breath catch at the sight of her. He stood in before her and placed his hands on her shoulders. "You're the most beautiful thing I've ever seen. That sunset can't begin to compete with you, my love."

She smiled shyly, and he was moved by her innocence.

"Thank you, Brody. I love you so much."

She lay her hands on his chest and lifted her face for his kiss before picking up the bottle and carrying it to the bed. Quickly stripping off all but his underwear and dropping his clothes over the back of a chair, he picked up the glasses and followed her to his bed.

Propping up the pillows, he sat next to her and held the glasses while she poured. With soft music filling the corners of the room, he placed his arm around her and ran his fingers over her hair, caressing her cheeks with his thumb. "Lindy, I brought you here for a reason tonight. I want to talk about something." His brows knit together, and worry lines creased his forehead.

"What is it, Brod? Is everything all right?"

"Honey, I have something I've been keeping from you. I need to tell you, because I don't want any secrets between us. We need to move on, and I think this is holding us back."

Frightened by his words, tears sprang to her eyes. "You're scaring me, Brody. What can be so terrible that you're not comfortable talking with me about it? I thought we discuss everything."

He stared into the amber liquid in his glass, unable to meet her eyes. "Everything but this. I've been seeing Dr. Collins. What you went through had a really traumatic effect on me, too."

"That's the big secret? That you're seeing Dr. Collins? Good grief, Brody. You really had me worried."

"There's more to it than that. I've been having dreams, but it's like they aren't really dreams." He shook his head in confusion. "I don't know how to explain it."

"Just take your time, hon. I'm on your team." She rubbed his arm reassuringly.

"Remember when you were in the hospital, and I asked what you picked up to eat at the road stop in Oregon?"

"Yes, I do, because somehow you knew what I was wearing and that I carried a drink. Then you went tearing out of there so fast. I always wondered how you knew."

"That's because the night before I asked you, I dreamed about it. The whole thing. I was there, Lindy. I saw you walking to your car in that parking lot, and I saw them come up behind you and grab you. I saw the

232

sandwich bag in your hand. I could read it. I even saw the car they put you in. Unfortunately, I couldn't see the important things—their faces and the license plate. When I got to Baker City, I recognized everything. It was exactly the way I saw it in the dream. I was there. I screamed to warn you, but you couldn't hear me. I tried to get to you, but I couldn't move. I was so scared. I felt like it was my fault you were abducted, because I didn't stop it."

She believed him without judgement. "No wonder you're freaked about it. Why didn't you tell me this sooner?" She slid her arm across his chest to embrace him.

"Honey, there's more. Listen to me carefully. I don't know how you're gonna feel about this, so please don't close up. Talk to me. Okay?"

"All right. What else is there?"

"I also recognized the cabin when I saw it. I've had numerous dreams of being there. I know pretty much everything that happened. It's like I'm always rooted in the corner of the room. I've seen the terrible things they did to you and made you do. You see, you don't ever need to tell me the horrors you suffered, honey, cause I've seen it for myself. I know he burned you every time he raped you so you'd be scarred for life by him, never able to forget."

She broke down and cried while he held her tightly to his chest, his own tears dampening his cheeks. His voice trembled as he continued, "I'm sorry, Lindy. I tried so hard, and I couldn't save you, and it's killing me. I feel like it's my fault, like there must have been something I could do besides throw up in the corner. I've struggled and tried. Every time I've tried. I'm so sorry."

They grappled together with their hurt and sorrow.

Finally she clutched enough control to speak. "You've told me a hundred times that what happened wasn't my fault, and you want me to believe it. It wasn't your fault, either. For some reason, you've been given the visions of what really happened. But remember, you weren't actually there at the time. You couldn't have stopped it any more than I could. I love you for sharing this with me and wanting to be my hero. As long as you're with me, I'm safe. I know you'll protect me from the evil things of this world as best you can. I trust you in that."

"Good. I want a relationship without any secrets. I don't want to mess it up. It's the first time I've ever really been in love. My sweet girl, you make me so happy just being in the same room."

They snuggled close and gazed at one other with pain and trust in their eyes. "Lind, does it bother you that I know all the details so completely?"

"Yes and no. I hate that you saw it. I didn't ever want you to know just how vile it was. I know how painful it must be for you, and I'm embarrassed by what they did. I wouldn't be honest if I didn't admit that. But at the same time it's a relief. Like you said, there are no secrets between us anymore. You'll be there for me in a way you couldn't have been otherwise. Maybe that was the point. So you could help me heal."

"Believe me, I understand how difficult it is for a woman to be close to a man after what you've been through. That you even want me to hold you like this just blows me away."

"I think it starts from childhood. When you hurt, you want something to cuddle that will comfort you, and you're the best teddy bear I've ever met. I could stay cuddled up to you like this forever."

They heard the back door open and close and footsteps moving around the kitchen. After a few moments, they approached the the staircase and stopped at the bottom step.

"Hey, Brody?"

Brody got off the bed and opened the door a crack. "Yeah?"

"Picked up a case of beer. Want to crack a few open?"

"Not tonight, thanks. It's been a long day, and I have early plans with Lindy."

"All right then." The footsteps walked away, and the television turned on before Brody closed the door.

Lindy felt a vague uneasiness at the thought of another man in the house with them. "That was David?"

"Yeah, who else would it be?"

"Could have been Braden, but didn't really sound like him."

Brody crawled into bed beside her and opened the drawer of his night table, pulling out a sketch book and pencil. "Tell me what you think of these, sweetheart." He opened it to a page of drawings and handed it over to her. She looked at the curlicued designs that flourished across the pages.

Her face lit as she studied them. "This is the gingerbread, isn't it?"

"It is if you like it."

"It's perfect. It's prettier than anything I've ever seen manufactured. We'll be so unique. Is it going to be difficult with all these little spindles?"

"They're shaker pegs. Just have to drill a bunch of holes and glue them in. The finials we can buy, and the rest is my own design and a lot cheaper than anything we saw at the lumber store."

"You know, every time I come out here I get such warm feelings about this house. Watching the changes slowly shape into the visions in our minds, I feel such a connection. It's a house with a great history, and it feels like we're preparing it for an even greater future." She rubbed her cheek against his arm. "I think I'll dream of that future tonight." With a smile she closed her eyes.

Brody set the book and pencil aside and turned off his light. He adjusted his pillows and lay with Lindy curled against his side, her head resting on his shoulder. "Goodnight, Lindy love."

"Goodnight, Brody bear." She smiled in the dark and kissed his chest before drifting off to sleep.

•

Tara and Meghan pulled into the driveway at Tara's garage apartment. She looked into the rearview mirror for a few moments after turning off the engine and saw a car idling on the street.

"Meg, do you see that car behind us?"

Meghan turned and looked back over her shoulder. "Yeah, I see it."

"Do you recognize it."

The car suddenly spurted into action and sped off.

The nerves on the back of Meghan's neck tingled as she turned back to face her sister. "Yeah, as a matter of fact I do. I thought it was my imagination, though."

"So, you've seen it before. Do you know whose it is?"

"No idea, but I've noticed it a few times.I feel like it's tailing me. After what Lindy went through, I guess I'm a bit paranoid."

"I don't think it's paranoia. He's been tailing me, too. I'm going to mention it to Rhett next time I see him. A dark green four-door Caprice Classic. Maybe he can find out who it is and why they're interested in us."

CHAPTER TWENTY-TWO

June brought a hot sun and warm winds to Lander. The gardens bloomed with the flowers Lindy bought and planted. Brody spent the spring cutting the gingerbread trim for the Victorian with his scroll saw, hoping to get it put up before the heat became unbearable.

Glints of sunlight broke through the rustling canopy of the cottonwood they sat beneath. Brody watched as it danced on Lindy's hair like little diamonds of light.

"David's gonna help me put up all your gingerbread this weekend. I've got a surprise for you in the library too. I think you're gonna be happy."

"I'm sure I will be. I finished the cushion for the window seat and made throw pillows for it, too. It'll be a really cozy nook." She smiled as her mind imagined the finished look, then a sudden, "Oh, I got some news today. My mother's house in Portland sold. The deal closes the end of July."

"I'm glad it's finally off the market. One less thing for you to worry about."

"It's like my whole life is falling into place here. I went through a nightmare to get here, but since my arrival

I've found love, a family and a home, friends, and hopefully soon a job I'll love too. My physio therapy is progressing so rapidly that I'm ready to start applying."

"You deserve good things, Lind. Hey, next week's your birthday. Any ideas what you'd like?"

"I want to spend the day with you, doing absolutely anything or nothing at all—just being together. Maybe some quiet music and a good bottle of wine. Sound good to you?"

"Sounds fabulous. We've spent so much time on the house lately it'll be nice to take a break."

She lifted his hands linked to hers and kissed them. "You've been working too hard, Brody. You don't have a deadline on the renovating, you know. We have years to make it just the way we want it. It's not like we're starting a family right away."

"I know. I guess I just want it to be a nice place for you. A princess needs a castle."

"Silly man." They sat quietly listening to the breeze in the trees and watching children across the street playing with the water sprinkler.

Lifting one hand, he brushed his fingers back and forth across her cheek. "Hey, Lind, you know what I love to do?"

"What?" She looked up at him over her shoulder.

"I love holding your hand. I love the way it feels when your fingers touch me. I love that you can do more things for yourself. You've worked so hard for that independence. By the end of the summer we'll probably be running together. We'll start small and gradually build you up again."

"I was resigned to the fact that I probably never would. And my hands…it's wonderful to be able to touch you. I think I'll probably never get tired of doing it." She reached up and stroked his face as she spoke.

"Well that's good, cause I don't think I'll ever get tired of you doing it. Did I tell you yet today that I'm in love with you?"

"I believe you mentioned it, but I like to hear it, so don't let that stop you."

"I love you, Lindy. I don't know how I got this far in life without you, but I never want to spend another day that way. I need you so much, sweetheart." He tightened his arms around her and kissed her earlobe.

She smiled and kissed his hand. He swallowed hard, fighting back the desire he struggled with every day.

•

"I think that's enough for today. I'm really pleased with the progress you're both making." Richard Collins closed his notebook. "Any questions before we finish here?"

"No, I can't think of any." Lindy stood, ready to leave.

"Actually, I do." Brody looked at Lindy, and she sat back down. "Doctor, Lindy and I have discussed the fact that we're making some real leaps ahead with you," Brody said, and Lindy nodded in agreement.

"My question is this. We don't want to get married until we're ready to have a complete physical relationship. I want to know when we can start working at that; put some of this progress to the test. I don't want to rush her, but I want to be able to at least touch her breast without her shooting through the roof."

"That's a reasonable desire, Brody. Are you willing to stop things at that point? Maybe I should rephrase that. Are you capable of stopping things at that point?"

"Yeah, I feel pretty confident about it."

"Lindy, what about you? Are you ready to try something?"

"I think so. I love Brody, and I want things to be natural between us."

"All right then. Here's what I want you to try. This exercise is totally about touch. Nothing oral. Not even kissing. What you'll discover are things most couples miss because they're in such a hurry to get to the finish line." He gave them instructions and they left, excited by the prospect of taking a new step on their journey.

•

Lindy woke early and quickly showered before getting dressed. She chose to wear a white blouse with a sailor collar and navy sailor's tie and a pair of navy shorts. After slipping on her ankle socks and Reeboks, she ate a quick breakfast. Brody promised to take her some place new for her birthday.

His truck pulled into the driveway just as the clock chimed nine. She grabbed her purse and ran outside to meet him.   "I've got news," she beamed.

"I'm figuring by the smile that it's good news. Tell me."

"I got a job."

His eyebrows raised in pleased surprise. "That is good news. Who was smart enough to hire my girl?"

"The Fremont County Library. I start the second week in July. All day on Mondays and late afternoons to closing the remainder of the week."

"That's perfect, Lind. You'll be working the same shift as me most days, and since the library is only three blocks from the Sheriff's Office, I'll pick you up each night after work and drive you home."

"Sounds like a plan. Life is good, Brody. I'm happy."

About thirty-five miles south of Lander, he pulled off the highway at South Pass City.

"This was originally a mining town. It's been restored to the way it was back in the late 1800's during the last big gold rush. A lot of these structures are original."

"This is excellent, Brody. Oh, look there's the jail. I'll bet that's your favorite building."

"My favorite building is whichever one you're in."

She stopped and turned to him. "That is such a sweet thing to say. It's no wonder I love you so much." She lifted her face and leaned into him for a kiss. Hand in hand, they toured the jail, the livery stable, the school, saloons, the South Pass Hotel, houses, and played a game of billiards at the Miner's Exchange Saloon on a restored table from the 1840's.

At the Interpretive Center, they learned about the mining process, the time period, and saw thousands of artifacts native to the town.

Brody suggested they try their own hand at panning for gold. They went out to the river where costumed workers conducted the activity. With pans in hand, they stepped into the water and began dipping and swirling.

Suddenly Brody straightened and called out to one of the staff members, "Hey, is it normal to find diamonds and emeralds in here with the gold?"

People clustered around him, eager to see. In his panning dish sat a ring with a large oval emerald and two smaller diamonds on either side of it. Lindy stared at the jewelry with saucered eyes and then up at him. He handed the pan to one of the onlookers and slipped the ring on her finger. "I love you, Lindy. Happy Birthday, sweetheart."

She blinked several times before she could find her voice. "It's beautiful. I love you." She grabbed his face and pulled him down to her. He put his arms around her waist and lifted her off the ground, kissing her as hard as she was kissing him while those gathered around clapped and cheered.

Before leaving the mining town, they stopped at the Smith-Sherlock General Store to buy a souvenir to remember their day.

As he reached to open the car door for her, she turned into his arms. "Thank you, Brody. I love it."

"I wanted an emerald because the first time you opened your eyes and looked at me, that's what I saw. Two sparkling emeralds. Most gorgeous eyes I've ever seen."

"Your eyes are the same shade. How much do you wanna bet our kids will all have green eyes?"

"You talking 'bout that little angel with the blond curls riding around on my shoulders?" He smiled at the memory. "I'm glad you're pleased. I wanna make you happy, Princess."

"Being with you makes me happy. Having you love me makes me happy."

"Wow! You must be the happiest woman on earth then."

"I believe I am." Her eyes drifted to a close, and her face reached for his kiss, soft and simple.

When they reached Lander, Brody took her to the Atlantic City Mercantile for lunch. Decorated as a saloon, it was reminiscent of the historical town they visited.

He held up a finger, and the waitress came to their table. He ordered two beers, and since Lindy knew what she wanted they ordered their food also.

"Brody, I can't stop admiring my ring. It's so pretty."

"I'm glad you like it. You don't really wear any jewelry, so I was taking a chance."

"I don't wear any because I don't own any. But don't worry. Every woman loves jewelry, especially from the man she's in love with. Hard to go wrong with things that sparkle."

"That's kind of what I figured when I fell in love with you. You sparkle more than any other woman I've ever met."

"Keep it up. Flattery will get you everywhere. What's on for the afternoon?"

"I don't know if I should tell you."

"Now you're getting my curiosity up."

"Good. You just go ahead and imagine all sorts of wonderful things. But the best part comes tonight."

"What happens tonight?"

Brody shook a finger and grinned. "Now, now. I can't give away all the secrets, can I? I'll only say it will be very different than anything else we do today." He sat back, very pleased with himself.

CHAPTER TWENTY-THREE

Following a lunch of steak and baked potatoes, Brody took her to Main Street Books so she could choose the first book to put in their library. She chose the newest Anne Perry novel, feeling quite certain he would enjoy reading stories about police inspector Thomas Pitt set in 1880's London. With only a minutiae of forensic evidence available, it presented a radically different world of law than Brody's.

When they returned to the truck, he drove through Lander and north on Highway 287 toward home. To her surprise, instead of slowing down to turn in, he passed right on by.

As they approached the town of Dubois, he turned onto a dirt road that trailed through trees, leading to a shining, blue lake. Sun reflecting off the water sparkled like the diamonds of her ring. A small boat tied at the water's edge bobbed gently. He sat her down in it, then retrieved the fishing gear and cooler from the back of the truck. After untying the boat, he pushed off before starting the motor. Maneuvering to the middle of the lake, he cut the engine and let the boat drift.

Lindy, having never fished before, was excited by the

prospect. After a brief demonstration, she managed to bait her own hook and enjoyed the challenge of casting, doing it several times just for fun.

He watched as she kept vigil over her line and saw the sweet contentment there. He noticed that her bouts of depression grew less frequent. The happiness blossoming inside her was no longer feigned or forced.

"Hey, Lind?"

"Yeah?"

"Love you."

She smiled and turned her attention back to her line. A breeze swept across the lake and gently blew her hair. He watched it swirl and remembered how she looked with it fanned out on the pillow around her.

"Hey, Lind?"

"Yeah?"

"Want me to be your husband?"

"I guess so. Don't see anyone else lining up for the job."

"Okay. Just making sure."

They sat in silence for fifteen minutes.

"Hey, Lind?"

"Yeah?"

"There's always Rhett, ya know. He'd still swipe you in a flash."

"Okay. I'll think about it."

"Don't bother."

"Okay."

She pulled her lips in and bit them to hide her smile. She loved it when this large, muscular officer of the law went all mushy inside. An absolute teddy bear. Her Brody Bear.

"Hey, Lind?"

"Yeah, Brod."

"I really wanna make love to you."

"I know."

"Don't forget."

"I won't."

Her line suddenly grew taut and she felt pull.

"Reel it in, darling."

She pulled it closer as he instructed. He set his own pole down to position himself on the bench seat behind her. He put his arms around her and helped her land the fish.

As he held up the sparkling Golden Trout for her to admire, his own forgotten fishing rod sailed through the air, diving cleanly beneath the water's surface.

"Brody, look!"

Too late—the rod was gone. "I guess that fish thought turnabout was fair play. He thought he'd catch the fisherman for dinner."

Lindy giggled. "I suppose that means we're done fishing for the day."

"Are you enjoying it?"

"Yes, very much."

"Okay. We'll stay." He grabbed his pliers and pulled the hook from her fish before dropping it into the cooler. She rebaited the hook and cast the line again. He remained seated behind her with his arms settled around her waist. She leaned back against him and propped her feet on the seat in front of her.

He slipped one hand under the hem of her blouse and let it rest on her stomach. Brody felt her tense instinctively before relaxing. She looked over her shoulder and kissed his cheek. He was a contented man.

After a candlelight dinner in Dubois, they drove back to the house. The evening sky was just beginning to blush with the shades of an artist's palette when they parked the truck.

Lindy developed a closer friendship with Bronwyn and the Shepherd sisters since he devoted much of his free time the past few weeks to working on the exterior of the house. Now she stood, admiring the transformation as it became the home of their dreams.

She ran back to the truck, remembering the book they bought earlier that day. "I want us to put it in our library. Make it official."

The room that greeted her tickled her with delight. "Brody, it's magnificent."

The shelving was stripped of the many coats of paint and refinished to a glossy shine. Soft lighting glowed from recesses in the ceiling all around the room. A cream-colored carpet spread beneath the large, cushiony chairs arranged for cozy reading.

"You've even got a start on the fireplace."

"I've got it roughed in. I'm gonna build it with rocks I'll haul down from the mountains."

With a small amount of fanfare, Lindy placed the book on the shelf before he led her to the next room where cardboard boxes sat neatly stacked against a wall.

"What's this?"

"All of our books." I stored them near the library so it would be easier to put them on the shelves."

"Ooh. This is so exciting."

"You're probably the only woman I know who would think so."

"Let's get them on the shelves for now, and I'll come back another time to have my play time organizing it all."

Pulling him toward her, she nipped softly at his upper lip. Her tongue trailed along his bottom lip as his hands tightened around her waist. When he began to reciprocate, she moved away from his mouth, kissed his neck and hugged him. "I love you, Brody."

Bouncing off the stool, she retrieved a box of books and unloaded the contents onto the shelves.

"Honey, I'll bring them all in. You just unpack, okay?"

"Sure. Where's David?"

"He said he was going into town tonight with some of the guys he works with. Won't be in 'til late."

When all the boxes were emptied, Brody wrapped his hands around her waist. "Honey, why don't you go upstairs and take your shoes off. I'll be right up behind you. Now we get to the best part of the day."

Hearing her skip up the steps, he strode quickly into the kitchen. Taking two wine glasses from the cupboard and a bottle of white wine from the fridge, he climbed the steps three at a time. Entering the bedroom, he kicked the door closed behind him. He set the glasses on top of the dresser and poured them each a glass. Handing one to her, he set the bottle on the night table on the far side of the bed, convenient for refills.

Lindy's shoes dropped to the floor, and she stretched her legs out on the bed.

Brody lit two lavender-scented candles, dropped some soft jazz into the stereo, and kicked his runners and socks off. He sat on the bed beside her and sipped at his wine.

"You've had a good day, darling?"

"I've had a great day. The best day."

"I'm glad. Are you sure you like the ring? If you don't we can go in, and you can pick something else out."

"It's very perfect. I wouldn't trade it for the world."

"Good. When I buy your next ring, do you want to come along and choose it? An engagement ring is pretty important to a woman, and I want to be sure you like it."

"I think I'd be self-conscious if I went with you. I want
248

you to choose it. You did such a fabulous job this time. I'm sure you'll choose the perfect thing."

"Give me clues then."

"I'm a pretty traditional girl. I guess I've always imagined a diamond." A small smile played around the corners of her mouth. "I'd prefer a solitaire. Any shape except a marquis. Is that enough?"

"How big?"

"I'm not going there. That's your decision, big guy. You know, I don't need a ring at all as long as I have you. You're all I need."

He gave her a quick kiss before setting his glass on the table. "Darling, would you like to take my shirt off?"

She set her glass down and knelt beside him. Grasping his shirt, she lifted it over his head. "I love looking at you, Brody." She ran a hand lightly across his chest. "You're so strong and beautiful."

Smiling, he sat up and took hold of the hem of her blouse. "May I?"

She focussed her attention on his eyes and nodded. He slowly raised the shirt, and she lifted her arms over her head. Left with her bra on, she relaxed back against her pillow. Brody lay with his head in her lap, and she placed one hand on his chest while the other hand caressed his face, his hair, his moustache. There was no need for conversation. They revelled in their quiet admiration for one another. The music was right. The mood was right. The people involved were right.

"Are you ready, Brody?"

"Mm hmm. Whenever you are, but let me kiss you first. Remember, no kissing once we start." He propped himself up on one arm and reached behind her neck. She leaned to his lips and felt his hunger. The kiss started slow and grew as they explored each other as though it was still new territory. A small moan escaped her throat, and his heart pounded when he heard it. With a groan of regret, he pulled away.

Lindy climbed off the bed and went to her microwave which he had set up in the bedroom. She pushed the buttons that would heat the container of oil he had put in it earlier in preparation. He spread a bath sheet out on the bed, then lay on top of it on his stomach. Lindy brought the oil, and sat straddling his hips. She poured a generous amount on his back and started the massage.

"Oh, Lindy, it feels so good."

As she progressed, he let her know when she touched a spot that felt particularly good while she told him of all the things she loved about him. Wanting to kiss all those spots, to love him, she struggled to maintain the rules. After twenty minutes on his back he turned over, letting her massage his abdomen and chest. He was amazed by the number of places she touched that aroused him. When she finished lovingly massaging every inch of his body above the waist, he sat up.

He held her to him for a moment, then asked, "Are you ready?"

She nodded and lay down on her stomach. He moved onto her thighs and undid her bra hooks. Pouring the oil on her back, he began the massage, always working his hands from the spine outward. He told her how he loved the softness of her skin, her long graceful arms, her delicate throat, her inner beauty.

When he finished she turned over, trusting him completely. He looked into her eyes as he poured oil on her stomach. He began to smooth it over her. After her stomach, he ran a hand upward between her breasts toward her shoulders. After massaging across her shoulders, his hands ran along down her sides so that only his thumbs brushed against the edges of her breasts. Finally his hands swept up around the outside of them. He gazed into her eyes and whispered. "I love you, darling. I think you're so beautiful, Lindy. I love to touch you."

"I love you too, Brody. I'm all right. I want you to touch me."

He let his hands work their way around, stroking from the outside edges to the centers, careful to keep his hands in a massaging mode and not allowing them to wander into a sexual touch. "Thank you, sweetheart. Thank you for sharing yourself with me. I'll love you for the rest of my life. I can't imagine ever being without you. I want to make love to you in this bed until the day I die."

"I want that, too. I want to be able to completely open myself to you. I want to be the wife you need."

Brody finished and moved away from her. "Do you want to soak in a hot tub for awhile? I'll go fill the tub if you want."

"I've got a better idea. You have a huge tub in there, why don't you take the wine, and I'll take the candles, and we can soak together."

"You won't mind seeing me naked?" He was afraid of frightening her and spoiling the relaxed atmosphere they successfully achieved.

"Are you kidding me? I've been waiting forever."

"Lindy Lassiter, it's no wonder I love you." He kissed her before going across the hall and turning on the water. She brought the candles and set them on the vanity. He went back for the wine, refilling both glasses. She kept her eyes on him as they took off the rest of their clothes, and Brody got in the tub. She sat in front of him and leaned back against his chest.

"Hey, Brod?"

"Yeah?"

"It was good. At first, like for five seconds, I was nervous. Then I looked into your eyes, and I know how much you love me. That was it. I relaxed and just allowed myself to feel your touch."

Brody lifted the sponge and squeezed the water out, letting it runnel down over her. "Were you worried the burn scars would bother me?"

"I think so. I wasn't gonna say anything, but I think I was."

"They're already fading."

"I suppose."

"You know I saw them before I ever fell in love with you. It hasn't stopped me from wanting you. I'm glad you enjoyed it tonight. We're one step closer to getting married, honey, I loved touching you because it's you."

"It goes both ways. I enjoyed touching you too. I've never done anything like this before. It was wonderful, but I found it hard not to bend over and kiss all the spots you enjoyed. I wanted it to go further."

"Good, cause I think that's the next step."

"I hope so. This tub feels so good. I'm glad you thought of it. You're always so considerate of me, Brody Bear. I don't know what I ever did to deserve you, but I don't ever want to let you go."

He kissed her behind her ear and let his hand rest on her stomach. They relaxed and listened to the music for half an hour.

"Honey, I think I'm gonna fall asleep," she murmured.

"Okay. Let's get out."

Lindy slid forward to pull out the plug and climbed out. Brody hoisted himself out after her. After drying off, they walked across the hall to go to bed.

He kissed her goodnight, curled up behind her and fell asleep.

CHAPTER TWENTY-FOUR

A piercing scream tore him from his dream. Brody sat up in startled panic and saw Lindy lying on the floor, curled up in a ball, crying and screaming and pulling at her hair. He nearly fell off the bed trying to get to her.

"Lindy, it's okay. Come here, honey." He tried to pull her up into his arms.

"No! Don't touch me! Don't touch me!

He tried to grasp her face to force her to look at him, but she only screamed louder. He stopped touching her and backed away, anxious and perplexed, helpless to know how to help her. She continued crying, so he went to the bathroom and closed the door which seemed to immediately console her. The screaming stopped, and a few minutes later he heard her scrambling.

When he returned to the bedroom he found her cowering in the corner. He crouched before her and tried to speak to her.

She glared at him with hatred in her eyes and spat her words out like venom. "Put something on. I don't want to see that filthy THING! You disgust me."

He stood and turned his back to her, her words cutting through his gut. Grabbing his jeans, he thrust his legs into them and glanced to see her face buried in her tucked up knees.

"There's obviously not much I can do here. Come downstairs when you feel safe. And, Lind, I still love you." He snatched a clean tee-shirt out of the drawer and trampled down the stairs. In the kitchen he poured some orange juice and tossed it down quickly. He grabbed a ball cap from the hook near the back door and slammed outside, retreating inside the barn and coming back out with a lawn mower.

Lindy heard the roar of the engine and crawled to the window to peek outside where she spotted Brody on the riding lawn mower. Her mind calmed. She knew he was hurting from her words, but she could not help it, and she could not take them back.

Hurrying across the hall, she turned on the shower and scrambled to get under the spray. She scrubbed herself, trying to erase the imaginary dirt. When the hot water finally depleted, she dried herself and dressed.

While brushing her hair, her eye caught sight of something glittering on the night table. Sitting on the edge of the bed, she stared at the ring he gave her the day before. What a wonderful day it had been; perfect and loving. He was the greatest blessing in her life, and she knew it.

She gazed back out the window at him, and her heart broke. Poor Brody—good, tender, and kind, and she repaid that by screaming at him, insulting him, and cowering from him. The feeling that she exercised no control over those actions frightened her more. She knew she hurt him badly, although he would try to hide it for her sake. It had been months now. She could not keep him hanging forever, waiting for a woman who could love him the way he needed and deserved. Her life must move forward. Struggling against her inner demons, she reclaimed control of her emotions and wiped away her tears. She knew what she must do, ready or not. With firm resolve, she ran down the stairs and out the front door.

She shouted from the porch, hoping he could hear her over the engine. "Brody, Brody."

He turned and saw her. Flipping off the mower, he hesitated before slowly walking to meet her. She flew across the lawn to him, throwing her arms around his neck.

"I'm so sorry, Brody. I'm so sorry. I love you so much. Can you forgive me?"

Beseeching green eyes gazed up at him with tears sparkling in the morning sun.

"Can I touch you?" he asked cautiously, needing her permission.

"I think I'll die if you don't."

He put his arms around her and held her snugly to him. Whatever prompted her agitation seemed to be over for now, and relief flooded through him.

"I love you, Brody. I'm so sorry, honey, I'm so sorry."

"It's okay. I love you." He tipped her face up to look at her. "No more tears."

She stood on tiptoe to kiss him—a gentle brushing of lips before she buried her face in his chest. "Please don't stop loving me. I need you. I couldn't stand it if you stopped loving me. Please, Brody. Please."

"Aww, honey, ya don't have to beg for my love." He lifted her in his arms and carried her into the house, sitting on the sofa and holding her on his lap. She cried, and he stroked her head while cuddling her.

"It's all right, Lindy. I love you. You aren't gonna lose

me, honey. I promise."

"I was so mean, and I know I hurt you," she sniffled. "I don't even understand why. Can we just stay like this for awhile?"

"Long as ya want. I'm always here for you."

She nodded and allowed the tears to flow and the stress to drain from her. When she finally felt relaxed and secure, she swallowed her fear and filled herself with determination. Brody said he would always love her, but she refused to take any chances.

She lifted her head to look at his face and found him quietly dozing. She slowly ran her hands over his chest, focusing on his nipples. Taking his bottom lip between hers, she gently sucked. His arms lifted above his head and stretched in a way that said he was becoming aroused. A growl of contentment rumbled from his chest, and she smiled. She would prove to him just how sorry she was.

When his kisses grew more ardent, she rose to her feet and slowly ambled toward the staircase, casting him a want-to look over her shoulder as she began her ascent.

He smiled as he watched her. She was so sexy when she wanted to be. He hoisted himself off the couch to follow. On the bottom step he found her shirt. Halfway up, he picked up her shorts. On the top step was a lacy, flowered bra, and when he got to the bedroom door he was greeted by the site of her panties on the doorknob. "I love this woman," he grinned.

He pushed open the door and went inside. She already had the music on and sat posed on the bed, her left leg curled around her and her right knee bent up in front of her. With her hands on top of her knee, she sat forward resting her chin on it. When she raised her head, she let her bottom lip seductively catch on a knuckle.

As he approached the bed with a crooked smile, she saw wonderful things shining in his eyes. Not lust or sleaze, but love and admiration.

"Oh, Lindy. You're beautiful, sweetheart." His voice trembled with reverence. He truly loved her.

She rose to her knees and inched to the edge of the bed. Kneeling in front of him, she lifted his T-shirt over his head and ran her hands over his broad chest and his tight stomach. She began to kiss his chest as she undid his jeans and slid them down. Taking his hands in hers, she backed away again, pulling him in her wake.

"I love you, Brody. I'll give you whatever you want."

"I don't want to scare ya, honey. I wouldn't want to hurt ya."

"I can't run scared for the rest of my life. I need to be able to be a wife to you. You said there were plenty of other ways for us to show our love without intercourse. I'm ready to try. Please."

He looked deep into her eyes, searching for reassurance that she could handle it. "All right. Some ground rules first. If you get uncomfortable, you say 'stop'. Okay? I'll offer, and you say yes or no. You have complete control, Princess. If we start something and you change your mind, you say so."

"Thank you."

He stretched out on the bed, his head on the pillow next to hers and pulled her snugly into his arms. Keeping his hips pulled away from her, he began to kiss her; short, playful kisses. She responded, and he felt her body relax.

Pressing against his chest, she rolled him onto his back and leaned over him, kissing his neck and shoulders. Teasing his nipples with her tongue, she kissed him across his chest and down to his navel, her nose slowly rubbing in the soft hair surrounding it.

He let his hand caress her back, drawing little circles and curlicues all over it with his fingertips.

"Brody?"

"Yes, darling."

"I'm sorry for what I said before. I honestly don't feel that way about your body."

"Honey, I would never use any part of my body to hurt you. I want to use it to bring us closer together. Sometimes when I hold you and kiss you, I feel like it's not enough. I want to give you a part of myself—my love, my joy, my passion. They're all gifts. Something special I only share with you."

She kissed her way back up his body to his ear. "I want that for us, too. I want to be able to open myself to you, physically and emotionally. I want your loving."

His hands stroked up and down her sides and moved her onto her back slowly. "Lindy, honey, can I touch your stomach?" She nodded consent, and he calmly let his fingers drift over her stomach, loving her softness.

Needing to please him, she encouraged, "You can touch me higher. Just don't hold my arms down."

He kissed her mouth with amazing slowness, and all her concentration was drawn to it. His thumb gently massaged her breasts while his hand cupped them in turn. His kisses slid across her neck and down her cleavage to her stomach, nuzzling and kissing as she had done to him. He continued to murmur during his ministrations, telling her he loved her and how precious and graceful and exquisite she was. Nothing about the experience even remotely resembled the assaults upon her.

Her breathing told him her excitement was blossoming. Watching her closely for any conflicting emotions she may be feeling, he let his tongue trail around the base of her breasts. Alternating between kisses and licks he worked his way to the center. When he captured it in his mouth and began to gently suck, she arched her back off the bed, and a small cry of pleasure escaped her. He repeated the routine on the other breast with the same results.

"Brody. Oh, Brody. I can't believe this."

"Want me to stop?"

"Don't you dare."

He smiled as he loved her, feeling her fingers weave into his hair. His hand drifted down her side to slide up and down her thigh, caressing it. As her excitement continued to grow, his fingers swept to the inside of her thigh and stroked it.

Lindy felt a million things happening to her all at once. She had no idea it would be like this. She wanted something more, but she was not sure what. Brody's mouth left her breasts, coming back to kiss her lips and whisper in her ear. She felt his hand leave her thighs.

"Brody, please don't stop. I want something. I want…"

"What do you want, Lindy?"

"I don't know. I hoped you would."

"I'll bet I do. Let's find out." His hand reached over to the drawer of the night table, and he pulled out a bottle of lubricant, quickly uncorking it and pouring some on his fingers. He cupped his hand over her femininity and held it there, letting her grow accustomed to the sensation and giving her a chance to say no. He returned to kissing her breasts, and she started to squirm beneath his hand. He slipped a finger in to rub against her and whispered a continuous stream of loving words in her ear, wanting his voice to keep her grounded as to who was touching her.

Amazed by the desire coursing through her, she felt frenzied right away, writhing under his loving touches, gasping and keening. When release came she cried out his name, over and over in ecstasy.

Grinning wickedly he removed his hand, kissed her cheek, and whispered in her ear, "Want more?"

Lindy could hardly breathe. She tried to open an eye to look at him but was too exhausted. "Un-uh," was the best she could muster.

He wrapped his arms around her and held her to him. "I love you so much, Lindy. I want you to find pleasures in our bed. There's no pain here, honey, only love."

She burst into tears and snuggled closer. "I love you, Brody. I love you so much."

"I know you do, sweetheart." He rolled onto his back and pulled her onto his chest to cuddle her. As the tears subsided, she kissed him and lay back down on his broad, hard muscles.

"Oh, baby, I've never felt this, I don't even know the right word, open, vulnerable, in my entire life."

"I know, darling. That's where the trust comes in. You have to trust me enough to allow yourself this freedom."

"That was my first time."

"You were beautiful. Honey, it made me feel so good to be able to give that to you."

"Is there something I should be doing for you now?"

"No, sweetheart. Another time." He smiled and ran a hand through her hair. "You wanna sleep or shower."

"I think sleep. Will you stay here with me?"

"I could lay here and watch you sleep all day. Get some rest, honey."

But she was already asleep. Brody lay looking at her, thinking. He had not realized she was a virgin at the time of the rape. A lot of things made sense now. Part of her reluctance was because she had no good experiences to relate to. No wonder she was so frightened. He hoped he gave her something to look forward to, knowing she trusted him because of the way she responded with such total abandon. "And that's just the beginning, my love," he whispered. "I have so much to give you."

When Lindy woke from her nap, Brody dressed and went back outside to finish the lawn. She stripped the bed, putting the linens in the washer before going into the library to organize the volumes they already unpacked. She found some books of Brody's about sex and sat down to read, amazed by how much she didn't know. As she became more engrossed, she turned sideways in the chair with her feet dangling over the side and a pencil in her mouth. She wondered how, in all her years of education, she managed to miss this stuff. By lunch she felt so much wiser than when she woke from her nap, and by supper she was a walking reference book.

Happily, she went to the kitchen to make dinner. After popping the casserole dish into the oven, she brought the dry sheets in from the clothesline along with six yellow roses she cut from the bush.

After tucking the bottom sheet around the corners of the mattress, she sprinkled the rose petals liberally over it, then finished making the bed.

CHAPTER TWENTY-FIVE

Taking the cordless phone from the end table in the living room, Lindy strolled outside to sit on the steps on the side verandah as she dialed home.

"Hey, Bronwyn. Is Mom there?"

"Sure. Just a minute."

Lindy heard the phone change hands and Bronwyn telling Gina who it was.

"Hi, honey."

"Hi, Mom. I need to talk if you have a minute."

Gina heard the hesitation in Lindy's voice. "Sure. What's up?"

"We had an absolutely fabulous day yesterday. It couldn't possibly have been more perfect."

"I'm happy to hear it."

"Then last night when we got home..." she stopped in mid sentence.

"Yes, then what happened? Something wrong, dear?"

Frowning, she twisted her mouth in a sudden dilemma. "You know, it's just occurred to me—I'll bet Brody wouldn't be too thrilled with me discussing our sex life with his mother."

"Well, honey, I know he's got one so you're not telling me anything new, and I don't imagine he's invented anything I haven't heard of before, so don't worry about that. I can tell somethings troubling you, though. What's on your mind?"

"Right, well, last night we tried what Dr. Collins told us to do. It was an upper body massage, back and front. Pants stayed on. No sexual touching, no kissing. It's supposed to help me adjust to someone touching me. He was so good about it. Kept strictly to the rules, and maintained constant eye contact with me, talking to me all through it so I couldn't dissociate. I guess escaping mentally like that is a pretty common thing to happen. It's how I dealt with the rapes."

"Okay, everything so far sounds fine. Why do you sound worried?"

"When I woke up this morning, Brody was sleeping curled up around me, and for some reason as soon as I felt him pressed against me down there, I totally freaked out. I started screaming and crying, and I couldn't stop. I was afraid of him, even though I knew it was Brody. I wouldn't let him near me. I crawled out of bed and curled up in the corner, and then…I'm afraid even though he was being gentle and helpful, I said a really cruel thing to him. He left me alone and went outside, and although he never said another word about it, I know he was crushed."

Gina's heart broke for the young couple. They were trying so hard to work through the pain, and it wasn't easy for either of them. "Do you want to tell me?"

"I told him to put some clothes on so I wouldn't have to see his filthy 'thing'."

"Ouch!" she winced audibly. "Okay. So I guess you're wanting to know why this happened after the

263

night went so well."

"I'm so confused. I want to stay over tonight with him, too, but I can't chance putting him through that again."

"Lindy, did Dr. Collins ever talk to you about body memory?"

"I'm not sure. That particular term doesn't sound familiar."

"Okay, let me try to explain. It seems that when the body has been abused, it holds the memory of it, like a protection. You might be just fine and dandy with something mentally, but if the body senses it resembling the bad memory too closely, it reacts."

"So, when Brody was curled up against me..."

"Your body remembered and was frightened. I know it sounds flaky, honey, but it's very real. It might manifest itself simply as cringing when being touched on your arm, or trying to turn away from a kiss."

"With my mouth taped shut most of the time kissing was never a part of what they did to me. I suppose that's why kissing with Brody has been comfortable." Thinking back to the morning, tears welled in her eyes. "Mom, I'm just scared. I don't want to hurt him like that again. I cried and said I was sorry, but it doesn't take it back. It doesn't make him forget."

"Lindy, talk about this with him. Your relationship will be a lot healthier if you do. Try to explain to him what happened. Ask him to try not to cuddle in that position. Maybe you can snuggle up beside him. That keeps your back end out of the danger range. Honey, this has never happened before?"

Lindy thought about it for a minute and recognition dawned in her mind. "I didn't think so, but hearing you talk about it, there were a few times when I was out in the garden. If I was on my hands and knees digging or planting, and I heard him coming up behind me, I'd instantly turn and sit flat on the ground. I never understood why at the time, but with what you're telling me now, I guess it makes sense."

"Exactly. It can surface at strange times from things completely innocuous. Now that you understand, it'll help some of your confusion, and you won't have to feel like you're the only one it happens to. It's pretty common for women who've experienced a violent crime."

"Thanks. I appreciate you being there for me. I love you, Mom."

"And I love you, Lindy. Listen, I want you to go onto the Internet when we hang up and look up both Yoni and Lingam Massage. They're based in old East Indian culture where the point of the massage isn't climax, although that can certainly happen. It teaches appreciation and honor for each others' body parts and to see them as something sacred rather than the lustful connotations Western society has put on them. It should help you get past your feelings about his "thing". It's very commonly used as therapy for helping rape victims reclaim their sexuality. If Richard hasn't already discussed this with you, you'll be a step ahead.

"Go print them off. Give the Yoni to Brody, and you read the other one. It's almost like a religious experience, and couples who've learned it say they still continue to do it many years after because it adds something special to the way they feel about each other. In fact, I think I'll go print it off to give Mike some bed time reading."

Grinning, Lindy wandered into the house to write it down before she forgot. "Mom, let's not tell Brody about this little talk. Then he won't be embarrassed. Dr. Collins is one thing. His mother is something else."

Gina laughed. "All right. I'll see you sometime

tomorrow. Just relax, honey, and have a good time."

Lindy put the telephone back on the charger and sat at the computer. A google search found the techniques Gina told her about straight away, listed among thousands of sites with information on sexual survivor therapy. She printed several pages of that material as well. When Brody came in for dinner, he found a set of stapled sheets sitting by his dinner plate.

"What's this, hon?"

"Some evening reading. I learned a lot today, and I want to talk about it after dinner."

"Sure," he shrugged. Pulling out the chair, he seated himself at the table and watched as she bustled around the kitchen. "You're looking like a mighty contented woman today."

She beamed a million watt smile at him. "You bet I am, Deputy. I'm getting a prize of a man when I get married!"

He grabbed her arm and pulled her onto his lap. "And don't you forget it, Mrs. Ashton."

"Oh, is your mother here?"

He tugged lightly on her hair. "Very funny. I'm just trying it out to see how it sounds. I think you look like a Mrs. Ashton. Suits you."

"Oh? Who said you were the prize husband I was talking about? Maybe I had someone else in mind. Maybe I'll be Mrs. Rhett Owens."

"Honey, you keep it up, and I'm gonna have to kiss some sense into you."

"Well, you know what they say. Women have a tendency to change their minds."

He looked down at her teasing smile as she sat with her arms looped around his neck. He kissed her nose and kissed her eyes and then softly kissed her lips. "Now, Lusty Lindy Lassiter of Lander, who are you gonna marry?"

"How about you?"

"Good choice. I love you, Lind."

"I'm glad, cause I plan on staying over again if that's okay with you. I just can't get enough of a good thing, and you're a very good thing." She tightened her arms around his neck and hugged him before getting up to put dinner on the table.

He pulled a jug of iced tea from the fridge and poured them each a glass.

She eyed the clock above the stove. "Shouldn't David be home by now? I made extra just in case."

"He must have stayed late or gone to town with some of the fellas. They might be calfing out at the Hathaways' ranch. They need the extra hands to stay on for that."

"Hmm. You know, I was thinking about it, and it just seems so strange. We've been together four months, and I live at your parents' home, but in all that time I've still never really gotten to speak to him other than a hello or goodbye in passing. He always seems to be coming or going opposite to us. I might just start to get a complex."

"Never thought about it, but I'm sure it's just a coincidence. And I'm sure he has no idea you've ever stayed overnight here. When he first arrived I gave him big spiel about how I absolutely never bring a girl home with me, under any circumstances. At that point in time it was true."

"And then I brazenly ruined your record," she smirked.

"No, then I fell in love and couldn't wait to bring you here. And since you can cook, I think I'll keep ya. This is delicious, sweetheart." His eyes strayed to the printed pages sitting next to his plate, and his eyebrows raised.

"This looks interesting." He picked up his iced tea and started to drink.

"Your mom's going to print off a set for your dad to read tonight, too."

He choked on his drink and started coughing.

Her head jerked up in surprise, and she reached out to slap him on the back. "Honey, are you all right?"

He continued to cough and sputter. When he finally caught a breath, he declared, "Too much information, Lind."

She looked at him, totally perplexed. "What are you talking about?"

"That thing you said about my parents. My parents are not sexual creatures, honey."

She rolled her eyes and giggled at him. "Oh, for heaven's sake, Brody. You're twenty-eight years old."

"That's right. Twenty-eight years of denial, and I'd like to spend the next twenty-eight the same way, thank you very much."

She gave him an amused look. "Oh really? How do you think you got here? And your brother and sisters for that matter?"

Brody chewed his dinner and eyed her in mock amazement. "Lindy, don't you know anything? Man, for a librarian you're not too smart. My mother was eating watermelon, and she swallowed a seed. It grew inside of her and when it got really big, the doctor opened the zipper in her stomach, and out came a baby. That's how we all got here, except Brooke. I'm pretty sure she originated from a sour cherry pit."

Lindy laughed at his absurd story. "Okay, so how do you figure a watermelon seed turned into a baby?"

"Hey, Thumbelina grew in a flower, so what's your problem? Honey, I think you need to put in some hours in the children's section at that library."

She continued giggling as he talked. "Okay, Brody. If it's as easy as eating a watermelon seed, how come we have to go through with all this sex business? I'll just wait until we want a baby and go pick up a watermelon at Safeway."

"Because, Miss Lindy, our generation came up with this better idea of how to make them. Besides, they stopped putting zippers in women a few years ago, so I'm afraid we're stuck with this new-fangled method."

"Well darn. I kinda like the sounds of the old way."

"I promise you'll love the new way." He gave her a sexy smile that sealed the promise.

With glittering eyes, she vowed, "I'll hold you to that, Mr. Ashton."

•

Two men walked into the Lander Bar and sat at a table in the back corner, not wanting to be noticed or disturbed.

"We're still free and clear?"

"Far as I can see."

He lifted his mug of beer and took a long drink. "I'm starting to get antsy. I want some action, and I don't want to wait forever to get it."

The dark haired one answered, "I still think you should reconsider. You're asking for trouble if you take the wrong sister. You may get more than you bargained for."

"I don't think so. I've been watching them for some time now. And I'm not finished with Miss Lassiter either. I don't care who her boyfriend is. If I want her, I'll have her. I don't take 'no' from anybody. Besides, she left before I was finished with her. She owes me. Big time."

CHAPTER TWENTY-SIX

"Well, how have things been since we saw each other last week. Brody? Bring me up to speed." Dr. Collins sat relaxed in his chair, coffee cup in his hand and his notepad balanced on his knee.

"I think they've been about ninety percent good," the deputy replied.

"I agree," Lindy added. "We had one negative incident, but still, I think a lot of progress."

Brody nodded in agreement as they sat side by side on the brown suede sofa holding hands.

"What do you wanna talk about? The ninety or the ten?"

They looked at one another in silent conference before Brody answered. "Maybe we should talk about it chronologically. That might be easiest. Friday was Lindy's birthday. We had a wonderful day together, and it seemed the right time for us to share some intimacy. We went to my place, and we followed through the exercise doing everything just the way you said. She seemed pretty relaxed through the whole thing."

The doctor nodded, then turned to her for

confirmation. "Lindy? How was it for you?"

"Brody made it really easy for me. He kept eye contact most of the time and talked to me, saying a lot of tender and reassuring things."

"No dissociation?"

"None. It was comfortable. I enjoyed it. I would have been willing to let him go further, but we stopped. I felt confident enough that we shared a bath together. It was very calming for me. He didn't try to touch me in any sexual way. I think we both felt really good about the whole thing."

"Yeah, we did," he agreed. "I felt great that she actually enjoyed it. Gave me a lot of hope that we can make it through this."

"Good. Your instinct was right in connecting with her. Women who've been raped often cope by going somewhere else in their mind so they don't have to deal with it, as Lindy said she did. It could easily happen by instinct when you touch her. By keeping eye contact and talking, it helps you know she's still there with you and helps her stay focused. You should continue with that."

"That's no problem. It's natural to want to reassure her that the touches are loving."

"Okay, so Friday went great. Then what?" Dr. Collins sat back in the chair, watching as they glanced at each other uncomfortably. "Brody, why don't you tell me things from your point of view, and then Lindy can give her side."

He rolled his shoulders as though wanting to get out of his own skin. "Okay. Saturday morning I woke up, and she was laying on the floor, all curled up in a ball and screaming and crying. When I tried to find out what was wrong, she just kept screaming not to touch her, so I left her alone and went to the bathroom. When I came

271

back she was in the corner and still pretty distraught. She seemed scared of me. She yelled for me to put my clothes on, so I did and left her alone. It was obvious my being there was making things worse for her."

Dr. Collins brows knit together, and he made notes on his notepad. "Lindy?"

"When I woke up, I felt Brody pressed up against my bottom. I called Gina later, and she explained to me about body memory. I'm pretty sure that's what it was. I just reacted to the idea of somebody touching me there. After he went outside, I calmed down enough to come out of the corner, and when I looked out the window and saw him, I was overwhelmed with guilt. I felt wretched for the way I acted and treated him. He's been so patient and kind, and I knew I hurt him."

The doctor let them sit quietly for a minute, then asked, "How did you deal with it, Lindy?"

"I thought about it and decided I can't keep running forever. I made up my mind that I was going to have to push myself into it, regardless. I went outside and apologized and asked his forgiveness."

"Brody? What about you?"

"I decided to just let her be. She'd let me know when she was able to be with me again. I knew it wasn't her fault, but I was confused about why it happened. I thought we made such progress. When she came outside later, I could see she was hurting over it. I took her in the house, so we could talk and make up."

"Then what?"

"Lindy said she wanted to go upstairs, and we did."

"Lindy? Why did you want to do that?"

"Because I felt guilty. Because I wanted to make it up to him. Because I love him and want to give to him. Because I needed to prove to myself that I could get through it. And," she hesitated, "I think maybe I was scared."

"Honey, what were you scared of? You never said anything about any of this."

"I was afraid that if I couldn't give you more, I would lose you."

"Damn it, Lindy. If we're gonna be together it's gotta be because it's something both of us want. You don't have to prove anything to me. You're not gonna lose me. Haven't I convinced you how much I love you?"

"Most of me knows it. Part of me is always afraid that if I can't give you what you need, you'll go find it somewhere else. So, I forced myself."

Upset and angry, Brody stood in frustration and stalked across the room away from her. He stared out the window, feeling once again like all their progress had just fallen apart.

Dr. Collins gave them time to think about Lindy's revelation. After several minutes of silence, he asked, "So, how did it turn out?"

Lindy answered. "It was one of the most beautiful moments of my life. We didn't have intercourse, but Brody's touch was magic, and I've never felt so loved. He gave to me so completely and lovingly." She crossed the room to him, placing her hands on his back. "Brody, I might have had the wrong motivation for the decision, but it was the best decision I ever made. If I sit here waiting for the right moment, it may never come. I decided the more important question was, am I with the right man, and the answer was a resounding yes. Sweetheart, please don't be angry."

"I'm not angry so much as hurt. How do you think it makes a guy feel to learn the woman he loves had to force herself to be with him. Geez, Lind."

"I think it matters more how it turned out rather than what my initial motivation was." She slid her arms

273

around his waist trying to comfort him, and laid her head on his back. "I'm sorry, Brody."

He lifted an arm for her to slide under, and he clasped her to his side. "I really thought we made some significant progress."

"We did. Instead of being terrified, I'm looking forward to being with you again. And that night was perfect, too. Brody, we've come a long way since then. Don't let my moment of fear destroy everything we've accomplished. Please."

"You're right. I'm sorry, too." He bent to give her a simple kiss, and they walked back to the sofa together.

Once they settled, Lindy turned her attention to the doctor. "So, back to the story. I learned about the Yoni and Lingam massages. We read about it and put it into practice."

The psychologist was surprised by this revelation. He was well aware of Lindy's justified reluctance up to this point. "Excellent. That's a real step, and the fact that you went ahead and took the initiative to move forward without my suggestion is very encouraging. Lindy, how was the experience for you as far as trust goes?"

"Actually, it developed it in two ways. It made me believe Brody sees me as something special. He's shown a lot of respect for me, for my body, and he's always touched me with decency and respect, but this did something more. I felt he treasured me, and something inside clicked, knowing he would never physically hurt me.

"In return, let's face it, the only contact I've had with a man's genitals has caused me significant pain. I never consciously thought of Brody's that way, and I was comfortable seeing him naked and having him in the bath with me, but this gave me such an appreciation for him. Now, instead of seeing it as a weapon, I can envision it as a vehicle for his pleasure as well as my own. It's helped me develop a whole new attitude." She cuddled closer to him and rubbed her cheek affectionately against his arm.

"Excellent. I suggest you make this a regular part of any intimate contact you have. If you choose to carry on after with further sexual activity, that's up to you. This exercise is particularly important for you, Lindy, both as giver and receiver. I'm glad you realize you're benefitting from it both ways. It also teaches each of you about sharing and not being selfish in the bedroom. Brody, do you have any thoughts or feelings you want to share about the experience?"

"Like Lindy said, I felt it was beneficial both ways. I felt it was a gift that she let me touch her so intimately, and I felt really special that she was able to touch me without recoiling. I wasn't aware until this past weekend that I was her first lover. It made me feel more hatred for whoever hurt her, and yet touched that she wanted me to be the one she shared herself with." He looked at her as he said the words, and she smiled shyly at him, making him fall in love with her all over again.

"Good. I think you're both doing great. Now, Brody, there's a few things you need to know. This body memory Lindy mentioned can kick in on her at anytime. It will usually come as a complete surprise to her, and it can still happen ten years down the road. It doesn't mean she feels any differently about you. It's her body's way of trying to protect her. She knows you won't hurt her, but her body believes that in order to protect itself it must respond negatively to certain things. You did well by leaving her with it. If you stayed, it would have only exacerbated the situation."

"That's what I figured. I knew that whatever was happening, she didn't suddenly stop being in love, so I just gave her the time and space to feel safe. She would come to me when she was ready."

"Exactly right. The other thing I want to talk to you about is Lindy's revelation this morning. Of course you're upset. What man wouldn't be? But I can tell you, her reaction was very normal. Many women feel they have to force themselves into performing sexually. They live with a constant fear that it will never happen naturally which leaves them with only two options. Either force it or be single and alone forever. Lindy already had a great deal of trust in you, and it worked to her benefit."

"Boy, I'll say it did. Brody gave me a whole new understanding of things. I'm not so scared of the journey, now. It helped me a lot." She squeezed his hand and gave him an encouraging smile. "Honey, it isn't that I didn't want you. I just needed a courage pill to go through with what I wanted. Haven't you ever wanted something so much, then been scared when the moment came?"

"I suppose if you put it that way, it's a different perspective. That's easier for me, but, Lindy honey, when you're scared you can tell me."

"What difference would it have made? You couldn't have treated me any better than you did, making sure I knew I had the power to say yes or no or stop. That gave me a lot of confidence, because I believed you. If you knew I was frightened, or that it was my first time being touched like that, you couldn't have handled it with any more tenderness than you did. You were perfect, and you gave me a special memory. I won't be scared any more, because I know what to expect now."

Dr. Collins listened to their discussion with satisfaction. They had both come so far and were comfortable talking openly with one another. That was three quarters of the battle. "The best thing you two have going for you is that you talk to each other. As long as you maintain that, you'll be just fine."

CHAPTER TWENTY-SEVEN

The Fremont County Fair brought excitement and commerce to Riverton as residents flocked from miles around for a week filled with rodeo events, exhibits, contests, a parade, and carnival rides. The bright July sun in a clear sky promised a wonderful day.

"So, this is Riverton," Lindy said, looking around as she stepped out of the car.

"You haven't been here before? Good grief, you've been in Lander almost a full six months now. Can't believe you haven't come here to the Wal-mart." Bronwyn closed the back door and frowned at her brother. "Brody, how come you never brought this gal to Riverton before? You've truly deprived her."

"Never thought about it. Never needed to I guess." He pocketed the keys and walked around the car to take Lindy's hand. "You haven't missed much, Lind. It's not nearly as prettyful as Lander." His eyes scanned the parking lot. "Wonder where Meghan and Holden are? Where are we supposed to rendezvous with them?"

"Meghan and Paige are picking Holden and David up from her grandparents ranch around supper time. She suggested we meet around six-thirty at the hog wrestling." Bronwyn took hold of Justin Cassidy's hand as the foursome made their way through the parked cars toward the front gate.

Lindy's ears perked, and her eyes skittered sideways. "We're going to watch men fighting with pigs? Hmmm. Sounds so —fun."

Brody missed her sarcasm. "Yeah, the catching and wrestling is good, but it's the stuffing 'em in the barrel that's fun to watch." His arm was suddenly jerked as Lindy came to a stand still, and he didn't notice. "What?"

"You can't be serious. They are not going to shove those poor animals into barrels."

"Sure they are. Butt-end first, of course. It's a race against the clock."

Again she eyed him with skepticism. "Hmm. Sounds exhilarating. I can hardly wait."

Brody threw his hip sideways into her and knocked her off balance. "Stop being a city girl."

"Me? A city girl? Why I'm the Lovely Lindy Lassiter of Lander? Nothing high-faluting and city about me."

He pulled his wallet from his jeans pocket and paid the admission fee to the park. "Okay, we've got about three hours before the others arrive. What do you wanna to do first?"

Lindy didn't even have to think about it. "Rides."

"There's a girl after my own heart." He turned to Justin and Bronwyn. "Sound all right with you two?"

Both nodded and the women stood chatting while the men lined up at the ticket booth to buy passes. They spent the next few hours riding the ferris wheel, the roller coaster, flying swings, and other amusements. The line-ups were long, and the foursome had plenty of time for gabbing together while waiting their turn. Justin wolfed down two burgers and wanted to get right back in line for another ride, but the others protested, needing time for their stomachs to settle first. They used the time to wander among the animal pens seeing who was taking home prizes for their finely bred livestock.

After a wild ride on the Enterprise, Bronwyn checked her watch. "We only have eight minutes to meet up with the Shepherd girls. We'd better get moving, or we'll be late."

They wound their way through the throng, smiling and answering calls of hello as they did. Lindy held tightly to Brody's hand, afraid of being lost in the crowd. Granted, Brody stood taller than most there, but she was not taking any chances.

Meghan spotted them first. "Hey, Ashton. Hi, Lindy," she called. As the distance between them grew short, the Shepherd sisters were ready with hugs for their girlfriends.

"Let's go watch the competition," Holden said. "My little brother's on a team."

Brody turned to Lindy, the question in his eyes.

"Of course. I was just funning ya before, Brody bear. But I want a good seat."

Ninth row up the bleachers was the closest they could find seats for all eight of them. Lindy was quickly swept into the excitement with the others as they laughed and rooted for the young wranglers who struggled to catch one of the slippery hogs and plunk him into the barrel. The shouting grew louder among them when Landon Nichols and his team got their shot at the prize. They worked together like a ballet in motion, making it look easy to capture the animal and deposit him accordingly. They set a standard that no other crew was able to beat. Some rivals were unable to even catch a pig. When the last team completed the task and the hog was barreled, the announcer declared

Landon's team the winners. The Lander group jumped to their feet with shouts of joy and applause.

As the bleachers emptied, and the crowd filtered out to the carnival area, Justin huddled the group together to get a concensus on what they wanted to do next. Poor Paige spotted the Haunted House nearby and noted the line-up to it was practically non-existent. Brody looked at it, and his nose curled up.

"Come on, Brod. It'll be fun." Lindy tugged his arm.

Leaning down to her ear, he complained. "I hate these things. They're so lame. You walk through, some lights flash, floors jiggle and mirrors distort things. Whoopee!"

"Spoiled sport."

"You go ahead with the others. I'll wait out here."

"Fine. And if I get scared in there, it won't be your hand I'm grabbing hold of."

He laughed at the very idea of anything in there scaring someone. "Knock yourself out, kid."

The group chose to stagger their entrance to the House of Horrors rather than staying all grouped together. The idea of finding their way through the dark maze on their own presented a more frightening challenge.

Lindy made it halfway through, tripping twice and bumping into walls as she went. Lights flashed on rubber masks and statues of demons. She turned a corner in the pitch black darkness, trying to find her way through with her arms stretched in front of her, reaching to feel her way along the walls.

The distinct feeling that Brody was right, and she shouldn't have come in here suddenly enveloped her. It was fine for the others, but Lindy was different. She had been kept locked in a closet for almost a month with her eyes taped shut. Panic started to set in as the memories of her own house of horror flooded her mind. She tried to move through quicker, wanting to get out of the maze and into the bright lights and Brody's safe arms once again.

As she turned a corner hands came from nowhere and grabbed at her body. Screaming, she tried to pull away. Walls everywhere: behind her, on both sides, in front of her. Trapped!

A hand clapped over her mouth to muffle her screams and arms pulled her tightly against a man's muscular body, the familiar scent assaulting her senses. A raspy voice whispered the echoing phrase in her ear. "I wonder if I'll kill you today."

The hands released their grip, and as quickly as it happened, it was over. The voice, the scent, the attacker — all seemed to dissipate into thin air, and she was alone. The fear, however, did not relinquish its grasp so easily. Adrenaline pumped through her system as she fought to once again find her way out of a sinister darkness that held her captive, screaming Brody's name over and over as she stumbled through the labyrinth.

A body collided with hers and arms once again reached to grab her. She refused to relinquish to them, swinging and screaming with all that was in her.

"Lindy? Lindy, it's me. Meghan. What's wrong?"

The familiar ring of her friend's voice cut through her frenzy, and she submitted to the soothing arms, sobbing and trembling.

"What is it, Lind? What's happened?"

"He's here. He's here."

"Who's here, hon? There's just you and me."

"No. My attacker. He's here. He touched me. He spoke to me."

"Brody's outside. Let's get out of here."

Meghan tightened her embrace around Lindy's shoulders and led her from the dark interior into the crowded venue where bright lights flashed all around them and fresh air filled their gasping lungs.

Brody stood waiting near the Wheel of Fortune tent, dropping a quarter on the anchor. The barker gave the wheel a hard jerk and people stood motionless, many with fingers visibly crossed as the wheel spun around and around, finally slowing to land on a black heart. The carnival worker swept Brody's losing quarter from the counter and called for the next round of betters before repeating his performance.

His eyes automatically swept the crowd as was customary with his police training, and he easily spotted Patrick Danvers approaching.

"Hey, Patrick. How's it going?"

"Not bad. Been here too long, though. Thinking of calling it a night and heading home soon."

"Been here all day?"

"Yeah, brought my little sister and her boyfriend up around noon. I think we've done everything there is to do about five times now. You here with Rhett?"

"Nah, me and Lindy came up with Bron and Justin. We met up with the Shepherd girls, Holden Nichols, and my cousin, Dave. They're all inside that stupid haunted house. Listen to that screaming, will ya? Sounds like someone's being murdered in there." He rolled his eyes and turned away from it.

"Brody! Brody!"

The blond man turned to see his sister racing toward him, alarm in her voice as she shouted his name. Unable to stop quickly enough, she crashed into him.

"Geez, Bron. What's on fire?"

"It's Lindy. You'd better come quick. She's really upset."

His head snapped around, searching frantically for her in the crowd. "Where?"

"Out behind the House of Horrors"

Brody dashed off with Patrick and Bronwyn sprinting closely behind. He rounded the corner to find Justin and Meghan trying to comfort her. David and Paige filtered out of the building, laughter and chatter rippling forth until they saw the commotion and joined the group.

The moment she saw Brody, Lindy collapsed into his arms. Tears glistened on her cheeks as she trembled convulsively.

"What happened, honey? What's going on?"

"He was in there, Brody. The rapist was in there."

The hairs on the back of his neck bristled as every nerve in his body jumped to life. "What the heck are you talking about? What happened? Was this one of those body memory things?"

"No, Brody. It was real. He was in there. He touched me. He spoke to me. He said it again. 'I wonder if I'll kill you today.'"

"Damnation. Justin, run around front and tell them to shut it down and turn the lights on in there. Nobody else goes inside until we've investigated. Patrick, you go in from this end and check it out thoroughly. If he's still around, we'll nail his butt to the wall this time."

Unbuttoning his shirt pocket, he pulled out his cell phone and placed a call to the Sheriff's Office, asking that more deputies be dispatched to help with the search.

He grilled Lindy as gently as possible, trying to find a clue in something she could tell him of the experience. She recounted her story to him four times before he asked the Shepherd girls and Bronwyn to take her back to Lander while he stayed behind with the men. Poor Paige was distraught for having suggested they ever go inside the attraction to start with.

After hours of an exhaustive search, they were no further ahead. Bronwyn had been the first in their group out of the building, but she had not seen anyone she didn't know come out after her, although she admittedly had been chatting with friends she met up with and not paying attention.

Brody drove back to Lander late that evening, dropping Justin and Holden in town before continuing on home with David. Frustration and anger boiled within him. He had once again been heart-stoppingly close to his nemesis, and once again failed to apprehend him. His confidence in himself as a lawman teetered on precarious footing.

CHAPTER TWENTY-EIGHT

July drew to an end, and Lindy threw herself into her new job, making every effort to push the events of the county fair out of her mind. Occasional warm breezes sweeping in through the open window offered the only respite from the stifling afternoon heat. A small clock radio sat on the window sill, tuned to the local station.

Lindy sat hunched over the desk in the back room cataloguing new acquistions as she hummed along. A favorite Kenny Chesney tune came on, and she turned up the volume. The final notes of the song were abruptly cut off as the DJ cut in with a late-breaking news bulletin. Disturbed by what she heard, she reached for the phone and called the Sheriff's Office, asking to be patched through to Deputy Ashton.

•

Brody pulled into the parking lot at Sinks Canyon, watching for a group of inebriated teenagers someone reported being destructive to park property.

The sound of static erupted from his radio, followed

by Jennifer's voice paging him. He picked up the microphone in response, and she immediately patched through a call from Lindy.

"Brody?"

"Yeah, honey. What's up?"

"Chris Adams penthouse in Nashville just exploded. Some kind of bomb, I guess. They don't know if he was home at the time or not. It sounds like there was extensive damage. The only way they could get rescue workers in was to lower them by helicopter. I know you and Chris are close friends and thought you'd want to know."

Brody leaned back into the seat and closed his eyes, stunned by the news. The thought of losing Chris gripped him with dread. When he could find control of his voice, he pushed the button on his mic and answered.

"Thanks for letting me know. I'm down at Sinks right now. I'll finish here as quickly as I can, then drive on out to the Adams ranch to check on his mama. This'll kill her if they find out he was inside."

"I'm sorry, Brody. Listen, if you can't make it to pick me up tonight, don't worry about it. You be where you're needed."

"Lind, if I can't be there in time, I'll call Braden to pick you up. Don't you walk home on your own. You wait."

"Okay. Be safe."

"Love you, Lind."

"Love you back."

He lowered the volume on the police radio and turned on the car radio so he could hear the news when it came on. His eyes scanned the area as he opened his car door. Four high school boys stumbled from one of the trails into the parking lot. They staggered to a red Pontiac Firebird and tried to climb over each other to pile inside.

"Hey, fellas. How's it going?"

"Just great, Ossifer. We had us a nice hike, and now we're going...wait—where are we going again?"

Brody chuckled at them. "Hey, don't worry, I know where you're going."

"You do? Can you tell me, cuz I forget?"

"Sure, I'd be happy to. If you get in that car and drive it, you're going to jail for DUI, and I'll take your license away. Your other choice is you can all come for a ride in my car, and I'll take you someplace where you can phone your parents to come pick you up. I think the second option sounds better. How 'bout you?"

"I don't remember the first choice again. What was it?"

Brody loaded the inebriated band into the cruiser and drove them to the Sheriff's Office, where parents were called to come collect them. When their parents arrived, he relinquished the Firebird keys to the father who owned it and was more than a little upset to learn it wasn't at home in his garage.

Checking his watch, he frowned as he strode quickly back outside to the cruiser. Once he cleared the town limits, he sounded his siren and sped the remainder of the way north on Highway 287, past his own home and on to the Adams ranch. As he neared his friend's property, he turned off the signal, not wanting to alarm the Adams' without just cause.

Parking near the corral, he noticed the ranch foreman, Dean, emerging from a nearby barn. Brody strolled toward him and nodded briefly in greeting.

"Hey, Dean. I just got word. Came out to check on Maddie. Any news?"

Dean stared at the hard earth beneath his feet, and his boot kicked at a stone. "I haven't rightly heard

288

nothing in the last hour or so. You'd better check in at the house with Maddie."

"How's she doing?"

"She's being Maddie. Tough on the outside, scared to death on the inside."

Nodding, Brody went to the house and knocked on the same kitchen door he walked through a hundred times as a kid. The door opened, and he took off his hat as he faced the worried mother.

"Hey, Mrs. Adams. I heard the news and figured I'd better come on out — see how you're doing and if there's anything I can do for ya."

Smiling tremulously in the face of her grief, she opened the door wider. "Matter of fact, there just might be. Come on in, Brody." She led him in to the den and offered him a seat on the soft leather sofa. "The good news is, I just heard from Christopher. He's all right."

"Praise God for that."

"The bad news is his girlfriend was in the apartment. This is the third attempt on her life this summer. He and Jeff Clayton both think it's one of his fans doing it. Chris' gal, Abby, was eight months pregnant and lost her baby in the first murder attempt. The second time, whoever it is got into her cottage while she was asleep and turned the gas on full blast. Chris got there just in time to save her. I'm very worried for both Abby and Christopher."

"Holy Hannah. I can't believe it. So, is this Abby the girl they were talking about him being engaged to last month?"

"Yes, and he's not. Well, not yet anyway. Her husband died less than a year ago and then with losing the baby, she's been through a hellish year. Chris wants to bring her home here to keep her safe. He doesn't want to risk a fourth attempt."

"Sounds smart. Do the police have any leads?"

289

"Not really. The first two incidents happened in Canada while vacationing and this third time in Nashville. The thing about it, Brody, is the killer wasn't present when the attempts were made, making it harder to prove who's behind it."

His forehead creased as he realized what she said was true. "That takes some planning. When is he bringing her to Lander?"

"They're coming on the Gulfstream tonight down at Hunt Field. I was gonna send one of the hands to pick them up, but I'd feel a lot safer if you would bring them. I wouldn't ask if it weren't for the danger they're facing.

He reached out and clasped his own hand over hers in reassurance. "It's no problem at all, Mrs. Adams. Anything at all you need, don't even hesitate to call."

"Thanks, Brody. This is a big load off my mind."

"Glad to help. Do you know what time he's landing?

"Not sure. If you call Hunt they'll probably know."

Brody stood. "I'll be right there waiting when he gets in. Don't you worry one more minute. I'll bring him home safely, and his arrival will be kept confidential."

"Thanks for stopping in, Brody."

"My pleasure. See ya later tonight, Mrs. Adams."

•

The oppressive heat continued for several days without grace. Warm wind dried the sweat on his back before it could drip in rivulets and dampen his clothes as he ripped out the two windows in the dining room and prepared to put in a large picture window with an antique stained-glass top light in it.

The ringing telephone interrupted his concentration, and he set his wood plane down to answer it.

"Brody. Chris Adams, here. Listen, I need to talk to

you. Any chance we can get together?"

"Sure. When?"

"Soon."

"Yeah. Can you come here? I'm in the middle of something, but I can talk while I'm working."

"Thanks, buddy. I'll be there in about ten minutes."

Brody hung up and returned to the task at hand. It was not long before Chris arrived.

"Hey, Brod. I wanted to talk to you without Abby around." Chris climbed the steps of the porch and helped hold the window frame. "Mama said she told you some of it when you were out to the ranch the other day, but I'd like to talk to ya about it myself.

"Sure. Better to hear it straight from you anyway."

"I'm hoping it's over now that we're in Wyoming. We're pretty sure we know who it is, but we don't know their real names. See, I've got these two stalker fans. They attended every single concert on my last tour, following us from city to city. We used to joke about them—called them Maisie and Daisy."

Brody set his tools down and went in the kitchen, pulling two beers from the fridge. "How serious were the attempts, Chris? Tell me more."

"Abby's husband died last fall and left her pregnant. We were only four weeks from delivery when they caused her to have an 'accident'. She lost the baby and would have died if her sister hadn't found her.

Chris sat on the porch railing. He leaned forward settling his elbows on his knees, peeling at the label on the bottle as he continued his story. "Two weeks ago I left her for about two hours while she napped and returned to find all the gas turned on and the pilot lights blown out. It was hours before she regained consciousness. We were on a secluded island, Brody. Just the two of us, and nobody knew I was there except

Jeff, Julie and my manager. After that second attempt I was too scared to stay, so we headed off to Nashville. Somebody sent flowers to the penthouse. That's where the explosive was hidden. Thank God she was in another section of the penthouse when it went off, or I would have lost her for good. I'm hoping she'll be safe here, but I wanted you to know. I don't want Abby hurt again."

"Maisie and Daisy, huh? Cute names. You need to be more selective in who you pick for fans, Adams," Brody said, trying to lighten the tension.

Chris half laughed. "Yeah, right."

"Do you have any pictures of those two?"

"No. We only…wait a minute. Let me check with Julie. She often videotapes before and during concerts. I'll bet she's got some footage with them by the stage. They had consistent front row center every performance. I don't know how they managed that. I can't even get tickets that good. If you catch 'em, I'll have to ask what the secret is. I'll call Julie to start looking through the footage."

"Great. We'll see what we can do about identifying them. I'll post their pictures at the office and send copies to the Police Department, too."

"Thanks, Brody. I really appreciate it. I'm so scared for Abby. She doesn't need this crap."

"We'll do our best for ya, buddy."

"Listen, we should get together with you and Lindy while we're home."

Brody took the empties to the kitchen and set them on the counter. "Sounds good to me, Chris. Let me know when you're available. Lindy works at the library same shift as mine, afternoons."

"Maybe you two can come out one morning, and we'll go out on horseback for a picnic in the mountains."

"She'll love it. Hey, I'm happy for you and Abby. You've been through quite a rough spell yourself with the divorce and all. Never was quite sure what you ever saw in that one."

"Yeah, she and Abby, though, just like night and day. Wait until you get to know her."

Chris picked up the tools and pitched in with the installation of the window. It was mid-afternoon by the time he went home.

CHAPTER TWENTY-NINE

Summer drew to a close and things gradually settled back to their standard routine. Bronwyn's summer hiatus from teaching ended, and it became possible to once again walk down the street without tripping over teenagers and tourists.

Braden strolled into his parent's living room on a Thursday morning and found his older brother and Lindy curled up together in the Lazy-boy chair. "How's our resident love birds doing today?"

Brody looked up in surprise. "What are you doing home this time of day, Braden?"

"I had a dental appointment this morning. Since it's getting close to lunch I thought I'd drop in and see what's up around here. So, what's up?" He flopped down on the sofa.

"Nothing much. We're discussing putting another bathroom in upstairs."

"What's wrong with the one you've got? Looks fine to me."

"It is, but I thought I'd turn the room next to our bedroom into an ensuite bath. Put in a nice whirlpool tub, separate shower. Make it really nice."

"Sounds like it. Call if you need a hand. I don't imagine you can get a whirlpool tub up those stairs on your own, and no offence Lindy, but I think he's gonna need bigger muscles than yours." He lifted his arm and flexed it for her, displaying a bicep close in size to his brother's.

"No offence taken, Muscle Man. You're welcome to the job. It's not imminent, though. We're still in the discussion stages. I don't feel the same rush that Brody seems to. We aren't gonna have kids right away, so there's plenty of time."

"What's up with you, Braden?"

"Not much. Working at the animal hospital is okay, but I like doing house calls best. When I open my own practice, that's where I want to focus. Large animals: horses, cattle, llamas."

Lindy listened with avid interest. Being raised as an only child, it was a treat for her to have siblings even if they were only sort-of adopted.

"That's great. Brody's been talking about getting a few horses one day. You can take care of them for us. It'll be wonderful having a vet in the family. Okay, work aside, tell us what we really want to know. How's your love life?"

"What's a love life? Hey, I heard Julie Clayton's in town right now. I was thinking of giving her a call. She's a hot little filly," Braden said.

"Yeah, we saw Julie at the Shady Eagle the other night. I don't know how long she'll be in town before she heads back to Nashville. I guess things are pretty much a mess right now. Chris and Abby broke up over something, and Julie's busy playing nursemaid to the broken-hearted man."

Lindy added what little she knew of the situation.

"Abby's stuck in Lander because all her ID was destroyed in the Nashville explosion, and she has to wait for the replacements before she can go back to Canada. She's come in to volunteer at the library, so we've gotten to spend some time together, but we never discuss Chris. It's a subject not open for discussion, but I can tell you she's just as devastated as he is. I hope they work it out soon. They're both so unhappy being apart. Maybe Julie can help them find their way back together again.

"I always hated that she went to Nashville to work for Chris. If she'd stayed in town I just might have married her."

"What am I hearing? You've actually thought of settling down?" Brody asked with surprise.

"Sure. Unlike some, I don't feel the need to date the entire female population of the county before I commit. I'm done with school. I've got some money put away. I'd like to find Miss Right."

"Well, Braden, I hope you find her soon, and that you'll be as happy as your brother and I are." Lindy smiled at Brody and they kissed.

"Hello! Somebody else is still in the room here."

"Sorry, Braden," Lindy apologized without taking her eyes from Brody. "We sort of like each other."

"I think I'll grab a quick lunch and go back to work. Brody, I don't know what you're waiting for. If you're gonna marry the girl, get on with it while you still like each other. Then you can make out at your own place. See ya later, guys."

"Bye Bray."

Lindy started to kiss around Brody's ear. "Want me to come out to the house tomorrow?" she asked.

"Yes, but no. I've got stuff to do. I'll pick you up at the library for dinner and take you home later, but that's all

I'll see of you tomorrow."

"Okay, well, I'll miss you. You've been so busy with the house I haven't seen nearly enough of you. I think Braden's right. We need to think about getting married so we can see each other more."

"I miss you too, baby." He kissed the tip of her nose and touched a finger to her pouting lips.

•

The Shady Eagle bustled with activity and seats became scarce quickly. Brody and Lindy arrived early to claim a table close to the stage. Meghan and her date, Holden Nichols, soon joined them. David and Poor Paige sat at a table with some of Paige's friends near the back corner.

After chatting while listening to the jukebox for half an hour, Brody excused himself. "I'll be back in a minute, honey. I need to talk to someone. Just a little business that need's taking care of." He kissed her cheek and left the table. She nodded before turning her attention back to her conversation with Meghan.

Ten minutes later, her head bobbed and ducked as she tried to catch sight of Brody. She finally spotted him at the bar standing next to Tara Shepherd with his arm tucked snugly around her waist and talking intimately into her ear. Tara's arm reached around him and drew him closer.

"Lindy, is something wrong? You just went white as a sheet." Meghan cranked her head around to see what had her friend so shaken. Discovering Brody and Tara looking too friendly upset her as well. She shot a dirty look at her sister's back. Turning back, she smiled and tried to reassure her friend in spite of her own suspicions.

"It's all right, Lindy. They're just friends. I'm sure it's nothing. He probably just saw her passing by and wanted to say hey. Don't worry about it."

"Sorry. I like Tara, but sometimes I still get jealous of her and Brody from before. You know?"

"Yeah, I know. My sister has a way with guys and can usually snag whoever she's interested in. I've walked in her shadow for years. But you don't need to worry about Brody. He's never been involved with anyone like he is with you. It's obvious he's crazy about you."

"I guess. I'm just being silly."

Brody returned a few minutes later, and Lindy kept her little green monster inside. They noticed Abby there waiting tables, obviously trying to make enough money to help get herself back to Canada. She handed her tray and apron in at the bar before heading for the stage. As she mounted the steps, the bar owner announced Abby would be singing. Everyone watched the shock and horror that darted over her features when he added that Chris Adams would be singing with her.

The room listened, mesmerized as the two performers took turns singing to the crowd. First Chris would sing about loving her forever, and she would return a song saying it was over for good. The cycle continued to repeat. On and on it went until Abby could not take it any more and ran off the stage in tears.

"Brody, take me home."

Brody saw tears glistening on Lindy's cheeks as the evening tore at her heart. He immediately escorted her from the night club. They sat in the Avalanche, and she cried.

"Brody, that was probably the worst time I've ever had. They're both in so much pain. Watching them being ripped apart like that is unbearable. They love each other as much as we do. It terrifies me to think that a couple so happy in love one day can be torn apart like that. Promise me it will never happen to us, Brody, because I couldn't take it."

"We'll never be apart, because we trust each other implicitly, and we have no secrets from one another. I promise you, you're in my heart forever, honey." He thought a change of subject would help her feel better. "You and Meghan seemed to have lots to talk about. I'm glad you get along so well."

"I've been lucky making friends here. My best friend is your sister."

"Bronwyn adores you. It means a lot to me that you and my family are close. Seeing how much they all love you just makes me love you even more. Even Brooke likes you, and that's something."

"I'm really blessed to have your family care about me. Believe me, I'm wallowing in it."

"Wanna come home with me tonight, or do you wanna go to Ma's?"

"Sweetheart, I never turn down an invitation to spend the night with you. You know that. I can't wait until I can be there every night."

"We're getting closer to it. Let's make the rest of the night unforgettable in a good way."

"I'd like that." She turned to stare out the window into the black night. "Brody, we'll always be together, won't we?"

He squeezed her hand tighter. "We may have days where we have to fight like hell for it, but I believe we can face whatever comes at us as long as we stand together. You're my heart, honey. Can't do too much living without one of those, now can I?"

When they pulled into the lengthy driveway, they saw David's truck parked outside the back of the house.

With a wink, Brody suggested they use the front door. They removed their shoes on the porch and quietly crept up the stairs. Lindy turned the stereo on when they were safely ensconced in Brody's room, hoping to cover any sound that would give her presence away. It became a game for them, trying to never let David know she had been there. Not that it mattered, but it made for an interesting little diversion.

Lindy pulled on her nightgown and crept under the covers quickly. Brody returned from the bathroom with his pajama bottoms and a t-shirt on. He climbed into bed beside her and snuggled against her, resting his head on her shoulder and a hand on her stomach.

"Hey, big guy. You need some loving?"

"Always."

She let her fingers run through his hair as they lay quietly together.

"It feels so good, babe. Just being next to you and feeling your touch. This is the best I've felt all week."

"I'm glad. Being with you always makes me feel special."

"You are special. That's why I love you so much."

She kissed his forehead and let a finger curl around his ear. "Brody, can I touch you?"

He chuckled quietly and turned his face into her shoulder to kiss it.

"What's funny about that?"

"Darling, that is something a man never says 'no' to." He kissed her lips and pulled her with him as he rolled onto his back.

She continued to kiss him as her hand slid down his body, stopping to brush her fingers delicately through the soft hair on his stomach first. By the time she finally touched him, he was ready to die from anticipation. She kissed him all over his face, his neck, his mouth, as she touched him.

"Oh Brody," she whispered, "I love touching you like this, sweetheart."

Brody was aroused. "Oh, Lindy. Oh, Lindy!"

She moved down to kiss his chest, and he pulled her mouth back to his for a last quick kiss before clutching her tightly to him as she loved him.

"Yes, Lindy, yes!" He gasped for breath and managed to tell her, "I love you, baby."

Lindy was thrilled that she touched him without any fear or revulsion. She felt nothing but love and adoration for him. "How was that?"

A deep chuckle erupted from his chest. "Another good reason to marry you." He held her face in his hands and kissed her. "It was perfect."

She smiled at his words. "Really? It was good?" She sounded like a child wanting approval.

"Yes, my darling. I love you for wanting to do that for me." He brushed her hair back out of the way as it fell around her face while she looked down at him. "Are you okay with it?"

Her eyes welled with tears. "I just wanted to love you. That's all I could think of. That's what I wanted."

He kissed her softly, letting her know how much he appreciated her gesture. It took seven months to get to this, and he knew the courage it took from her. "Would you like me to touch you now?"

"Maybe in the morning. I just want to enjoy this moment. Do you know what part I liked best."

"What's that?" He could not help smiling at her.

"You were saying my name at your 'big moment'. I can't tell you what that meant to me."

"Ah, Lindy. It will always be your name."

She lay her head on his shoulder and let her hand roam over his broad chest. "Me too, Brody. Only you—

for always."

"I'm glad we agree on that." His hand stroked up and down her arm. "Should I go shower, or do you want to share a bath?"

"Share. It's nice to relax together."

"Good answer." He kissed her one last time before getting up to run the water. He lit the candles that became fixtures in the bathroom and got two fresh towels out of the closet. She came in and locked the door, refusing to relinquish the intimacy of their evening. An intrusion from David at this point, however accidental, would be most unwelcome. She stepped into the deep tub and stood while Brody got in behind her. Instead of leaning back against him like she had in the past, she lay on her side with their legs entwined so she could wrap her arms around his waist and rested her head on his chest.

If life could always be like this— quiet, soft, intimate— how wonderful it would be. A deep contentment settled in her soul. She gave him something tonight. It was good to be on the giving side for a change, and she hoped soon she would be able to give him everything. She was not quite ready, but as each day passed, it came closer. Soon. Soon, she would be his completely.

•

Brody's birthday fell on a work day, so he and Lindy waited until Saturday when they were both off to celebrate. On a beautiful day in early autumn with a touch of briskness in the air, Lindy picked him up. They drove to Sinks Canyon with backpacks and embarked on Lindy's first long distance journey on foot since her hospitalization.

"This is a terrific view, Brody. I can see for miles."

"It would be great to build a house up here with this view, wouldn't it?"

"Amazing. But I suppose if we saw it every day, it might lose some of its wonder. And I wouldn't want to try to get a car up this hill in the winter."

"You're right. I guess we'll have to settle for the house we've got. No troubles with the driveway there."

"I don't consider our house 'settling' for anything. It's a beautiful house, and one we can grow in. You see, on my way into town that first day, I saw it and thought to myself, 'I love that house. I'd better find the owner and make him fall in love with me so I can live there.' So, I waited until you were on your way home and threw myself down at the side of the road so you'd have to stop for me."

"Is that how it happened? Gee, good thing I'm the owner then, isn't it? If somebody else owned it, we wouldn't be here right now would we?"

She reached into her pack and pulled out a small package. "And you wouldn't be getting this birthday present, so you should appreciate that house."

He took the gift from her and unwrapped it. When he opened the box, his eyes grew large in stunned surprise. "Oh, honey! This is too much."

"It's what I wanted to give you."

"But, Lindy. A Rolex. I've never even seen one before." He flipped it over in his hands, reverently inspecting it. "Wow! 18 kt. gold. This is magnificent."

"I'm glad you like it."

"I love it. It's beautiful. I just wish you hadn't spent so much on me."

"You won't let me pay off the mortgage. I have a huge bank account just sitting there. I guess if I want my future husband to have something neat, I can get it for him. Besides, it's nothing compared to what you've given me."

He kissed her. "You are the sweetest woman in the world. Love you, Lind."

"Love you back."

He slipped the watch onto his wrist. "Holy Hannah, Lindy. This thing costs as much as my truck."

"Enjoy it. Every time you check the time, I want you to know I'm loving you at that very moment."

"And I'll be loving you, sweetheart."

CHAPTER THIRTY

October settled in with crisp cool winds and clear skies. Warmer clothes came out of closets and autumn decorations adorned homes and businesses. Days grew shorter and children arrived at the library with rosy pink cheeks.

The woman who tried relentlessly to kill Abby Lockner made one final attempt and died at her own hands, but Chris and Abby were still apart.

Tuesday morning marked six days since Lindy last saw Brody, and she missed him to the point of distraction. Braden picked her up from the library each night as Brody claimed to suddenly be too busy.

Unwilling to face one more day without him, she decided to drive out to the house and surprise him. She put the curtains she made for the dining room window in a bag and set them on the passenger seat of her car. Stopping at the bakery on the way, she picked up a Dutch apple pie and fresh kaiser buns.

As the miles clicked by on the highway, she passed the spot where Brody first found her and contemplated how her life changed that night. From the moment he rescued her everything consistently climbed uphill. Each successive day she believed she could not possibly be happier or more in love, and yet each day it got better.

She pulled into Brody's driveway and parked in the back by the kitchen door, surprised to see Tara's car before nine o'clock in the morning.

Lindy set her groceries on the kitchen table and wandered through the house looking for them. After searching the entire main floor, she stared at the staircase, perplexed. With a shrug of her shoulders, she started the climb.

Voices emanating from Brody's bedroom stopped her dead in her tracks.

"Tara, you are amazing. This is absolutely incredible."

"I'm glad you like it."

"Are you kidding me? I love it."

"Good. I wanted you to be happy. Are you sure Lindy doesn't know about this."

"No way. She's totally in the dark, just like I wanted. It's been hard, especially the last week. I haven't even been to see her."

"Maybe that wasn't such a good idea. She might start to suspect something."

"I couldn't see her and still do this. I had to make a choice."

"I hope she forgives you."

"No problem there." After what Lindy considered a rather pregnant pause, he continued, "Tara, I appreciate ya coming out here like this. Don't know what I would have done without you."

"I'm happy you asked me. I've certainly enjoyed doing it."

Pain ripped through Lindy, leaving her unable to breathe. When she could not stand any more, she

306

quietly hurried back down the stairs. Passing through the kitchen she picked up her pie and rolls, refusing to leave them for him.

Quickly pulling back out onto the highway, her drive home couldn't have been more different than the trip there. Speeding down the highway, she tried to find a spot where she could pull off and fall apart. How could Brody do this to her? All those months of telling her how much he loved her. All those months of sessions together with a therapist. All those months of learning to trust again. All broken. Shattered. Slipping the ring from her finger, she dropped it into her purse. After a good long cry she pulled back onto the road and headed for town. She needed to get back to town. It was all she could think of. One step at a time.

What to do? Where to go? Bronwyn would be at school this time of the morning, and she could not talk to Gina about it.

Meghan. She would go to Meghan.

•

Meghan answered the door, and as soon as Lindy saw her she fell apart. Inconsolable, she could not even begin to tell what happened. Meghan led her to the sofa, distressed to see Lindy so upset. When Lindy pulled a tissue to mop at her tears, Meghan noticed her hand.

"Your ring. Lindy, where's your ring?"

Lindy shook her head no, trying to find her voice. "Brody," she tried, but it came out choked. "Tara."

"Brody and Tara? What about them?"

Lindy just nodded and fell onto her shoulder, burying her head while Meghan held her. It took a few minutes of pondering the situation for her to understand. "Lindy, are you saying Brody and Tara are seeing each other?"

She nodded again. "… sleeping with her."

"NO! Lindy, no. It just can't be true. He worships the ground you walk on, girl."

"I found them there together this morning. In his bedroom."

"I can't believe this! I mean, I'm not saying I don't believe you, I'm just finding the whole thing mind boggling. You're sure?" Even as she asked the question, she remembered seeing them that night at the Shady Eagle when they stood with their arms around each other, Brody whispering in Tara's ear. Right there with Lindy in the room. Now realizing what it really meant, she could not stomach how brazen the behavior had been.

"Positive." Lindy relayed the conversation she overheard, and Meghan had no other choice than to see it for what it was.

"I'm sorry, Lind. I'm so sorry. No wonder you're heartbroken. This is such a shock for me, I can't even imagine how awful it is for you. I don't understand why they would do this. I've never known Tara to be part of something like this before, and Brody…I thought he was far above this kind of thing."

"I don't know what to do, or where to go. I'm so lost. My whole life here in Lander was because of him. I'm scared, Meghan. I trusted him. I believed him. I suppose it's my own fault. He needs a woman who can be everything for him. I haven't been that. I'm damaged goods, unable to fulfill all his needs. He told me before he liked going to bed with her."

Frowning with worry, Meghan shook her head in denial. "Lindy, you haven't talked like this in a long time. Don't you dare blame yourself. This is not your fault. The only thing you've done is to love someone we all thought was worthy of it. He has no excuse for this. He knew before you ever got involved that you had things to work out, and he accepted it."

Lindy stared listlessy at her hands in her lap. "What am I supposed to do now?"

"I'll call in sick for ya so you won't have to deal with work today. What do you want to do?"

"I haven't got a clue. I don't feel comfortable staying with Mike and Gina anymore. I love them, but I'm not marrying their son—not now. I'm not gonna be a part of their family any more, so I really don't belong. And what am I supposed to say? 'I found your son in bed with another woman'?" Another storm of grief swept over her in a deluge.

Meghan retrieved a new box of tissues for her. "All right. Why don't you stay here in my second bedroom? At least until you decide what you want to do about things."

"Thanks, Meg. I don't know where else to go. Even this, well, I was kind of scared to come to you," she admitted.

"Why? Why would you be afraid to come to me? We're close friends."

"But she's your sister."

"And she's acted like a whore. I'm absolutely disgusted with her. You are welcome to stay with me as long as you want."

Lindy nestled her head against Meghan's shoulder. "Thank you. This means a lot to me."

Meghan took Lindy to the Ashton house and helped her gather her belongings. After packing them into her car, Lindy went back inside to leave a note for Mike and Gina, thanking them for all they had done for her.

At three-thirty Meghan called Bronwyn asking her to come to the apartment. Upon arriving, she became immediately upset as soon as she saw Lindy, who had not stopped crying all day.

"What's going on here? Lindy, what's happened?"

The woman burst into another round of sobs, leaving Meghan to recant the story. Bronwyn and Lindy hugged and cried together a good fifteen minutes before Meghan interrupted them.

"Listen up, girls. We have a job to do, and sitting here crying won't get it done."

Bronwyn sniffled. "What do we need to do?"

"Most of Lindy's things are out at his place. We have to get them out of there for her."

Lindy had not even thought about it, but it made sense. She never wanted to darken that doorstep again, but she was the only one who knew which things were hers leaving her no alternative.

Meghan continued with her plan. "We'll need all three vehicles, and we'll probably have to make more than one trip. She had a trailer full of stuff. We can store the things at my parents' place."

Bronwyn stood and wiped her eyes. "I'm gonna drive over to the Sheriff's Office and trade my car for his truck. Get a lot more in that way. Besides, it's poetic justice to use his truck to take her things away."

"Oh, Bronwyn, please don't tell him. He'll want to talk to me, and I just can't deal with it. This day has been too much already," Lindy pleaded.

"I'm not even gonna see him. I'll just make the switch. Besides, I don't have a single thing to say to him. I may never speak to him again for the remainder of his miserable life."

They gathered coats and purses together. Meghan placed a hand on Lindy's arm. "Are you gonna be all right to drive?"

"Yeah. I'll manage. I just want the day to be over."

Lindy and Meghan drove straight out to the house. Bronwyn stopped at the Sheriff's Office, happy to find the cruiser that Brody drove, missing. She parked near Brody's truck and went inside to see Jennifer at reception.

"Hi, Jen. I'm gonna take Brody's truck and leave my car here for him, just in case I don't get back in time. He can switch back at my mother's place after work if that happens. I'll leave the keys here with you."

Jennifer looked at Bronwyn's tear-stained face. "Sure. You okay, Bronwyn?"

"No, not really, but I can't talk about it. Thanks, Jen."

Bronwyn left, finding Brody's spare keys right where she knew they would be. Looking neither right nor left, she put the key in the ignition and left the parking lot.

Lindy took Meghan to help her retrieve a stack of empty boxes she knew Brody kept stashed in the barn.

"Meg, if you could go upstairs and clear my things out I'd appreciate it. I can't go up there. Oh, and leave this on his dresser." She handed Meghan her emerald ring.

"Okay. What am I taking?"

"In his bedroom I have my stereo and microwave and some clothes in two of his drawers and the closet. That's about it for that room. I can't think of anything in the bathroom that I can't replace. One of the other bedrooms has a bunch of my stuff still in boxes. Maybe clear his room out first. Then when Bronwyn arrives she can help bringing down the other boxes."

"All right. What are you gonna do?"

"I'll pack up my books in the library. He's not getting any of my treasures." She turned with a purpose and began her task. When she heard Bronwyn come in, she asked her to help Meghan.

Bronwyn was on her way out the back door for the

311

fifth time when David came home.

"Hey, Bronwyn. What's up? I see your brother's truck here. I thought he was working tonight."

"David, I'm glad you're here. I have the truck because I have to move a bunch of stuff out of here. Brody was keeping it for me, but now I have a place for it. Appreciate it if you could lend a hand."

"Sure. No problem at all. Let me grab a sandwich, and I'll be with you in two shakes."

"Thanks, David. I'm bringing things downstairs from the front bedroom." She continued out to the truck with the box in her hands and deposited it in the back.

Lindy stayed in the library, packing her books. Glancing at the window seat, she remembered the night he brought her to show her the bookshelves he refinished for her. He bought her a novel so she could put the first book on the shelf in their library. It had been her birthday. They unpacked all these books that night. It was the night she started to feel it would truly become her home.

"Oh, Brody, why? I tried so hard for you. I've loved you so much. I'll die without you." She cried, remembering the nights she spent here in the house. The nights she gave him her love as best she could. The days she spent planting flowers and bushes, and painting the house trim. Planning for a future that would never happen.

Slowly, she started the heart-wrenching task of lugging boxes to her car. Moving things out meant saying goodbye for good. She sat in the car and cried some more, unable to believe things were over between them. She did not want it to end. She wanted to go back to the early morning hours when she did not know. Things were better then. Maybe she could just pretend. Maybe if she forced herself to go all the way, he would stop seeing Tara. Then again, maybe not. He told her before that he enjoyed sleeping with Tara. He said she was sexy, and fun, and pretty without a truckload of problems. All the things Lindy was not. She leaned against the steering wheel and sobbed.

Meghan finished collecting Lindy's things from Brody's room and quickly perused the bathroom. She found some make-up and hair things in the cabinet. She dropped them into a shopping bag and tucked them in a box, stacking the boxes she packed at the top of the stairs.

David climbed to the top of the stairs and carted the boxes back down and outside to the cars. As soon as Lindy's and Meghan's cars were full, they left for the Shepherd's home in Lander to unload them, leaving David and Bronwyn to finish loading the truck.

CHAPTER THIRTY-ONE

Brody arrived at the library just before closing time to pick up Lindy. He had not seen her for days, and he missed her. He watched as the other librarians came out and locked the building behind them. Lindy was not among them. He stepped out of Bronwyn's car to speak with them.

"Where's Lindy?"

"She didn't come in today, Brody. Called in sick."

"Okay, thanks."

Worried, he got back in the car and drove to his parents' home, hoping it was nothing serious. When he arrived, he found the house ablaze with lights. Curious, he hurried inside and found his mother in tears.

"What's going on? Ma? What's wrong?"

"What have you done, Brody? Tell me what you did to her."

"Did to who? I haven't got a clue what you're talking about. Where's Lindy?"

"Lindy's gone. She's taken all her things and left. I came home and found her note."

None of it made any sense to him. "What do you

mean she's gone? Gone where? What note?"

Gina practically threw the letter at him.

Dear Mike and Gina

This is so awkward for me. I love you both and wished with all my heart to be your daughter, but things have changed. Brody and I are no longer together, and I'm uncomfortable living here in his family's home. After all, he had you first.

I truly wish things worked out differently. Brody is my whole heart and soul, but he doesn't feel the same about me any more. I haven't decided whether I'll stay in town or not. I'll let you know either way. I'm just suffering too much right now to think straight.

Thank you for all you've given me and done for me this year. I have loved being part of your home and your family. It's meant more to me than you'll ever know.

> *With deepest affection,*
> *Lindy*

Brody raised his eyes to meet theirs in total confusion. "What the hell is this? Lindy and I haven't broken up. This is crazy. She knows I wanna get married. I don't understand any of this. I went to the library to pick her up, and they said she called in sick. None of this is making any sense at all. And what does this mean?" He slapped at the letter. "I don't feel the same way about her any more? Where does she get these ideas? I've been killing myself for her."

In the midst of Brody's bewilderment, Bronwyn arrived full of anger and hurt. When she saw her brother, she stood before him and slapped his face as hard as she could. He grabbed her wrist and yanked her back when she tried to walk away from him.

"What was that for?"

"I hate you, Brody Ashton! You disgusting piece of filth. I've always been proud to be your sister, but no more. I'm ashamed to even say I know you. In fact, I vote we kick you right out of this family."

His eyes squinted in confusion as he faced her. "What are you talking about? Has the whole world gone to hell in a handbag?"

"Don't even bother trying to pretend with me. I know everything, so stop the lying. Be man enough to admit what a sleazeball you are." She wrenched her hand from his grasp, picked up her car keys, and slammed out the front door.

Brody looked at his parents, shock written all over his face. "I have three questions, and I'd really appreciate someone providing some sensible answers here. Where is Lindy? Who was that witch that just flew through here? And third, seeing as how I've been totally lost since I walked in that door, can somebody say something that makes sense?"

Gina counted off the answers on her fingers. "We have no idea where Lindy is. She took all her things and left. That was your sister Bronwyn who just flew through here, and I'd say seeing how angry she is, she probably knows something we don't, and third, you know as much as we do. She's gone because of something you've done." She folded her arms and glared at her son.

"Are you for real? Lindy's really gone?"

"That's what I've been saying."

"Why? Why would she leave me? We've been so happy. I don't understand any of this." As the reality hit him that she really was gone, he plunked himself down on a chair, stunned. "She left me?" Tears filled his eyes. "Why, Ma? Why? I've been so good to her. She's never said nothing about being unhappy with me. She kept

316

saying she couldn't wait until we were married." The tears slowly coursed down his cheeks. "I love her, Ma. I'd never hurt her. I cherish that woman."

Mike studied his son carefully. "Brody, you really have no idea why this happened? She must have some reason for believing you don't want her anymore."

"I really don't know, Dad. Geez, what am I supposed to do now? What am I supposed to do without her?" His chest hurt, the aching inside unbearable. "I love her so much. I have to find her and straighten this out. I can't be without Lindy."

•

Tara and Justin wheeled a patient with cardiac arrest into the emergency department at Lander Valley Medical Center where a hospital team took over. When the patient had been transferred to an examination table in the trauma room, they toted the gurney out to the ambulance.

Tara saw Meghan at the desk and stopped to speak with her. "Hey, Meg. What's new?"

Meghan looked up from the chart she was making notes on, and her face filled with emotion. An eyebrow raised in distaste as she replied, "What's new? I guess my opinion of you."

"What's that supposed to mean? What's going on?"

"We all know what's been going on. You're a bitch with no principles. I used to think you had some class. I was wrong." Meghan abruptly walked away, leaving Tara totally nonplussed.

She noticed her father down the hall and decided to question him. His face tightened when he saw her.

"Dad, what's up with Meg? She's got a bee in her bonnet about somethin."

Matt got straight to the point. "Tara, can you deny that you've slept with Brody Ashton?"

"Dad! We don't generally discuss my life in these terms."

"Have you slept with Brody? Think very carefully before you answer me."

Tara stood gaping at her father. He had never asked her such a thing before, and she reeled from the shock. "Yes, I have. Why?"

"Then if you find people don't have any respect for you any more, it's all your own doing. I have patients who need me." He stepped around her and ducked into a treatment room, ending their conversation.

Angry, Tara saw Meghan turning into the staff lounge and followed her inside. "Meg, you're mad at me because I slept with Brody? Why do you even care? It had nothing to do with you, and who I sleep with is my business."

"Your whole attitude disgusts me, Tara. I know, you've always been the wild Shepherd sister, but I believed you had boundaries even you wouldn't cross. It appalls me that you don't even feel guilty about it. Have you no shame at all?"

Justin pushed the door open and stuck his head in to talk to his partner. "Come on, Tara. We've got a call." Deciding that talking to her sister was an exercise in futility, she shrugged it off and followed Justin outside to the ambulance.

•

"Thanks, Bronwyn. I appreciate you telling me, honey. When you talk to her, you tell her Daddy and I love her."

"She knows that, Mom. It's been really rough for her.

She's cried non-stop all day long. I doubt she'll even speak with him. She's so torn up. I think she needs some time on her own."

"All right, darling. Try and get some sleep. See you tomorrow." Gina hung up the telephone and started crying again herself. She grabbed a tissue and blew her nose as she walked back into the living room where Mike tried to console his son.

"Well, Brody," she started, "I don't see how you can undo this one. I just spoke with Bron."

"What did she say? What happened?"

"Lindy found out you've been sleeping with Tara Shepherd. No wonder she's destroyed."

"No, Ma, I haven't. I wouldn't do that to Lindy. Never."

"Apparently, Tara admitted it to her father and sister tonight at the medical center."

"No! I haven't been with her since last winter, before Lindy and I ever got together. I swear."

"Brody, Lindy went out to the house this morning. She found you in bed together and overheard you talking about how amazing Tara is, how you've been keeping it all a secret from Lindy. Even about you not seeing Lindy all week just so you could be with Tara. You made her sound like a fool for not even suspecting your deceit. 'Don't worry. Lindy'll forgive me.' What's that supposed to be? I've never known you to be so arrogant."

Mike went to his wife and put his arms around her, his sympathy for his son evaporated.

Brody gaped at them, bewildered. "It's not true."

"Are you telling me Lindy's putting herself through all this grief over something she made up out of thin air? I don't think so, Brody. She heard the whole conversation, and why would Tara admit it if it wasn't true? You have to face up to this one. You've made your bed, so to speak. Now you'll have to suffer the consequences, and that means losing the best woman you've ever known."

"I'm telling you, I haven't been sleeping with Tara."

"Was she at your home this morning?"

"Yeah, but..."

"No buts, Brody. Were you or were you not upstairs in your bedroom with her?"

"Yeah, but..."

"Have you been keeping it all a secret from Lindy?"

"Yeah, but..."

"Then you deserve to lose everything. I'm so ashamed of you." She turned to her husband. "Michael, please get him out of my home." She stalked down the hall to her bedroom, closing the door emphatically behind her.

"Dad, do I get to say something here? It isn't what it sounds like."

"Make it good." Mike stood planted in the middle of the room with his arms crossed, anger in every feature.

"I built a new bed for Lindy. A huge four poster. I wanted it to be a wedding present for her."

"So you thought you and Tara would just try it out to make sure it works?"

"NO! Listen to me. I asked Tara for help. She made the canopy and curtains for it, and matching drapes for the window and a duvet cover. I haven't been in to see Lindy because I've been working hard to get it finished. Tara came out this morning to finish putting it all together. I planned on proposing to Lindy this weekend. I've already bought the ring. Dad, she's the only one I want. I love her. Please, help me. I need her."

"You're sure that's all it was? Don't you lie to me, boy."

"I promise, Dad. Lindy's my whole world. I don't want to be with anyone else but her."

"All right. You go on home and try to get some sleep. I'll talk to your mother, and one of us will talk to Bronny. She's obviously in touch with Lindy. Somehow we'll get this all straightened out. I'm mighty relieved you haven't been cheating on her. Your mother and I adore that girl. We want her in this family for keeps."

"So do I, Dad. I don't know what I'll do if she doesn't come back to me. She's the only woman I ever met that I can't live without."

•

Brody sat at his kitchen table nursing a bottle of beer when David's bedroom door opened. "Sorry, David. Did I wake you?"

"Not really. I was only half asleep anyway. Haven't seen much of you the last week or so."

"Yeah, I've been building a bed. Supposed to be a wedding present."

"Really? Who's getting hitched?"

"I was hoping it was gonna be me. I was gonna ask her this weekend."

"You're not going to now?"

"Don't know. I think we broke up today. She's pretty upset, and I don't know if she'll listen to me. She moved all her stuff out of my parents' place today."

David winced and faced his cousin with squinted eyes. "I think I helped her move her stuff out of here today, too. Bronwyn was here with Meghan, and they moved a lot of boxes out. Your girlfriend spent most of her time sitting out in her car crying. Real upset about something."

"Lindy was here tonight?"

"Yup. Sorry. I figured you knew what was happening since Bronwyn used your truck to move the stuff."

"Damn that sister of mine." He stood and picked up his beer. "I'm going to bed. Maybe tomorrow this world will make more sense." His feet felt as heavy as his heart as he trudged up the stairs. He pushed open the bedroom door and leaned against the door frame, glowering at the bed. This morning it had been a wonderful thing. So proud of his handiwork, he could not wait to show it to her. Tonight, it served as an icon of tragedy.

On top of his dresser lay the glittering emerald ring. He remembered the day he gave it to her. It had been a perfect day for both of them. They were so much in love.

He opened a drawer and found her belongings gone. He sat on the edge of the bed and took his shoes off, letting them drop to the floor. Curling up on the bed, he ached for his Lindy, and the large bear of a man cried himself to sleep.

•

The events taking place in the Ashton family provided him with better circumstances than he had been waiting and hoping for. The time to pluck the blossoms from the vine was finally at hand.

CHAPTER THIRTY-TWO

It was late afternoon before Gina managed to reach Bronwyn. It required a lot of talking and cajoling, but she finally convinced her daughter to listen to Brody's explanation.

"You know, Bronny, it sounds a lot more like the Brody we've always known, and it's easy enough to prove. I'm sure all we have to do is show up and see it for ourselves. Lindy obviously overheard them talking about the bed and jumped to what seemed the logical conclusion. She needs to be told the truth as quickly as possible. I'm assuming you can handle that?"

Torn between lingering anger and sheepishness for not trusting her brother, she agreed. "All right, Mom. I'll talk to her. If Brody's telling the truth, I guess we have a lot of apologizing to do. Especially me."

"You should have seen him last night after you left. Cried his heart out over losing her. These two need to be together."

"I'll see what I can do. I'm so glad it wasn't true. I always liked Tara, but Lindy's my sister, and that's where my loyalties lay. I'll do my best."

•

Lindy walked to the library from Meghan's apartment. She still wanted to die from the pain, but managed to dredge up some of the courage that brought her through the last crisis in her life. She lived with responsibilities now and could not just curl up in a ball and retreat, no matter how badly she wanted to.

Lost in her thoughts, she failed to notice a dark green Caprice Classic slowly swerve to a stop at the curb beside her. The heavily-tinted electric window on the passenger side slid smoothly down, and the driver leaned toward her in invitation.

"Hey, Lindy, get in. I'll drive you to work."

With a half-hearted attempt at a smile, she stepped across the boulevard and got in. "Thanks. The wind is a lot colder than I thought when I started out. I should have worn a warmer jacket."

"Hey, happy to help. How's things with you and Brody?"

"We're not seeing each other any more."

"Oh, geez, sorry. That must be new."

"Yesterday." Turning her head away so he wouldn't see her eyes misting, she noticed the Safeway grocery store, it's parking lot bustling with activity. "Wait a minute. This isn't the way to the library."

"Don't worry about it, I'm just taking a different route. You'll get there."

"Okay."

Hands rose from the floor behind the passenger seat. One gripped her forehead and pressed it back into the headrest while the other held the chloroform-soaked cloth over her nose. Within seconds she fell unconscious. The car continued on its course, speeding quickly out of town.

●

Bronwyn called Meghan and relayed Brody's explanation. "He says he hasn't slept with Tara since last winter."

"Oh, no." Meghan closed her eyes in dismay as she realized her blunder in the whole fiasco. "I asked her last night if she'd slept with him, and she said yes. She had no idea why that upset me so much. You see, I never asked her when, only if she had. She didn't lie. I just asked the wrong question. He must be telling the truth, Bron. There was a beautiful huge bed in that room when I was packing her things."

"Mom did the exact same thing to Brody last night. She said he was destroyed over Lindy leaving him. Meggie, we need to tell Lindy as soon as possible. He already bought her engagement ring."

"I'll call Tara and talk to her, just to confirm everything Brody said. After that I'll pick you up, and we can go to the library and talk to her together."

"I'll be ready in about half an hour."

"I'll be there. Thanks, Bronwyn. I'm so relieved it isn't what we thought. Now we just have to convince her."

●

"Mom, have you heard from Lindy at all today?"

"No, but I'd sure like to. I've been home all day, but she hasn't come by or called. Did you talk to her yet?"

"No, not yet."

Gina detected worry in her daughter's voice. "Is something wrong, honey? You're sounding a bit strange."

"I'm just hoping nothings wrong. Meg and I are at the library. Lindy left Meg's place four hours ago, but she never arrived. The girls here haven't heard from her."

"Was she walking or driving?"

"Walking. She just had a jacket and her purse. Nothing else. It's not like she was skipping town. She was definitely headed here."

Lindy was too dependable to simply not show up for work, and Gina knew it. "Bronwyn, I think you should call your brother."

"I'll walk over to the station and see him. It's only three blocks away."

"Keep in touch. I'll worry until I hear from you."

Bronwyn hung up. "Meg, I'm gonna go tell Brody. Maybe you should go back to your place in case she calls or shows up there. Brody can take me home."

"All right. Stay in touch."

Bronwyn ran to the Sheriff's Office, nearly knocking two deputies down as she tried to push past them in the doorway. Breathless, she stopped at the reception desk. "Jennifer, is Brody here?"

"Yup. Looks like he got run over by a truck. He should be back there at his desk." She pointed over her shoulder with a pen toward the squad room.

"Thanks." Bronwyn scurried through the double doors and found her brother seated at his desk. Staring into space with a glazed expression, he appeared oblivious to the activity surrounding him. She placed a hand on his shoulder and gave him a gentle shake. "Brody, I need to talk to you."

Blinking rapidly, he returned to the present and turned to face her, his eyes dull and listless. "Coming back to take another swing at me, are ya?"

She sat on the edge of the desk. "I'm sorry, Brody. Of all the people in the world, I should have known better than to take it at face value. I'm sorry I deserted you. She was absolutely certain about everything she overheard, and it destroyed her. In the same situation, most anyone would have come to the same conclusion."

"No, Bron. If she trusted in my love for her, she would have walked into that room knowing she wouldn't find me in bed with anyone, including Tara." He turned away, feeling betrayed by those who should have known better.

"I need to talk to you."

"What do you want?" he asked, too distracted to pay attention.

"Brody. Focus here. This might be important."

He turned to look at her. "Okay, I'm listening."

"Lindy left for work at two-thirty and never got there. Something happened between Meghan's and the library."

He leaned forward, instantly alarmed. The pencil twirling nimbly between his fingers snapped crisply in half. "What do you mean she never got there?"

"Just what I'm saying. She left Meg's place to go to work. The library says she never got there. I'm worried."

"Holy Hannah! Lindy's too responsible to simply not show up. I'll start at the library and walk the route back to Meg's place. See if I can learn anything. This is really a case for the police—their jurisdiction, but nobody's gonna stop me from looking for her." He rose from his chair and threw on his jacket. "Wanna walk with me? Can always use another pair of eyes." He took a picture of Lindy from his desk drawer and tucked it into his pocket.

On the way out he stopped at Jennifer Dexter's desk. "Hey Jen, Lindy's missing. Never made it to work today. I'm going out on foot to see if I can find her. It's not an official case yet. She's only been missing for," he turned to his sister for confirmation, "what Bronwyn? Almost five hours, right?"

Jennifer hid her concern and kept her tone business-like. "I'm sorry to hear it. Stay in touch. I'll radio if we need you."

With twilight already descending, Brody took along two flashlights, giving one to Bronwyn. As they stood on the sidewalk in front of the library, he laid out their plan.

"Okay, I'll take this side of the street, you take the other. We'll walk the route Lindy would have used from here to Meg's apartment. Keep your eyes open. Look for any sign, anything at all that might be out of place. Anything that will let us know Lindy's been there."

"Got it. Good luck, Brod." Bronwyn crossed the street, and even though there was still enough light to see without it, she turned on the flashlight to scan the sidewalks and surrounding areas for any indication of Lindy's passing.

When they arrived without acquiring any clues, Brody went inside to question Meghan and learn what Lindy wore when she left the apartment that afternoon. She also provided two additional snapshots of her missing friend.

"Okay, we each have a picture of Lindy. We retrace our steps back to the library and knock at every door along the way. Ask if anyone saw her today. It might jog someone's memory to see her photo."

The women nodded in agreement, willing to do whatever they could to help find Lindy.

As she neared the end of the fourth block, Bronwyn climbed the steps of a wooden porch and knocked at the door. A woman in her late fifties answered.

"I'm sorry to trouble you, ma'am. We're searching for a woman who went missing today. She would have walked down this street this afternoon, and I was wondering if you could tell me if you saw her at all." She handed the woman Lindy's photo.

Eyebrows raised in recognition. "This is that nice young girl who works at the library, isn't it? Isn't she dating Brody Ashton?"

"Yes, that's right. I'm his sister."

"Oh, yes. I can see the resemblance." She looked back at the photo. "Yes, I saw her today. I was digging up my bulbs out in the garden when she came along. A car pulled up to the curb. The driver spoke to her, and she got in with him. Then they drove off. Can't help you after that."

"Are you sure?" Bronwyn's hopes escalated.

"Of course I'm sure. I saw it with my own eyes."

"Thank you so much. I'd like you to tell Brody what you saw. Could you hold on a minute while I get him? He's just across the street."

"Certainly."

Bronwyn shouted across the street, and Brody came running. The woman recanted exactly what she saw as he took notes.

"Can you describe the car, ma'am?"

"Let me think a minute. Seems to me it was dark green. Not a sports car. More an executive style."

Brody instantly became alert. "Could it have been a Caprice Classic?"

"Yes, it might have been."

"Could you identify the driver?"

"No, I couldn't see inside. It had those tinted windows."

"Thank you, ma'am. Oh, one more question. Did you get a chance to see the license plate?"

"Only that it was a Wyoming plate. I'm sorry. I didn't know it was important, or I would have paid closer attention."

"You've been a tremendous help. Thanks."

Brody and Bronwyn met with Meghan back on the sidewalk. "Okay, girls. No sense going any further if this is where she was taken. No one beyond this point will have seen anything. I'm going back to the station. Thanks for your help."

"Call if you learn anything new."

They each gave him a quick hug, before he turned on his heel and left. Within minutes he was seated back behind his desk. His thoughts threatened to spill in a thousand directions at once, and it took all his effort to stay focussed. Pulling a business card from the center drawer, he picked up the telephone and placed a call to Denver.

His call was answered on the second ring. "Northrup."

"Bracken? Glad I reached you. It's Brody Ashton."

"Hey, Brody. How's it going?"

"Not good, I'm afraid. Lindy was abducted today."

"Well, Hell. Again? Are you certain?"

"We've got an eye witness this time."

"I'll be there later tonight. Can you connect me to Jennifer?"

"Sure. Thanks, Bracken. I'll put you through." He stabbed at the button on his telephone to connect to the switchboard. "Hey, Jen. I've got Bracken on line 12. He wants to talk to you."

"Thanks, Brody."

When Rhett and Patrick arrived at eleven, Brody was still hunched over his desk, totally consumed.

"What's up, Brody? Anything interesting?" Patrick asked.

"Lindy's been abducted again." He raised his eyes to meet theirs, and they saw the agony in his face.

"What!" Rhett perched on the side of the desk in

330

disbelief.

"I called Northrup. He'll be here in a coupla hours. It was the same guy, Rhett. He's been keeping an eye on her all this time. First he found her at the hospital and attacked her there. Today he nabbed her on her way to the library—the one day she walked instead of taking her car."

"How do you know it was the same guy?" Patrick asked, wanting to know how Brody could be so certain.

"Same car that took her in Oregon."

"I don't remember reading any evidence in the report that we knew of what kind of car it was."

Brody squirmed, unable to give the officer a straight answer. "Trust me. I'm telling you it was the same car."

"What do you want me to do?" Rhett asked, eager to be of assistance.

"I already drove out to the cabin at the Clayton's ranch where they held her the last time, but it was still vacant. I'm gonna drive out again now to see if they've taken her back there. We can't be sure they know we're aware they used it before."

"I'll run out with ya. If they're there, you'll need back-up."

Brody grabbed his coat. "Let's go."

The deputies each drove their own vehicles to the Clayton ranch, finding the cabin engulfed in darkness. Flashlights in hand, they approached the building and went inside. A quick glance confirmed its barrenness. Brody arrived holding his breath, hoping against all hope to find her. Now, it escaped his lungs in a rush of chagrin. With no inkling of where else to possibly search for her, his spirit crumbled.

•

Lindy woke in the dark, unable to open her eyes. She recognized the sensation instantly and knew — they were taped shut again. Her hands and feet were also taped together, but her clothes were still on. One small detail for which to be grateful. The cold and damp floor beneath her made her shiver. Concrete. They must have brought her to someplace new.

Shock gripped her as she remembered the event that brought her here. At least she now knew the identity of one of her captors and wondered about his level of involvement in her abduction back in January.

A door opened above, and footsteps thudded softly on the wooden steps of a staircase. She turned her head toward the sound. The visitor stopped in front of her and roughly ripped the tape from her mouth.

"Food."

A hot spoon was pressed to her mouth. Reluctantly, she opened her lips, remembering the unpalatable slop of her previous captivity. To her surprise, the food proved edible. She knew she needed to eat to maintain her strength. She managed to escape before. She would again. Brody always told her he admired her bravery and strength. She would prove him right.

Where was he now? Did he know she was missing? Would he care? Of course he would care. Silly question. In spite of everything, she believed he loved her on some level.

"Brody, where are you? Come for me. Save me. One more time, save me. I need you now, more than ever. I love you. Whatever you did with Tara, I forgive you," her mind whispered.

"Wanna use the bathroom?"

The voice pulled her from her thoughts. "Please."

He slid a metal bucket next to her and tugged her slacks and underwear down from her hips. With his hands under her arms, he lifted her and set her on it, then waited for her to use it. It took her several minutes to relax enough to urinate in front of him, but since he didn't seem to be leaving, she finally managed. When she finished, he pulled her clothing back up and pressed a fresh strip of duct tape over her mouth. She listened as the footsteps retreated up the staircase, and the door at the top opened and closed.

Her world reverted to silent darkness once again.

•

The deputies sat with chairs tipped back and feet propped on their desk tops as they discussed the abduction, hoping a brainstorming session would offer new places to search. They talked endlessly in circles, and in the end all remained flummoxed. When Bracken Northrup finally arrived from Denver, Brody gave up his vigil and went home.

Tossing his keys on the kitchen counter, he passed through to the living room and found David lounging on the couch watching television. After the stessful events of the past two days, Brody's temperament was anything but social.

"Hey, Brody."

"David, I'm going on up to bed. Been a bad day, and I'm in a foul mood."

"Okay. I take it you didn't manage to straighten things out with Lindy?"

"Nope, she's been kidnapped. I have to get some sleep, so I can start fresh tomorrow."

"Wait a minute. What do you mean she's been kidnapped? You can't just make a statement like that and walk out of the room." Setting his coffee mug on the table in front of him, he asked, "Are you sure?"

"Yeah. She never made it to work today. I got a witness who saw her getting into the car."

"Geez, I'm sorry, Brody. Are you okay?"

"Nope. Listen, I really do just want to go to bed."

"Sure. Let me know if there's anything I can do."

"Night." Brody trudged up the stairs, took off his uniform, and turned on the shower. He ducked his head under the faucet, letting the hot water spray his head and down his shoulders. It did nothing to relieve his stress tonight.

After toweling off, he climbed into his bed. Lying on the same side where Lindy always slept when she spent the night, he whispered to the night air, "Lindy, my love, where are you? Talk to me. Tell me how to find you. Help me, Lind. I have to find you before they can hurt you again. Talk to me."

His eyes closed, and he envisioned her walking down the street. A car pulled to the curb and the passenger window slid down, but he could not see the driver. Lindy stepped closer and spoke through the window. She smiled and willingly got in.

She knew the person!

Suddenly everything faded to a deep blackness – devoid of all light, and he perceived that he had swiftly been transported to Lindy's awareness. Her eyes were taped shut along with her mouth, and her feet and hands were bound. He sensed she was still clothed, and he breathed a quick word of gratitude.

"Where are you, Lindy? I'm coming for you, but I need to know where you are. I love you too, honey. You don't need to forgive me. I've never strayed. I'm still yours, and I always will be. Find out where they're keeping you, and I'll be right there. Help me, Lind. I'm trying."

·

Brody woke early and skipped his morning run. Peanut butter quickly slathered on a slice of bread to eat while driving to town, sufficed as breakfast.

Northrup arrived shortly after. Brody sat in front of his computer monitor, printing off a list from the DMV of green Caprice Classics with Wyoming tags. Bracken reviewed the list, whittling it down to those in Fremont County, while Brody contacted radio stations and county newspapers, following up by faxing a photo of Lindy to run in the papers. Bracken and Brody split the thinned list between them with the intention of tracking down the owners. If the cars registered within the county did not pan out, they would enlarge the search circumferally.

Brody quickly perused the squad room and noticed an office in the corner with the lights out and the door propped open. "Bracken, I need to talk to you. Something I probably should have done when you came last spring. Can we go over into the office there?"

Bracken felt a sudden sense of foreboding. If the deputy possessed information that could have solved the case months ago, Bracken would strangle him. He followed the blond man into the office and closed the door.

"What's up, Brody? What have you been holding back?"

"I didn't know how to explain this before. It's pretty strange, and being that Lindy had already been found…" he squirmed uncomfortably. "Frankly it just plain sounds flaky."

"What is it, Ashton?" Bracken put on his blank FBI face.

Brody told of the dreams he experienced over the last eight months, and that all the details turned out to be accurate.

"And now?"

"Last night when I went to bed, I witnessed this last abduction. It was definitely the same vehicle that took her in Oregon. When that car pulled up next to her yesterday, she spoke to the driver. It's someone she knows, or she wouldn't have gotten in. After everything she's been through, she's too cautious for that. Her eyes and mouth are taped shut again, so she can't see where she is. She feels the cold dampness and believes she's in a basement. She hears him coming down a staircase to feed her, and there's a door at the top of the stairs. I know this sounds crazy but things have always been so damned accurate before."

"I've heard of stranger things. My instinct says to go along with you on this. I wish you'd told me about this last time I was here. Let's get out there and start looking. Jennifer and I are supposed to be flying back east to Connecticut in a few days. Let's get this wrapped up in time."

"Thanks, Bracken. Appreciate your help."

CHAPTER THIRTY-THREE

"I wonder if I'll kill you today."

The words brought so many memories flooding back readily to her mind and body. She wanted to respond to his words. She wanted to say she knew he would not kill her because he enjoyed tormenting her too much.

Thoughts and memories of Brody kept her sane and gave her strength. He had been so much a part of her healing and personal growth. Instead of worrying and allowing the fright to rule her mind, she chose to dwell on positive things. Brody would find her soon. She felt confident of that.

Last night when she thought about him before falling asleep, she swore she could hear him speaking to her. He said he loved her, that he had not cheated on her. He told her he was searching for her and promised to find her. Some might call it wishful thinking, but she remembered how he connected with her before. Her faith in him kept the fear from enveloping her.

•

Brody picked up the ringing telephone. "Ashton."

Jennifer spoke clearly, yet quickly. "Brody, I just took a call from Jefferson Clayton. Chris Adams has just been shot out at his ranch. They need you out there. A chopper's on the way to airlift him."

"He's still alive, though, right?"

"It doesn't look good. Jeff said it was a sniper shooting. Got him in the head."

"I'm on my way."

Brody ran outside to his cruiser, threw on the lights and the siren, and sped out to the Adam's ranch. He saw the chopper landing, and he turned off the highway and headed overland to reach it. He arrived as the medi-vac copter lifted off again, heading to Salt Lake City.

Jeff Clayton, the only witness, was unable to provide much in the way of clues. He could tell Brody where Chris had been sitting when shot, and speculated on which direction the bullet came from, though he saw no one. Distracted and antsy, Jeff hurried to board a plane for Salt Lake.

After sending Clayton on his way, Brody calculated angle, time and distance before calling for a back-up unit to scour the mountainside for evidence. Calculating the sniper's location at the point of firing, Brody jumped back in the cruiser and drove to the projected area. The officers hunted for several hours before finding a bullet casing. Depositing it into an evidence envelope, Brody tucked it into his pocket and drove to the Sheriff's Office.

After submitting the shell for ballistics testing, he requested another deputy be assigned to assist in the investigation. He was torn, now. Two cases of personal importance to him. He could not put one aside for the other without an avalanche of guilt descending upon

338

him. The best he could do was to partner up on both cases.

At 7:30 he stopped by his mother's house for dinner, needing to talk with someone who could understand his dilemma.

"Brody, you don't look well. You'll find Lindy soon. I know you'll get her back, honey."

"It's not just that, Ma. Somebody shot Chris Adams today. Bullet lodged in his brain. He might not make it. The press is gonna be all over us on this one. Probably TV cameras and reporters everywhere by tomorrow. Celebrities don't get shot without the whole world taking notice. There's gonna be a lot of pressure, and it deserves to be a top priority case. But with Lindy still out there somewhere, how can I focus on anything else?"

"Put someone else on Chris' case."

"I've brought Burnett in on it. Maybe I can pass it to the sheriff, it being so high profile and all. Not that I don't want to do what I can for Chris, I just can't give him my best right now, and he deserves nothing less."

Gina took the milk jug from the fridge, refilled his glass, and set it before him. "Lindy will be back with us soon. I can feel it."

"I hope so, Ma. I'm going crazy without her."

•

Tara Shepherd walked out the back door of the house at the Hathaway ranch. Her mother stepped onto the porch next to her and pulled her car keys from her purse.

"It's okay, Mom. Go back to town without me. I'm gonna stay and ride for awhile. I haven't taken Jezebel out for a few days, and I think we could both use a good long run. Don't worry, I'll get one of the hands to bring me back. I don't work tonight anyway, so time isn't a factor."

"I don't know, Tara. I don't like you going out alone like this—not with what's happened to Lindy and Christopher the past few days. I'd rather you didn't.

"I'll be fine, Mom. This is Grandpa's ranch. I grew up here. I know every inch of this place. I'll be careful, I promise."

"Well Chris knows every inch of his ranch just as well, and it's right next door. The trouble's too close to home, honey."

"Mom, I'm not ten years old. Stop worrying." She did not want to admit to her mother that her friend's kidnapping and her cousings shooting were a large part of the reason she needed to get away and think. Tara was the tough cookie in the family. She kept her fears hidden.

Angie looked at her daughter and saw herself thirty years earlier. She knew Tara inherited her own stubborn streak and that her objections were pointless. "All right. Just see that you're careful. Maybe you should have someone go out with you."

"Sure. If it will make you happy."

Angie dropped a kiss on her cheek and got into the car. Tara watched the car drive away down the long laneway to the highway and shook her head in amusement. Her mother could be so over-protective. It worked fine for Meghan, and let's face it, Poor Paige needed it, but not Tara. When would her mother realize she was a grown woman with a mind of her own and the intelligence to look after herself. She strolled to the stable and saddled Jezebel.

•

340

Isabelle Hathaway walked to the stables to see if Tara had yet returned. Her granddaughter had been gone several hours, and unless she was working with a herd, that was a monumental amount of time for Tara to be out on horseback. When she saw Jezebel's empty stall, her fears were confirmed. Tara was still out there somewhere. Frowning, she turned to retrace her steps. She really should call Angie and let her know.

"Howdy, Mrs. Hathaway. Something I can do for ya?"

Isabelle jumped, and a small squeal escaped as her hand flew to her chest in alarm. "Oh, David. You startled me." Her racing heart began to slow to its normal rhythm. "Tara went out riding quite awhile ago, and I'm rather worried. She doesn't usually stay out so long, and she's by herself today. I hate to trouble you…"

"I'll ride out and see if I can track her down. Glad to be of help." David grabbed a saddle from the wall and went to Blitzen's stall. He was a good, solid ride with plenty of speed, even in the hills. David loved riding into the foothills ever since his first time with Meghan and Paige. It offered a magnificent view for miles around. Within minutes he had the stallion saddled and ready. He led the mount to the barnyard and told his employer, "Don't worry. If Tara's out there, I'll find her."

Two hours later, David returned with a single horse tied behind him. "I'm sorry, Mrs. Hathaway, but it looks like there may be trouble. The only sign of Tara I found was Jezebel roaming aimlessly on her lonesome. There was no trace of Tara anywhere in the area. I did a pretty good-sized radial search, and it was out on the open prairie land. I would have found her if she was there. I've brought the horse back with me, but I'm afraid I have no idea what's happened to your granddaughter. Let me get Jezebel brushed down and watered, then I'll show you on the map where I found her."

341

·

Two full days went by and Brody and Bracken were no closer to finding Lindy. Brody felt more frustrated than usual with a case. This one held his future in its hands. He still believed she was being held in a basement somewhere. The deputies visited just about every basement in the county over the last forty-eight hours, without success.

The telephone at the station rang, and Jennifer forwarded the call to Bracken. Now, Tara Shepherd was missing, and the Hathaways were worried. Every hand on the ranch was searching and using radios to keep in touch, but to no avail. It appeared that Tara disappeared. The Hathaways were concerned about the possibility of it being related to the Lassiter kidnapping.

Bracken drove out to the Hathaway ranch with a total disregard for the speed limit. He did not want to say it out loud, but he was afraid they were right.

·

Normally on a day off, Brody would have spent the day with Lindy or working on the house renovations. Today, he spent it searching for her. Feeling bushwacked, he arrived home far earlier than usual. He noticed the absence of David's car and attributed it to being a Friday night. His cousin was probably out drinking with the other hands from the Hathaway ranch, as usual.

Brody was glad to be alone in the house. He needed privacy to grieve for Lindy. Feeling distraught, he skipped the shower and lay on his bed fully clothed. His hand lay on his chest, where the pain pounded, steady and cutting.

"Lindy, love, I'm gonna lose my mind without you. I need you back with me, baby. Can't you tell me anything else? Talk to me. Lead me to you."

Though the evening was still early, he was exhausted—mentally, emotionally and physically. Almost too tired to sleep. Almost. Sleep crept in so slowly, he was not even sure if he was awake or asleep. A voice whispered in the somnolence, and he edged closer to make out the words.

"I'm all right, Brody. They haven't hurt me this time. I'm waiting for you. They moved me today. I don't know where, but I'm out of the basement. I love you. I think about you all the time I'm awake. They can't hurt me as long as you're with me. I know you can hear me, sweetheart. Please, come soon."

•

Dane Grant sat astride his horse on the mountainside overlooking the Clayton ranch. All the hands on the ranches that neighboured the Hathaways' had been out on horseback for several hours searching for Tara Shepherd. Bill Clayton had a large map of his property spread out on the work table in the tack room. He systematically assigned a section to each of his hands. Darkness fell quickly, making their task more difficult.

Dane held a lantern high overhead, trying to dispel the encompassing gloom. A glimmer of light in the distance caught his attention, and he nudged the horse in that direction. As he rode closer, he realized from where the light emanated and used his walkie-talkie to alert the main house.

The telephone startled Brody awake. He reached into the dark and snatched it quickly.

"Yeah?"

"Brod, it's Rhett."

"Hey, Rhett, any news?" he asked hopefully, sitting up and dropping his legs over the side of the bed.

"We think we know where she is."

"Where we going?" Brody reached for his pants and started to pull them on.

"The Clayton's cabin."

"We've already been there."

"They know that. That's why they waited until tonight to move her there. You'd better run out and pick up Northrup from the Hathaway's. He'll never find his way to the Clayton's in the dark."

"Good. Is Patrick around?"

"Not right now. Want me to find him?"

"No. Don't tell anyone where you're going. We need to keep this under wraps until we have her safe. And listen, make sure you approach inconspicuously. No lights, no sirens."

"Of course. I'll meet you there."

"Thanks. I won't go in until you get there. And, Rhett, I'm afraid it's gonna be a tough night—for both of us." Brody disconnected and ran downstairs, grabbing his keys to the Avalanche on his way out the door.

Rhett turned on the heat in the cruiser as he pondered Brody's warning. Was he referring to more than Lindy's rescue? He sped out through the countryside. As he turned off the main highway he doused his headlights, driving the remainder of the distance by moonlight. He saw Brody's Avalanche in the shadows and parked beside it.

"Tara's gone missing, too," Rhett stated. "Think they might both be in there?"

"Geez, let's hope so." Brody pointed to the dark green Caprice Classic parked near the front door. "Rhett, take a gander at the perp's car. Look familiar?"

"It's the car we've been looking for. You scored on that one, Brody," Bracken observed.

Rhett gawked at the car, his expression a mixture of confusion and worry. "Matter of fact, I do recognize it. Tell me he's here to help."

"Sorry, Rhett. That's what I tried to warn you about. She knows him. It makes sense she'd feel safe getting in a car with him."

"Brody, no. It can't be. It can't," Rhett objected.

"Well, Hell. Of course. We naturally discounted this one. How utterly stupid of us. " Bracken was agitated he made such a negligent slip.

"I just can't believe it." Rhett felt as though the world just tipped off its axis.

"You have to believe it before we go busting in there. I'll go in first. That okay with you, Bracken?"

"We're right behind you." He reached beneath his suit jacket and extracted his Sig Sauer, ready for action.

•

Lindy lay on the bed. She heard two of them coming into the bedroom together. One tied her bound hands to the headboard before lifting her sweater and camisole up over her head. The other yanked her pants down around her ankles. The first leaned against the wall, ready to watch until it was his turn. To his pleasure, he would have the first go at taming Tara Shepherd.

Lindy took herself away in her mind. Brody would be here soon. He would not let her down now, and she knew in her heart he never had.

The second was in the process of prying her knees apart and climbing on her when the door burst open. Brody stood with his feet braced, arms extended, ready to fire. "Stop right there, David. Get away from her now, or I'll shoot."

David felt the barrel of the gun digging into his back, and he backed away from Lindy. "What's the matter, Brody? You don't want to share with family? You told me she left you."

"Get away from her, now. I won't say it again."

David stood still, and Brody shoved him across the room. Knowing Rhett and Bracken had his back, he holstered his gun and tended to Lindy, hastily pulling her clothes back on her.

She heard Brody's voice in the distance and allowed her mind to come back, concentrating on what was being said.

The one who stood against the wall moved slowly, almost imperceptibly, as he drew a revolver and aimed at Brody. Before Brody realized what was happening, Rhett put a bullet through the villains heart.

"Rhett...buddy." With a hand over his chest, his legs buckled beneath him, and he crumpled, a trail of blood smearing the wall behind him.

"You're no buddy of mine, Patrick." Rhett looked at his partner, the man he worked side by side with for six years. He wanted to cry, but was overwhelmed by betrayal and anger.

Turning to the closet door beside him, he swung it open and found Tara Shepherd huddled inside. Kneeling next to her, he undid the ropes and gently pulled the tape from her eyes and mouth. "You're safe now, Tara."

Tara flung herself at him, and he held her. "I was so

scared."

"It's all right. I've got hold of you now, girl. They can't hurt you. Just hold on to me."

Brody rose to his full six-foot-three and stared hard at the man who lived in his home for the past several months.

"Well, David. By the way, what is your real name? I know you're not my cousin."

The man dropped the affectations of his feigned western drawl. "Very clever, Deputy Dawg. Say, if you're such a great lawman, why didn't you find her when I had her stashed right there in your own basement?"

Stunned by the revelation, Brody turned away, not willing to allow his antagonist the satisfaction of seeing his personal defeat as he swallowed the bitter bile that filled his throat. Returning his attention to Lindy, he asked, "Are you all right, darling?"

She nodded as he untied her and removed the tape from her eyes and mouth. With her arms free, she threw them around his neck and sobbed.

"I've got you, sweetheart. They aren't gonna hurt you ever again. I love you, Lind." He clutched her tightly, rejoicing at the feeling of her within his arms again. He kissed her and whispered reassuring endearments in her ear.

Bracken stood in the doorway of the small room, eyeballing the perp as his own anger roiled within. "You thought it was a lot of fun, didn't you? The beating, the raping, the torment. A real good time, right?"

David looked Brody square in the eye. "You should know she's a good time. Does she struggle and pretend to fight when she's with you the way she does with me? She likes it that way." He grew cocky, wanting to rub it in Brody's face. "And what an appetite that woman has.

347

She just can't get enough—always pleading for more."

Bracken carried on, egging David along. Pushing him like he was trying to do to Brody. Tit for tat. "I'll bet the time in the hospital was really great. Knowing someone could walk in on you at any moment? Probably heightened the excitement for you, didn't it?"

"You know it. You should have tried it there, Brody."

Brody released Lindy and rose to his feet. Turning to face David, he casually grasped his weapon and drew it. Sarcasm bubbled within as he responded to the prodding jibes. "Yeah, I get what you're saying. She's not a real person anyway, so it's okay to use her. In fact I should probably beat the daylights out of her for trying to leave me." With his back to Lindy, he could not see her looking up at him in confusion.

"Now you're talking. I knew you'd understand."

"Yeah, I do. So tell me, was she better than the one in Pennsylvania?"

"Sure was. That broad was no fun at all. Found out about that one, did you?"

Bracken interrupted, "What about the one in Oklahoma? How long did you hold on to her?"

"She was only good for a few weeks before I tired of her. But Lindy here, she was worth coming back for—again and again."

A cold shiver ran down Brody's spine as he listened. "I'm glad to hear it. And I really do understand. I understand what a cold inhuman bastard you are." He raised his gun and pointed it straight at David's head. "Rhett?"

"Go for it, Brod. His kind ain't welcome in this part of the country. We can't let people do this to our women folk and just walk away."

"Northrup?"

"If you don't, I will."

"You won't shoot me, Brody," David stated, with absolute confidence.

"Oh, really? And why is that?"

"You can't shoot me without provocation. That would be murder. You're too goody-goody for that."

"Don't count on it. There's nothing I won't do to keep my woman safe and happy. Absolutely nothing. You so much as look at her the wrong way, and you're a dead man."

Brody's peripheral vision caught Rhett pulling Tara from the closet, and his eyes shifted slightly at the distraction. David took it as his opportunity and hurled himself at Brody, trying to knock the gun away. Without hesitation, Brody pulled the trigger.

Lindy screamed and jumped from the bed when she heard the gun go off. "Brody!"

David fell to the floor, his final breaths rasping.

Brody looked down at the fallen man, blood pooling around his head. "Thank you, David. You just made it a legitimate shoot." He smiled as he remembered his mother's kitchen. "And I have it on good authority that even God will shake my hand."

Lindy flung herself into his arms as he holstered his weapon.

"It's all right, sweetheart. It's over for good this time." He held her close and rocked her while she cried. "Never, ever again."

"I love you, Brody. I'm so sorry." She clutched him as tightly as she could. "I heard you. I knew you were coming."

"Everythings okay, Lind. I've got you, and I won't let go." He kissed her hard, letting her know she would be his forever. They clung tightly to one another as the impact of their ordeal engulfed them.

Bracken gave them a moment before asking, "Lindy,

have you been hurt at all?"

"No. Except for keeping me tied up, they didn't do anything this time. You got here just in time. I'm all right, Bracken. Thank you. "

"I'm just glad it's over. You and Brody go home now. Rhett will see that Miss Shepherd gets back to her family, and I'll tie things up here."

Brody supported her trembling body. "We'll both be in to the station tomorrow to give our statements. She needs some rest now." He lifted her in his arms, then turned back. "Rhett, I'm sorry about Patrick."

"Yeah, so am I. Thanks."

Bracken clapped a hand on Brody's back. "Good job, Ashton. It's been a pleasure to work with you."

"Thanks, Bracken. I'll talk to ya tomorrow."

"Great. Take your time, and take care of her."

Brody carried Lindy out to the Avalanche and placed her inside. Once he was securely belted behind the wheel, he pulled out his cell phone, dialed it, and handed it to her. "I think there's some people who need to know you're safe, and it can't wait until morning."

She took the telephone and heard the other end pick up.

"Hi, Dad. It's Lindy."

"Lindy! Are you all right?"

"Yes. I'm with Brody, and everything will be just fine from now on."

CHAPTER THIRTY-FOUR

Brody bided his time for three weeks until the emotion and pandemonium abated somewhat, relieved that Lindy's recovery proved much easier this time. The fact that she had not been raped again counted for a lot. With trust restored between the couple, the entire incident only served to bring them closer together.

He arrived at his parents' home on a Saturday morning and found the family gathered around the breakfast table. He poured himself a cup of coffee and pulled up a chair to join them. "I've got good news," he announced.

All eyes turned to him, and Lindy answered, "Good news I hope. What is it?"

"A coupla things. When Bracken ran my dear cousin, David's, picture through the computer, we got a positive ID on him along with several aliases on drivers' licenses from nine states. His real name was Bruce Avery. And another point of interest for you, he was really Patrick's cousin, not mine. Aside from the two other victims we knew about in Pennsylvania and Oklahoma, he faced rape charges in seven other states. A total of fifteen women. We closed files all over the country."

Lindy lifted her coffee mug and stared into it, not willing to meet anyone's eyes as she confessed. "I'm glad you killed him, Brody. I never thought I'd be pleased to see someone die, but I am. I still get nervous; I still get scared. I suppose I will for a long time, but you've given me a sense of peace knowing he can't ever come back and hurt me again. I'm finally safe."

"Yes, you are." He draped his arm around her shoulder and pulled her closer. "The other good news is we got the guy who shot Chris Adams." He paused before adding, "And better still, Chris and Abby are back together. He's being moved from Salt Lake to the hospital here in Lander."

"That is good news." The family smiled with relief. Life in Lander could finally relax and return to its Mayberry-like quality of life. Sensing the couple wanted to be alone, the rest carried their dishes to the sink and left to pursue their own plans for the day.

Smiling like a cat with a secret, Brody revealed his piece de resistance. "One more thing. I heard from Bracken Northrup yesterday. He and Jennifer Dexter are visiting his parents' place in Connecticut, and he called to say they're getting married next Friday. And, being as he's apparently quite wealthy, he's sent airline tickets so you and I can be there for the wedding…if you want to go that is."

"Of course I want to go. This will be our first trip away together, and Heaven knows we deserve a break." Lindy put her arms around his neck and gazed into his green eyes.

"I want to take my sweetheart for dinner tonight at the Carriage House. Would you like that?"

"Sounds perfect."

He kissed her lightly and ran a finger down her nose. "Tonight is gonna be special," he whispered.

"Silly Brody Bear, any night with you is special."

He tightened his arms and held her closer. "You know, we haven't discussed what happened between us."

"There's no need. You told me you didn't cheat on me. I don't understand what really happened, but I believe you."

"Wait a minute, when did I tell you that?"

"When you were looking for me. You said you loved me, you needed me, and you hadn't cheated. You asked me to help you find me. I don't think it was the kind of moment you'd lie to me."

"You heard that?"

"Of course I did. I heard you in my head all the time. I talked back. I tried to tell you as much as I could. I knew you were looking for me. The only surprise was that you brought me here afterwards instead of to your place." She snuggled her head onto his shoulder and let her fingers stroll around his neck.

"Well, I did spend the night here with you." He ran a hand through her hair, and she smiled. "Ya know, I heard you too, Lind. We really are connected, honey. Listen, would you come to the house tonight? There's something I'd like to show you."

"Can I stay over?"

"I hope you will." He tipped her face up for his kiss. "I was scared I'd never hold you like this again. I think you were braver than I was."

"Only because I felt you with me. I trusted in you, Brody. Do you realize how significant that is? I wish I had that same trust when I went to the house that morning. I should have let you know I was there and talked to you about it. I just felt too hurt and betrayed.

I'm sorry."

He slid a hand up and down her back, relishing the fact that she was in his arms. "I was shattered when I found out you left me. I couldn't understand why, and when Bronwyn finally spilled it, I couldn't have been more shocked. I've never betrayed you, and I never ever will. Tara Shepherd can't hold a candle to you in my eyes, or my heart. Don't you know that?"

"You've never said so. I remember you saying how much you enjoyed being in bed with her, and I figured since I wasn't..."

"Since you weren't what?"

"Able to give you what you need." She turned away, feeling inadequate and embarrassed.

Brody lifted her chin until she looked him in the eye. "Honey, you do give me what I need. I'm very happy with our loving. It's like a slow blossoming that grows stronger and deeper each time we're together. The thought of being with another woman doesn't even enter my mind. I told you I never loved her. You're the only one I've ever loved." He kissed her firmly to punctuate his point.

•

The maitre'd at the Carriage House showed Deputy Ashton and his lady friend to their table in a quiet secluded corner. Flickering candlelight cast a romantic aura while music quietly serenaded.

"This is a beautiful restaurant, Brody. Thank you for bringing me."

"My princess deserves the best always."

She smiled and looked up coyly at him through her lashes. He felt his heart skip a beat. She was perfect in his eyes.

After the waitress took their dinner order, he reached across the table and took hold of her hand, admiring the emerald back where it belonged.

"You look very nice tonight, Brody. I don't often see you in a suit and tie. Makes me wonder how long it's gonna take to get you out of it again."

Brody blushed and smiled at the mental image she portrayed. He started to wonder the same thing, and his anticipation for the evening ahead escalated.

"I haven't seen you blush in a long time. It's so cute, and I've always been partial to that dimple."

"You keep it up, Missy, and we'll be out of here before we even get dinner."

"Promises, promises." Her eyes twinkled in the candlelight as they gazed into his, and they held. His fingers tightened around her hand.

He raised an eyebrow in a teasing manner and tempted, "I bought you chocolates." Thoughts of the night ahead ignited a slow burning desire.

"I suppose you want to watch me eat them," she countered.

"I suppose I do." He gave her a lazy, seductive smile. "Sexiest thing I've ever seen."

After dinner they both passed on dessert, anxious to be alone together. They left the restaurant with their fingers loosely linked together. Instead of opening the door of the Avalanche for her, he leaned in to kiss her. His hands held her face as he lingered over her lips, tittilating her with promises of more.

They remained silent the entire drive to Brody's farmhouse. He parked the truck and walked around to open the door for his princess.

"I love you, Lindy." He kissed her before setting her on her feet. Picking up her overnight bag, they went into the dark house. He snapped on a lamp as he led her into the living room, and hung her coat in the front closet with his own. She sat down while he went to the kitchen for a bottle of wine. He sat beside her on the couch and poured them each a glass.

"Thanks. It's nice to know we have the house all to ourselves, and that no one will be arriving later."

"I like it much better this way, too. I'm really sorry, Lindy. It's been hard knowing I've been harboring' your attacker all this time. I feel like such a jackass, like I've betrayed you somehow."

"I'm just glad it's over. Let's not think about it any more. This will be our house. We'll make it a home together, and we'll banish any trace of him ever being here."

"Is that what you want? To make this our home together?"

"You know I do. It's all I've wanted from the day we met. Well, not quite the first day, but it didn't take long."

"I'm glad you moved your things back here from the Shepherd's place. I want you to start unpacking and putting them all around the house."

"Okay, I'll do that. I love this house. I think we've done a lot to make it ours instead of just yours."

Brody set his glass on the table and knelt in front of her. "I love you, Lindy. You know I do. You are my heart and soul and everything good in my life. I want to spend the rest of my days with you beside me. Lindy, will you marry me, and spend your life with me? Please?"

Lindy saw a tear sparkle in his eyes. Her own heart pounded a million beats a minute, and she felt her throat tighten. "Yes, Brody. I'll marry you and spend forever with you. I feel like my life started the day you found me. I love you in every way a woman can love a man."

He pulled the ring box from his pocket and opened it,

revelling in the delightful way her eyes glittered when she saw it.

"It's beautiful. Oh, sweetheart, I love it. It's perfect." As tears slipped from her eyes, she took off her emerald and moved it to the other hand, so he could put the diamond on her. She admired it and fell to her knees in front of him as they kissed, softly at first, growing deeper and more passionate.

"Lind, can we take this upstairs? To our room?"

They picked up their wine glasses and slowly climbed the stairs, leaning against one another.

He stopped her outside the closed bedroom door and told her, "I'm glad you said yes, because I have your wedding present in here. Are you ready?"

"Am I gonna love it?"

"I sure as heck hope so. I built it for you. Course if ya don't like it, I can probably sell it at a yard sale or something."

"Let me see!" Excitement bubbled, and she was thrilled he took the time to make whatever it was himself. He opened the door and she could not believe her eyes.

"Brody! This is truly the most magnificent bed I've ever seen in my life. Look at all the woodwork on the head board. You even carved our initials into the design. I love it. I absolutely love it."

"Needed a bed worthy of the princess who would sleep in it. Honey, this is what I was doing with Tara. She made the canopy and the drapes for it. It was for you."

She closed her eyes in chagrin. "I feel so stupid. All I put myself and the two of you through. I'm sorry. She's done a beautiful job. And the matching duvet and shams with it. I really owe her a huge apology."

"I think she understands. As for me, what do I care

now? You're gonna marry me, and I couldn't be any happier. You're gonna be the most beautiful bride that Lander, Wyoming, has ever seen."

She smiled as he took her glass and set it with his own on the night table. Sliding his fingers into her hair, he lifted her face to his. He kissed her eyelids and her small nose. He worshipped her with his lips, kissing and caressing her. He felt her undoing his tie and the buttons on his shirt. She slid it off his shoulders and kissed his chest.

"Oh, my Lindy. I love your touch." He slid the zipper down the back of her emerald green dress, and with his fingertips lifted it off her shoulders. It slid to the ground in a silky puddle, and she stepped out of it. As she climbed onto the bed, he watched the way she moved in her black satin camisole and French cut black lace panties with black stockings and heels. He practically leaped to the other side of the bed and made quick work of removing his shoes, socks and pants. He crawled across the bed on all fours and fed her a chocolate from the open box on the night table beside her. She lay back against the pillow and savored the candy in just the way he loved.

"Did I tell you how sexy those heels look on you? You're driving me crazy."

"I hope so. It would be awful to marry someone who wasn't attracted to me."

He pressed his lips to hers, and she pulled him closer. They knew each other well, and he knew the kind of kisses she liked best. Her fingers wandered through his hair and held him tighter. His hand slid down to her breast, and she arched her back, wanting to fill it. The satin was smooth under his fingertips, and he enjoyed the sensation of touching her through it.

Her hands began to move lower, trailing over the

warm skin across his back. "I want to love you forever." All her senses were aflame, and she was excited.

He slid her lace barrier off, and she in turn removed his boxers. He kissed her neck, her cheeks, her lips and pulled her on top of him. He pulled his mouth away and gazed into her eyes.   "It's all up to you now, Lind. You have the control to make it what you want it to be; how deep, how fast, everything. I love you, sweetheart."

That was all she needed. "I want to be yours."

He popped another chocolate into her mouth as she moved onto him, and they consummated their love with a tenderness that turned into total abandon as the passion grew. He was hers, and she was his, and she gave herself without reservation. When they finished, she lay repleted against his chest.

"Oh, sweet darling. I love you."

"I know you do. And before you ask, it was perfect for me. I feel so loved and cherished. It was beautiful. Like you."

"Like you. You'll always be loved and wanted in this bed, Lind. I'll never get enough of having you like this."

"You'll make a fine husband. I'll always want you, too. I'm glad we finally made it to this point. You've been so loving and patient. I'll always love you for that, for taking one step at a time and never pushing. It means more than you'll ever know."

"You were worth waiting for. Besides, I'm glad we took it the way we did. We've learned so much about each other, and our relationship is a lot stronger for it. Honey, live here with me now. I don't want to come home to an empty house any more. Let's get married right away."

"Really?"

"It's what I want. I guess it's really up to you. You've probably always dreamed of a big she-bang. You set the date, and I'll be there, but make it soon."

"The only people I have are your family, the Shepherds and Rhett. Bracken and Jennifer if they can be here. My guest list is pretty small."

"Sounds like a perfect number. You talk to Ma, and she'll help with whatever you need."

"How about Christmas Eve?" she suggested. "You'll never forget our anniversary that way."

"What makes you think I'd ever forget it?"

"Men always do. Anyway, what do you think of the date?"

"I think it's good. By Christmas Day, you'll be Lindy Ashton."

"Or you'll be Brody Lassiter. You never know, it could happen."

"Well, the headboard says A, so it's gonna be Ashton," he said with finality, then realized she really might have different ideas. "Unless you want to keep Lassiter."

"I'm afraid I'm not quite that liberated. I want to have the same last name as my children and their dad. Definitely Lindy Ashton. Besides, if I have your name, maybe women will quit asking you out!"

He laughed. "I'm glad. If you wanted to keep it Lassiter I wouldn't have argued, but this way definitely makes me happier. And you know, the number of invitations is dwindling. I don't get asked out nearly as much as I used to. I guess the word is out that I only want to spend time with one woman."

"Good. I think we should put our engagement announcement in the paper so they all know to back off. You're mine, Brody Ashton." She kissed him possessively, making her position clear.

"Yes I am, Lind. All yours forever."

"I love my ring." She cuddled against him and held

her hand out so they could admire it. "I've never seen another like it. I didn't even know they cut diamonds in a heart shape. It's very pretty. Very delicate in design."

"Soon as I saw it, I knew that was the one. You are my heart. I want you to remember that every time you even so much as glance at that ring."

"I keep waiting to wake up. I'm not used to having so much happiness in my life, and there's been a lot since you. I don't know what I've done to deserve so much."

"Honey, you've had enough grief to last your entire life. It's time for happiness." He kissed her and was instantly pulled back under her spell. "Lindy, let me love you again."

"Oh, yes, and I think we can turn out the light this time," she whispered.

"You sure about that? We've never had them off before."

"I'm very sure."

He turned off the lamp before covering her with his large body. He loved her to completion, and again she gloried in the fact that it was her name on his breath as he climaxed.

She fell asleep later that night secure in the knowledge that she was loved and wanted and needed. She was not sad any more. She was not lonely any more. She was about to marry the most wonderful man she had ever met.

•

"Hi, Ma. Me and Lindy are here. Where's Dad?"

Gina called from her bedroom where she was putting laundry away. "I think he's down in the workshop."

Brody went to the top of the basement stairs and called down, "Dad, you down there?"

"Yup."

"Can you come upstairs? I need to talk to ya."

"Be up in a minute."

Gina came into the living room and found Lindy sitting on the end of the sofa next to Brody, holding hands.

"How was dinner last night?"

Lindy beamed, "It was very nice. We went to the Carriage House, and the food was excellent. It's quite different from any place else in town. A real touch of elegance."

"Really? What did you order?"

Embarrassed, she looked sideways at Brody. "Umm, actually I don't remember," she giggled.

They heard Mike's footsteps ascending from the basement. He smiled at the couple as he came into the living room and sat next to his wife.

"I'm here, what's up?"

Without any preamble, Brody proclaimed, "I asked Lindy to marry me last night."

They looked at him expectantly.

Puzzled by their lack of response, he asked, "Well, aren't you happy? I thought you guys would be excited."

"You haven't told us her answer yet," Mike pointed out.

Brody rolled his eyes. Lindy laughed and told them, "I said absolutely yes."

Mike and Gina jumped to their feet and pulled the young couple from the couch for a round of happy embraces. Lindy proudly showed her ring, and she and Brody remained fixed on each other, both wearing perma-smiles.

Gina called the rest of the Ashton clan to congregate at the family home, not giving out the secret.

Bronwyn was the first to arrive. "What's going on?

You guys are all talking a mile a minute in here."

Lindy rose to face her. "You're my dearest friend, Bron. I'm hoping you'll agree to be my maid of honor."

"You're getting married?"

"Christmas Eve," Lindy beamed.

"Yee-haw. This is the most excellent news. Yes! I would be so honored to stand up with you. I'm so happy for you both." The women hugged tightly, and both started to cry. Then she was swept into Brody's arms for a bear hug. "Smartest thing you've ever done, big brother."

"I'm just happy she said yes."

"Lindy, let me see the ring," she said as she reached for her friend's hand. "That's gorgeous. I'm so happy we'll be sisters for real, now."

"Me too, Bronwyn. Thank you for everything."

Braden arrived ten minutes later, walking into the beehive. Brody asked him to be best man, and Braden was happy to take on the job. No hand shakes in the Ashton house. Just more hugs. Brooke and her husband, Jim, arrived with their two little girls to join the festivities.

It was after ten o'clock before everyone went home after non-stop talk about wedding plans. Things took shape quickly, and Lindy realized she was going to be a bride.

"Ready to go home?" he asked, tired and hopeful.

"Honey, I know you want me to move in, but I'd like to stay here at Mom and Dad's until the wedding. You know, tradition and all that. I'm an old-fashioned girl, remember."

"I won't say I'm not disappointed, but if that's what you want. It's only six weeks. I guess I can live with that. Besides, we leave for the Northrup-Dexter wedding in a few days, and we'll get to be together there."

"Thank you. It's important to me, and it'll be easier to plan the wedding if I'm here in town with your mother."

"Okay, I already said you win. But I'll miss you."

"I'm counting on it."

He held her close, kissing her long and leisurely. "I'll go now before I change my mind. Love you, Lind."

"Love you back."

CHAPTER THIRTY-FIVE

Close friends and family gathered together at the church on Christmas Eve. Lindy and Brody agreed they wanted to keep the evening small and intimate. Lindy asked Meghan and Jennifer to be bridesmaids, while Brody asked Rhett and Bracken to join Braden in standing up with him.

Candlelight glowed, adding to the intimate ambience as Mike escorted Lindy down the aisle. When the minister asked, "Who gives this woman to be married," he answered, "Her mother and I do." He kissed her cheek, placed her hand in Brody's, and gave his son's shoulder a squeeze before sitting in the pew next to Gina.

Brody looked at his bride, a small tiara on her head and fingertip illusion veiling her beautiful face. Her gown was styled from the 1700's. The corseted bodice laced up the back by satin ribbon with a scoop neckline and lace-trimmed, elbow length sleeves. The full skirt draped to a train in the back. She truly looked like a princess tonight. Brody stood proud and tall with conviction in his tone when he spoke his vows to her.

When it was her turn, she began by saying, "I can't believe this is really happening to me. I love you so much, Brody." He smiled at her, and she repeated the vows to him.

When the words were spoken and the rings exchanged, the minister declared, "Forasmuch as Brody Michael and Lindy Louise have consented together in holy matrimony, and have witnessed the same before God and this company, and have pledged their love and loyalty to one another, and have declared the same by the joining of hands and the giving of rings, I pronounce that they are now man and wife. You may kiss your bride."

Brody lifted the veil and happily settled his lips on his new wife.

The Landau Room at the Carriage House filled with wedding guests for dinner and the celebration of the marriage. Lindy became emotional as she listened to toasts and speeches by the various Ashtons, realizing she had done more than marry Brody—she became a part of a family. One she could rely on for the rest of her life.

After dinner they danced, giving the bride the chance to spend time with every gentleman in attendance. At the end of the evening, Lindy threw her bouquet. Tara Shepherd caught it, and Meghan and Lindy looked at each other and grinned, both thinking the same thought: how happy the women of Lander would be if Tara was no longer available to its men.

Instead of driving back to their home that night, the bride and groom stayed at the Pronghorn Lodge. They hung the "Do Not Disturb" sign on their door and closed it firmly, cloistering themselves from the rest of the world.

•

Christmas morning dawned, and Brody and Lindy surfaced to spend the day with the family at Mike and Gina's house. Having newlyweds in the family and all the excitement that entailed made it the best Christmas they could remember. When the last gift had been given, people realized Brody and Lindy had not given each other gifts.

"Lindy, my present for you is at the house. You'll just have to wait until this evening when we go home."

She smiled. "I think you'll find your present out front."

"Yup. It's there all right," Braden confirmed.

"What are you two up to?" Brody eyed them suspiciously before striding to the front door and turning the knob. Shock rippled through him, and his eyes bulged. A brand new, cherry-red Lamborghini Gallardo with a huge white ribbon on the top dominated the street in front of the Ashton home.

Lindy perched on the edge of the sofa by the Christmas tree, waiting. Brody did not speak. Brody did not move. Brody stared out the door. Everyone else ran to the door to see what turned him into a zombie, and Braden squeezed Lindy's hand. Wild exclamations filled the house. Brody did not speak. Brody did not move. Brody still stood staring out the door.

Lindy got up and went to him. "Honey, don't you like it?"

"HOLY HANNAH!"

"I think he likes it," Braden pitched in. "Man'd have to be crazy not to."

Brody picked Lindy up, squeezing her until she could not breathe and kissed her until she was dizzy. He carried her outside, setting her in the car, then jumped into the driver's seat like Tony Stewart.

"Better put on your seat belt, darling." Turning the key, the engine purred, and he was off. "Holy Hannah, Lindy!"

"Does that mean you like it?"

"Holy Hannah!" He shifted gears and drove out south of town where he could open the throttle and let it fly. Grateful snow had not fallen and closed the highways, he wanted to push the odometer above a hundred and fifty miles an hour, but restrained himself to a mere 70. Spring would be here soon enough, and the engine would be broken in by then.

After fifty miles of highway, he turned it around and headed back. Once he reached Main Street, he pulled in at the hotel they already checked out of earlier that morning. Dragging her by the hand, he stopped at the registration desk long enough to demand just one thing.

"Key."

The clerk handed him a room key, and he called over his shoulder, "Just add this to my bill."

When he got her into the room, he kissed her, and kissed her, and kissed her. He pulled her down onto the bed and had their clothes off in record time.

"Holy Hannah, Lindy!"

He made love to her, kissing her the whole time, and the only words he ever uttered were, "Holy Hannah, Lindy."

When they finished with the room, they passed back through the foyer, dropping the key off at the desk as they left. They got back into the car and drove to his parents' house.

"You two were gone a long time," Braden commented.

"Um, we had to stop so Brody could thank me," she blushed.

"I'll just bet he did." Braden gave her a knowing grin.

"Ya done good, Lindy."

"I hope so. He hasn't said anything except 'Holy Hannah', and 'Do up your seatbelt'."

Everyone laughed, and Brody asked, "Who's next?"

Braden grabbed his coat, and Brody took him out for a ride in his new car. He was followed by Bronwyn, Brooke, Jim, Mike and finally Gina. After the rides were finished, he spent the remainder of the day staring out the living room window at his new car.

When they arrived home late that night, Lindy did not see the Avalanche parked in its normal spot.

"Honey, where's the truck?"

"I sold it."

"Brody, you love that truck. Why would you sell it? You never even mentioned it. That's not like you. We talk about everything."

"I needed the money for something else."

"I can't imagine what you would need that kind of money for that you couldn't just ask me for it."

"Lindy, did I say thank you?"

"Every time you looked out the window I took it as a thank you. I'd say I've been amply thanked. And poor Hannah is now extremely Holy, probably ready for sainthood." She smiled as she leaned across the stick shift to kiss her husband.

"Let's go in the house." He jumped out of the car and came around to open her door for her.

Lindy turned on the kitchen light as they went inside, and set her purse and their presents on the table. "Honey, want some hot chocolate?"

"Don't you want your present now? We can have the chocolate after."

"I forgot all about it. I've been so excited watching you all day."

"Close your eyes." She did as he asked, and he took

369

her by the hand and led her into the living room. "You can open them."

When Lindy opened her eyes, she knew exactly how Brody felt earlier. Totally nonplussed. A beautiful, mahogany grand piano sat in the middle of her living room. "Oh, Brody! I can't believe it. I never expected anything like this." Tears glistened in her eyes. "This is what you sold the Avalanche for?"

He nodded, pleased. "Play for me, Lindy."

She sat on the bench. "I haven't played for a full year, so I'm pretty rusty. Don't be disappointed."

He seated himself on the edge of the Lazy-Boy as she stretched her fingers and ran up and down a few scales and arpeggios to warm up. When she was ready, she played Tchaikovsky's Concerto No. 1 in B♭ Minor.

Mesmerized, he listened to his wife play. His wife. And she could play the piano like an accomplished concert pianist. He shook his head in wonder. It was one thing to know she could play, it was quite another to witness it. When she finished he sat on the bench next to her and kissed her.

"Honey, that was worth every penny. Holy Hannah, honey. You're incredibly talented."

"Thank you, Brody. A piano like this is something I never dreamed of owning. I'll care for it, and cherish it."

"I'd say our first Christmas is one we'll never forget, and probably never be able to top. Let's go upstairs."

She took his hand and followed him.

•

Late February they received an invitation to the wedding of Chris Adams and Abby Lockner. People were thrilled by upcoming nuptials as Abby was already quite large with twins. Chris' physical therapy was progressive, and he learned to walk and do simple things again.

The wedding was a star-studded affair with hundreds of big names from Nashville in attendance. Brody and Lindy were happy their friends managed to overcome their problems and find their way back together. The greatest wish they could offer the couple was to find as much happiness together as they themselves found.

When the seven course dinner was over, the stars took turns performing one or two songs while people danced. It was a huge thrill for the guests from Lander, hearing so many of their favorite singers, up close and in person.

When Tim McGraw and Faith Hill sang "Let's Make Love", Brody led Lindy onto the dance floor.

As she swayed gently in his arms, she bit at her lip nervously. "Brody, there's something I need to tell you," she said, somewhat reluctantly.

"What's that, honey?"

"Remember the night we got engaged?"

"Of course I do. It wasn't that long ago."

"Do you remember what else happened that night?"

He looked into her eyes and smiled with the memory. "Yeah, we made love. All the way for the first time," he said softly.

"Exactly. Do you remember anything else about it?"

"I remember everything about it. What in particular are you referring to?"

She mustered up her courage and spilled it. "The fact that we made a baby that night."

He stopped dead in his tracks. "What did you say?"

"I know we planned on waiting a few years before this happened, but we didn't use any protection that night."

"We're having a baby?"

"That's what I'm sayin."

He picked her up in his arms and twirled her around. "I love you, Lindy Ashton."

"You're not mad?"

"Of course I'm not mad," he grinned ecstatically. "My wife is pregnant. We're having a baby!" He kissed her passionately, then threw his head back and laughed.

She allowed herself to relax for the first time in weeks. She had been so afraid he would not be happy about their plans going awry. "I'm happy about it, Brody."

"So am I. I'm delighted. I know we wanted to wait, but what the heck. We have a family on the way. When?"

"Early August. Honey, if it's a girl, I kind of have a name picked out already."

"What's that, darling?"

"My mother's maiden name. Brindley. I know it's unusual for a given name, but I'd like it."

"Brindley. Sounds like an Ashton name to me. Brindley Ashton." He smiled and kissed her. "I absolutely love you to pieces, Lindy."

"You know, it was just a year ago this month that you found me on the side of the road. Now, I'm married to a man I adore, and we're having a baby. It's hard to believe all that's happened in a year. Back then I was sure I'd never recover. You were so patient, and you saved my life in so many ways. I thank God every day for you."

They cuddled together as they danced. "You know, I think I'll have to buy your Avalanche back."

"Why?"

"There's no room for Brindley's car seat in the Lamborghini. We'll need a family vehicle as well as Daddy's toy, so we may as well make it a practical one.

It was really useful when you were renovating, and now we'll be doing up a nursery."

"Daddy!" He beamed at the word. "Girl, I think you've knocked my socks off."

Brody took her by the hand and tugged her along behind him out of the wedding reception with only one thought in mind — how hard was it going to be to make love in a Lamborghini?

www.ingramcontent.com/pod-product-compliance
Lightning Source LLC
Chambersburg PA
CBHW060154260626

47160CB00001B/263